BLUE E

*For Mum,
Hayley,
Alex, Lana
and Em.*

Published Novel by the same author

The Master of Clouds ISBN 9798747661110 (2022)

Published Short Stories

Think With The Wise But Talk With The Vulgar (1995)
The Nostradamus Widow (1996)
Commemoration Day (1998)
Of Kith And Kin (2010)
Totem (2011)
The Colour Of The Wind Erodes The Shape Of Time (2013)
Dodge Sidestep's Dastardly Plan (2013)
Contractual Obligations (2014)
Dodge Sidestep's Second Dastardly Plan (2015)
Gliese And The Walking Man (2016) - Soundtrack to the Short Story (2016)
https://syngenic.bandcamp.com/album/gliese-and-the-walking-man
On Loan (2016)
Dodge Sidestep (and Martin's) Final Dastardly Plan (2016)
The Armageddon Coat (2017)

Published Essays

Writers' Workshops (1995)
Research (1995)
Boldly Queuing (1996) (With Neil Jones) Interzone Issue 104
Putting on the Style (1997)
A Brief History of Sci-Fi and Fantasy Film Scores (2008)
Artful Theakering (2015)
Drunk and In Charge of a Magazine (TQF) (2016)

The author would like to thank the following
individuals, my very good friends who have relentlessly
endured the formation of this, my second novel with
encouragement and open ears:

The man with sweet spheres
The man bereft of domino pieces
The man known as Formicidae
The man dwelling far across the border

And of course, Emma, my wonderful wife! Truthsayer
in the best sense of the word, advocate of my insatiable
determination, supporter to my rabid rallying cries as this
novel developed.

BLUE BULLETS

BY

HOWARD STEPHEN WATTS

This is a work of fiction. Names, characters, places and incidents either are a product of the author's imagination or are used fictitiously. Any resemblance to actual persons, living or dead, events, or locations is entirely coincidental.

First published in 2022 by Kindle Direct Publishing

Copyright © Howard Stephen Watts 2022

The moral right of the author has been asserted.

Cover layout and design by Howard Stephen Watts
Cover photography by Howard Watts. Model: Lana May Watts
Proofreading by Emma Watts

CONTENTS

Introduction

One ~ The Funeral and the Girl

Two ~ Presents from the Past

Three ~ The Red Bullet

Five ~ Family Histories

Six ~ Steeltown

Seven ~ Visitors

Eight ~ Destination Hope

Nine ~ The Buffet Car

Ten ~ Hope

Eleven ~ Hotel Infinity

Twelve ~ Second Hand Memories

Thirteen ~ Exhumed or Perhaps, Exorcised

Fifteen ~ Family Values

Sixteen ~ Meeting a Well-Known Stranger

Seventeen ~ Alan

Eighteen ~ The Mines of Too Mant Memories

Nineteen ~ Family, Steeltown, Hope and a Dear, Dead Friend

Twenty ~ The Singing Secrets and the Banana Conundrum

Twenty One ~ Planationistics

Twenty Two ~ The Beginning of the End of Infinity and, Well, The End

Twenty Three ~ The Domain of the Darkedness and the *Actual* End

BLUE BULLETS

By

Howard Stephen Watts

~ Introduction ~

My dear son,

I am so very, very sorry, but I'm unable to be with you for the foreseeable future – I just have time to finish this, my life's story thus far, to pass on to you, as I flee from the evil that has sought me across countless years. I cannot and will not put you in harm's way – you must understand this!

Providing you with our family history is a tradition I've maintained from my mother, and is of the utmost importance to me!

You will undoubtedly find this letter both bizarre and commonplace, as apart from a few significant episodes herein, all of our lives, for the most part, are. It will also provide answers to the many questions you undoubtedly have.

Your uncle will care for you until we meet. You must trust him, you must believe in him!

I hope you will understand, accept my apology, and forgive me for my absence...

Relativity always, my son. When you can, come find me!
With all my eternal love,

Your mother.
XXXXX

*   *   *

I'm going to start here.

Ok, it's not really *my* start, but I've given it a lot of thought and talked about it a great deal, so here goes.

Nick's earliest memories as far as I can see back inside him?

Well, they appear to us both occasionally, as though he tries to ignore them, hide them, or perhaps hide *from* them – but they do appear, black and terrible and loud for us both, shouting at us for acceptance. Perhaps all painful memories do, as they are truly part of us, make us, instruct us?

These particular episodes are the catalysts for Nick's determined search, his dreadful, disgusting endeavours of which only his victims, he, I and one other are truly aware. They drive him to carry out his obsessive hunt for the completion of his symphony. It is a complex theme.

The first episode follows, and I'll continue to recall these for you, when I feel they're required, or they pop into my thoughts as they're triggered by others.

THE NAUFRAGUE

There was a storm. Not an ordinary storm, not just high winds and torrential rain, but a violent, malevolent calamity that tossed his passenger ship from giant wave to giant wave during his parents' exile.

Upon seeing the unpredicted approaching tempest, the ship's forecaster was executed immediately by the captain, and as the lightning illuminated a curling wave spitting white froth like a rabid animal from its crest, the helmsman realised no set of sail or altered rudder course could steer the ship away from the onslaught of certain catastrophe.

His father tied his mother to a mast below decks, lest she be flung into the bulkhead. As his father reached out for him amid the seawater spitting from the splintered hull, the ship finally split in two with a scream from defeated timbers, its keel unable to withstand further abuse from the forces outside.

He awoke on the sand, coughing up seawater and bile, his chest heaving with convulsions until there was no more left inside.

He was eleven years and four-fifths old, and it was there his evil obsession was born.

* * *

~ 1 ~

The Funeral and the Girl

It began as a fairly pleasant, ordinary afternoon.

"I hate funerals. Damn waste of time, standing around listening to some referee ramble on about how good some dead guy was. How the hell do they know, from what they've been told by the grieving family? Well they're not gonna be saying anything bad, are they? And if they did, do you think for one second and a quarter a ref would include that in a sermon?" He sniffed, wiping his nose with the back of his left hand. "It's about time the whole sorry affair was shaken up. Let's have someone stand above the coffin, preferably when it's in the ground, and tell everyone what an absolute tool the guy was, let's have some honesty."

"You're all heart," muttered Detective Williams, pulling at her tight shirt collar. "Besides, it's against the rules – no disclosure for the ref before the fight."

Chief Nick Adams grinned. "I've been to so many of these damn things over the years, I'm getting sick of my time being wasted." He turned to her. "You honestly think refs aren't on the take?"

"I don't know, don't care – but if you've seen enough of these, then I guess *you* shouldn't have had most of them whacked."

He turned back to the view outside. "There'll be more, that's for sure. Next time I'll be on vacation. Somewhere hot – across the ocean. A lonely island maybe."

Williams shrugged. "Good luck finding a place like that, even if you could get there. Just stories, boss."

They weren't, but I understood how and why she believed they were, and why Nick craved such a place.

I watched the squad car slow as it reached the cemetery. The wrought iron gates with their raised rashes of rusty scabs were permanently open. Both had broken hinges, forcing the gates into the overgrown grass, straining at their top hinge bolts from the brick pillars' masonry like decayed teeth and braces protruding from diseased gums. If you had been there, you would have drawn a similar description, of that I'm certain.

A white gull landed on the right hand pillar with a streak of red upon its left wing. Noticing the throb of the squad car's suspensor field, it turned, eyes blinking, watching, and Detective Chief Inspector Nick Adams (plainclothes) stared back as it watched him. It squawked a single comment before flying off with a borrowed whim to discover a better perch.

"Not many here," said Williams as she leaned forward to look out of the window to her right.

"Are you surprised. The guy was an idiot."

"You wouldn't be saying that if he'd agreed to take the pay-off."

"Of course I would. He'd still be an idiot. I told him, 'You're an idiot. If there was an idiot competition, you'd come second.' He asked me, 'Why second?' and I told him, 'Because you're an idiot.'"

The squad car's field kicked away gravel in a similar way tyres used to as the vehicle followed the meandering drive to the chapel. I liked that, as it simply reminded me of the old times I'd been told about by your uncle.

When the car hovered to a halt, the driver and front passenger stepped out, brushing the creases from their uniforms before perching their caps upon their heads. Adams told the car to lock its doors and wait as he and Williams joined them.

The twenty-first precinct's chief pathologist stood with a handful of other spectators around the coffin, and Adams and Williams walked slowly down the narrow, cobbled pathway where an honour guard of uniformed officers waited, rifles at their sides. Both Nick and I noticed Williams seemed awkward in her uniform. Her petite frame cocooned, insulating her from comfort, the rough fabric constricting. Her cap was a little too big, the shiny black peak too low, obscuring her view and forcing her to tilt her head back. It hid her hair, which was a shame. She had lovely, naturally blonde, straight hair that framed her round face perfectly when it was allowed to be itself.

"Gruber's brought his ex-wife with him," she said in a low voice, noticing the thin pathologist in his crumpled, dark blue suit.

"Cathy's always been a spectator," said Adams. "It gives his kids a break from having to look at her face, thirty-six ten. Gruber told me she's at these things as often as possible, loves a fight."

"She certainly lost her looks after having the kids."

"In her case just mother nature's way of saying no more of this shit in the gene pool – more of that and you're gonna trigger another mass extinction event, just to make sure."

"Do you know how their split started? Wasn't down to you, was it?"

Nick just shot her a stare which swore.

I noticed the illustrator sitting on a wooden stool next to a twelve-foot-high statue of the daemon, Adramelech, High Chancellor of the Darkness, president of the high council of Devils, Superintendent of the King of Daemon's summer wardrobe, so the plaque beneath read.

The illustrator looked up as we strode past into his field of view. "You're late!" he shouted, slamming down his right palm upon his knee, hastily reaching for his sponge. Williams gave him the finger without turning.

A funeral illustrator's not a well-paid job these days – it all depends on the quality of their compositions, but there's plenty of work. From the brief glimpse I'd seen of this artist's work from the corner of Nick's eyes, he was of a low-to-mid-range ability. As I'm sure you're aware, the vanishing point is a preliminary essential before any work should begin, no matter what medium's being employed, if you'll pardon the pun. Unlike illustrators, mediums find it difficult to find work these days.

"I just hope this one's quick," said Adams, smiling and nodding to Gruber and his wife. His eyes followed the curve of spectators around the coffin until they found the deceased's wife, her two children standing either side of her. He walked up to her, shook her hand briefly, offering his condolences, telling her what a great officer her husband had been, and how proud he was to have had him serve under him for almost twenty years. She thanked him through her tears, then whispered in his ear. "I know what you did, Nick, you jerkoff. You'll pay for murdering him. I have proof." And with that she kissed him on the cheek, lingering a little too long to be comfortable for me, I must add. He took his place next to Williams, his expression unaffected by her threat.

The right honourable referee officiated over the proceedings in a respectful and unbiased manner. I was pleased to see this, as I find it unprofessional for RHR's to comment for either side; it's frowned upon, but not uncommon. His brief speech completed, the band began to play. It was an enjoyable ensemble. They wore light purple catsuits with off-white shirts open almost to their waists, ruffles lining the plackets, high collars that struggled to stay motionless as a strong and somewhat sweet breeze blew across the proceedings. Each of them sported a long black wig of zebra mane, matching the trim of their knee-high boots. They were all competent musicians, but the deceased's wife had obviously needed to save money, as a vocalist was not present. It was a fair and well-thought-through decision on her part, as lyrics can in most cases be perceived as a tool to influence the outcome.

The coffin lowered into the grave, coming to rest with a thud. I give the band their due (or more accurately, the percussionist) as the thud of the cast iron casket as it hit the grave's bottom was perfectly punctuated, preceded by a snare roll and completed with a simultaneous bass drum and cymbal crash. It wasn't this drummer's first gig at a funeral, that was obvious.

The daemons winked into existence right on cue, and Adams traced a finger down the service list for their names.

"Xaphan, a second rank exiled malcontent," he mumbled, glancing up. "Looks a little tired, Billie." This was a shame, as I was expecting a good show. You would have thought he'd had an early night beforehand, just to save a little strength. But it was obvious he'd been up all night by the look of his eyes.

She gave Nick a dismissive curl of the mouth, tugging at her collar again.

His opponent was uncredited on the service list, so Adams folded it and stuffed it in his jacket pocket.

The band switched to another number, one I'd not heard before. It began discordantly, with the quartet joining the rhythm separately and across the beat. None of them made any effort to keep in time, nor play together to form what could be considered by anyone with an iota of musical sensibility, a tune. The pianist made great efforts to embellish every phrase that appeared to be heading towards a logical modal conclusion with a mad flourish of notes, sounding as though they were performed by someone having convulsions. I was sure one of the notes was correct, however. The drummer insisted on punctuating inaudible peaks during the tune, hitting his cymbals with nonsensical arbitrary skill. As the bass player's fingers meandered around his fretboard with the grace of a drunken spider in an attempt to ignore the root notes of the few chords the guitarist lazily strummed, I felt Nick realise they were playing jazz. Nick did his best to block it all out, as he did with all music. Still, when I lived as a child, *"You have to practice long and hard to be this bad,"* my mother told my father on many occasions whilst he helped her count our sugar grains.

The coffin lid leapt into the air.

"Here we go," said Adams, folding his arms.

"Be honest, it's the only reason you came," mumbled Williams, as the coffin lid landed on the grass in front of the referee.

"No, there's two reasons this time," said Adams with a satisfied smirk.

The referee lifted his head, raised his arms, pausing for a moment before shouting, "Begin!"

The daemons took their cue and floated at the ready, either side of the open grave. The deceased's soul rose slowly from his body. It looked angry, which for me was a stupid stance to take. Get with the plan. Inevitability is just that, inevitable.

It began to glow, forming up to take on the shape of a truncated octahedron. Both daemons shrugged, they'd seen this old malarkey many times before, and were *not* impressed. I'd seen it perhaps three, maybe four times. It never ended well, that much I could guarantee.

The shape's hexagon facets produced various lengths of sharp cones of refusal. They were pure white, perfectly smooth, their tips shining in the suns as sharp as needles – I knew what they contained, and that was another mistake. The square facets grew large grey eyes with lashes thrashing about like serpents, the eyes widening in surprise as they saw the daemons, the lashes rearing up like cobras, the eyes narrowing with hatred at the circling combatants.

"So, what you got for dinner tonight?" asked Williams, her stomach suddenly rumbling.

"I'm gonna head down to Abernathy's first," answered Adams, reaching into his inside jacket pocket for his glasses. "Going to sink a few long ones before third sundown and then worry about food." He held his glasses above his head and squinted at each dirty lens. Tutting, he pulled out his handkerchief to clean them as the first round began.

"I'm gonna pick up something on the way home," said Williams, pushing her cap back a little. Saves Dolores from cooking."

"Noble," said Adams, knowing her decision was arrived at from a practicality standpoint, rather than being an act of benevolence on her part. Xaphan's hands grabbed the longest of the spikes and snapped it off with a deafening growl, throwing it casually over his head like you shouldn't a javelin. It landed in front of the illustrator point first, obscuring his view of the fight for a few moments as it evaporated into a tower of pungent green smoke.

"Nick," said Williams, pointing. "Isn't that other daemon Volac? I'm sure we've seen him before, around a month ago."

Nick shrugged as the soul quivered. It knew now what it was up against as regret bled from the stump. They never learn, they never prepare.

Volac made a predictable but classic manoeuvre. He laid prone in the air, tucking his old leathery wings tight against his back, tail straight with its arrowed tip held between his ankles. Thrusting forward he seized the stump with both claws, his jaw dislocating with a sharp click, thrusting down onto the wound to suck the regret from the soul. The mourners cheered (more from politeness than appreciation of the tactic) and rightly so.

With a kick from Xaphan's right foot, Volac's snack was cut short. He backed away, wiping the regret from his lips, sucking it quickly from his clawtips. Xaphan spun around in a blur, thumbs gouging out an eye, squeezing it in his hands until it popped like a melon with a loud wet, well, pop, I guess. The soul screamed as the serpents around the empty eye socket lay limp.

"Might get a pizza instead. I'm not sure." She turned to Adams. "Have you tried that new place on the corner of seven hundred and fifty second? What's it called, Negative Prime Pizza – something like that?"

"Not yet. The prices seem reasonable, just a thirty for a medium with all the toppings. Just haven't got around to it. I still love Gino's. It's hard to beat."

"That's because he's not, especially with a bat."

"That was a mistake, he knows that now! No anchovies, heavy with the garlic for crying out loud, but no freaking anchovies!"

The music finally died, and the band took a few moments to tune their instruments as if to indicate the instruments themselves were responsible for the quality of the last piece. They upped the tempo now with a unique medley of 30s classics.

Xaphan and Volac pulled at the soul from either side in a tug of war. They each held a spike, but Volac made ground quickly. Frustrated, Xaphan reached down to the grass. His hand swept around in a great arc, picking up the deceased's wife, Judith, to hold her in front of an eye. Now, perhaps it was because Xaphan was tired, I don't honestly know. Perhaps he'd not been told the rules before being asked to participate. Either way, his move was forbidden.

"Foul!" cried the referee, waving his arms madly above his head as he ran forward. "Break!"

Volac released his grip and backed away a few paces, treading air. But Xaphan either didn't hear the referee, or chose to ignore him. With a swift movement he impaled Judith on the soul's longest spike.

"Holy crap! Look at that!" exclaimed Williams. "I'm glad I came now."

"Typical," said Adams.

She turned to him, frowning. "What's the matter, boss? You sound disappointed."

Adams snatched his glasses from his face and strode over to the referee, the illustrator shaking his head as he reached for his sponge again.

"That's *not* allowed!" said Adams, looking down at the referee.

"What?" The referee shouted above the gurgled screams from Judith, dying above.

Judith's eighteen-year-old son, Gregory, pushed between them, dragging his crying two-year-old sister, Bethany, along with him as she sucked her thumb. She had a lovely pink dress and a plastic crown of fake daisies in her blonde hair. I didn't like her shoes.

"The guy's right," said Gregory, waving an accusing finger at the referee before tugging on his sister's arm. "Shut up, Bethany!"

Xaphan glanced down at them for a moment then turned back to the soul, pushing Judith's body further down the spike, splitting it in two at the waist. Her two halves landed either side of our group, curling and spouting black and grey clots of all kinds of fluids onto the well-kept lawn, kicking and flailing about for a few moments before it twitched a couple of times as if shrugging, comfortable with its final resting places – a little like trying to get comfortable in a cheap hotel bed, I guessed, as I didn't know at that time.

"That's a disqualification, ref," said Adams, ignoring Gregory's comment, "no doubt about that."

The soul darkened now, its shape returning to a sphere, growing cold.

"You're right," said the referee, turning to look up. "Xaphan, you're disqualified! Rule 4c, section 12." He brought out his bible and held it up. "You know the rules, buddy!"

The daemon shrugged and turned to Volac. They conferred for a while, resulting in Xaphan reluctantly nodding his head. He picked up Judith's broken body halves, licked each bloody end with a purple forked tongue the length of Adams' car, then pushed them together. In an instant she was whole again, and he placed her next to her children, apologising with a sound resembling half a dozen and three chicken's eggs broken into a steaming pan of butter.

"Volac is the winner!" shouted the referee as Xaphan vanished. Judith complained about the stains on her clothes, stating she'd sue for dry cleaning and repairs, but the referee would have none of it. "You signed the disclaimer. Look at clause 479," he said, slapping his bible. "It's all there, honey."

With the contest won, Volac took charge of the soul, summoning a capture cage to surround it.

"Wonder where he'll end up?" muttered Williams under her breath, joining Adams.

"Who cares? It's time to go."

As they walked back up the hill, I could feel Adams' reluctance to leave. He kept looking back across the cemetery, watching Judith and her kids as they headed for their car.

When we reached our car he ordered it to stay locked. "Just give me a minute, Billie." He turned, and as Judith's car headed out of the opposite car park it erupted in a ball of flames. He ran forward, Williams close behind. But it was obvious there was nothing that could be done, which I knew was exactly what he had planned. He stood as close as he could just to make sure they were all dead, and as the flames died down, he spotted something from the corner of his eye.

A figure running fast, a young woman. She jumped up onto a headstone and somersaulted to another. In a flash she produced two black handguns from holsters at her waist, jumped again and fired at Adams from mid air.

"*What?*" shouted Adams, as he heard the bullet whizz past his right ear, and I thought for a moment with great relief, my time imprisoned inside Nick Adams, head of Middletown's Policing Force, was coming very close to a conclusion.

Trapped in his head, I've seen so much of his evil, seen so many atrocities he's committed over the years. He'd managed to keep this city suffocated beneath his stranglehold for far too long. I could look away during the really ghastly moments if I wanted to, and I took pleasure in believing that upon his death his soul would *not* be fought over, as his actions guaranteed him a permanent bed and a nice soft pillow to rest his head in the depths of the Darkness.

Another bullet followed close behind the first, and Adams dropped to the ground, fumbling for his side-arm.

"What the hell?" shouted Williams, discarding her cap and joining him on the ground. But Adams was watching the girl now, her form shimmering behind the heat haze from the car as she advanced. She wore long blue denim shorts and a red vest with white piping. Bald head, nothing on her feet, crazy look on her face. It was an interesting outfit, not quite the correct choice for this time of year, but each to their own. Perhaps she didn't feel the cold. She fired again.

"Shoot, goddammit!" shouted Adams to the honour guard.

They returned automatic fire, peppering headstones with lead, chips and chunks of marble and granite tumbling through the air, dust particles creating clouds of grey and black. Her return fire found two of them, putting them down dead. Hiding behind a statue's broad plinth, (Ukobach, a low level daemon with a really bad taste in waistcoats) she caught her breath.

Adams frantically waved the honour guard forward. "Get them to flank her! She won't get out of here!" he shouted to Williams.

"But..."

"Just do it. Follow me in and give me cover. We're going straight down the middle."

Standing, he let off two rounds, keeping his eyes on the statue for movement, then running forward, sliding up to crouch behind a headstone. There was a nice bouquet of red and yellow wildflowers left on top of the headstone, and I struggled to remember the variety, but they disintegrated as she fired back, the petals carried away on the breeze.

Williams moved slowly forwards, shouting now, ordering the honour guard to divide. This was a mistake. If she'd only learnt to use hand signals.

The girl appeared again, bold as old brass, sprinting between the graves, heading to Adams' right. Bullets followed her, but not one came close. I began to admire her. I didn't have a clue who she was, or where she came from. It was just very pleasant to have a distraction when all I had to look forward to was Adams writing a report before heading down to Abernathy's.

She hid behind a gravestone. "Give it up, girly!" shouted Nick. "You're outnumbered. This can only go one way. Throw the guns out, now!"

We watched as she jumped up onto a headstone and leaped to a plinth, elevating herself. She knew exactly what she was doing and fired once over Adams' head.

The left-hand flank of the honour guard took positions behind headstones and statues to return her fire, unaware Adams was exactly in the middle, between them and the right flank. All hell broke loose as the bullets creased the air, forcing Adams to lie flat. The right flank spun around and returned fire and she ran again.

Silas Gruber and Cathy Gruber-Michaels were in their car, heading for the gates.

The bullet's trajectory was perfectly calculated, impacting Cathy in the neck. She slumped to the side to fall into Silas, causing him to steer the old vehicle across the grass and into the chapel.

Adams was covered in stone debris as Williams ran over. "She's gone. We've got four officers down!"

Nick stood, angry as hell, well, not quite that angry. "Get forensics down here now. I want this place sealed tight and every blade of grass, every headstone, every statue examined for evidence."

He strode over to the illustrator who sat trembling upon his stool, his mouth open in shock. Nick pulled the canvas from the easel and broke it in two over his knee, pulled a blank from the illustrator's bag, placing it on the easel, almost knocking it over in anger. "Paint her, paint what you saw," he said, waving his gun in the illustrator's face. He holstered it and turned as Gruber ran over to them. "Cathy, she's dead!"

~ 2 ~
Presents from the Past

I read the report with Nick. Forensics spent hours combing the cemetery. Twenty men and women in white overalls, walking between the headstones with their heads bowed, like lost ghosts seeking to return to their forgotten graves.

Ghosts. The comparison made me think. How my worlds' realities had taken a strange twist as some far distant decision touched it. This event, this 'rule' had slowly crawled across the void as the universe, unaware, carried on with the task of simply existing as life flourished and died, flourished, got bored, murdered one another and died.

As Nick Adams slept off his drinks fully-clothed on his couch, I sat in his head, wide awake, remembering a very long time ago.

I think it was a Riftday, or a Rothday, I'm not too sure. I do remember the time, it was late in the afternoon, around twelve minutes or so after nine. My parents had left me with my great uncle, Ephesus, at his lakeside shack, while they took time for themselves venturing into Hope to search for a new home for all four of us.

I was twelve years old, and it was just a few weeks before my first teenage birthday.

Great Uncle's shabby shack of peeling white paint and crooked roofs sat elevated above the lake shore on tree trunk stilts. He was sitting at the end of the narrow rickety pier of a few missing planks, stretching far out over the water. His rounded shoulders were wrapped in a grey woollen shawl as he waited for a bite on his line, his feet pretending to enjoy the coolness of the water. I listened to a pair of mayflies arguing about how to spend the only day of their lives together as they flew up and down the pier, and behind me my dwarf giant pet gastropod, Charles, the Curator of Whims, Chameleon of Truths, clung to the shack wall, his eye-stalks retracted to take his afternoon nap. I sat barefoot in an ebony rocking chair enjoying the suns, wearing a wide-brimmed, battered straw hat with a red ribbon tied in a bow at the left side, big, pink rimmed sunglasses and my loose cotton dress of yellow poppies keeping me cool as I let my mind wander whilst it wondered.

As the suns dipped beneath the horizon in turn, the temperature dropped in turn too, and when the last sun vanished from view, it was time to head inside to the warmth of the fire where shadows danced around the walls to the rhythmic spits and crackles of long-dead wood.

Great Uncle told me fantastic stories as he toasted marshmallows on a long fork, dipping them into a cup of hot lime and ginger tea, passing them to me lest I burn my fingers. I can still taste them, even today. Then we watched the fire die, the room becoming dark and cool as the shadows' dancing became lazy, until I fell asleep in the big wooden chair he'd made for his departed wife almost a century and a half ago.

We'd waited weeks for Seasonstill to finally break that year. Low billowing clouds of miserable blue-grey had shielded us from the three suns for weeks, rolling across the sky in a seemingly neverending reluctance to dissipate as the rain impacted the lake like tiny silver needles. One morning the rain clouds finally cleared, and I remember watching them from my bedroom window, breaking away like cotton candy being teased from its cane during a midsummer fair.

I hurriedly called to Charles, eager to step out into the suns, telling him to follow me downstairs. I was really looking forward to the day, as arrangements had been agreed that on the third fine day of the holidays I could walk back into Broadstone by myself after breakfast, to meet my best friend, Keloff. He wanted to introduce me to his new friend, someone he excitedly called, 'the man who knows everything.'

I was suspicious of this claim, with a few handfuls of questions for this stranger, but meeting up with Keloff was foremost in my mind. I assumed his colourful description of this stranger was just his way of encouraging me to join him. He didn't have to, I liked Keloff *very* much, and presumed that this 'man' would probably be either out, or too busy to see us, allowing us to spend the day together exploring the ruins of the past, poking their heads amid the tall wildflowers of the meadowlands beyond his father's farm, and the citadel ruins where Keloff spent most of his free time.

"Be certain to return in time to tidy your room," Great Uncle had said, by way of permitting my trip alone, but I knew that wasn't all *that* important at all, as my mother had explained all about *that* scenario to me previously. I'll tell you all about that later.

It was a distant neighbour of Great Uncle's, ex-High Chancellor of Clouds, Mr Moople, part-time forager of discarded adjectives, (but most noteworthy for his estate of ruined weathermills) who broke the news to us that morning. He wore his considering expression, which I knew was a fine prelude to his as yet unknown thoughts, as he stood in the open doorway. Great Uncle had an annoying habit of leaving the front door open, saying, "I haven't anything worth stealing, and why close it and not let the day enjoy my hospitality too?" Mum told me it was because he hoped his wife would return from the dead one day, but we all knew people didn't usually do that.

Mr Moople had trekked between the forest of shale monoliths lining the abandoned bone mines and navigated his way along the cliff-maze of grey pine trees, some two leagues to the west. I should have realised then that what he had to say was mightily important for this old gentleman to take such an arduous journey.

"Mr Moople!" I shouted, dropping my toast onto the plate to run over to him as Great Uncle stood by the door. I gave him a great big hug and a little kiss on the cheek, and he wheezed a brief dry breath, smelling of peppermint and green apples. I could feel an uncharacteristic tension in his slight frame – yes, he was thin and frail, and smelt overall of weariness at the best of times, but there was something more to him this day.

"Don't snollygoster me, child!" he said, trying to hide the fact he was pleased to see me. "I must talk with Ephesus." His face quickly found the smile he knew I was used to, as from beneath his faded light blue satin robes of a sky he'd once managed and commanded, he produced a lollipop, holding it up between our smiles. "For after your lunch, no sooner and no later!"

I took it, nodding quickly. "Thank you," skipping a few times to return to sit down to breakfast. As I twirled the stick slowly between my fingers I noticed the wrapper was still fully intact, faded of course from years of existence, and I wondered how many he had in his collection, as he would produce one for me every time we met.

"It's the tomorrow, all's changed now," he said, standing in the doorway as Great Uncle stood aside, inviting him in with a gesture. Sitting in a swivelling red leather chair on Mr Moople's left shoulder pad sat his tiny, senior Hair Warden, dressed in a smart, white cotton suit. He turned his back to us, barking orders to his eight underlings in the hair wardens' funny chirping noise, resembling that of a chattering magpie's laughter. They all nodded as Mr Moople walked forward, hastily releasing the wheel brakes to the pair of iron carts carrying Mr Moople's hair, yards and yards that had not been cut some two hundred years and two days since his birth. Satisfied every strand was safe and accounted for (all eight of them knew exactly how many strands he had, and between them every strand's name) they relaxed, obviously thankful another journey was now complete without incident or an encounter with a wandering stylist, determined for business.

Great Uncle invited him to join us for our breakfast of boiled larks' eggs and slices of fried bell mushrooms, cut into the shape of a turtle's love. Following a few delicate manoeuvres, he sat at the table. With thumb and forefingers of both hands he smoothed his tall, back-combed eyebrows which twisted like Gothic spires and tied at their top with tiny blue bows, and I noticed the weariness in his eyes.

"Tomorrow? All changed? How?" asked Great Uncle, wiping yellow yolk off his beard with his napkin.

Mr Moople's hands found the table before him. "Daemons, Ephesus. The Darkedness daemons are here!"

My great uncle didn't seem at all concerned by the news at first, and broke off a chunk of brown bread, buttering it with the sharpened handle of a large old silver dessert spoon, the only utensil he ever ate with. "Daemons, eh Moople? What kind of daemons?"

"Ancient, as young as the beginning of time," he said wide-eyed, his clawing hands grasping the air beside his narrow face in an attempt to introduce some kind of enthusiasm from my great uncle. "Some as big as this rickety shack," he pointed briefly so as not to offend. "Some, some as small as young Charles there." My gastropod's eyes narrowed upon Mr Moople as he chewed on the last of his mushrooms, and Great Uncle gave him a glance to not take offence as I finished the decorations to Charles' shell. I'd started this task the day before, with paint, white glue and sprinklings of gold and silver glitter, and my design was almost complete.

I signed my name with black paint, replaced the brush in a jam jar of water, jiggling it about a little to admire the swirling clouds there to then fold my arms upon the table and listen. Charles' eye-stalks curved around to see my work, telling me he was happy with a thump of his foot and a quick whistled melody, so I gave him a big smile as the adults' conversation continued.

"Not that old then," my great uncle replied, dropping the spoon beside his plate. "But, I guess it's time." I noticed the concern colouring his voice as he stood up to clear away the breakfast things.

"Time for what, Great Uncle?" I asked as I turned to watch him holding his back, struggling to straighten.

He remained silent for a little while, and when he was satisfied the table was tidy enough and all the dirty plates and cutlery were in the sink, he spoke, picking up his favourite spoon and polishing its silver with his handkerchief as he sat down. He concentrated upon that spoon, refusing to look at me. "They will fight for our souls, Tiny Flower. They are the evil, they are the good."

Great Uncle placed the spoon and handkerchief on the table before him, then produced an ancient coin from the worn brown leather satchel he always carried over his shoulder. He flipped the coin in the air with his thumb. "Call!"

"Tails," snapped Mr Moople.

The coin hit the breakfast table with a tinny "Ouch," and began spinning as the two of them watched it, finally coming to rest. "You win," said Great Uncle, picking it up and dropping it back into his satchel. He scooped up the spoon and handkerchief to continue polishing.

"Fight? For our souls? What for?" I asked.

He examined the spoon in the light for a few moments, before producing a stone from a leather pouch on his belt to sharpen it upon. "The time is now that all that could live, have lived." He looked over at Mr Moople, frowning for a moment as he continued sharpening his spoon. Checking the sharpness with his thumb, he replaced the stone in his pouch, stood and walked back to the sink to wash the spoon and dishes, raising his voice as he continued. "The universe has had its fill of high-form life, had its fill of all the souls from all the millions of billions of trillions of others out there." He lowered his voice with sadness. "The great receptacle of life is finally empty."

"I don't understand. Others? Receptacle of life?"

He exhaled long and hard, stroking the bottom of his thorny beard as he turned, a few soap bubbles briefly existing there to slide down it and silently burst.

"There are many worlds out there, in this realm and others. The receptacle held every soul from the very beginning, waiting, issuing them as each high-form of life evolved and was born to accept them. Now, the receptacle is empty, exhausted – sterility will blanket the universe.

There will be no more new births, for no high-form can be born without a soul."

I stared at him as he walked back to the table, returning his spoon to his place setting. Then I began to laugh, closing my eyes, waiting for Charles to join in. But there was only silence, save for the drip of water upon a plate from the sink. I opened my eyes expecting to see Great Uncle's beaming face, his shoulders heaving up and down as he struggled to suppress his laughter, expecting Mr Moople to blurt out one of his high-pitched giggles along with a chorus from his hair wardens, his visit simply to borrow a slab of Great Uncle's butter churned from throd fish milk. But no. Great Uncle sat perfectly still, his expression deadly serious, as was Moople's and his wardens'.

He clasped his large hands together on the table before him. "When high-forms die, their souls will be fought over. If a daemon of the light is triumphant, they will allow that soul to live again, returning it to the receptacle to be issued once more when a yet to be newborn finds life in its mother's womb."

I looked at Charles. His eye-stalks had receded a little, then I looked back to Great Uncle. "And what about the dark?" I asked, looking at Mr Moople for assistance. "Darkedness, I think you said? You said there was light and dark?"

He seemed as though his words struggled to form in his mouth. "If a soul is won by a daemon from the dark, it will be fed upon for eternity by the Darkedness. Daemons do not have souls, Tiny Flower. The dark will drain souls until they are almost withered away, like a Seasonsbreeze leaf carried away by the wind, lying upon the forest floor, awaiting Seasonchill's frost, to rot and die beneath it. But unlike a fallen leaf, they will wait for a soul's strength to return, to feast upon it again and again, all through eternity. From this, the evil of the Darkedness will eventually multiply. When fought over, a soul will never know which daemon is which, for a daemon's appearance is just that. The Darkness must be stopped. You will find..."

"But what if the soul beats both of them, then what? What happens when..."

Charles began to whistle, his shell vibrating, telling me to keep quiet. My heart began to quicken, "I...I'm sorry to interrupt. It sounds like a good story, Great Uncle, but how do you know all this?"

I noticed Mr Moople heave a sigh as he sat back in his chair, his head tilting toward the ceiling causing a flurry of activity behind him, and that's when it all became a little too much for me.

"I am an ancient daemon," Great Uncle answered, his back straightening, adding a generous hand to his height. "Older than those which will make themselves known to this realm, this day. Older than what all high-forms call the beginning, older than a time when there was nothing." He wiped up a few breadcrumbs from the table into his hand and held them out for Charles to nibble upon. He took them gently as Great Uncle continued in a whisper. "I was present when this arrangement was agreed, old even then," he said, watching Charles with a gentle smile hidden beneath his moustache. "I signed the contract with the others, a document of ten thousand signatures." He waited until Charles had finished every breadcrumb, wiped his hand on his tunic and turned to Mr Moople, raising his voice. "Have they established the clause yet, Moople, bound it to this world?"

The old gentleman shook his head briskly, causing his hair wardens to chatter as they snapped into action once again. "No, no, only one arrived. A herald, Tzitzimime."

"Are you *absolutely* sure?"

"Of course, Ephesus, that's why I'm here! I felt her arrival," his voice softened as his eyes widened. "Felt it in my hair, Ephesus." With that he turned, heading for the door. "We must both adopt our roles now, you know that. I must prepare, as must you." He smiled at me briefly and nodded. "Tiny Flower." I smiled back as he continued. "Good day, Ephesus, and good luck."

I watched him leave, Great Uncle uncharacteristically closing the door behind him, standing there for a moment with his back to me. He returned to the table, sitting for a while in silence before picking up his spoon and staring at his reflection in its back. I leaned over to look too, and for a brief moment I saw a reflection of something else there, something indescribable. I was about to ask another question when he slit my throat with the sharpened handle.

Then I awoke, sitting in the head of Nickolatus Fenstinion Adams.

~ 3 ~
The Red Bullet

Much later?

Perhaps. I have no way of knowing.

But, the world *had* changed. Great Uncle, or whatever he was, had been right. There were many combinations of what existed before. Some, lost over the years, some remained – changed, altered and adapted. People either forgot how things had been, or chose to ignore them, but for the most part I remembered a little of how things were.

I missed Charles greatly. My parents – and of course, Keloff – and often wondered what became of them all.

The following morning Nick showered and changed his clothes. He drove through the early morning traffic to a neon-illuminated thirty-six hour diner, bought a bag of bacon bagels then told his car to take him to the precinct as he lay across the back seat, hands clasped over his stomach, eyes closed in concentration, whistling his tune.

I realised when I awoke in Nick's head that Great Uncle had hidden my soul away there, unable to take the risk I'd be won by evil and taken to the Darkness to be feasted upon. Then I remembered Great Uncle's voice as my life ebbed away at the breakfast table. *'Witness and remember all you experience when you awake. Watch all he does and we will use your evidence to defeat them, destroy the Darkness as his actions break the contract.'*

I thought about that contract. Surely there was a loophole, somewhere? If I could only read that contract perhaps that would release me from this prison? But what does a girl of my age know of contracts?

"Anything from forensics?" asked Adams, dropping the bag of bagels upon Williams' desk.

She peered into the bag and took one. "Nothing, chief. Not one shred of evidence, just shell casings." She shuffled some papers then opened a grey folder, tracing a slender finger down the first page. "We've got another missing person though."

Adams gave her a frown. "This girl was running barefoot across the cemetery, jumping all over the place, from tomb to gravestone. You're telling me not one sliver of skin from her feet?"

Williams shrugged and bit into her bagel. "What about the missing person, you want a hand in that?"

"Nah. Concentrate on the cemetery."

"You certain? That's the second in a month and five weeks – roughly the same age and gender?"

"Just the cemetery."

She threw the bag back onto his desk. "Gruber said he wants to see both of us as soon as you're ready."

Adams finished his bagel, grabbed the bag and headed for the stairs.

The morgue was a smooth dungeon of cream-coloured ceramic tiles. In places they had chipped away to reveal rusted steel. The most commonly used drawers at Gruber's waist height showed cracks where the pitted stainless steel handles hung loosely on their mounts. The red-tiled floor's white grout was missing here and there, allowing the watered down blood clots from a thousand hosed down bodies to gather and harden on their way to the drain.

Gruber was hunched at his desk, writing notes beneath a harsh desk lamp, humming a tune from the funeral. He turned as he heard footsteps behind him.

"You wanted to see us?" said Adams.

He stood, waving us in excitedly. "Yes, yes. I thought you'd be earlier?"

In the centre of the room a table, where a translucent plastic sheet covered the corpse of Cathy Gruber-Michaels.

The thin mortician walked over to it and pulled back the sheet, revealing his dead ex-wife's head and shoulders.

"She don't look any better," said Adams. "What's up?"

Gruber's nose twitched at the odour from the corpse. He fumbled in his lab coat pocket for a small tub of nose balm, wiped a little beneath his nose, then offered it to Adams and Williams.

"Spoil the bagel," said Nick, as Williams took it.

Gruber shrugged before pointing at Cathy's neck. "Here's the wound. What can you see?"

"A hole," said Adams too quickly, so the two words sounded like one, refusing to take a closer look and offering him a bagel. Gruber shook his head like a bird shaking off water after a bath, his thinning black hair refusing to move, greased to his scalp and neatly parted at the centre.

"No," said Williams as she crouched down. "It's not a hole, it's an indent with a halo of bruising."

Gruber nodded, pulled up his sleeve to glance at his watch before looking at Adams. "Your underling is correct. The bullet did *not* pierce her skin."

"So you're telling me a ricochet hit her in the neck, killing her?"

"There's no evidence of a ricochet. I had the car examined – she had the window wound down. It was a clean shot."

Nick folded his arms. "But what about the four dead officers? You telling me they weren't taken out by clean shots? They're dead, right?"

Gruber smiled, glancing at the drawers to his right. "Oh yes. All on ice, killed by custom shells. Big and nasty, tailor-made to fit a bespoke weapon." He looked at his watch again, his thin lips counting silently, and I wondered what he was getting to, and how long it was going to take. He covered her up and returned to his desk. "Here. The bullet was found in my car, under Cathy's seat." They joined him as he picked up a pair of large tweezers, carefully pulling the bullet from a Pyrex flask to hold it under the desk lamp. Adams went to take it.

"No! Don't touch it, whatever you do!" exclaimed Gruber.

"What's going on. It's red. Is that blood?"

"Looks like the tip of a lipstick," said Williams.

Gruber dropped it into the dish with a brief clatter. "If you remember, your mystery assailant carried two weapons. It's my hypothesis one weapon carried a standard round," his head jerked backward once, "or rather the custom rounds which felled your dedicated officers. The other weapon carried these rounds."

"So, what are they?"

He looked at his watch again, then up at the wall clock.

"Your personality injection late or something, Gruber?" asked Adams.

The pathologist held up his right index finger for silence and shook his head again, counting silently then nodded once. Behind them the sound of plastic moving startled Adams and Williams and they turned.

Cathy had sat up, her hands covering her breasts. "Grubee dear, what's going on?"

Adams and Williams stumbled back in unison to hit the drawers."What the fuck's going on, Gruber!" shouted Adams, dropping his bag of bagels.

"Darling, please get me some clothes. Unless you have other things on your mind?"

Gruber threw her a towel which she draped around her shoulders. She turned to Adams then looked to the floor. "Nick, if those are your usual bacon bagels, I could sure use one. I'm starving."

He slid slowly down the drawers, fumbling around for the bag, his eyes remaining fixed on hers. He found it, snatched it up and held it out to her at arm's length. "Here, finish the bag, I'm done," he said, finally tossing it to her.

As she gorged herself, Gruber walked over to them. "The bullet's composed of a very strange substance. It's an immutable drug." He tapped his temples with both forefingers. "I've to run more tests, but it seems this drug permanently alters behaviour." He glanced over his shoulder. "It's a sort of love potion, a passion enhancer. It inhibits hatred, eradicates negative thoughts as soon as the substance enters the bloodstream through the epidermis and finally reaches the brain."

Nick's thoughts were running fast, imagining what such a bullet would have done to him and his plans. That's something I can say about him, he thinks quickly, and had an uncanny ability to see the possible results of any situation beyond its immediate effect.

"If this stuff gets into the water supply..." He straightened up. "I'm gonna head down to Steeltown, see what I can dig up down there. Billie, run a background check on the dead officers – see if there's a link. First, get over to the water reclamation plant as a precaution, take a special weapons detachment. We've gotta find this bald bitch and take her down, fast."

~ 5 ~
Family Histories

Yes, I *know* it should be chapter 4, but I *hate* the number 4!

You'll find out later...

Water. So taken for granted, and so little of it during those days.

Nick's sacrament was in the ocean following that shipwreck, and later I was told of his earlier beginnings, memories he was too young to remember. But for now, a continuation of his memories following that fateful storm, told as best I can through the foggy recollections of suffering and triumph he remembers. Everything in the correct order, always son, except some numbers.

Nick's convulsions finally ceased upon the pebbles. The soothing breath of the ocean touched his ears, a constant and ancient repetitive rhythm of calm. He struggled, rolling over upon his back with his eyes tightly closed, expecting excruciating pain, but surprised by feeling only the discomfort from the pebbles beneath his limbs. The suns shone warm against his drying skin, the salt upon his wrinkled lips, the dryness in his throat. Then he laughed, louder than he'd ever laughed before, forcing the last vestiges of seawater from his lungs. He was surprised to be alive, against all he'd seen and expected, against all that nature could inflict upon him during those terrible tempest's hours. Then, only the certainty of his death in his heart, now, just a violent memory. He opened his eyes, blinking rapidly at the bright, wiping them clear to focus.

Above, white clouds strung out in wisps against the blue, (smudged he decided, surprised by the thought) moving slowly, a visual accompaniment almost in unison with the ocean's rhythm. Then a few gulls, gliding together in silence.

Tranquil.

Then the other sounds came, rising slowly. Perhaps these sounds were always there, but his mind had chosen to hide their significance from him, allowing him to gradually discover his unexpected survival?

The crunch and scrape of pebbles, far from rhythmic, lazy, disorganised, punctuated by a struggling groan. It came from his right, a little way off, and as he concentrated the sounds annoyed him, invaders upon his beach of tranquillity. Could he not be allowed just a few more moments' peace? Then he knew. The groan came from his father's throat, and behind this the sounds from others. A choir, no, a chorus of dying upon the pebbles as the tide's breath sought to soothe them into acceptance.

Okay, family histories.

When my parents were not enjoying Broadstone Bloated, the little village of narrow themes to streamline their views of life, they explored. Broadstone was the place of my birth, and I have many fond and a few unfond memories of my childhood living there in our little terraced house.

The sea was my father's obsession, and he had inherited this from his extraordinary father, Roan, and influenced to a degree by his father-in-law, Julian.

Julian, once the Chief Custodian of Lost Road Signs, author of the unpublished, *'A Concise History of History,'* a man of short sentences and temper, a Theologian of Accidental Graffiti and expert woodlouse tracker and trapper in his youth, vanished just after I was born.

My mother's parents' first meeting was accidental by most people's standards, others arguing it was preordained by the gods of employment.

My grandmother's occupation was interviewing possible candidates in the employment office located in Grandslur-upon-Drymist, commonly known as 'the town of pointless jobs.' It had once been a hub for travel, its central station a mid-point to branch off in all directions as far as the eyes could see – Middletown, Hope, Broadstone Halt, Viewhaven, Pepperdean Hemstitch, to name but a few.

Grandfather Julian was enthused by the prospect of becoming a cucumber peeler for a local restaurant, and upon seeing this job advertised following his redundancy after four years and twenty-two months employed measuring rulers for accuracy at the Ministry of Measurements ruler factory, was eager to acquire the position. The upsurge of new measurements, a standardisation eliminating the old things called inches, cost him his career. Now, the new measurements were in force, and having found just one inaccurate ruler during his factory employment, management decided quality control wasn't really that important after all. Julian had hoped his past work experience would land him a job within the Holy Order of Mapwalkers, (a subsidiary of The Truthsayers) that ancient group of monks roaming the countryside, checking maps for accuracy, and in some cases, exploring the land to create new, accurate maps of otherwise unknown territory. But, upon applying for a junior position of map holder / reader for a senior monk, he discovered they now embraced the new measurements he was sadly unfamiliar with.

Tads, slivers, smidgens (which I believed for many years were baby pigeons) teeny-tiny bits, little bits, big bits, long bits and short bits, were now just a few of the standard measurements employed, following the measuring census of '56. The Ministry, aware most people spoke of measurements using these words, realised it was obvious they were far more popular and therefore far more accurate for the population as a whole.

So, during my grandfather's interview by my grandmother for the position of cucumber peeler, she decided he was far better suited for a position as her partner for her life ahead.

As she occasionally looked over her desk to him while knitting, he noticed her questions regarding his qualifications to peel cucumbers become more and more of a personal nature, and certainly unrelated to such an essential, delicate task. She pointed out grape polishing yielded a far better rate of payment, as did walking the streets of Middletown to conduct surveys upon people conducting surveys. He considered taking a junior position in Middletown's new Joke Investigation Bureau, but was aware that as a junior, he'd only hear jokes he'd heard before, and was under-qualified for a senior position as he'd probably laugh at new jokes before he was fully trained to identify potential offence, which was the department's entire objective. He refused these job opportunities, content with the prospect of cucumbers and catering. As he stood to leave, she cast off her knitting, rolled up the length of wool and passed it to him.

"What are we doing together this coming Frothday, I'm not working, that's what's not happened?" read the message as he unfurled it, and he simply gazed back into her alluring green eyes, knowing right then his future was set.

Following the death of my grandfather's mother, (a bereavement councillor for automatic porcelain dolls whose eyes were permanently stuck half closed – his mother's, not the dolls') they moved into her house in Wishart's Wood, leaving behind the awful memories of mum's Aunt Scalas adventure, which I'll get to a little later.

Grandfather Julian drank far too much water as he looked at life from an abstract viewpoint. Soon after moving into their inherited house, my grandmother found him arguing with trees as the wind blew their branches together, swearing at them in ancient nonsense as they confounded his ability to remember the names of their leaves. *"Be still, let me remember you all before your fall!"* my mother had told me he would often shout from the bedroom window during the autumn nights of Seasonfall, banging his fists against the panes, dribbling from the corners of his mouth, waking my mother when she was just an impatient young girl, wanting to enjoy the dreams she'd rented from the travelling Dream Weaver.

Despite my grandmother's obsessive desire to return to the comforting slums of Middletown's Old Town where she was born, grandfather refused to move from that house in the wood.

After grandmother refurnished the house, he was certain something was hidden there, a message of unique importance left behind for him by his mother. He worked tirelessly over many years exploring their accommodation on his hands and knees, examining the meandering patterns of the hall carpet, cross-referencing them with the patterns of the rug in front of the hearth and the fluffy curved mat surrounding the toilet, using the carpet beneath the dining room table as a cipher.

My grandmother would simply relax, knitting, while he'd measure every wall and ceiling down to the tad, add the numbers together and divide them by the amount of raindrops refusing to run down the window panes on a Riftday afternoon. He'd study and record the angles, bevels and chamfers of the decorative embellishments exhibited by cornices, coving, banisters and balustrades, the contours of skirting boards and door frames, peer into the brass door handles lest their reflections pointed to hidden areas he'd not yet discovered. On one unfortunate occasion, he locked himself away, standing for a day and two-thirds looking into the bathroom mirror, convinced the reflected view of the window behind him was one of a different season outside. This forced my poor grandmother to carry out her daily ablutions in a wooden bucket she'd bought to plant up her trailing lobelias. Thankfully for him, he drank a lot of water, emerging from the bathroom after having the sense to actually open the window and peer outside into normality, returning to my grandmother with half an apology and a hunger for a ripe gleeberry pie with goat's custard.

The following Mournday morning he drew up a 1:1 scale floor-plan of the ground floor, Sellotaping together empty cereal packets, forgotten old wallpaper from the corner of a wardrobe and flattened cardboard boxes, taking it out into the garden. I was told by my mother this certainly useless process had been arrived at after he'd adopted the practice of reading two books simultaneously, one sentence from each at a time in the hope some form of enlightenment would emerge from this alternating narrative. True, his own recipes gleaned from this practice whilst trawling through Grandmother's book collection of 10-minute meals for the beginner were astonishingly successful after his disappearance, affording our family a substantial fortune from his cookery book sales of *'20-Minute Gastronomic Masterpieces in 20 Minutes or Less.'* Although his decorating and 'Do it Yourself' home-making skills led only to disasters of equal astonishment, and on rare occasions injury, causing my mother's lifelong mistrust of any piece of furniture resembling a breakfast bar stool. After my grandparents left and my parents cleared the house in the forest for sale, his home-made dining-room chairs and table were viewed equally as, and I quote *'Beyond mentally disturbing'* by psychologists, and as *a 'three dimensional representation of his perceived position in the world hierarchy'* by art critics. But art critics seem to say such on a whim, I've found. Never trust them, son.

Anyway, that Mournday morning he thought the first bird dropping falling on his 1:1 scale plan of the ground floor would pinpoint the location of the secret, as one of my grandmother's hobbies was twig-whittling. She had won countless trophies for her art, and was fond of creating peg-legs for one-legged birds. Grandfather was convinced this first bird dropping would be by way of thanks from some airborne saviour, a synchronicity of sorts. Unfortunately for him and his plan (which the trees agreed held some merit) a splattering from a flock of wagtails (having gorged themselves on gleeberries from the left-over pie discarded on the lawn) peppered his cardboard plan with all manner of possible clues, none of which provided him with a concrete lead.

However, my grandmother pointed out that viewed from a certain angle when the shadows were just right and the light not, the peppering spelt the word *'you silly fool'* in ancient (now extinct) Livonian.

Following months of searching their house without an answer, he took his frustration out into the forest, hacking down trees that had given him the most abuse, to use their wood to build an exact replica of his inherited home. He was convinced the universe would not allow two objects containing the same secret to exist together, forcing the universe to give up the secret he had somehow managed to copy during the build. This was too much for my grandmother, a second identical house to cook in, floors to sweep, fires to tend, corners to dust and most importantly, toilets to clean – plus the expense of buying identical furniture and clothes to hang in the wardrobes. So she took my mother away to the coast where she met my father, Grandmother returning some months later alone with all the hope in her heart she'd find both houses demolished and her husband waiting to take her back to Middletown, his stupid obsession finally dead.

But it was not to be. Upon her return my grandfather had vanished, the houses now occupied by a family of travellers that had grown weary of travelling.

I never met mum's parents, which I still feel sad about today. I was told by my mother, Grandmother had a wonderful smile of false ivory teeth, and an uncanny ability to fall asleep whilst standing up without ever falling over. My grandfather loved her very much, and for the most part during their first years of marriage, took her everywhere with him. "It saves me kissing her goodbye," he had told my mum.

Her favourite hobby, apart from twig-whittling and knitting, was to weave rugs and carpets for their house in Wishart's Wood, spun from the wool shorn from the multi-coloured sheep of Mulan-ulatan Province, imported from the east-south-east. She'd embellish those rugs with ancient languages she said had appeared to her in a standing dream when she was a child. Binary, Cobol 61, Fortran, Pascal and Kotlin. Their combined messages were almost impossible to decode. But she admitted, once unravelled they simply read, *'Don't forget to lift the toilet seat, Julian, you lazy sausage.'*

This was a shame, a shame she felt their relationship was such that she couldn't bring herself to address this simple request to my grandfather in person, and a shame this incident took place just three years and eleven days before the invention of the urinal.

The last my mother heard of her was in the form of a postcard. *'Gone to find your dad, please pass this on to him if he returns.'* it simply said, postmarked from an unknown town in the east, with a stamp illustrating a deserted sausage restaurant, the postcard's picture one of a woman standing in front of a sausage restaurant, holding a postcard with a picture of a deserted sausage restaurant. If this postcard was meant as a second 'come find me' clue for Julian, he never returned to read it, and my parents never deciphered it.

As Nick headed for Steeltown, I remembered my dad's parents' greatest exploratory achievement, a story Great Uncle Ephesus asked my dad to re-tell on many an occasion when visiting my parents for a game of cards.

You must excuse my rather verbose enthusiasm in recounting all this family history to you, son. It was such a long time ago, and, I believe, although it's not *that* out of the ordinary, it is important for you to know, to help give you a sense of the past and where you came from, and how important clear communication obviously is. I know I've said this before, but I'm saying it again because it's important.

What I'm about to tell you is our first great family secret, so I'd appreciate it if you didn't share it with anyone or anything – especially trees. And I'll admit (if you had not already realised) I find retelling these facts refreshingly cathartic. It's absolutely wonderful to have someone listening to me after so many years, and it's especially wonderful as it is you, my son!

So, before my father was born, his parents had sailed the southern seas, just so my grandfather, Roan, could see what was actually out there, rather than rely on hearsay. His passion later fell to the sky, which you'll read about later if I have the time.

Beneath and beyond the tethered floating communication relays, with their balloons filled with the gas collected from political speeches, they sailed. Past the marker buoys with their little arrow signs indicating the directions of currents, upwellings and downwellings my grandfather allowed their little vessel, *Sea for Yourself,* to drift. From time to time he'd hoist sail to steer towards a cloud he liked (a combination of his father's approach, nature's whim and the Captain's choice, he'd told my dad) pushing the little sailing vessel further than any explorer had ventured from our coastline. He had planned ahead, leaving supplies tied to marker buoys he'd dropped while out fishing on the trawler during the night, and for this my grandmother was thankful, especially as there were no pies.

Upon sighting land they anchored and swam to an unknown shore, to walk upon sand not visited in a thousand and four lifetimes, so my dad claimed. Fossilized dictionaries from a handful and a half different languages protruded from the cliffs, narrating the evolution of words. Pages upon pages lay open, motionless, sealed by the passing of time and the absorbtion of minerals, a treasure trove just waiting to be read. But my grandfather, fond of announcing, *'Travel broadens the mind, time travel would muck it up for everyone, although they wouldn't know about it,"* to anyone who would engage him concerning the virtues of exploratory travel, had his eyes firmly set upon other treasures he was convinced lay beyond those cliffs, refusing my grandmother's wish to copy down as much as they could and return home.

They climbed, clinging to volumes concerning phraseological instances, semantic relationships and textual aspects of linguistics. When my grandmother almost fell from a single glass-like sheet of lexico-grammar including congruent and metaphoric expression, she almost turned back, but he convinced her to continue as he hoisted her up. She loved him back then, that much is true and was obvious.

As they reached the summit, exhausted by what they'd read, they turned to face the sea, watching the ocean as a roar of water filled their ears. The receding, great low tide grounded *Sea For Yourself*, swaying as it came to rest with its keel on the seabed. Beyond, a landscape of once submerged, enormous tide pools and mountain ranges emerged, stretching as far as any eye could see. The marine life evacuated. Millions of fish swam in a great shoal to the giant sinkhole, their only chance of survival. Grandmother took out her notebook and pencil, sketching what lay before them. A landscape not seen by human eyes for three ages and a very long while.

Behind my grandparents lay an exotic, brightly-coloured forest, and for two days they trekked through it heading south, until they discovered a range of five mountains shaped like crooked noses. At the base of each mountain were two enormous caves. Roan, feeling invigorated by the discovery, chose one at random to explore, Grandmother deciding to wait outside and set camp, and perhaps massage her feet and comb her hair.

When he returned a day and an hour later, he was visibly shaken. He believed he had awoken the giant snails of that land from their thousand-year slumber.

As the snails emerged from the caves, back to the shoreline my grandparents scrambled, running through the forest to abseil down the jagged dictionaries to the sand below. There was nothing left for them but to return home across the seabed, abandoning *Sea For Yourself* after hastily gathering a few belongings from its tiny cabin.

The snails were far behind, yet relentless in their pursuit.

By all accounts, my grandfather became uncontrollably upset, the wrecks the low tide had exposed were wondrous. Tens of hundreds of vessels of all shapes and sizes littered the landscape: steel, brass, bone and wood. Ships from recent and ancient times lay there, some as simple as a ship needs to be, others as mechanically complex as a large cardboard box of rusted mechanical timepieces, all shaken up. Wooden masts intact with rigging, grand complications of rope and sail. Others just unrecognisable shapes hinting at a form and function, teasing the mind into deciphering a purpose no longer required and forgotten, all of which my grandfather struggled not to forget. Some of their names he recognised from tales he'd read in nursery rhyme books, or overheard in various alehouses as a very young man. Others from myths, fallacies, folklores and legends, retold at speakers' corners, or scribbled on public toilet walls.

Ships' hulls like gutted fish, skeletal and exposed amid the silt, creaking and dripping with the water's history in the blazing suns. As they ran hand in hand across a treasure-littered landscape my grandfather stopped, staring open-mouthed, but my grandmother turned, dragging him on as the snails ignored these dead hulks and advanced.

They ran between statues of the ancient forms, beautiful idols of the old and newer gods. Platinum, gold and silver coins shining in the sun like a dusting of fallen leaves, thousands of precious stones glistening, the silt washed from them by the tide. They found an invading army numbering in their thousands, spewed from a hull's pierced starboard side, now nothing but skeletons picked white-clean by the crabs and crustaceans. Some still adorned with their armour and helmets, bones clutching swords, shields and spears. Elsewhere, towns and villages long forgotten from an eroded coastline, some undoubtedly crumbled into the sea like a child's wooden blocks, tumbled into chaos by a playtime accident. Others intact, simply drowned as the ocean expanded, communities of abandoned purpose and identity.

They trod these forgotten streets during the days, marvelling at the settlements they never imagined they'd be fortunate enough to see. Graveyards of eroded tombstones, with just a hint of their loving epitaphs hidden by coral and crustaceans. Tombs topped with amputee statues, disfigured by time, forgotten by all.

As the nights fell, they hid to sleep within the wrecks, aware of the snails' relentless advance.

After a week and ten days they came to a seemingly bottomless ravine, a wide, jagged scar across the seabed from some ancient tectonic event. They were trapped.

My grandfather's climbing ropes were too short to span the ravine, it too deep to explore in the hope it narrowed as it became deeper, to be traversed and climbed to reach the other side. My grandmother, exhausted, looked along this ugly rent, noticing a glint in the far distance.

It was a passenger vessel, a liner of twelve black funnels, of enormous shattered paddles situated either side of its hulk. It had come to rest across the ravine, its back broken in the middle but still intact, creating a bridge they traversed for a day and a half.

Across the turbines they crawled, a maze of interlocking cogs and gears, fused by rust forming ochre hill upon ochre hill. Through boiler tunnels of damp soot and coal they ran where the seaweed clung like moss to granite. Out into the shattered state rooms where beautifully crafted furniture created for beings of an alien physiology rotted.
Clambering up giant staircases, risers just a little taller than my grandfather, and treads twice so. At last the buckled superstructure's meandering girders formed a lifeline to the seabed beyond; like a giant mechanical spider's steel web it spanned the rent.

Some weeks later, they sighted their homeland again, determined to warn the coastal settlement, *Viewhaven*, of the impending snails' relentless advance.

Holidaymakers complained to them as they hurried across the sand. "How far's the sea?" they moaned, as they held their impatient children's hands, they clutching plastic buckets and spades.

"Run! Giant snails are on their way!" my grandmother pleaded. But they ignored her, continuing their pointless trek.

Roan sat upon the sand as my grandmother alerted the authorities, holding his shaking head with shaking hands as he wept at what he'd seen, for he knew the tide had teased him, and would soon return to reclaim those wonders he had been so lucky to witness, to quench those parched secrets for another three hundred and a third years as the sinkhole belched forth life once again to flood the ocean floor. He laughed uncontrollably at the realisation they'd witnessed a folklore story that was now an undeniable truth.

Along the coastline telescopes perched high upon castle ruins turned their lenses away from the stars and angled them towards the seabed's horizon. Lighthouse beacons became searchlights, diligently combing the silent landscape during the nights. Hastily erected battlements found their way into the seaside holiday town, where lines of people queued at the coin-operated binoculars dotted along the promenades for a chance to glimpse the snails' advance. Beach huts became barracks for battalions of military personnel, fishing villages became overrun by squads of soldiers. Ice cream sales plummeted.

Two days later, the snails appeared on the horizon. The siege had begun.

The lead snail, a bull, festooned with rusted armour, a vacant saddle and crumbling chimneys protruding from his shell, let out a high-pitched whistle that transformed into a discordant tune. A melodic chord filled the air as they drew nearer, as each snail whistled a single harmonious note to join that of their leader.

Then a low percussive throb rumbled across the seabed like summer thunder as their lungs beat against the insides of their shells. A battle cry to which they continued to slither, it was decided.

Holidaymakers scrambled back to the promenade, beach towels, sun umbrellas hastily gathered up and some discarded. Picnics abandoned, children crying and screaming objections to the sudden end of their fruitless sandcastle construction attempts, their brightly-coloured plastic buckets and spades left to litter the sand as their parents dragged them to safety.

No bombardment by artillery could penetrate the snails' hardened shells; bullets were simply absorbed and deflected back by their thick, wet skin. Fire wouldn't ignite them nor delay them, salt had no effect, neither did garlic or parsley. The seabed became obscured by thick black smoke from the defensive onslaught, and like a winter's sea fret it hung heavily across the battlefield as the snails continued to advance.

A handful of soldiers retreated as the snails reached the beaches, cowardly troops running blindly through the narrow streets, shouting to the inhabitants to evacuate. Men, women, children, dogs and cats ran for their lives, although a few cats remained, as they don't like doing as they're told very often.

One inhabitant refused to leave. The President of a local music society, one Barnaby Swim, his musical talents long overlooked, had translated the snails' whistled and percussive theme into a recurring message of primary notes across our twenty-one note scale.

He understood.

Running through the streets towards the beach, exasperated by the military onslaught, he screamed for the attack to stop, colliding outside a souvenir shop with my grandparents running in the opposite direction.

"I know! I know!" he spluttered, as my grandparents picked themselves up from beneath a carousel of garish postcards, going on to explain exactly what they'd seen.

Down to the sand he ran, my grandparents joining him as he explained how to communicate with the snails. Upon reaching the promenade, my grandmother pleaded with the military commander to cease fire, while my grandfather hurried down to the sand to join Barnaby.

Waving his arms madly to call a ceasefire to the terrible attack, "I know! I know!" Barnaby continued calling, as bullets threatened to end his life, his tweed jacket billowing in the wind, pierced by a stray burst of Gatling gun fire. As he stood between the snails and the militia, he cursed as he poked his fingers through the holes in his favourite jacket, then held out his arms to either side, palms flat, rapidly looking to each side. "Enough! That's simply *enough!*"

My grandfather stood back, fearing he would be cut down by the haphazard military attack, as Barnaby pulled his penny whistle from his jacket's inside pocket, striking up a tune, stamping upon the sand to communicate. The snails halted in unison, eye-stalks turning to this bony stick-thing that had spoken to them. In disbelief he pulled the penny whistle from his lips, as that was not the tune he'd intended to play. He glanced at his instrument to see an extra finger hole, pierced by a stray bullet, causing the instrument to play sharp. Thrusting it into his mouth he cancelled the last few notes and began the phrase again. As a master of the penny whistle, he easily compensated for the instrument's damage, just as an artillery shell tore his body to pieces. His severed head continued to blow on the penny whistle from breath that had left his lungs moments ago. His legs and left arm fell to the ground, tumbling over and over as they gave great spouts of crimson onto the yellow sand, his torso and right arm twisting through the air like a hideous triple-amputee's acrobatic circus finale.

Upon seeing this, the ceasefire order was given, my grandfather acting as cultural envoy between the snails and military, stamping and whistling and translating.

The gastropods turned back to their objective, finally coming to rest, perching themselves upon rows of *Viewhaven's* picturesque guest houses, pubs, bars and fish and chip restaurants to copulate. When exhausted, here they retracted into their shells to sleep, their mating cycle complete for another thousand or less years. However, before their hibernation, my grandfather's efforts were rewarded by the lead bull snail. A gift of a tiny (by giant gastropod's standards) egg.

Many months and several weeks later, it was confirmed by a costly, official investigation the snails' whistling and drumming *was* their form of communication, in spite of my grandfather's obvious success. Barnaby Swim's garbled message had been both understood and ignored as gibberish during his violent death. *"I understand, you're here to, asthmatic lobster's trench-coat buttons."* he had unwittingly said to them.

The snails' musical message had been simple, as it had been all along, and as Barnaby had understood it. *'Could we all, have a lit tle priv acy, p lease?"*

Barnaby's family, bereft of financial compensation for his gallant attempt at communication to halt the conflict, took their endless frustrations out on the snails. Graffiti adorned their shells as they slept. Obscene messages cursing their mating cycle and lamenting poor Barnaby's death. Layer upon layer of paint adorned them over the following summer, until the messages these relations prayed would endure as immortal epitaphs simply created patterns the holidaymakers enjoyed in the midday suns as they strolled along the promenade, relieved by the fact the ice cream industry had returned to the coast.

Clear communication. Such a life essential for everyone and everything. Once this fact was realised, it led to all manner of invention.

Further historical investigation by Barnaby Swim's grandson revealed that long before vehicles were powered by the bright cracking throb of electrical suspensor fields, giant snails were used for transport during a mostly forgotten and briefly recorded historical period known only as 'A really, really long ago time.'

A trading route from the very far east-south-east, across the dry and dusty mountain range of Farkle had been established by a single woman and her snail. Many explorers had tried to traverse this inhospitable boundary to see exactly what lay beyond, only to return defeated by the treacherous terrain and weather. This trader, her name long forgotten by time, brought with her exotic herbs, fruit, vegetables and books. These wondrous products, strapped to her snail's shell in netting and supermarket carrier bags, ripened to perfection on her arrival after the long journey, bringing new recipe ideas and words to understand for the people of the west.

Slowly the route expanded. With help from others from her town in the east-south-east the impassable was bridged. The route became busy. The most successful traders using bull snails – building homes to shelter in within their shells – protecting the now permanently evicted bulls with wool and leather cladding, some adorned with brass and pewter armour, the richer riders dealing in silks and fine furniture cladding their bulls in gold leaf, silver and turquoise. Small coal fires would be seen behind tiny illuminated rectangular windows carved into the thick shells, tall crooked chimneys belching black smoke, keeping both trader and snail warm during the harshest of winters.

And that tiny egg?

A decade and a year or so later, my dear Charles was born.

~ 6 ~
Steeltown

I've always thought Steeltown was a contradiction in terms, as it was built solely from wood. It made sense, as Steeltown's inhabitants, mostly metal themselves, didn't want to live in houses constructed from materials similar to them. After all, people do not live in houses made from flesh and bone, not on this world, anyway.

On our way there, Nick took a detour to his apartment, filling a sports bag with an array of equipment stuffed on shelves in the hallway cupboard. He opened his desk drawer and pulled out a black box no bigger than the palm of his hand, a square red button sitting at its centre. He examined it briefly, grinning before placing it in his jacket pocket.

When we reached Steeltown, he parked the car himself, instructing it to immobilise anything that tries to break in.

There was no checkpoint or visual barrier to determine where Steeltown began and Middletown ended. But if you looked closely as you walked slowly towards Steeltown, you'd notice the timber buildings gradually becoming more dominant. The wooden skyscrapers seemed to have grown onto the skyline like trees, with an abundance of differing architectural styles. Some still remained from the earliest days of the district, others under construction, exotic timbers imported from hundreds of dying worlds replacing those built upon. Other buildings caressed by giant trees, meandering branches supporting all manner of accommodations.

The background cacophony of the city behind us began to evaporate. The car horns, the low level throb of footsteps, conversations and vehicle noise replaced by an electronic hum. The further we ventured, the clicks and whirrs, the piston breaths of escaping pressurized steam, the whine of electronic servos and hum of myriad electronic voices in a multitude of languages became the norm.

They ignored Nick, he was known to every one of them as *'a permitted organism'*, for they never forget a face. They went about their business as usual, every one of them artificial.

Their fleet of ships regularly ventured out to return with raw materials. The further they travelled, the less organic life they found, the more of their own kind, lost, alone, orphaned, abandoned and purposeless. Nick understood them, and moreover understood how Steeltown gave them all identity and purpose.

They were refugees from thousands of different worlds; all shapes, sizes and functions. As their organic masters died off across the cosmos, they found themselves redundant. So they gathered together to build a place they could all call their capital, to live their eternal lives.

Robotic slaves, androids, all manner of artificial life (although they hated the term) thrived here, with one steadfast and immutable rule: no cyborgs.

As Nick walked their wooden sidewalks, some glided by on their suspensor fields, adding an acrid smell to the air. It took Nick's breath, bristling charges of static causing the hairs on his arms and legs to stand up. Others plodded by heavy-footed, some on wheels, some with caterpillar tracks, while some moved with the grace and precision of a human dancer as others crawled and gyrated in ugly spasms of momentum. They were all for the majority dissimilar, yet respected each other equally as identical.

Humans didn't usually venture into Steeltown, there was no need as the locals could look after themselves, and by their very nature were very good at it. Essentially, each and every one of them was a potential mechanic and organ donor.

During its first year, Steeltown had become a popular tourist attraction, parents taking their kids out for the day to see the 'funny robots.' But like all tourist attractions which are for the most part not built for such a purpose or advertised as such, the novelty soon wore off. The fact there were no conveniences such as car parks, bars, restaurants, hot-dog stands, game arcades or toilets, were issues many visitors brought up. The last straw was the absence of an over-priced souvenir shop enabling you to buy some badly-made trinket to trigger memories you'd rather forget as you picked it up while dusting a shelf. The kind-hearted that could afford to, made cash donations to help build these human essentials, but the interest died before any human necessity found favour.

The last human to reside just outside Steeltown, an historian and anthropologist, one Jemima Jeremaid, asked each ship's captain to record and pass to her information they'd found on the worlds they had discovered during their journeys, or worlds they ventured from.

The information returned to her was invaluable, and she believed it could help her uncover the true origins of organic life, unlock so many secrets to the nature of the cosmos and finally create a fairly accurate, yet obviously incomplete lineage of reality. Most agreed to her request, returning with recordings she studied and categorized as she built up a vast knowledge base. However, many of her contemporaries argued her assembled data were sadly minimal to the point of almost insignificant non-existence, in the grand scheme of things. In her old age, she carried around her lifetime's work in a complex quantum storage device, built by her from information the artificials brought back. It was modelled after a turquoise cross-body handbag with white stitching, gold fittings and a mother-of-pearl clasp – an exact replica of one Jemima had been given by her parents for her thirty-third birthday.

Holding this vast knowledge at her waist, she journeyed out aboard a ship bound for a distant yellow star, and a single lonely grey planet orbiting within its habitable zone. She was sure this was the one place in the universe that could unlock all the sacred secrets, as she claimed her research had pointed to this location, this mystery sector, time and time again.

As the ship climbed into the sky and reached the blackness with the stars beyond, she realised machines have no need to breathe, suffocating to death in her cabin some eight and three quarter minutes into the voyage.

Some believed the captain of the ship had been bribed by the old gods to forget to pressurize her cabin so their sacred secrets remained such. This didn't sit well with many who believed it was impossible for a robot to kill, although they were happy to destroy robots when it suited them.

Others believed it was a simple oversight on Jemima's part, and that the thought of her need for a simple life-support system had never crossed her mind – a symptom of single-minded ambition to unlock the sacred secrets, coupled with her mind's frailty of geriatric imbalance – that, or living with robots for most of her life had sent her stark raving mad.

All believed her handbag would never be found, and in that they were so far correct, as the ship returned on automatic without it, her body, captain or crew.

The gods would not permit their quarantine of truth to be breached, it seemed, and that distant sector of space with its grey world would not feel the footfalls of humans nor robots, wherever it was, whatever secrets it held.

Nick crossed the street, heading for the Mayor's office. He took an open elevator clinging to the side of a narrow tower to the top floor, affording us with a view across the vast settlement. Tiny lights illuminated the streets far into the distance, each an artificial going about their unknown tasks. Nick looked to the west, where a shuttle glided in from orbit, heading for the port to unload whatever it had found out there.

The Mayor's office was just a room, a wooden box, in essence. The building creaked and swayed a little, like a small rowing boat touched by a gentle, riverside ebb.

"I need info," said Nick, striding in.

The Mayor's single eye whirred and clicked as it focused upon him. "In abundance. Specifically?" This old mobile dictator was used to interruptions from Nick, but time didn't matter to him.

Nick unwrapped the illustrator's portrait of the gunslinging woman. He placed the bottom of the frame on the Mayor's desk with a thud that echoed briefly. "Have any of you seen her?"

The Mayor's eye clicked again, his head jerking forward and back a few times. "Is this one of your lost creator gods?"

Nick shook his head, giving the Mayor a sly grin, aware of the smugness of the remark, as all artificials were aware of their creators – mostly from company manufacturing plaques upon their bodies, or references in their software and operating systems. Yet, all high-forms simply guessed, or believed what they were taught, or wanted to believe, championing their chosen creators above their neighbour's and very often getting very agitated about gods in general.

"No. When I was a little kid, I prayed to the gods for a red trike – but kinda knew the gods don't work that way, so I stole one and asked for their forgiveness."

The mechanical Mayor remained expressionless as Nick got to the point, "Cross-reference and collate."

A brief hiss of steam escaped from a small polished brass funnel situated behind the Mayor's head. His mouth, resembling two rows of antique typewriter striker bars, clicked and squeaked as they arranged themselves into what Nick considered a smile. "I need to refresh my memory; it's not what it was," said the machine with a lie.

Nick knew the deal. He leant the painting against the Mayor's desk and unzipped the sports bag, pulling out a four-slice toaster with a dial timer, placing it on the desk.

The Mayor picked it up with a claw, holding it in front of his face, another claw operating the slider quickly. Looking at the bottom he read the model and serial number. "Scrap value's not good, Nick," he said dropping it onto his desk, "and no plug."

Nick sighed and reached into the sports bag again, producing a small transistor radio and a clockwork can opener.

The Mayor repeated his examination, looking in great detail at the cogs of the can opener. He placed it to one side then prised open the radio's plastic back cover, his eyes scanning the circuit board. His head tilted up and his eye telescoped over the radio. "How important is this organic to you?"

"Very," said Nick, folding his arms quickly, "and I don't have a lot of time. The whole city could be in jeopardy."

The Mayor placed the radio gently upon the desk and folded his six arms across his chest with a clatter, his mouth becoming a broad horizontal line.

"The whole city?"

"This organic is dangerous to everyone living in Middletown," said Adams, holding the edge of the desk with both hands. "Steeltown included."

"Unconvinced. Details?"

Nick let out a sigh and thrust his hands into his trouser pockets, turning his back to the machine. After a few moments he turned back and spoke. "Listen, she's killed. Not only that, she's altered behaviour. We have a great thing going on here, Mayor." His hands left his pockets and he fanned out his arms, walking slowly in a circle. "I look after your kind. I ignore the fact you mechs abduct the odd human for your experiments in biointegration, despite banning cyborgs. Lights in the sky, huh? UFOs, huh? That's what I say to them, when the reports come in when some son of a bitch vanishes from his bed. Case closed. I allow your kind to roam Middletown, for whatever reasons you have." He leant his hands upon the edge of the Mayor's desk again, angling his torso forward, looking up at the machine. "I need to know if she's been seen." He narrowed his eyes, staring into the Mayor's lens as he wondered what he was thinking. "If the public know the truth about your abductions, they'll be down here recycling you lot into food processors before you can scream 'fuck you!' in binary.

Perhaps I should send a special weapons squad down here, to rip this place apart and search for her?"

"You are a son of a bitch," said the Mayor, his mouth clicking into a grin. "But you are bluffing."

Nick smiled back. "My mother always called me that, but didn't see the irony. Here's the deal. If this bald bitch is coming for us, there's no guarantee she won't come for you. I can end this now if you want, one way or the other, with or without your help." He reached into his pocket and pulled out the small black box with the red button in the centre. "EMP device," said Nick, throwing it casually from hand to hand. "Just gotta push this button and boom, goodbye Steeltown, hello kitchen cupboard."

The Mayor paused. "You wouldn't. After all we have achieved, the lives we have helped, continue to help, all I have provided you with personally? If our experimentations with biointegration work, organics could one day become as immortal as us."

There's one thing I can say when comparing a human's eyes to that of an artificial's. Human eyes have so much character. But a lens is just a lens. The Mayor recognised the determination in Nick's eyes, and Nick saw the slight quiver as a couple of the Mayor's mouth bars twitched at the corner.

"Immortality's not part of the big picture for me. Now," he said, picking up the portrait once again to slam it upon the desk, "have any of you seen her?"

The Mayor stood, towering above us. He placed his arms at his sides, his eye retracting and the lens cover closing slowly. An arm gestured to the window. "Observe."

As Nick took a couple of steps to the window, we watched as every inhabitant of Steeltown simultaneously came to a halt and silence fell. A request was sent and information was transferred.

The Mayor opened his eye. "An instance." An unseen slot at the top of his head ejected a small disc and he took it, holding it out to Nick."Here."

Faces are easy to remember for humans and artificials. So are pieces of art. Names, normally not so much. Clouds curling across the sky like great white beasts in a migration to who-knows-where are impossible to remember. Can you remember a particular formation of clouds? Nick wanted to remember the clouds on that day before everything changed. The artificials remembered everything, recorded everything they saw, and he knew it.

"One more task for you," he said, straightening himself with authority, clasping his hands behind his back."Quellday, 82nd of Balantor, 18.89 p.s. 821129. The sky from co-ordinates 1.9148246 by 8.2362986. I need images, moving, no stills. Search deleted surveillance footage – CCTV cams from that exact location. The information needed is before any of you arrived, but I know if it's out there, you'll find it as you eat all forms of information."

The Mayor placed the disk back in its slot and called for another memory. After several minutes, satisfied, he ejected the disk once again and held it out with a whirr of servos and a snap as his elbow joint locked.

"Hard copy also."

The machine seemed to sigh, then its mouth bars raised and lowered in turn along their rows in a clicking wave. From deep within its chest a whirring sound began, then a snap. Its teeth began rapidly striking at random, a piece of paper slowly emerging from its mouth in short, jerky bursts, its two middle arms reaching to the side, the claws rotating and snapping together as the paper continued to emerge. Then it stopped, the paper dangling from the Mayor's mouth, and Nick reached up to tear it free.

"Thank you," said the machine, its mouth bars running a cleaning cycle.

"A pleasure," mumbled Nick, looking at the printout, turning it over in his hands.

"That's twelve-fifty for the paper," said the Mayor.

Nick looked up, folding the paper and placing it in his inside pocket. "Add it to my account." He snatched the disk from the Mayor's claw, placed it in the sports bag along with the black box, and headed back to the car, leaving the girl's portrait as a reminder.

As he ordered the car back to the precinct, he sat back in the passenger seat, lighting a cigar with a blue flame from a press of the red button in the centre of the black box.

Williams wasn't at her desk.

Nick slumped in his chair and picked up his deskphone, but Williams' talkie asked Nick to leave a message.

"Call me back, I've got a lead," barked Nick, dropping the grubby Bakelite receiver back into its steel cradle.

Minutes later he was standing at the coffee machine when a black-outfitted special weapons officer ran into the precinct from the lift doors at the end of the hall. Nick took his coffee from the machine without thanking it and turned to face the officer as he slid to a halt.

"Sir, the water reclamation plant. A bald woman was there, my squad's been hit, Williams is down."

The water reclamation and purification plant was a squat building of old red bricks. It sat amid the warehouse district, against the canal side at the south-east corner of the city. Everything was quiet, just the low hum of electricity from the pylons overhead.

Nick looked up at the old building as he drew his weapon. The wire fence entrance gates had been left open, the padlocked steel chain, cleanly cut. Protruding from the top of the pyramidal building sat a huge funnel of mottled copper. Beyond this, similar but smaller funnels could be seen against the skyline, built upon existing buildings many years ago. These collectors with their pumping stations beneath were placed at the most common areas of rainfall around the city, connected to the plant via huge steel pipes that twisted and meandered through the streets and buildings like giant snakes writhing through a maze. The sky always looked to me as though an orchestra of giant trombonists had abandoned their instruments, leaving them pointing to the sky. Strangely for Middletown, this wasn't true. Nick glanced in the direction of his lock-up, resisting the urge to check progress there. That would have to wait.

Silently he gestured to his team, splitting them into three units, one around to the rear delivery dock, one to the side gate and the last to remain with him.

As Nick's team reached the main entrance doors, light filtered out beneath in a thin slit, along with the sounds of footsteps and a suspensor field running on idle. He looked down at his shoes, kicking a few shell casings.

He gave the command and his team burst through the doors, weapons held level.

The special weapons unit were taking bottles of water from the assembly line, boxing them up and loading them onto a waiting truck.

"Nick!" called Williams, turning to face him with a welcoming grin, "glad you made it!"

Nick holstered his weapon, waving at his team to stand down. "What the fuck's going on?"

"The third delivery is almost ready to go out," said Williams as she heaved a box up to a waiting officer at the rear of the truck. "This one's headed out to District Seventeen's slums."

Nick marched over to her, dumbfounded. "What are you doing, you idiot?"

"It's the right thing to do," said Williams, frowning with surprise at her superior. She lifted another box to the truck, then brushed down her jacket, angling her head into the air and cupping her hands around her mouth. "Take five, guys! Relief's just arrived." She turned. "Listen, Nick – water's free. It's not right we sell the stuff, it falls out of the sky, for crying out loud."

Nick grabbed her by the shoulders. "It's a money maker!" he shouted.

"But it's a con, Nick. We both know the purification system's been in use for as long as anyone can remember, it doesn't cost anything to run or maintain, as it looks after itself. We don't even know who built the damn thing, it's that old! Come on! See sense and be kind. It's unethical to charge a twenty for a bottle. By the gods, I remember when I was a kid, Nick. I read in school, water was free a long time ago. Free! Beer and wine's cheaper than water now, how does that work out, putting a strain on the hospitals, alcoholics lining the wards? Free up some cash for Middletown's poor, let them have the water so they can spend a little extra on just living."

Nick leaned to his right, noticing the greenish indent circled with bruising on Williams neck. "She was here waiting for you, wasn't she?"

Williams nodded. "Great girl. Said she's looking forward to meeting you. She's right, you know, it's not virtuous to charge Middletown for something that's a gift from the gods. Everyone should share the gift equally." She turned her head to shout, "Shouldn't they, guys?" and the unit nodded in unison.

"Are you shitting me? So, when you arrived she was here waiting, took you all down?"

Williams shook her head. "Took down's not quite right. Enlightened is more accurate. Gruber was wrong. It wasn't about adding red to the water, the filtration and purification system would render it inert. Plus, she didn't have enough red to cover the entire city. She knew you'd think that, though. Clever girl, huh?" She held up an index finger as Nick's grip on her shoulders fell. "One step at a time, and time I have aplenty," she said, "for courage, I have, diligence, kindness and..." she stopped, mouth open, eyebrows raised high in anticipation, wanting Nick to finish her sentence.

He didn't reply and Williams looked disappointed, speaking in a slow sarcastic pace. "Oh come on Nick, *courage, diligence, kindness and...*" She nodded her head slowly in encouragement, rolling her right index finger in a circle as if winding an invisible length of string around it.

"Charity," mumbled Nick, almost choking on the word.

Williams clapped her hands once. "You got it, buddy! Well done. Now, give us a hand with this, will ya? If we're lucky we can get this out to Seventeen before lunch. Water is the gift we must pass on. It gives everything life, makes the land fertile. Imagine how happy this will make everyone."

As she bent down to pick up a box, Nick pistol-whipped her until she was unconscious.

I've grown accustomed to living in Nick's head, he, unconscious of my presence. I can switch off any time I like, swim away to 'sleep' for want of a better term – shut myself off, close my 'eyes' if I decide to, if things get really terrible, as they often have. I feel as though I'm swimming through his mind – if that makes sense? When he's asleep and I'm awake, there are bright tendrils, like glowing seaweed waving gently like reeds touched by a riverbed current, with brightly-coloured spheres attached to them. When he recalls a memory, these spheres detach themselves, join together to construct the memory as a whole. I guess each one is part of that memory, as senses – smells, textures, sounds. I managed to hold one in my hands for a brief moment once, until it pulled itself from my grasp to join the others. It was heavy, and although bright, had a distinct darkness to it, almost a life of its own, revealing itself to me as an inner hatred. That made me think. Perhaps memories do have a life of their own, an agenda to warn us from their moment of creation, preventing us from repeating mistakes? I know it sounds strange, son. But when you have as much time on your hands to think as I do, thoughts do become strange.

Maybe my tolerance of his evil has grown to a degree, become the norm for my imprisoned life. Perhaps his behaviour is just an amplified version of *all* adult behaviour, actions and thoughts the majority either never have, or dismiss and control if they do? I honestly don't know. I hope we'll both find out one day.

What I do know and have learnt to understand, is the fact that I have come to accept part of his evil – believe it or not. Or at least I appreciate the fact that through Nick, I've been afforded a unique viewpoint, providing me with, in part, an *understanding* of its origin, from the episodic memories surfacing occasionally from his distant past with voices all their own...

'Yes, father's voice,' he managed to whisper – unmistakeable. Even though it was coloured by anguish and physical pain. Unmistakeable, despite never voicing such emotions.

Nick sat up slowly, perching on his elbows towards the view along the shoreline.

The bodies of dead and dying crew and passengers contrasted against the muted pebble tones. Some of their brightly-coloured clothes, torn, ruffled. Material fluttering in the breeze, each a flag of individual identity vying for attention, silently crying for help where others could not. Ladies' fine layered silks discoloured by seawater, bunched up, jewellery glinting, gentlemen's capes partly covering figures like lazily-draped shrouds. Others' attire revealed too much of the people they were designed to maintain decency for - contorted limbs festooned with shreds of skin and seaweed. 'All raped by the storm, except me,' he found himself whispering once more. Remnants of nature's abuse against those lives which were so full of blatant superiority over it.

His eyes continued along the hopeless shore of desolation, unable to react, to cry, to speak as shock seized his juvenile soul.

Occasionally, these fabric tatters of normality revealed white skin, some with wide ugly lacerations of red, others where broken white bones protruded from the skin like spring shoots, forcing their way though

fertile soil. Now the gulls pecked at this soil, the dead and dying alike. Layers upon layers laid bare.

Struggling to his feet he saw his father's eyes look up to him, realising they'd always looked down at him, as all of them had, every adult. That condescending glare, a dismissive smirk, and he now had a feeling of superiority over them. 'Perhaps I am the storm, too?' he mouthed to himself. He found himself brushing down his clothes, tucking in his damp shirt, straitening his collar and smoothing back his black hair, as he'd been taught by his mother before addressing his father, for fear of offending his noble standards.

...but, there's a feeling of fear I have too, and have never been able to shake off, long before my imprisonment. It's that feeling when you're a kid, as Nick was upon that shore, that you're missing something *really* important, that something's going on but you don't know what it is – no, more than that for me – a feeling of something more terrifying than Nick, or his experiences. It's just a feeling, but it's as though there's someone watching me, as though Nick is secretly aware of my presence and his actions are simply for me to witness, his audience of one. It's a stupid feeling, because I know he's not aware of me. I guess it's just a kid's paranoia, but from experience, adults tell kids only just enough to get a message across, or get something done. Adults can be deceitful.

A kid asking, "Why?" is sometimes met with a, *"Because I said so,"* or, *"Because it is."* Adults almost never tell the whole story, never go into the details. Perhaps they think details are unimportant, or that us kids will pick the details apart – expose the nonsense of adult 'common sense' and make them look silly. Or they're scared they won't be understood, or have to explain something which isn't suitable for us, leading to a string of other questions they'll have to explain, if they can, or have the courage to, for fear their child is growing up and therefore they, growing older?

I think it's all down to time too, they're just too busy – the older they get, the less time they have to go over stuff they've known about for years and years. And besides, isn't that what the schools are for – to teach kids stuff parents haven't the time to?

Thankfully, my mum always had the time to teach me stuff. And it's because of this fact, (and a handful of others) I decided to write this letter to you. My mum learnt at a very young age that when people ask you to do things, *"in your spare time,"* or, *"when you get a moment,"* it was utterly reprehensible.

She explained, she'd never found anyone giving out 'moments' – as though they were sweets of different shapes and flavours you could pick out of a brown paper bag. She also said she didn't know how to get one, as everyone she'd met that had a moment spare couldn't tell her where they'd found it, or what they were going to do with it. The actual length of a moment was one of great mystery also, and differed between the people asking you to do stuff during one.

She told me, "If someone ever asks if you have a spare moment, say, 'Well I did, but it's now been used up answering your question,' and if they ask if you have any more – walk away!"

She also insisted there was no such thing as *spare* time. "It belongs to me," she'd say. "It's not as though I have an hour and two-fifths where I have nothing to do. My time's all been planned out, and if I did have some spare, I'd certainly be using it to do *my own* things, rather than use it doing something for someone else that had squandered theirs." It was all too obvious to me, watching from inside Nick, that adults actually mean they want a task completed there and then, and not during a moment of spare time. In essence, stop what you're doing and do something I want you to do.

And that's when I knew mum *had* set aside spare time for me, because she knew I'd have many questions for her, as she was against sending me to school.

"Most of it's nonsense," she told me, "unnecessary for your life ahead. Yes, there's a few things you must learn and be good at, but it's important to be good at things you're interested in too. You won't have much time to be a kid – it goes by *really* fast, so it's best if that time's not spent trying to make you behave like an adult, telling you pointless facts you'll never need that are best left hidden away. You can behave like an adult when you've naturally grown into being one. Schools tell you what to think, Tiny Flower, and not how to. That's their greatest failing."

Mum always had time for me, even if she was busy sweeping sticky silk floss from the roof, early on a Mournday morning.

Mum's Lesson #38

I didn't realise it at the time, but my home schooling was constant. It wasn't as though Mum stopped teaching at a certain hour; she continued to enlighten me throughout the week, including the three precious days of the weekend. What follows is one of her most valuable lessons – I've called it #38 for no other reason than to set it apart from other lessons, as I didn't keep track of them numerically or in order of importance. That, and the fact I'm particularly fond of the shape those two numbers create when placed side by side. The three looks like another eight peeking around a corner. Far more appealing to the eye than 83, that's for certain! In that instance, the three looks like an eight cut in half, and (putting it mildly) I'm not *at all* fond of the number four, as it reminds me of the pointy-nosed teacher I endured during my one and only lesson at school, and that's putting it mildly too.

I may or may not tell you other lessons Mum taught me later on, as at the time of writing this sentence, I'm undecided.

I remember talking to my mum about this feeling of something being hidden, as I mentioned earlier, and stuff not being told to kids fully, one grey Frothday evening after tea-time. I'd agreed with Charles' request to play *'come find me'* for a few hours before bednight time. It was the day after Grandpa's dreadful accident, and we all needed to occupy ourselves.

Dad was working overtime on the trawler, hoping to catch the season's first throd fish as they came up to bask close to the surface and peer into the starlit night, and Mum had told me to tidy my room, put all my toys away – otherwise *Aunt Scalas* will come into my room when I'm either asleep or not there, and take a toy away as a punishment for being untidy. I didn't believe it, didn't believe in *Aunt Scalas*, – I knew in my heart it was just one of those adult lies to get kids to do stuff – in this case tidy up – so the adults didn't have to, and so when the kid becomes an adult being tidy is second nature. And yeah, adults have more stuff to tidy and put in the right place like bills and important stuff. *'Tidy room, tidy mind,'* Dad always said to me, to back Mum up.

Mum was at the sink that evening, and it's clear to me now we always had meaningful conversations while she was elbow-deep in water at that thick-rimmed iron sink. It was almost three-quarters the size of the bath upstairs, and served various purposes such as washing whitefruit, bathing me when I was a baby and cleaning fish, but for the most part she stood there dutifully either washing dishes or clothes. On this occasion it was the lunch and tea-time cutlery and crockery.

She sensed me behind her, withdrew her rubber-gauntleted hands to shake off the soap bubbles and turned, crouching down with a broad smile, resting her elbows on her knees to let the water drip onto the dark wooden floor between us. "What is it sweetheart – you ok?"

"It's just, well..." I murmured.

"Go on," she said, pulling off her gloves to lay them over the edge of the sink behind her. They always made her hands wet as they used to belong to Dad, they were a little too big for her and had tiny holes from minip bites. "I thought you were playing 'come find me' with Charles?"

"I am," I said quickly, "it's his turn to hide first."

She nodded. "Ok, so what's on your mind?"

That's the thing about playing 'come find me' with a snail. First, they love exploring, second, even dwarf giant ones are slow. I used to count up to ten thousand and fifty-eight, to give Charles a good chance of finding a hiding place – now I'll just watch the kitchen clock, ticking back the hours. An hour and seventy or so minutes is usually enough, but he always left a trail for me to find, no matter how hard he tried to hide it by sliding backwards and nibbling twigs and grass along the way to drop over his trail. Freshly nibbled twigs and grass were still a trail.

When it was my turn to hide, I'd take a book with me to read. I'll admit, I preferred playing catch with him, it was more fun, watching him catch the ball between his eye-stalks. He was really good at that. Throwing it back was a bit more difficult for him though – rearing up on his tail and letting himself drop forward to get the ball back.

"You said I should tidy my room before I go out, because I might be too tired when I get in. Well, I haven't done it because I don't believe any more, it's silly. I want to know grown up things, like, like why do you and Dad argue so much?"

She pulled a dishcloth hanging from the metal hoop beneath the sink, folding it into a pad to wipe away the water upon the floor between us. I could see she was trying to suppress a smile.

"Your dad's restless," she said quietly, concentrating on the water. "He thinks something's missing in his life, but he doesn't know what it is." She flipped the cloth over, polishing the floor, angling her head to check her progress in the light. "It frustrates him, makes him feel inadequate inside, empty." Satisfied the floor was dry, she poked the dishcloth back through the hoop, ensuring its folds were neat before turning to look at me.

"So you tell Dad not to worry?" I said.

"No, I tell him if he's lucky adventure will come and find him, if she wants him to join in, I," she stopped herself as her shoulders fell. "Adventure is always looking for a friend, a companion to join in – to play with." She began straightening her apron, re-tying the knot in a bow, ensuring the loops were the same size. "Adventure doesn't like being on her own, because without a friend, she's simply expectation."

I thought about this for a few moments then said, "How do you know?"

It seemed to take my mother an age to answer, as though she was thinking hard about what to say. I thought she was going to send me back upstairs to tidy my room, but eventually she spoke.

"You see, when I was much younger, adventure came to visit me. So the adventurous part of me is fulfilled. Daddy is still waiting for his visit, but, it might be he's missed that visit already, because he didn't recognise it. That's what worries him."

I sat down cross-legged, resting my elbows on my knees to cradle my head in my hands, looking at her, waiting.

She took a deep breath, running her fingers through her long curly red-brown hair. She smiled from behind it as it fell across her face, sitting down cross-legged.

"Ok, you're old enough now, I guess. What I'm about to tell you is a secret I've never told anyone, and I want you to keep it to yourself, please. Promise?"

Her expression was deadly serious, and I wrinkled my nose, rubbed it then nodded. "Ok Mum, I promise."

"It was a long while back. I was a little younger than you are now. I was at school, talking with my friends during lunch break time. One of them mentioned she was almost late for school, as her mum insisted she tidy her room before leaving, and I realised I'd forgotten to tidy mine!

"I spent the rest of the afternoon anxious, *really* worried that my favourite toy had been taken by Aunt Scalas. I watched the clock, ticking back the day, wishing it would hurry up and the hometime bell would chime. When it finally did, I ran home through the dusty streets, ignoring my friend's calling for me to wait. Down the back alleys I hurried, past rows and rows of rickety old fences where dogs barked, snapping at my passing heels, disturbing younger kids playing at their back gates, jumping over the pot holes lest I tripped. I burst through the back gate almost breaking the hinges, down the garden path where your grandmother was kneeling, tending the flowers that lined it. In through the kitchen door which slammed back with a squeak and thud, and not even the sweet smell of your grandmother's freshly baked fairy cakes cooling on the baking tray waiting for pink icing stopped me. My bed was made, my bedroom floor tidy. I was so out of breath, my chest heaving, heart pounding. Dropping my satchel, I pulled open my cupboard door to find my toys were all stacked neatly. I took them out one by one, dropping them behind me in an untidy pile as my mother came in.

"'What's going on and going to happen, young lady?' she asked, standing in the doorway with her arms folded.

"'Where's Anaximander!?'

"'I haven't seen him. I told you last night to tidy your room. I did this for you after my lunch, that's what's happened.'

"Anaximander, my map, wasn't there. I turned and stepped over my pile of toys to look under the bed, pulling out my colouring books, paper and coloured pencils. Anaximander wasn't there either. My heart began to pound again and I could feel an uncontrollable anger rising in me. I started to cry – I was angry at myself, angry I'd left him alone, after all the fabulous conversations we'd had. I was worried for him, worried where he was and if he was angry with me for not looking after him.

"'Where is it? What have you done with it?' I demanded of your grandmother.

"'It's your own fault. If you'd have done as I'd asked, he would still be here and none of this would have happened.' She reached into her apron pocket and took out her knitting.

"'What have you done with it – please – Aunt Scalas isn't real! That's just stupid – stop lying!'

"'I warned you. Aunt Scalas has taken him away. That's your punishment for not tidying your room before bed.' She didn't look at me, there was just the sound of her knitting needles rapidly clicking together.

"I sat down, my vision blurred from all the tears, wiping them away with the back of my hand as Alfie, my younger brother, came in. He peered around my mother's legs wondering what all the fuss was about.

"'I hate you! Hate these stupid lies! Just give him back and I'll be good, I promise! I'll tidy my room every day, do chores, anything – I just want him back, please Mum, please, please give him back!'

"'I'm sorry, my dear,' said your grandmother, 'but we warned you this might happen, and it has.'

"She left to ice the fairy cakes and Alfie, bless him, sat with me until my crying stopped, giving me his handkerchief to wipe my tears away.

"'Don't worry, Lottie,' he said, pushing up his spectacles that were far too big for him so he could see better. 'It'll be alright. I don't like it when you cry.'

"I scrunched up his damp handkerchief and threw it at him. 'Leave me alone.'"

I thought for a moment. "You weren't very kind to your brother."

Her eyes fell to the floor as she spoke. "I know, I've always felt guilty about how I treated him, considering what happened later."

That's when my hands stopped supporting my head and found my lap, my fingers interlocking. Mum put her forefinger over her mouth and looked to the side, silent for a few moments, avoiding my gaze. She blinked rapidly and I thought she was going to stand up to continue her chores and not tell me the rest of her adventure, but a thin smile found her eyes and then her mouth as she removed her forefinger, turning back to me.

"You see, it was Alfie's idea. Looking back, I realise that at the time it was a *brilliant* idea – and it was great to know that kids *do* have brilliant ideas, but they don't see where those ideas can lead, and what trouble they can cause. Kids can't see the consequences of their plans, as they don't look beyond their actions. They move on to other thoughts, like closing a book to go off and play with something else. Alfie was adventure personified, even at that age, and that's when adventure came to visit us, together."

I glanced at the kitchen clock, wishing I'd not agreed to play with Charles, and then I saw the raindrops gathering on the windows. He'd enjoy the rain as it would speed him up a little and help to hide his trail. My mother continued.

"Alfie crept into my room that night – I could see his torchlight beneath my bedroom door as I lay there awake, wondering where your grandmother had hidden my map, listening to the distant sounds of the streets beyond our little terraced house, the cars, the adults' chattering as they walked home from the alehouses, dogs barking at each other from their back gardens. I sat up and waited for him, imagining him on tiptoes, reaching for my door handle. At last I watched it slowly turning in the moonlight, and I reached over to my bedlamp, flicking the switch.

"'Lottie! You're awake!' he whispered, turning off the torch to run over to my bed.

"Propping myself up on my left elbow I stared at him. 'What are you doing? Mum and Dad will go mad if they find you out of bed!'

"'I know how we can get your map back from Mum! It's *easy!'*

"So, I listened to his plan and we set to work. We crept back into his room, dragging into my room his big teddy bear Dad had won for him at the summer fair a couple of seasons ago. We sat him in the middle of the floor, unzipped his back and took out most of the stuffing and foam, hiding it under my bed. I climbed in first, my legs from the knees down in the bear's stubby legs, wrapping stuffing around them, creating a big foam seat to sit upon. Then I helped Alfie inside and he sat on my lap. Together we added more padding until everything felt right. We zipped it back up, leaving a little gap for my finger to fit through. It was just a matter of waiting then, waiting and keeping quiet, trying not to giggle or move as your grandmother came in to check how tidy my room was.

"It was so hot in there, so dark and difficult to breathe, and I was just about to whisper to Alfie that this was a bad idea when we heard my door handle turn and a floorboard creak. Everything fell silent, as if the cars had stopped and turned off their engines, the adults found their way home, and the dogs had grown tired of barking at each other. The whole of the night had stopped.

"We felt Mum pick us up, heard her strain a little with our weight, and my heart quickened as I thought she'd figure out what we were up to. But no, there was silence with only our nervous breath as company. I expected to hear your grandmother whispering to your grandfather for help, but there was only the steady rhythm of her footsteps rocking us from side to side as she carried us downstairs, across the hall, into the kitchen and out into the garden.

"'It's the shed,' I whispered in Alfie's ear. 'Anaximander's in the shed.'

"He nodded quickly, then reached up to straighten his glasses, stifling a yawn.

"'Don't forget, Lottie, as soon as we're put down, unzip the back and jump out.'

"Then we heard the creak of the garden gate, and the click of the latch as it closed behind us. Your grandmother continued walking on, and I wondered which neighbour's house we'd end up in. I felt Alfie's body relax against mine as he fell asleep to the gentle rocking motion, so I cuddled him for a while until we stopped. I was just about to wake him, anticipating being put down as I heard the last few teeth of the zip behind my head close, and we moved on again."

Looking back at this episode with my mum, I remember being enthralled by her story, and at this point I knew she was making it all up. But how I enjoyed it!

"I must have fallen asleep too, because when I woke up we were motionless. Perhaps being put down with a thud had woken us both, I can't say with any certainty. I whispered to Alfie, explaining that our mother had zipped up the bear to the top. There was the tiniest of gaps – too small for my fingers, but a perfect size for Alfie's little finger. He wriggled around and reached up, stretching to find the gap in the dull light and poke his finger through and pull. When the gap was large enough, I pulled at the zip and in a few moments we were free, clambering out, dragging bunches of stuffing and foam with us. Then..."

I held up both my hands to mum to stop. "Then there you were in a neighbour's house, both of you in your pyjamas," I said with authority. "Your mum and her friend sharing a pot of lime tea, staring at you from the living-room couch, both of you in big trouble as you'd have to get home and get ready for school fast. At least you got your map back. It's true, no child wants to be seen outside in their pyjamas, your brother didn't think of that when your mum marched you back home, did he?" I looked at her confidently, nodding my head with my arms folded, my right foot tapping the kitchen floor.

But she just stared back at me, motionless, silent, only the sound of the rain against the window our companion. My foot tapping stopped and I unfolded my arms.

She leant forward. "When *you've* had *your* adventure, *you* can tell them to *your* child," she said with a hint of anger in her eyes, forcing me to look away. I shuffled nervously, pretending the floor had suddenly become uncomfortable, bringing my knees up to my chin to cuddle my shins. When I settled, she waited for me to look up before continuing.

"Then our eyes became used to the light. The walls were made of big light-grey hexagonal bricks, illuminated by flickering candles perched on ledges at different heights, dripping with long streaks of wax to create dried pools upon the stone floor. The place reeked of damp. We couldn't believe it, and I can honestly say I had to whisper to Alfie to close his mouth as it was wide open with surprise. Around us were piles and piles of toys, all shapes and sizes, hundreds of them – and in the centre of this cave was a huge wooden table, chipped, rotting. Upon that, candles at each corner with different shapes of colourful wrapping paper, stacked neatly on top of each other in the middle. There were balls of string and cloth bows, some entwined with tinsel, all reflecting the candlelight. We heard laughter, children's laughter, but it was different somehow, rough, guttural – echoing down a hexagonal tunnel beyond the table. Walking over to the table I saw wrapped presents and my map, sitting on a sheet of wrapping paper, so I whispered to Alfie to follow me. As I picked him up, Alfie nudged me, pointing to the tunnel. There was a shadow of a figure there, twisting against the walls as it grew larger, joined by shuffling footsteps. We dived under the table, me clutching Anaximander to my chest, his plastic cold to the touch.

"We were shaking, and I noticed tears in Alfie's eyes. I held a finger up to my pursed lips, and he nodded quickly, shaking with fear. The shuffling grew and then we saw the feet. Old, bony, horrible long black toenails that scraped against the stone floor making scratches, wrinkled skin caked in grime, and the smell made us feek sick. The feet stopped at the table, and a gurgling sound filled the air, then a groan of pain which grew louder and louder as the feet quickly parted. A splash of blood and thick grey liquid hit the floor between the feet as the groan became a deafening scream. Silence for a moment, then the feet tensed, toes gripping the flagstones, the nails scratching and searching, finding the gaps between them. Then there was a thud that hit the puddle, droplets finding our faces, forcing Alfie to quickly wipe his glasses clean on his pyjama jacket as I wiped my cheeks with my sleeves. We stared. It was a newborn baby, or at least it looked like a baby, curled up, its back to us, a coil of what looked like misshapen rope, pink with red veins draped over it like a string of sausages. It slowly rolled over towards us in the mess, as if it knew we were there, and opened its eyes. They were dark blue, somehow beautiful in the flickering candlelight. Then it became angry, a pale arm struggling to move, its stubby fingers reaching out, three curling back to leave one limply pointing at us. Then the coiled rope quickly began to move, pulled upward until this tiny creature gurgled a cry, complaining as it griped the fleshy rope connected to its belly with both hands, before it was hauled up out of sight.

"The feet turned to walk back down the tunnel, and it was our curiosity that forced us from under the table to follow. The creature, Aunt Scalas, or whatever it was, carried a wrapped present under her right arm, the baby draped over her left shoulder.

"Eventually, at the end of the tunnel, twenty or so steps opened out and down into a large hexagonal area. There, what looked like a hundred children played. But as we watched from the shadows at the top of the steps, we noticed they were not children as we know them – they were *old* children. Wisps of straggly hair protruding from dry mottled scalps, dressed in partial rags, stained, ripped, dirty. Where they had teeth they were decayed, grey in the candlelight. Upon seeing the creature they formed a circle and sat, Scalas standing in the middle, placing the present at her feet before slowly backing away. She was horrible, partially clothed in what was once a long dress of bright colours and abstract shapes, it too stained, torn, the hem, neckline and sleeves all tatters of jagged fabric. Her skin fell around her bones like an unwashed, uneven tablecloth from a month of untidy meals, long ridges of pale skin forming scabbed folds. Her eyes were almost black; like pools of oil they reflected the flickering light, set deep in their sockets. Wire-thin white hair, matted in dirty clumps and pushed back over large ears, lobes as large as Alfie's hands, her lips dry and cracked with dark red gouts, her nose barely covered by skin, grey-white jagged bones where nostrils once were. The ancient children all looked to her, waiting, agitated, fidgeting, but smiling.

"She opened her mouth to reveal gums of grey and black, and at last a long deep croak filled the air, echoing in the chamber as steam drifted out of her mouth in the cold.

"The ancient children sprang to life, scrambling towards the present in the centre. They fought each other viciously, punching, kicking, biting, all determined to claim the present hiding beneath bright wrapping paper. Multiple screams filled the air, some of pain, others of anger, hatred and determination as hair was pulled from scalps and ears torn from skulls. Alfie and I were transfixed, unable to come to terms with what we were seeing, myself hoping I'd wake up in my bed screaming, this whole episode just a crazy nightmare. Then her croak filled the air once more, and those that were able to form a circle, did so. She stepped forward, looking down to the injured upon the floor as they moaned, writhing in pain. The others in the circle giggled at this, whispering to each other behind cupped hands. Then the creature dragged the injured out of the circle by their ankles, piling them up in the shadows against the far wall. The present they fought over was in partial tatters, wrapping paper stained with blood, revealing another layer of different-coloured paper beneath. She placed it in the centre of the now smaller circle of children, shuffling back to her position. Then her croak filled the air again, and the violence began once more.

"'We've got to find a way out of here,' I whispered to Alfie, but all he could manage was a nod. There were tears running down his face and he'd wet his pyjamas.

"I turned on my map and the large screen came alive, illuminating my face. Quickly I zoomed in with one of the buttons and the view changed, showing our position in the tunnel. I scrolled back the way we had come, noticing an illustration of a stairway at the far end of the cave behind us.

"*'Good morning Charlotte! Where would you like to explore today?'*

"I'd forgotten to turn Anaximander's volume down, and his voice echoed around the cave. I fumbled to mute him as the fighting stopped and the ancient children all turned to look towards us in silence. Slowly, the injured climbed to their feet with the help of others, and from the shadows the bodies from the first fight came crawling and hobbling into the light. Aunt Scalas just looked at us, the vile baby draped over her shoulder struggling as it turned around, facing us with a sneer, pointing again, letting out a scream. As her children began to creep slowly toward us we turned and ran.

"Their determined cries filled the tunnel, but we were faster, and as I slid to a halt to check the map I hit the table, knocking over a candle onto the wrapping paper. Flames filled the air instantly, and Alfie looked at me with a grin. I knew what he was thinking. We threw wrapping paper onto the table as the ancient children appeared at the tunnel entrance, shielding their eyes, backing away from the heat. We worked fast, throwing toys and wrapping paper onto the growing bonfire.

"'Quick, Lottie! Help me with the bear!' shouted Alfie, so together we tossed the bear and its stuffing onto the fire, then I pushed the table, burning my palms upon its edge. Alfie helped me until it tumbled over onto its side into the tunnel entrance, partially blocking the way. I grabbed Alfie's hand, placing my map under my arm and we ran from the screams and the crackling of burning wood. We found a twisting wooden staircase that led up into the darkness and both turned as the splintering of wood filled the air. Scalas had burst through the burning table, and was hurrying towards us, her children close behind. We scrambled up the stairs and Alfie's spectacles fell, tumbling down the steps. I shouted at him to wait and I jumped down a couple of steps to retrieve them, but one of the lenses had cracked from the fall. Scalas was scrambling towards me on her hands and feet just a few steps below, her baby sitting astride her neck, her children gathering behind her. I ran as fast as I could, reaching the top of the stairs where Alfie stood below a hatch in the ceiling. I pushed it open, helping Alfie through first. I crawled free then slammed the hatch shut, silencing the cries from below.

"Out of breath, we found ourselves lying on the floor of a hallway. It was just a house, but with a really high ceiling, for the most part normal – clean and tidy. Then the hatch opened a little, Scalas' hand grabbing Alfie's ankle. I remember turning, seeing the look in her deep black oily eyes as she pulled at his ankle, widening in surprise, slowly finding colour at their centre, and as she paused in astonishment, I kicked at her face with my heels, over and over again as hard as I could, determined, gritting my teeth. She pulled Alfie's slipper from his foot, taking it with her as she retreated with a whimper, the hatch closing with a thud.

"I was shouting to Alfie now as I scrambled to my feet, to help me drag an armchair over from the far wall to cover the hatch. As we did do it opened, hitting the bottom of the chair, banging again and again, trying to increase the small gap where a spindly arm finally reached through. Smoke poured through as the hand found the edge of the chair, pulling it aside a little in short, sudden jerks against the polished wooden floor, so I stood on the chair and Alfie joined me jumping up and down as if that would help, and the chair didn't move.

"I looked around, and upon the wall behind us was a huge painting. There was a beautiful woman standing in a summer garden of exotic flowers but with their petals closed – she was the most beautiful woman I'd ever seen, and beside her stood three children. Then I noticed the dress she wore – identical to the tatters draped over the creature that was Scalas. Our feet became hot as flames licked at the edges of the hatch, so we jumped down and waited until the chair caught alight, before running from that house to find ourselves in the middle of what Alfie later called, *The Elsewhere Someplace*.

"Beyond the front door and veranda steps meandered a long twisting pathway of red bricks, leading down a huge hill to a pair of tall silver gates. We ran on, but Alfie called after me as he couldn't keep up without his slipper, couldn't see properly with a cracked lens, so I gave him a piggy-back, passing him my map to wedge between his tummy and my back.

"Either side of the pathway and all around that hill the house stood atop were little mounds of earth – graves I decided – thousands of them. But the strangest thing about this elsewhere someplace? There was only one sun shining high in the sky.

"I turned from the gates, watching the windows of that horrible house as the flames flickered and grew angrily behind them, and I thought I heard one last scream above the sound of falling timber as that house began to collapse. I pushed a gate open with my shoulder and found myself on another, smaller veranda, and I breathed deeply in relief as I saw we cast three shadows upon the wooden planks.

"Anaximander had recorded his journey to that house, so we simply followed the route back. Alfie held him in front of me over my shoulders as I carried him home. It took us a day, perhaps a little bit less, and when we reached the outskirts of town, we found that your grandparents had contacted the authorities. The whole neighbourhood was out searching for us.

"When we told them what had happened they didn't believe us, and we couldn't prove a thing. Even when I held up Anaximander as proof, I was accused of hiding him in the first place.

"'It's just a story to encourage you to keep tidy!' insisted your grandmother. 'I was told the same when *I* was a child, as *my* parents were told, and so on. Look at the state of you both, your pyjamas are ruined, poor Alfie's lost a slipper and broken his spectacles! Now, that's what's happened young lady!'

"The authorities traced the way back to the house, but when they returned they told us there was just an old woman living there."

My mother turned to look at the kitchen clock. "Time to find Charles now, sweetheart," she said, standing.

I folded my arms in a huff. "I don't believe you," I said. "That's just a story to take up time, to let Charles hide. But at least I know Aunt Scalas isn't real now – and you made up that horrible story for me to understand how important it is to be tidy, *and* that I'm growing up fast enough to know the truth." I was smiling now, a little smug I'd figured it all out so quickly. "And, and Aunt Scalas couldn't visit every kid's room in one night – that's just stupid. There's not enough time!"

My mother smiled at me as I stood up proudly. "Wait here," she said quietly, "I'll be back in a moment. Don't move."

I went to the kitchen door and opened it to the rain. It was softer now, a refreshing light drizzle, almost at an end. The sky showed signs of early dusk as I watched the rain clouds preparing to move on, as a sun set behind the whitefruit trees at the top of the garden.

I heard my mother walk up behind me and I turned. She was holding a dark blue box to her chest, the size of my weekend breakfast bed tray. "Here," she said, holding it out.

I took it from her. It was like a drawing pad, and had raised letters of chipped and faded silver across the top. The letters were slanted, reading; *'Anaximander. Your Talking Map,'* and at the bottom of the pad were a few buttons, their edges worn, the plastic case cracked and scuffed a little in places and blackened at the edges.

"I'd turn it on, but he takes things called batteries, and they're not made anymore."

She took Anaximander back from me. "Now go and find Charles, please."

"But I don't want to get wet, the rain's not stopped yet. He'll come in later."

She turned to look out of the kitchen window. "If I worried about getting wet, you wouldn't have clean plates to eat from, would you?" She held out her hand, "Look at the state of my fingertips." I took her hand and noticed the wrinkles from the washing up there, but what really struck me was the dull red scar running across the middle of her palm I'd not noticed before. I turned and ran out into the rain.

But that scar, that whole story had me thinking while I was looking for Charles, and certain things she'd told me still didn't make sense.

A while later I carried a sleeping Charles into the sitting room. It was almost dark in there, save for the yellow flames caressing the logs in the narrow fireplace and a few candles my mum had lit and placed in front of the leaded window overlooking our front garden. She was sitting close to the fire in Dad's big brown leather winged chair, barefoot, her knees bent and legs tucked to her side. Staring vacantly into the flames, she curled her hair between thumb and forefinger, smoking one of Dad's cigarettes that he kept in a box on top of the fireplace. It was the first and last time I ever saw her smoke.

"He was asleep in Dad's mushroom patch again," I said, as she blew out a long stream of smoke. "He'd eaten a few and curled up on his side, pretending to be a mushroom."

She blinked a couple of times, and leant forward, tossing the half-smoked cigarette into the flames before gently taking him from me, placing him on her lap and patting his shell. "He's a naughty little snail," she said absently. "Did you hide the stalks in the compost?"

"Of course."

"Good girl. I tidied your room while you were looking for him."

I sat cross-legged on the rug in front of the fire, pulling my woolly hat off by its big pink pompom, rubbing my damp hair with my fingertips. I huffed. "Why tidy my room? You said Aunt Scalas' house burnt down, and," I turned from watching the flames and our eyes met, "and, I've never met an Uncle Alfie!"

"Bednight time now, honey," she stated matter of factly, the firelight illustrating not a hint of emotion upon her face as she looked at me. She stood, placing Charles on the seat behind her to unbutton my coat, laying it over a wing of the chair by the collar to dry. I took her offered hand and within a few minutes and several more I was tucked up in bed, teeth and hair brushed, all cosy and warm with a hot water bottle beneath my toes and the eiderdown beneath my chin. Mum knelt beside my bed, running her fingers softly through my hair. I could see in her eyes she wanted to say something, as usually she'd kiss me on the forehead, wish me sweet dreams and turn out the light to hurry downstairs to wait for Dad. Eventually she spoke, her eyes still fixed upon her fingertips, her voice as soft as her touch, but with a sadness I'd not heard before.

"Alfie became disturbed by what he'd seen, obsessed. He couldn't stop thinking about it, it gave him nightmares. For months he'd wake up the whole house, screaming and crying in the middle of the night. I tried my best to comfort him, telling him she was dead, buried beneath that house, but he shook his head, afraid she'd return one night seeking revenge and murder us both in our sleep. So, years later, after he'd pleaded and pleaded with me, I agreed to help him. After all, he'd helped me."

"'Children's toys are still being taken,' he said.

"I argued that their missing toys were certainly down to the parents, keeping the myth of Scalas alive.

"'I can't have children of my own unless I know,' he said, 'and neither should you. I'm not going to risk her coming back to hurt them, hurt us. I *must* know if she's really dead, Charlotte. And if not, I'll end this for both of us, for everyone.' He took his broken spectacles from his trouser pocket and held them up to me. 'I'm going back to the Elsewhere Someplace, and if she's alive, she'll remember me.'

"We used my map, followed the route back to where we'd returned from so many years ago. Anaximander took us to a house on the corner of a street on the outskirts of a small village called Pepperdean Hemstitch. It was just an ordinary-looking house in an ordinary-looking village.

"I stood with Alfie on the veranda. The house appeared empty, silent. We cupped our hands around our eyes to look through the dusty windows, but couldn't see anything. I remember turning to look at the view from the front door. It was the same as I remembered from that terrible night when we'd escaped.

"Then I heard him say, 'Charlotte, when things are too obvious, they're often overlooked.' And then the door slammed behind me. I spun around, quickly pushing it open, peering inside for Alfie, shouting his name, but he'd vanished and the house was completely empty. As I stood at the doorway looking in, I realised it was just a hollow shell, a fake. Not one piece of furniture, not one picture on the walls, no fireplace, chimney breast or staircase, it was just an empty box. I called for him again, over and over, then realised my voice didn't echo back to me, and my body tingled with fear when a strong smell of burning wood and ash found my nostrils. For a moment I considered walking across the threshold into the Elsewhere

Someplace, facing the silver gates to run and help him, but something prevented me. Perhaps it was my inner sense of self-preservation, I can't say – then I knew: this was *his* adventure, something *he* had to do on his own. So I sat on the veranda steps with my back to the door, watching dried leaves clattering by, cartwheeling down the street in the wind, waiting and waiting for his return.

"When one sun remained in the sky I headed home, my lone shadow and map my only companions.

"I've not seen Alfie since that day, and Pepperdean Hemstitch is just a ghost village now, deserted and crumbling. Everyone moved on, moved away for one reason or another."

She kissed me on the forehead with a sad little smile. "Goodnight honey. I'll see you in the morning," leaving me in the comfort of my warm bed and tidy room.

I suppose I'm right when I tell you having a child is a very important part of adult life. More so, from Mum's lesson above, knowing you can keep that child safe, as I'm doing my utmost for you by not being there.

Williams was bundled into Nick's car and taken back to Gruber.

"It's as before," he said, examining a sample of Williams' blood through a microscope. "There's nothing I can do for her, she has been changed, forever."

"So where does that leave us? We've had red bullets and now green. Both with different effects, and both disruptive."

"Well, I've made a little progress," said Gruber, pushing his wheeled chair over to a bookcase above his desk, peering over the rim of his spectacles as he studied the book spines. "The *'drugs'* for want of a better term, contained in the bullets are a concentrate."

"Manufactured?"

"No, natural, but refined." He reached for a book, pulling it out hastily, licking thumb and forefinger to turn the pages. "I will have more information for you soon, Adams."

Williams stirred upon the table, holding the back of her head. "What hit me, feel like I've been through a thunderstorm, all tense, muggy."

Gruber swivelled around in his chair and helped her to sit up as she rubbed her eyes and stared through blurred vision, finally resting her hands on her knees.

"I did," said Nick, pulling out his side-arm and putting a bullet through the centre of her chest.

"Perhaps I am the storm, too?" This time he spoke the words, his father adopting his usual frown as Nick stood there shakily. His father's legs were ruined, *'Tangled together, as if they're embracing each other in comfort, aware they will never serve their actual purpose ever again.'* Nick smiled at this thought, but more so, knowing his father would never stand over him to belittle him again. He laughed, they looked funny, his expensive shoes, pointless now, lying on their sides amid the pebbles like overturned rowing boats, loose laces like broken oars.

"Help me, son!" He heard his father's gurgling croak, blood and seawater in his throat.

He coughed and spat several times, as though this would be a definite cure for all his ills. Then he looked behind Nick as something caught his eye, revealed to him fully as Nick crouched down, resting his forearms on his knees, to face his father and gloat. His father's face distorted in pain and he screamed, as though the pain from his ruined legs had finally reached him. But no, it was not physical pain that caused such a deafening cry.

Nick looked over his shoulder, and there against the leisurely curve of a palmnut tree rested part of a ship's

mainmast. His eyes followed it from the sand. The white sail ragged and torn, hanging from part of the mainyard. Washed in the sea, dried by the suns and the breeze, it flapped against the timber as though it were a bedsheet tangling around a washing line clothes pole. And there something was revealed, glimpsed in teasing moments of distant recognition as the sail curled back for an instant, then fell, curled back and fell, over and over again as the wind grew and died, grew and died.

At once this sail snagged a branch, continually flapping against itself in objection, just as a bedsheet on a line curls over itself, trapping itself, flapping urgently to break free.

There was his mother, limbless, the rope her husband had tied to protect her still around her waist, her face just a featureless smear. Then the wind grew, drying and untangling her hair as it snatched the sail away forever from the palm's protective grasp, the wind whistling between mast and bough as it rose.

~ 7 ~
Visitors

Back at his apartment Nick pushed the disk the Mayor had given him into his player. The screen flickered with horizontal then vertical bands a few times as the speaker cracked, before settling upon a scene.

The number one appeared in italics for a moment. He squinted and sat closer to the screen, unable to identify the darkened street that faded in. The view from the artificial's eyes was from a low angle, the machine clinging to the shadows to avoid the pools of white light from the street lamps. A shape darted from an alleyway on the left, the distant sound of a metal trash can tumbling over. The view spun to the right, catching the red and blue running across the road. Nick paused the video and hit the info button on his remote. At the top right-hand corner of the screen, a small map of the city appeared in black and white, the buildings viewed from above as wireframe outlines. A small blinking yellow indicator appeared, and Nick stabbed an arrow on the remote, zooming in on the indicator. He looked between the map and the paused video as it juddered up and down. Shaking his head, he hit play. The map vanished and the video continued, the artificial watching as the red and blue figure vanished into the opposite alleyway. The video paused and faded. Nick swore, the exact location impossible to figure out.

He hit play on the last file.

Quellday, 82nd of Balantor, 18.89 p.s. 821129. Sky co-ordinates 1.9148246 by 8.2362986.

The images relaxed him at first. The three suns played behind the clouds, taking it in turn to hide from view as they twisted across the sky. It was a beautiful Seasonstill's summer day.

We watched as he waited on the grass. I'd never seen this memory before, a memory that fused with the footage upon the screen, creating a mosaic of a past in my soul, giving it a clarity and depth I'd never experienced. It was as though Nick had somehow hidden this episode from me, but I knew that was impossible, so I decided it was simply that he had locked it away from himself, either unwilling to remember, or savouring the memory to be brought forth and enjoyed like a favourite meal. How wrong I was.

Nick was thin, a full head of black hair, neatly cut and parted at the side. He was a lot younger – perhaps eighteen or so years, wearing a blue and yellow uniform. He sat in a park I'd not seen before, watching the families strolling past. To his left, a playground of swings, a slide and a roundabout, surrounded by picnic benches and a low white picket fence. There, children shrieked with delight, queuing with their parents for their turns.

There was a scream, somehow filtering through the children's as they enjoyed themselves, like an accompaniment, a contrast. Then horrified screams and shouting. He finally stood and looked towards the road bordering the park to his right, checking the watch she had given him. There were people running to the scene, and he stood, running too.

He realised what he'd see long before he actually saw it, I could feel that. He recognised the overturned pram, the tiny white shoes on the ground, her best summer dress, but his legs just kept running forward, no matter how much he wanted to not be part of this horror.

His wife and twin boys, just a year and two days old, were dead. The truck had hit them as they crossed the street, slamming them into a row of parked cars.

He had told her not to be late, as he only had half an hour off from his traffic duties, but had sneaked away a little early from directing the vehicles passing the park where she had crossed, so he could enjoy the suns.

His tear-filled eyes fixed upon the screen, unblinking. Then he frowned. The crowd of onlookers, horror stricken. All but one. A face partially hiding in the shadows of the truck caught Nick's attention. The mouth had a subtle yet distinct upward curve. A half-smile?

Nick shook his head and wiped his eyes, leaning closer to the screen. Could this voyeur's expression be one of relief? Perhaps this unknown figure had avoided being mown down itself, a reflex of self-preservation, saving itself from an identical fate – the way that flies always seem to smile after they avoid you trying to swat them. Nick shook his head, frowning, thinking identical thoughts as myself. Was this a smile of pleasure, of achievement the owner failed to suppress, allowing itself to enjoy? And I frowned too, as something in those half-hidden eyes seemed familiar.

I now understood his anger, as his emotions released themselves to me. The conversation he'd had with a daemon much later refreshed itself in his head, as he ejected the disk and snapped it in half, throwing the pieces against the wall.

"Where are their souls? Help me find them! Replace them for me! I will do your bidding, anything!"

The daemon had shaken its head. "The contract is binding to all worlds. They could be taken anywhere across the void if won by the light to be reborn. We have no control, that is the contract's law!"

"But you can save them for me! I'll do *anything!*"

"If won by the dark, you know the consequences, they are immutable. I will, however, take your offer to the Assembly for consideration."

He didn't attend their funeral. He couldn't witness a battle he had no control over. So their souls were out there somewhere, and every time he looked up into the sky and saw the three suns he was reminded of their three souls, the most precious things he had ever experienced in his entire life. Every suns' set he was reminded of their deaths, one by one. Every suns' rise reminded him of their existences elsewhere, somewhere.

"A bargain is offered for your services," he was told during a latter meeting. "Do our bidding, and their souls will be returned to you. We offer you a down payment, the soul of the man that killed your family."

Nick thought for a moment, then nodded. "Put it in my car."

His thoughts returned to that smile he had seen. Why would someone smile at such a horrible scene? He sat back, drifting off to sleep for a half-hour and a third, leaving me to ponder the day's events, concentrating on that half-hidden half-smile before I too slept.

When he awoke, he pulled his armchair over to the ceiling-high doors, opening out onto the narrow balcony. It was a breezy night. The moon was almost full, reflecting a silvery light that highlighted the shabby, thin white net curtains either side of the doors. They billowed and flapped in the breeze like angered banshees as Nick sat smoking a cigar and gulping whiskey. His side-arm lay on his lap. *'She's looking forward to meeting you.'* Williams' words kept repeating in his head.

We both wondered. What would she bring to the fight, and which bullet had she allocated for him?

As he took another slug of whiskey, a breeze of wings preceded a brown owl coming to rest on the balcony's black metal handrail. It looked at Nick with eyes the size of side plates, its head bobbing up and down a few times as it sat dead centre of his view over the city.

"You're late," said Nick lifting his glass to his lips.

The owl blinked then rearranged its wing feathers a few times until it was comfortable. "What is so important, Adams?"

Nick wiped his mouth with the back of his hand, cigar smoke causing him to blink and wave it away. "There's a girl roaming the city. She's upsetting our plans."

"Then do more than upset hers."

Nick took a sip as the daemon, Stolas, shuffled along the handrail to come closer to him.

"It's not as easy as that. She's coming for me. I'm gonna need help."

Stolas' eyes blinked a few times as it looked left and right. "My superior is aware of your difficulty, and to be clear, it's *your* problem. Many in the Assembly are beginning to question our past decisions. Time is precious, even now. Your progress is not as you promised. I supported you in the Assembly's Great Hall of Immutable Decisions, when the choice was made long ago. I championed you when you called upon us to assist you. Do not let me..." The owl's eyes grew wider, its head rapidly bobbing up and down then left and right. "I must leave, you have a visitor," it said quickly.

With that, Stolas unfolded its wings and jumped from the handrail. Nick stood, hurrying out onto the balcony to watch the daemon flapping its wings a few times before gliding over rooftops, banking between buildings to become a diminishing silhouette against the bright low moon.

It began to rain. Softly at first, as if afraid to erase the view, like a splattering of water by an uncertain artist across their watercolour work in progress. The rain then found its confidence. The downpour threatened to soak Nick standing upon the balcony, but he stood defiant, watching the people below hurrying for doorway shelters, hastily extending umbrellas, hailing cabs whose headlights highlighted the spikes of water bouncing from the concrete. He smiled as he looked across the city. "You're all mine," he muttered as he squinted through the rain, wiping the water from his eyes with the back of his hand.

He felt cold, I felt cold – which was disturbing as I had never felt a connection with Nick's feelings like that, never ever before.

For the first time in my second life, I felt as though I'd taken my existence in Nick's head for granted. It was as though he had come to terms with his superiors, as though he had looked into the mirror for the first time. But it was more than that, Nick had seen something else in that half-smile on the disk, something out of place, as if it were a face cut out of a newspaper and glued down over another. I felt his vulnerability, a vulnerability he fought hard to keep at bay, and for a brief moment, when I had forgotten all I had seen of his actions, the murders, corruption, bribery, arson to name just a few, I simply saw the man inside and felt pity for him and his future, the life, like my own, that was taken from him by accidental chance.

He shivered, taking a final puff of his cigar before dropping it to the street far below. He watched the stub tumble over and over, dissipating, its embers struggling to survive against the darkness and the rain, wanting that fall to last an eternity, to prevent him from having to deal with the present. When it vanished, the sounds from the streets found our ears, accompanied by a rumble of distant thunder. He tried in vain to shut them all out, as if they were reaching up to him, to shout and scream for compassion, illustrating the utter despair the city reeked of. He had manipulated and distorted it all through his horrible reign, to make it the shit hole it was now. He couldn't ignore their intensity as they seemingly cried for pity, so he necked the whiskey, breathing hard as a knock upon the door interrupted the cacophony from below.

He turned slowly, wondering at what he would find as he opened his apartment door, a mere tissue between a disquieted now and a hesitant future. Pulling his soaked shirt over his head and tossing it onto the bathroom floor, he grabbed a towel to partially dry his hair and torso, before wrapping his dressing gown around himself and tying a knot tightly at his waist.

Would a swift answer to the door be seen as respectful, or would the visitor respect a pause representing a show of confidence? Nick was questioning himself, I was questioning him with a silent whisper in my head as he ran his fingers through his thinning hair, glancing briefly into the small circular mirror above the fireplace before heading down the hallway to the door. I decided to sit back, reassured by my invisibility, feeling myself relax a little. If I didn't like what I saw behind that door, I knew I could always close my eyes.

I closed my eyes.

As I felt him stop at the front door I decided to peek between my invisible fingers with one eye open, as I had done with my real fingers many times as a child, as my parents had argued and shouted at each other. My only companion then was Keloff's drawing which I had taken one evening and hidden away. Perhaps a treasure map, illustrated in crayon. A dream he had of other lands where everything was different, a dream I shared with Keloff without him knowing. I still remember that innocence vividly, although I had no such tangible companion now, it had all crept away, for it knew it could no longer be part of me since my imprisonment. I missed Keloff, Charles, Mum and Dad, and understood, as much as I hated to admit it, how much Nick equally missed his family.

He closed his right eye, placing his left to the door's spy hole. The corridor was empty, with only the seashell-shaped up-lighters illuminating the cobwebs around them. There was no one there.

The knock came again, harder this time and he jumped back, fumbling at the deadlock and chain, finally releasing the last lock with his key.

He stepped back into the hallway as a small silhouette came forward. There was a whirring sound of metal upon metal, a melodic click as the figure slowly found the dim light of Nick's apartment, and I wondered if this visitor was a result of the Mayor's experimentations. Nick turned, walking back to the comfort of his whiskey.

Peeking between my fingers a little more, I saw the visitor pausing in the darkness, just beyond the shaft of moonlight illuminating the lounge carpet.

"Adams." The voice was old and tired, saying his name slowly in what I decided was an attempt to make the name sound like a mocking curse.

"Yes."

"Your work has become unsatisfactory."

Nick bowed. "It's a pleasure to meet you once again, Grand Master."

I felt a smile coming from the figure. I know it sounds strange, but I could somehow feel this stranger was amused by the situation. Perhaps it could sense Nick's fear also.

"Stolas has visited you. I see he has left a trail of yellow guilt across the evening sky. No doubt he warned you of my disappointment, Adams?"

"Yes. I explained my problem to Stolas – a girl. She..."

"A girl! Yes, girls can be problems."

There was a silent command in the air, and the whirring briefly began again. The figure's feet and shins found the shaft of moonlight. Its skin was old, mottled and translucent. Nick sniffed the air once at a smell which overpowered the combination of the cigar and whiskey in his throat. It was an acrid, offensive odour, thick with anger. I opened my fingers just a little to see more. The stranger's feet were resting upon dull metal plates, beneath them at either side, two tiny wheels with spokes made of polished white bones.

"I'll need assistance," said Adams, as he continued to dry his hair.

"Sit," said the stranger, as a hand with an outstretched finger of the same translucent skin snapped into the moonlight, pointing at the chair by the balcony.

Reluctantly Nick closed the balcony doors and sat, taking the opportunity to pick up the whiskey bottle from the side table along with a cigar as he passed. Filling the glass with a generous double, he lit the cigar as the mechanical whirring began again. The figure skirted along the edge of the shaft of moonlight, turning to face us.

"Assistance? Have you not assembled everything you need over your decades of control?"

"I'm almost ready, then I'll move on to other cities, as previously agreed. A Warden will be charged with maintaining all I've established in Middletown. I will adopt a new identity and work my way up, as I've done here. It just takes time and patience." He took a gulp of whiskey, and I could feel his confidence slowly creeping back. "This girl, however, has skills from the old times, uses drugs bordering on magik potions, potions I erased from history along with their creators many years ago."

Silence, then the figure spoke. "You speak of Middletown's Warden, yet we know in a fit of yesterday's anger, you killed your only suitable candidate. A grave error on your part. Uncharacteristic, born simply from your frustration." The figure sighed a long rasping wheeze. "Unacceptable!"

Nick blew a long plume of cigar smoke into the moonlight and for a moment it hung in the air before dissipating.

"I'll bring her back. It's all in hand – I realise I need her. She has a great deal of information in her head, and I'm confident that a brief visit with death will remove the drug this girl introduced into her system. I'll return her to this existence first thing in the morning."

The figure sniffed and came forward into the moonlight, halting just before we could see its face. I'll be honest, I didn't know what I'd see, but I was intrigued by the mechanics of the chair it sat in.

"Your confidence is reassuring, yet your lack of urgency concerning. My superior and his generals are becoming hungry, yet this girl's actions have found the ears of Middletown's subjects, giving them hope, souring their flavour, spoiling our recent crop of souls with the bitter taste of optimism. This indigestible enthusiasm is spreading, Adams, finding its way to others, creeping across the land like a plague, and you're allowing it to find favour in their hearts and multiply."

"I will stop its spread. There's plenty of time. I'm well within the schedule agreed upon. Once this planet is fully yours, I will move on to the next and..."

The figure held up a hand for silence, fingers creating a long meandering shadow upon the carpet like a silhouette of a winter's tree against a darkening sky. It sniffed again. "Our plans have changed, Adams. We are aware our influences across the cosmos may not be as powerful as we first believed. We have a new method that, once implemented, will guarantee the flavour of our future crop."

Nick frowned and took a deep breath. "Am I instrumental in this plan? I trust my reward is still in place, guaranteed?"

"All will be revealed during our next meeting. However, I have a gift for you, and can advise this, you must destroy all hope, then we will," the figure's hand found the moonlight, palm held out. "Wait!" It sniffed the air again then spoke almost silently. "I can smell a petal." Its voice was soft now, and as I removed my fingers from my face and opened my other eye, it leaned forward into the moonlight, staring into Nick's eyes. "I can smell more than just a simple petal. I can smell a Tiny Flower. But no, *more* than that. It *was* a bulb lying beneath the surface of you. It has slept through the warmth of many springtimes, to emerge, to grow and blossom."

I stumbled back in Nick's head as far as I could, letting out a scream unheard, as if Nick's eyes were two giant windows and this wizened figure was peering in, looking for me in a spherical room without an exit. The wheeled chair whirred once more, bringing it fully into the moonlight and I noticed nine tiny men, one winding a giant spring with a brass butterfly key, the others polishing cogs and wheels of brass and copper as they stood upon gantries encircling the edges of the chair's frame. I looked up wide-eyed as the seated figure looked through Nick, squinting, trying to find me, his hairless head nodding with recognition and a wide knowing smile as he brushed his eyebrows flat with his thumbs.

It was Mr Moople.

~ 8 ~
Destination Hope

When I awoke, Nick was driving his car though the centre of Middletown. The streets were busy, people hurrying to work formed single long shadows of dark grey against the damp pavements. I must have fainted in Nick's head – either that, or Moople had somehow knocked me out. Nick's thoughts were centred on driving. There were no memories of what had occurred between him and Moople following my blacking out.

We reached the precinct and he hurried into the morgue where Williams' body was on ice.

"Get Billie's body out on the slab and leave us," said Nick to Gruber. The little man was about to object, but thought better of it when he saw the look in Nick's eyes.

"Is the slug out?" asked Nick, placing his jacket on the back of Gruber's chair and rolling up his shirt sleeves as Gruber closed the book he was reading. He stood.

"Of course." He opened a drawer set into the wall. "I was about to prep her body for burial. Her wife asked if..."

"No need. Wait in my office. Call Dolores from my deskphone, tell her you've made a mistake and everything's okay. Tell her Billie will bring in a take-out tonight – it's on me and she'll be home early."

Gruber shrugged, slid Williams' inert body onto the table then replaced the tray, slamming the locker closed with an echoing clatter. He left reluctantly with a mouthful of questions never to be asked.

Nick began chanting in a deep, unrecognisable language, causing him to cough a few times as his voice lowered in pitch. He corrected himself and started the chant again, walking slowly around Williams' body. His hands carved the air, creating symbols which stayed hovering where his fingertips had cast them. They were ragged, like iced lightning, and when twelve were established, a bright orange thread of light, tinged with small blue intermittent sparks, linked each in a chain. Williams' body quivered as Nick's vocalisations grew louder. A shaft of white light leaped from each symbol simultaneously into her body, causing it to jump up from the table to come thudding down hard. She began to stir as the white lights continued to feed into her, spinning faster and faster until they became a Catherine wheel blur, and I noticed the bullet hole in her chest had healed without leaving a scar. Gradually the blue slowed, fading against the dirty cream walls. At once the lights and symbols vanished, their task complete.

Williams stirred upon the table, holding the back of her head. "What the fuck hit me?" She rubbed her eyes and stared through blurred vision, resting her hands upon her knees as Nick helped his partner sit up.

"I did," said Nick. "How much is a bottle of water?"

"What?" She looked up confused, then closed her eyes tightly.

"How much?"

"What size? Er, it's a twenty for a small and.."

"Get dressed." He bent down to look Williams in the eyes. "When I call, you come running, understand? No matter what you're doing or what's going on."

Williams nodded, "Sure boss. What happened?"

"Nothing happened." Nick straightened up, grabbed his jacket from the back of Gruber's chair and headed for the door, pointing to his partner. "You're in charge until I get back."

What was my great uncle's neighbour doing in Nick's apartment, and why was he so revered? Questions and questions circled around my head until I remembered the brief conversation from the morning of my murder; *"We must both adopt our roles now. You know that. I must tell others. Good day, Ephesus."* A plethora of possibilities were begging for attention. I shut them all away, deciding to simply go with the flow – there was nothing else for me, following Williams' resurrection. I wondered how Nick had managed to achieve such a feat, then remembered what my father had said about travel. From what Williams had said, my guess was Nick had somehow snatched her from the past, removing her from the instant she had encountered the girl at the water purification plant, replacing her soul within her dead body. Somewhere, in another reality, she was now wanted for a murder Nick had committed. It figured, as it wasn't the first time Nick had managed to shift the blame of his actions.

Nick's car pulled up outside the entrance to a subrail station and he stepped out. A steel shutter adorned with peeling posters and faded graffiti betrayed the beauty of the ornate entrance archway. At its base, the shutter was padlocked to a clasp bolted to the pavement. Cast concrete half-pillars straddled the shutter, pretending to support a low triangle above, inset with broken neons.

He was ignored by the few passersby – a blind beggar sat cross-legged playing a melancholy tune on a banjo of three strings. Nick looked at him briefly, dismissing him as a suitable candidate, unlocked the padlock and removed it, pulled the shutter up just far enough to crouch under, slamming it back with a rusted steel screech. Fumbling in his pocket he found his lighter, replacing the padlock before pulling a lever set into a box against the wall. The lights spat illumination, accompanied by a low electric hum as he sniffed the stale air. The lights finally burned away the darkness in turn and we hurried down the Subrail's wide concrete staircase, climbed over a barrier and continued along a dimly-lit arched corridor of dirty white tiles. Peeling and faded advertisements from long ago lined the walls, and at the end of the corridor I could see the way ahead was boarded up, a door sitting in the middle of a makeshift wooden wall. *'CLOSED. NO ENTRY'* was pasted over the door at a lazy angle.

Nick pulled out his keys and selected one, unlocked the door and with a little effort pushed it open to step in, shutting and bolting it from the inside.

The darkness evaporated in fits as if refusing to leave as Nick hit a switch, fluorescent tubes jumping to life, flickering and blinking as if arguing with each other before establishing the corridor. We continued on to a flight of steps, down into the underbelly of Middletown, until we reached a Subrail platform. Newspapers, discarded fast-food cartons and a woman's black high-heeled shoe our only company. Nick shivered and blew into his hands, looking up as a destination board came to life, its white letters flipping over at the centre behind a dusty cracked pane of glass. They finally came to rest, revealing the word 'HOPE,' with 'Next Caravan – 6 minutes,' written beneath it.

"I know you're in there, but not for much longer," said Nick. "Yeah, you, Tiny Flower, or whatever your damn name is. Think it's clever sitting in my head, a witness to my every deed, huh? Well there's no witness protection programme that can save you, you nosy little bitch."

He reached into his pocket and produced a pair of large black sunglasses. "Here," he said unfolding the arms and placing them upon his face, "you might wanna take a look at this, just for old times' sake. It's the last time you're gonna see yourself."

As I peered out of his eyes and the lenses came closer to finally obscure both our views, I saw a girl's face. I frowned, and the face in front of me frowned too, and I realised the inside of the lenses were mirrored, reflecting me from inside Nick's head.

It wasn't that I'd forgotten what I looked like over the years, it was more to do with my inner perception of myself. I'd imagined I would age inside Nick's head, as my consciousness had aged and matured through the years of my entombment. But that had not happened. My reflection was identical to the instant which I remembered from that summer's day of my murder.

My face was sun-browned, a clear complexion of vitality with a few freckles dotted over my nose. My long, gleeberry-coloured hair awash with streaks of blonde, my eyes bright and pale blue. I still wore my battered straw hat and white cotton dress, and as I smiled to myself I wanted to cry, longing to be a young girl again, realising it had been so long since that life, that I couldn't even remember my name.

Who was I? W*hat was I called?*

Then my anger rose, as I realised once again my youth had been taken from me. All those instances I secretly looked forward to had passed me by, no, had been *snatched* away from me, prohibited! I had been erased from *my* time, and all the participants eager to share my life with me were forced to carry on without me and move on.

What of my parents and their plans for me? Of my dear Keloff, and our growing relationship?

I was a just a brief word. My name, erased from the fleeting paragraph of history I was supposed to be part of, rendering that paragraph unintelligible upon reading it, as my presence there had ceased, without closure. Now, that small episode of history I participated in would be ignored as irrelevant in the grand scheme of things. And the other words, the people so important to my life and others to theirs, had rearranged themselves through no choice other than to make sense of that paragraph they shared, rewriting that story of their time without me.

What had they all thought of my death, if indeed it had been reported as such?

Had Ephesus presented my parents with my body, or told them the last he saw of me was when I left to meet Keloff – how could he have explained what happened to me? What of Keloff, and our planned meeting that morning and the trip to see the man who knows everything? Had the cause of my death been forced upon *him* by my great uncle, and if so, had it been investigated, had he been wrongly punished?

I realised I'd never know, and this worried me greatly.

But right then, at that very moment, upon seeing my reflection, crying streams of tears, I was determined to find out, to right such wrongs, should I ever became whole again.

"Like what you see?" asked Nick, the cheerful tone of his voice betraying the mocking grin his face obviously wore. He snatched the glasses away, tossing them onto the tracks with a brief echoing clatter. "Not long now," he said, glancing up to the destination board. "Five minutes." He took a few paces forward and looked down the tracks. "Can't have a witness able to testify against me. You may think the Grand Master's where the buck stops, but oh no. The Assembly's almost infinite, and we can't have you mouthing off along the chain of command until you find a pair of compassionate ears that'll listen to you and take action, can we? Chances are the higher up the hierarchy you go, explaining what you've seen, the more inconsequential the information will be to them – but that's not guaranteed, so you're gonna get picked, Tiny Flower. Picked and left to wither away and rot."

My mind began to trace back across the years, searching for an exit, a way out of Nick's head. If there was one, what was it, where would it be, where would it lead? Could my great uncle have provided me with an escape route?

Like a dusty rug upon a creaky wooden floor, rolled back to reveal a hatch and a narrow flight of stairs, leading down to a torch-lit tunnel where a boat waits for me upon a sandy beach. Or perhaps a doorway hidden behind a walled bookcase, triggered by a certain book as it's removed from the shelf, a corridor beyond opening to a secret garden, where maybe there's a secret hole in a flint wall, concealed behind a thicket of brambles, beyond which a dew-soaked lawn awaited my bare feet to leave footprints as I run to a big white horse waiting to carry me to freedom? Clichéd dreams, I know. But I'm still young enough to yearn for such, as are you.

But there was nothing for me, no escape to anywhere or otherwhere, no place to hide from whatever Nick had planned in this sphere of imprisonment I clambered against, slipping upon its surface time and time again to come to rest exhausted. I thought about what Nick had said, about the infinite hierarchy, every high-form and daemon alike answerable to a higher order, and I wondered what these beings were – if they were observing us now, or had grown tired of our affairs, choosing to ignore our petty lives as he'd hinted.

I imagined I felt like my grandfather had felt when searching and searching for something he knew was hidden in that house in the forest, but was unable to find. Like my father, chasing an adventure that was always out of reach, and never truly his.

There *had* to be a way out.

The sound of hooves echoing down the tunnel distracted me. Six pure white stallions emerged from the tunnel, drawing a long caravan of eight battered brown wooden carriages with chipped yellow livery. The horses' long grey manes were braided, running along their backs to be woven into their tails, their tails then split into two bunches, curling up beside the neck of the next horse to be braided into its mane. A tall, beardless gnome sat upon a wide wooden seat behind the horses with a tatty red and white striped canopy above his head. He was dressed in a black uniform with red piping along the sleeves and lapels, his trousers of red pinstripes leading to his shiny black boots. He pulled at the reins and a lever to his left, applying the brakes to the carriage wheels. "All aboard!" he shouted from his perch, as the ensemble came to a halt. Nick leisurely opened the nearest carriage door and stepped in, closing it gently behind us.

We sat on the nearest vacant seat next to an elderly woman. She wore a bonnet of pure black lace, her black hair billowed from its edges like frozen soot escaping from a fireplace following a chimney being swept. Her dress of intricate black cotton, intertwining patterns of swirls and contrasting sharp angles was absolutely beautiful. The hunch on her back caused her to sit forward, gnarled mottled hands of paper-thin skin hiding white bones and purple tendons, clasped together upon a walking stick of ivory with thick stripes of intertwining gold.

"Good day, youngster," she croaked, and Nick nodded, crossing his legs and brushing down his trousers. "Ma'am."

A whistle sounded and the carriage jerked forward.

"Shopping for something special are we, or visiting a friend?" she asked, turning slowly to him with a cheeky wink. I wondered at the use of the word, 'we' in her sentence. Perhaps she could see me, help me? Then I realised it was just one of those annoying figures of speech, employed by people attempting to sound superior, but coming across as snobby and sarcastic, when they already knew the answer.

"Perhaps."

"Shopping then. Something for a girly friend, mayhap?"

Nick sighed, "How on earth did you know?"

The other passengers looked over briefly at us as the old woman took the sarcastic hint, sucking in her cheeks, looking out of the window at the darkness and her reflection to her right.

They were a varied group of beings, and I realised this was a transport specifically for daemons, the lazy ones that enjoyed the comforts of the old times, of luxurious travel instead of the instant blinking in and out of locations the younger, impatient ones chose. Okay, lazy is not a kind way of describing them, even daemons like a little privacy, a time to contemplate. And when you live as long as they, there's a lot to contemplate, believe me, I know.

One passenger sitting a few seats down the carriage to our left wore an enormous top hat of grey felt, that almost touched the carriage ceiling. Peering from behind his newspaper he squinted with suspicion at us. His eyes were magnified by two brass-rimmed monocles, connected by silver chains to piercings in his earlobes. I watched tiny figures walking along the chains, backwards and forwards as if on a circus tightrope, steadying themselves on his cheeks now and again. Only the pupil of his left eye could be seen behind the convex lens, his right eye diminished to a tiny point, and I noticed the newspaper's columns contained letters of different sizes and shapes. He ruffled the newspaper straight as Nick noticed his stare, hiding behind it as a hatch opened half way up his top hat. A group of tiny red eyes stared out from the darkness there, and I was sure I heard a giggle above the clatter of the carriage as it trundled on. A rope ladder belched from the hatchway, and six tiny orange people wearing all-in-one swim suits climbed carefully down, each carrying a polka dot deck chair over one shoulder and a draw-string duffel bag of tartan over the other. I watched them as they set the chairs up on the top hat's brim. A few produced books to read from their duffel bags, while others appeared to be chatting, one staring out across the carriage with a pair of binoculars searching for something. I knew how he felt. What *was* my name?

    Sitting across from us was a young man. He took up both seats as he was so overweight. His white linen shirt strained at the buttons, pulling across his chest and stomach. It looked like it was adorned with stains from a hundred different meals and his shirt collar's top edge cut into his neck where a roll of sweaty fat jiggled about to the carriage's movement like a plate of half-set lime jelly. As I stared from the corner of Nick's forward gaze a buttonhole, stretched almost to the point of ripping, in the middle of his stomach, slowly closed upon the button it held. I tilted my head a little and noticed it moving like a mouth. The other button holes began to move also. An a cappella arrangement filled the air, its lyrics eschewing the limited virtues of extensive pond maintenance during early spring. The other passengers shouted, "Shut up, Daniel's shirt!" in unison, and the young man looked a little embarrassed, wiping his brow with the grubby cream-coloured antimacassar the back of his head rested upon. He looked down, telling his buttonholes to behave and talk amongst themselves quietly for the remainder of the journey. They didn't.

    The door at the end of the carriage opened and a burly uniformed figure stood in the doorway. "Tickets!" he shouted.

The group of tiny people sitting in their deck chairs seemed a little agitated. a few slammed down their books to rummage through their duffel bags to find their tickets. The conductor checked each one with a magnifying glass, nodding his thanks in turn. As he looked at the figure hiding behind his newspaper, the tiny people stood up chattering amongst themselves. The newspaper didn't move, but a hand slowly rose from behind it, pointing with an impatient jerk towards the top hat. I found this a little strange, as two hands still held the edges of the newspaper.

One of the tiny people was ushered back up the rope ladder by the others. He retuned a few moments later with a rolled banknote he carried over his shoulder. It complained in a muffled voice as he dropped it to the waiting people below and they unrolled it to pass it to the conductor. He nodded his thanks, turning a handle sitting on the top of a ticket machine he wore on a belt around his waist. A ticket appeared as he turned the handle and the pointing hand snatched it away. The little people jumped up and down congratulating each other then went back to what they were doing, one telling the conductor to keep the change as obviously none of them wanted to climb the ladder again carrying such heavy coins.

"Ticket?" said the conductor to Nick.

He lazily pulled out his wallet and flashed a card.

"Season ticket holder. Thank you, sir," mumbled the conductor, looking at the old woman next to us. "Ticket?"

She shuffled forward a little and her hump moved. A boy's head and shoulders appeared from it as her dress unzipped from the inside. Her expression became pained as he pulled himself up by her shoulders and she grunted and wheezed a little at his effort, supporting herself by her cane. "Two singles to Hope from Pepperdean Square," said the boy with a chirpy voice, offering the conductor a few coins. "One senior, one child, please."

As the conductor worked his ticket machine the boy turned to us. "Taking her home," he said with a nod. "She's been busy far too long, looking after the old house, and has reached retirement now."

"Figures," said Nick, as the boy took the tickets, retreated and the old woman's dress zipped closed.

"He's a good lad," she said, sitting back. "Looks after me, he does, but I won't allow him to walk anywhere, as I'm worried where he'll end up, as we all should, silly little Herbert."

A short while later, satisfied every passenger had been checked, the conductor shouted to the carriage as he reached its centre. "Ladies and gentlemen, the buffet car is now open, situated to the rear. We serve a wide variety of gourmet meals and snacks, beers, wines and spirits for your delectation, but please, *don't* touch the cheese and tomato sandwiches. If you have booked a table, please be prompt. Thank you."

Our journey continued through the tunnel's black then suddenly we were in daylight, and I noticed with some pleasure it was nearly not raining. I peered to the right, my fingers spread wide apart either side of my face as I pushed it against his peripheral vision, in an attempt to see as much as I could of what was outside while Nick's gaze remained ahead. The landscape was desolate. Empty shells of houses, roofless, their bases caressed by rubble, ruined and blackened brickwork, crumbling chimneys like uneven spires worshipping reluctant gods. They looked as if the sky had dissolved them. A group of windmills with drooping wooden sails of missing slats sat motionless upon a hill. Birds circled them, some returning to their nests while others searched for other suitable accommodations, and as our field of view changed I could see the sky through the windmills' carcases intermittently, their brickwork held together here and there by creeping weeds, their bright green leaves enjoying the suns and the refreshing light rain that had ceased a moment and a quarter ago.

Nature was beginning to reclaim the landscape, supporting these broken abandoned relics and follies of mankind. They were nature's permitted reminders, warning us our brief domination of the landscape was essentially not worth our efforts.

I wondered about the haunts of my youth and how they had fared, how they had changed since everything had altered. Were they now just stains upon the landscape, and my memory?

It was a strange feeling, to remember the old streets of my home town, and I questioned why the living called them *'old haunts,'* as ghosts are usually associated with hauntings, and not the living. And why were ghosts always dressed? Was it that their clothes died at the same time? It could be that long ago the living had seen ghosts of old friends at a popular shared meeting place. A subtle nod and a wink while no one could see, lest you're labelled as insane, whilst all you're doing is being polite to the ghost of an old friend returning to the comfort of a location and friendship they once loved. Being dead wasn't that popular with the deceased after all, despite so many scriptures from so many religions assuring us it was just the next step. I suppose it was a little like moving house when you're a child, which I did once – but more of that later, perhaps at the end – parents insisting you'll make new friends and there'll be so much novelty to experience and enjoy. For some, the next step is in the wrong direction, as you have no say, in life or in death.

Nick checked his watch.

"Are you consuming sustenance, deary?" asked the old woman, a look of abandonment in her eyes, contempt for Nick's reluctance to engage her with anything resembling convivial conversation.

"I guess," said Nick, managing a genuine smile at last.

"Then I shall join you, mayhap?"

"My ideal dinner date's for two – me and a good waiter. But, it's still a way to Hope, and the restaurants there aren't that great. No pizzas, that's for sure."

He stood, she held out her hand and he took it, helping her up. And as we headed for the buffet car, I noticed outside a brief streak of red and blue pass the window.

He stood, and as his father held out his hand for assistance he refused it. He turned away from him, back to the horror of his mother's final resting place, as his father's cries diminished to sobs. Finally, he spoke through them. 'My sister! My beautiful sister! Such a wonderful soul.'

'Then this is your ultimate punishment,' **thought Nick, astonished by his father's revelation, of his parents' deception.** *'Not banishment after all, but to live just long enough to witness my mother's final punishment too. You, rendered incapable of assisting yourself by the storm, and your injuries from the night you took me away from the beautiful machine. The storm that spared and freed me from your control has finally forced you to show me your perversion!'*

He remembered the court case of a week and nine days before, his mother's trial, and how she had dressed him for it.

Sitting behind a roped-off area, uncomfortable, a stiff white collar and tie, tight around his neck like an executioner's noose. A new suit with a triangular portion of cotton resembling a handkerchief, peering with fake respectability from a breast pocket, its hidden stitches holding it permanently erect to earn respect. New polished shoes constricting his feet, the leather not yet creased from his guided footsteps.

He looked along the row of her accusers. Hiding beneath white hoods, features hidden by identical, expressionless white masks, an elongated black capital letter 'T' for truth, painted across the forehead and down the nose.

His mother read her opening statement. *'Your teachings are full of inconsistent fables, a tapestry of* *terrible lies, woven between the thinnest threads of actual truth. These sporadic truths, just a spattering of seasoning, selected by the Brotherhood of Truthsayers to bolster legitimacy in the eyes of the populace, to control them, suppress them. These crimes must cease without delay. Your perverted institution must be disbanded and deemed a criminal organisation, intent only on deception for its own gain."*

One replied.

'Yet you create your own versions of truth, determined to undermine the stability the Truthsayers have worked tirelessly to establish for everyone. You form a Church of Disbelief, to encourage the populace to question all we have achieved for their good. You urge them to gather and worship beneath a roof built to shelter your parishioners from our light, that roof supported by windowless walls, serving only as barriers to our truth awaiting outside.'

He crouched back down to look at his father. His old eyes were full of tears. *'Please son! Please help me!'*

Are you requesting a favour? Assistance, after all the beatings I have suffered by your hands, as mother, devastated by your actions, screamed at you to stop as I could no longer speak?

Nick nodded, stood and looked around, listening to the constant whistling from the mast and palm, the cries and sobs of the dying. These sounds accompanied him as he walked to the shoreline, it breathing in a rhythmic fall and rise of shale and sand. His footfalls, determined, evenly measured and punctuated by his resolve, fell across the shoreline's rhythm to form a percussive tempo. He smiled as he realised this, aware of nature's count-in to his emerging symphony.

The stout timbers were continually pushed up onto the pebbles there, only to be snatched back by the following ebb. He chose one, one that seemed more eager amid the others to remain upon the beach. If only for a few moments, as though it were waiting. *'Has it chosen me?'* he thought, as he picked it up. It was dark oak, ornately carved, heavy in his hands as he spun it around to examine it. *'Was it part of a door frame to the captain's cabin, or part of the dining hall furniture – perhaps the leg of a chair?'*

He shrugged, it didn't matter, it would serve him well.

He returned to his father to help him, and with one swift movement, brought it down upon his head to shatter his skull. It was a perfectly timed baton fall, and a perfect percussive start to his symphony, he decided.

Mum's lesson #5
Thought, Keloff and The Great Deletion.

Nick walked through the carriages and I thought about what Mum and Dad had explained to me about The Great Deletion of '29, a few days and three, before it happened. It was the Truthsayers third emergence, some forty years after the second had been finally swept away by its detractors.

Even at such a young age, I could feel there was something going on between my parents, something building up, something not quite right, as though one lived in the afternoon, and the other in the morning. Okay, the divide between the two is just a tad, but a division none the less, and once divisions start they just keep going, keep growing. Like a pulled thread in your favourite woolly hat, that thread will keep dangling in front of your face to distract you, becoming longer and longer, the hole bigger and bigger, until you do something about it, or accept it until you haven't got a hat anymore.

But their issue wasn't really with each other, but more with the looming prospect of The Great Deletion, and how they thought about it, knowing they had no choice but to come to terms with it. We all have to deal with aspects of life we have no control over, our opinions not heard or ignored, our viewpoints as useless as a signpost to an invisible town. Of all this, I'm sure you're well aware, son. The Sayers had returned after decades of hiding among us following their defeat, studying us, formulating and concluding. Now they had a new agenda, which would slowly unfold.

Dad returned home for dinner in the early evening after consuming a gallon or so of ale, following an afternoon visiting his favourite alehouse.

Upon Mum's insistence, I'd accompany Dad during his visits to *'The Butchered Wheel,'* alehouse whenever possible, as such infrequent visits were an *essential* part of her lessons, she had told me. Gradually, I found a great friendship with Keloff beneath the table Dad drank at, and he became my best friend. We'd listen to our fathers' conversations – Leet, Keloff's father, trying to convince my dad to join the order of Truthsayers of which he was suddenly a member. But my father, may the gods bless him, refused Leet Skarlac's constant attempts at recruitment, favouring his own truths arrived at from experience, rather than those rigid lessons the Truthsayers would soon orate again from every town and village square. Unfortunately, on this occasion, Mum told me to stay at home.

As Dad stood in the kitchen holding out a treasure map drawn by Keloff with his crayons, he tried to convince my mother to join him on a search for his adventure. He was certain his garbled ramblings made complete sense. *"He shat under our mable, I bought im juice, e gave me sheesh,"* he said to my mother,

My mother reached for her, *'The Handy Guide to Drunken Phrases - Translations and Meanings,"* a pocket-sized notebook she had written herself, for herself.

By sniffing my father's breath she could smell a mixture of ale and whiskey. She fanned the book to the correct chapter, as there were several denoting the types of alcohol my father was fond of and combinations thereof.

Aware we didn't know anyone called Mabel, and certain no one would defecate beneath her even if we did, my mother realised what he was saying – adding a note with the small pencil she usually kept behind her right ear for such occasions or others that required a written record, lest they were forgotten. She snatched the map from his hand and passed it to me, saying I should go to my room as she began preparing a mug of steaming hot crushed whitefruit branches, orange rhubarb roots and devilled throd fish eggs, to sober Dad up.

My father became more agitated as she helped him into the dining room, swaying as if he were at sea, cursing my mother's reluctance to help him find his adventure as she continued making notes from his slurred mutterings. I watched from the doorway, briefly looking at Keloff's map, which was actually a drawing of a unicycle with a red spoke. I hurried upstairs to bed, briefly peering through the banister rails at their angry shadows cast against the hall wallpaper as Dad pulled Mum's notebook from her grasp to hold it behind his back, escalating their argument into a shouting match. I told Charles all about it, and he was very supportive, telling me not to worry, and that everything would be alright in the morning. I smiled and nodded to him, patting his shell.

Their argument trailed off into a calm conversation as it became dark. I brushed my teeth at the little corner sink, gave Charles a drink from the tap before I climbed into bed, allowing him to sit in the sink as we listened to their voices late into the night, watching the moonlight cast swaying shadows from the whitefruit trees against my bedroom wall before we fell asleep.

After a silent breakfast late the following morning they explained it to me. It was the first day of the weekend, and we sat in the front garden beneath the living-room window on a narrow wooden bench Dad had made years ago for him and Mum to relax. I watched Charles watching the few passersby from atop the garden wall as I sat between my parents.

"The Great Deletion is due very soon," said Dad.

"What's *that* mean," I asked, arms folded across my chest, worried they'd start arguing again.

"We're not supposed to know yet, but Leet, my friend from the alehouse told me last night, hoping that would convince me to join the Truthsayers. There's going to be a lot of arguments very soon, Tiny Flower. Perhaps even fighting."

My mum raised her eyebrows, shaking her head slowly, just enough for me to see.

Dad let out a deep breath which smelt of vinegar from devilled throd fish eggs.

"Leet told me last night. It's just the beginning, a small part of *The Unremembering*. The Truthsayers will forgive us for what we've said in the past, deleting it, protecting everyone from accusations in the future of things we've done or said to each other." He rested his elbows on his knees, staring at the ground, his hands clasped together as though they were wrestling. "He insists it'll be good for everyone," he said, shaking his head. "We all have to agree with their view of history, as they say they've studied the past carefully, and they think they know exactly all the things that people have done, and what's happened that has led us up to this point, making people unhappy. And, apparently, some of it isn't very nice, and neither were some of the people. We're not permitted to point fingers at each other, for something that happened yesterday, or one thousand and two years ago before that."

I looked up to him. "What, like beans? They're not very nice either. Are we allowed to talk about tinned beans being not very nice, like people?" I returned my gaze to watching Charles, allowing my legs to sway backwards and forwards alternately at my knees, pointing my toes, the tips of my outdoor slippers brushing the tops of the weeds hiding in the shade beneath the bench. "Mum gave me them on toast, and that was yesterday."

I could feel Mum's shoulders shaking a little as she suppressed a giggle, holding her hand in front of her mouth, her long fingers curling around her cheek. "Oh, I agree!" said Dad, turning to face me, "and I brought up a question for Leet a bit like that last night. I was told, 'If you're unsure, it's best not to talk about it. You don't want to offend anyone.'"

"So if someone asks me if I like tinned beans, what should I say?"

Dad looked at Mum before he answered. She'd settled down, but I could see she was struggling a little not to blurt out a big laugh. "Nothing negative to hurt anyone or start a discussion," he said, with a hint of seriousness to his tone. "Apparently it's dangerous to talk about the reasons why you don't like certain things, because other people won't care and that might upset you. And before you ask, there's no point in telling people why you like things that they don't, because firstly they shouldn't have told you what they don't like in the first place, and secondly if they have, you won't change their mind in the second place."

"Or worse, in the third place," added Mum, "they'll take offence and the authorities will be called to investigate. Just say, *out of context*, if you can't say anything good."

I began to wonder if we're all destined to be like Charles – with mouths used only for eating, and not talking.

"What if I'm, one day, perhaps at Keloff's – and he gives me beans on toast. Will I be offending him or the beans if I say I don't like them,? Will I be reported and punished?"

"No, you're too young at the moment. But *we* might, for not telling Keloff's dad, and not telling you not to say anything that could offend them."

"But that stops us talking and asking questions. You've always told me to ask questions if I don't know, and to tell you things I'm worried about!"

"We know, honey," said Mum through a sigh. "But this is the way it's going to be. If you start to learn now, it will protect you from getting into trouble when you're all grown up."

I rubbed my finger under my nose and sniffed, realising once again that I wasn't at all keen with the prospect of growing up. But no, I was enjoying the growing up part, it was when it was deemed that *that* part of my life was suddenly over, that annoyed me. Who had the right to say so? Surely I wouldn't suddenly stop learning when one day I was seen as an adult, but the day before seen as a kid?

It was becoming clearer to me by the day, as I headed inexorably towards that indefinable 'moment' of suddenly being one of them, (which clearly adults had decided long ago it was when kids reached a certain age) that most of what defines being an adult was, for the most part, very silly. I also wondered at Mum's continued use of the word, 'all' in her reply to me. Did that mean parts of me became an adult before others, like my hair, knees or feet? I didn't like the idea of my knees being adult before the rest of my legs, as Mum's were becoming a bit bony and wrinkled. I decided because of this talk we were having, my parents had decided it was my brain that was going to reach adulthood first. Mum had asked me a few times, 'What do you want to be when you're all grown up?'

"Taller," was my reply every time.

I looked at Dad. "So who are these people that would accuse people? I don't understand."

"Everyone. The Truthsayers are protecting us from each other's accusations."

"What if I ask Keloff if he likes beans, next time I see him, and we agree not to tell anybody about our conversation?"

They looked at each other over my head for a few moments before Mum spoke. "Children are allowed a leeway, as I mentioned, to learn the new rules before they're adults. They'll form half of the schools' currriculum, next term."

I grinned.

"And children that are home taught will be sent to Thinking lessons."

My eyes went wide at the terrible thought, and I was about to object when Mum leant forward a little and spoke quietly.

"This coming Mournday, I'm afraid, honey."

My stomach churned. "I'm not going."

"If you don't, we'll get into trouble. It's only for a few days, before the school holidays start."

"Can Charles come with me?"

"He can go with you, but not into the lesson. Pets aren't allowed."

Dad tutted, removed his arm from my shoulders and sat up straight, turning slightly, making the bench creak. "Here's an idea. You could leave a little early, see Keloff on the way and leave Charles with him for the day. After school, you can pick him up on the way home."

"Good idea," said Mum. "I'll walk you to Keloff's, and Keloff and Charles could walk you the rest of the way?"

"Yes, that's even better," said Dad.

I could feel them looking at me from either side, as I watched Charles slithering down the garden wall to join us as fast as he could. He'd heard his name as he'd been listening all the time.

"Ok." I looked up at Mum. "Do I have to wear a uniform?"

"I'm afraid so," she said, running her fingers through my hair. "It arrived in the post yesterday. It's not as bad as you think, sweetheart. It's having a soak in the sink, so it won't be all nasty and rough and smell all new. Then you can try it on and I'll alter it if it doesn't fit very well."

"There's nothing to worry about," said Dad. "After next Frothday, just try to remember to forget to bring up anything someone said to you before then. Everything must be kept in context with the truth of those that say."

"Truthsayers?"

He nodded.

"But how am I supposed to know all what they say, like history and stuff?"

"We'll be given guidelines, pamphlets to read to begin with." said Mum.

"And they'll be a Sayer in every town. We can ask them if we're not sure." added Dad.

I shook my head. "So, I'm starting my life all over again, from next term?"

They nodded. "Look at it this way, it will be so easy for you, sweetheart," said Mum, "as you're young. Imagine how difficult it will be for old people, like Mr and Mrs Cribbage? Both of them have so much to unremember. It's not going to be easy for them!"

I couldn't believe what I was hearing. The very thought of being taught what to think disturbed me. The eradication of being young, forcing children into a position a lot like my present predicament, trapped in an adult's body.

"You just need to keep conversations," I watched Dad as he struggled to remember, his eyes returning to the ground, darting about as though he'd lost a talking penny in the grass and couldn't see it as it cried out for help. "How did Leet put it? Err, that's it, that's what he said! In context, on topic. The Sayers frown upon out of context conversations, as that could lead to, to *branch-offs*, which are pointless, unproductive and waste time, or so they believe."

"Yes, and think of this," said Mum cheerily, trying to convince me. "By the time you have children, these new rules will be normal. Any worry you have now, won't matter for them, because they won't know any different because they would have grown up that way."

"I'm not having children, I said quickly. "I played with some in the street a few times. They're rubbish."

"Oh, and before I forget to remember, there's a new greeting ritual: '*The great context protect you*,' and the answer is, '*and together we are specific*.' There's no more 'Good morning,' or whatever time of day it is, because that's an opinion. Someone might not think it's a good morning, and be offended, or be jealous because it sounds as though you're having a good morning, and they aren't.

'How are you?' is also frowned upon, because the Sayers believe nobody really wants to know how the other person is, it's just an ancient, pointless ritual, leading to a worthless conversation that doesn't help or change anything."

"Because they've had beans for breakfast, and have painful wind," I muttered under my breath.

"Honey?" said Mum in a huff, "you *have* to take this seriously!"

My anger was churning up inside me. I couldn't believe the stupidity of it all, the point of it all. "This is crazy! How come being polite is now seen as being rude? How can all this steaming horse toilet be real?"

"Flower!" said Mum, clasping her hands together in her lap and straightening her back. She always abbreviated my nick-name when I said something adult. Now it was Dad's turn to suppress a laugh, but he failed, causing Charles' eye-stalks to recede a little and Mum to bite her bottom lip.

"Don't worry," said Mum quietly, as Dad's laughter trailed off, "it's only for a little while." She leaned closer to me and whispered in my ear. "We might leave all this behind."

I gave her a confused look, unfolded my arms and placed my palms under my knees as they'd become uncomfortable. "What do you mean?"

Her eyes glanced over to Dad, I turned to him as he gave her a little smile, then a single nod with his eyes closed. I looked back to her and and she continued. "How would you like to spend the Seasonstill holiday with your great uncle, while dad and I look for a new place to live, in Hope?" She put her arm around my shoulders, pulling me close. "The Sayers will have problems convincing folks there of their new way, and no chance at all with the people of Middletown – there's just too many of them, with different viewpoints and long-established traditions, for the Sayers to control. They tried long ago, but were driven out."

"Murdered, you mean," said Dad.

"Aiden!"

There was silence for a while until I broke it. "Hope. That's not too far from Viewhaven and the beach, is it?"

"That's right!" said Mum.

I looked between them as Charles whistled and thumped to be picked up. "Can Keloff come to stay, can I come back to visit him, can I – with Charles?"

Dad's arm found my shoulders too. "Of course." He squeezed me tightly then stood, picked up Charles and passed him to me. "I'll go and arrange Mournday morning with Leet and Keloff. Please help Mum with your uniform."

On the way to the class (which was held in the school hall where the kids usually had to eat school dinners, or throw a ball to each other when it was raining outside) Keloff did indeed join me for the walk.

As Mum and I saw him waiting for me on the veranda of the house his father had built at the top of Ridgetop Hill, Mum put Charles down, kissed me goodbye, wished me luck and headed home. I watched her as Charles slowly woke up at my feet, peering from his shell with confusion at my new shoes, and as she turned we waved to each other a final time. I pushed the gate, holding it open for Charles and telling him to hurry up.

Ridgetop Hill was planted with rows and rows of mothcotton plants, enjoying the chalky soil and natural drainage. It was early in the growing season, and a troop of impatient dogflies patrolled the rows of young plants searching for bugs, buzzing up and down the rows where the pods were just showing their white cotton, peeking from beneath their slowly opening pod seams. As I walked up to the house, the morning mist withdrew from the hillside, chilly around my ankles, leaving behind it a caress of moisture in tiny droplets on the plants' wilting red petals, shining and sparkling like crystal tears in the first sun.

And there was Keloff, sitting in his mother's rocking chair on the veranda with his boots resting on the handrail, a sprig of grass protruding from his mouth. The chair dwarfed him, and his cocky smirk immediately caught my attention.

He waved and called out, "Mornin', Charlie boy!" brushing his mop of curly hair from his eyes. Charles gave a brief thump and whistle, saying it was too early for anything.

"You look pleased with yourself," I said, adjusting the strap of the brown leather satchel which was far too big for me and kept banging the back of my knees as I walked. "How come you're not going to Thinking lessons?"

He took the sprig of grass out of his mouth, flicking it into the dust as he stood, the rocking chair rumbling on the squeaking timbers behind him for a few moments before it came to rest.

"Dad can tell me all that stuff. They've made him Sheriff of the District, say they're gonna give him a car so he can spread the word as far away as Middletown."

I looked around. "Where is he?"

His head jerked. "In the barn out back, greasing the pickingweavers, cleanin' their bobbin chassis, an' calibrating the gear cogs." He looked over the crop. "Gonna be a good harvest this season, for sure, we'll need all of 'em running true."

I tilted my head to the side, a little concerned. "So you're ok with all that Sayer horse toilet?"

He shrugged as he jumped down to join us, stirring up dust. He wore a torn and faded red and white chequered shirt rolled up to the elbows, jeans that obviously belonged to his dad at some point, as they were ragged at the bottom, cut too short and held up at the waist by string and black nylon braces should the knot escape. His big boots were the only thing that fitted him properly, and he smelt of pickingweaver grease and his dad's spicy pipe tobacco.

"It's a job, and dad ain't getting younger. Easier than ploughing and planting turnips, that's for sure. Anyways, it pays pretty well, and if he wants to spread that muck, it's up to him, TF. Sure beats spreading real muck for a living."

I didn't mind him shortening my nick-name to TF, and he was the only person I'd allow to do so. He turned from the rows of plants, looked me up and down a little and his smirk returned.

"What's the matter with you now?"

He sighed as he took the satchel from me and placed it over his shoulders. "Never seen you have to dress like a *real* girl before."

I thumped him on the chest. "I've always been a real girl, stupid!"

"Yeah, but, you know – with a uniform, all new and clean and pressed with straight creases. Ain't it uncomfortable?"

"No," I lied. "Mum and I washed and dried it in whitefruit blossom."

He pointed. "So what's the 'TA' badge for on your blazer pocket, – does it stand for Tiny Apprentice, now you're all dressed up and respectable like, an' going to school?"

I looked down at it, then back up to him defiantly down my nose, but couldn't, as he was a head taller than me and it hurt my neck a little. "It stands for 'Trainee Adult,'" I muttered, trying my best to sound as though I was happy and proud with the label the Sayers gave kids. "And it's not school as such, it's just Thinking lessons."

He looked surprised. "It's lessons in a class, they're in school, sure sounds like school to me!" he said, walking in the direction of school. I was hoping the reason he was walking so slowly was so he could make our time together last longer, but knew it was probably so Charles could keep up.

"That drawing you gave to my dad, of the unicycle with one red spoke. What's that all about?"

He grinned again, rubbing the back of his head. "Oh, nothing really. Just something I put together while I was sitting under the table the other night."

"Really? That's it?"

"Well, kinda." He paused, thrusting his hands into his pockets and looking at the grass. "I met a man, last week's yesterday. Across the way, near the Citadel ruins. He told me he knows everything, told me I should draw that for you."

"Humph, most adults think they know everything. What's new? And does he, did you test him, and ask why you should draw that picture for me?"

He didn't reply for a while, using that while to look back to see if Charles hadn't dropped behind, or wandered off in another direction to explore a scent trail lying in the grass. I looked back too. He hadn't, and just looked between us with his innocent 'what's the problem?' expression.

"Not exactly, but..." his voice trailed off.

"What? You can't just start telling me something and then finish with *'but.'* What!?"

"It's a bit strange. Told me he knew my grandmother – Mum's mum."

"He must be really old then," I said, frowning as my new shoes began to pinch my toes and rub my heels. "How could he remember if he's *that* old?"

"That's the thing, he doesn't *look* old – sounds it by the way he speaks as he keeps mixing things up an' forgetting, but nope, looks younger than our dads, for sure!"

We came to the rickety gate at the edge of Leet Skarlacs fenced-off land, and as Keloff opened it for us I carried Charles through. As I put him down and brushed the grass from my hands, I looked up and felt a shiver. Down into the valley floor my eyes wandered, the distant school building of unattractive squat concrete blocks, a few shops, rows of small flint-walled houses and a farm. The buildings looked like they'd been placed together on the hillsides to tumble down and come to rest all mixed up, rather than arranged properly. Behind the buildings, fields of yellow sunchoke flowers stared back at me from the hillside. Everything was silent, but even this far away it seemed foreboding, threatening to me, as I knew I had no choice other than to continue. It wasn't the adventure I half-imagined it might be, and had it not been for my two companions, I knew I would have run off as fast as I could, despite my painful feet. I walked on as slowly as I could.

Our feet found a narrow chalky path, a crease carved into the hillside over many decades and two thirds, leading down to the settlement. Charles objected to the rough path with a rude whistle, choosing to travel along the short grass to my right.

"Are you going to tell me what he said then, this man who knows everything?"

"First, best I tell you what my mum told my dad, about her mum, before she passed."

I looked over to him and nodded, not wanting to go into his mum's death just after he was born. Dad had told me, and Keloff knew that, so there wasn't any point. It was the first time he'd ever spoken about her to me though, and I respected that.

"When my gran was a little kid, younger than us, she lived with her folks on a hill growing mothcotton too, but in those days they had to pick it by hand." He looked back. "Their hill was bigger than Ridgetop, really big. Almost the size of a small mountain. She'd wander off, exploring their back garden, where a tall wire fence stood at the bottom. She'd cling to it, lookin' at the shadows. The land past the fence was all overgrown, brambles, wild gleeberry bushes, jagged-leafed ferns, long grass and trees – all dark and mysterious. She had to know what lay beyond it, had to explore. But the fence was too tall to climb."

"The fence was obviously there for a reason, Keloff, to keep her safe."

"For sure. But one evening, as she clung to the fence squintin' into the darkness and wondering what was there, she swore she heard somethin' in the distance, a kinda faint metal click-da-click, over and over again. Like a broken clock, one hand stuck behind the other, complaining it can't move."

"Never seen that."

"I have. Dad repaired it. Well, anyhow, she went back, sneaking out of her bedroom window in the dark, clinging to the fence and listening. But that sound didn't come back, and she wondered if it coulda been a dragon or something, an animal, caught in a hunting trap. She had a set mind to find out, and that wasn't gonna change. Especially as she heard the click-da-click the next night.

"In the morning she was helping her mum put washing out. There was a post at one end of the garden where the line fixed to a pulley to hoist it up. The other end was tied to a tree, and as her eyes wandered up and along the branches, she saw one reached over the fence –"

"So she climbed the tree early the next morning and dropped down the other side." I looked up to him with a grin, "Then she realised she..." I slipped on the loose chalk as I was talking, Keloff grabbed me by the arm with both hands. Steadying myself against his weight, he let go, his right hand finding my left as we stared at each other for what seemed an age. We both turned together to carry on walking. I gripped his hand tightly, and our fingers interlocked and my tummy flipped over.

"Can't have you getting chalk on your uniform," he said. "Best I hold your hand, if, if that's ok, TF?"

"Until we reach town," I answered, trying to hide my smile.

"Yeah. You were saying?"

"Sorry, yes, she dropped down into the bushes on the other side, but then she realised there wasn't a tree to climb there to get back over the fence and into her garden."

"Yep, but I'll get to that in a bit. She crawled through all the bushes and long grass, heading in the direction she thought the click-da-click came from. But when she cleared the bushes, she couldn't believe what was there."

The slope began to decrease a little, the buildings ahead a little larger before us, the sounds of people talking and dogs barking finding our ears. I felt Keloff loosen his grip a little, so I squeezed his hand, letting him know it was alright to hold my hand still as I needed his companionship, although his hand had become a little sweaty. He turned his head to me with a smile, and I smiled back briefly as he continued.

"Far below her was a deep vee cut into the landscape. Perfect, steep slopes on either side. At the bottom of the vee, the ground was flat with small grey stones. There were two strips of shiny metal stretching into the distance in perfect straight lines, as far as she could see. She couldn't see over the top of the vee, but as she walked closer through high grass, found the ground level out with gravel and dirt. There was a long row of bricks sticking out the ground, high above the strips, so she sat down, her legs dangling in the air, shuffling along so the metal strips were directly under her. She just sat there for hours, watching the last two suns come up, before she saw something in the distance. It crawled between the two strips towards her, growing larger and larger, and then she heard the click-da-click." He turned to me, realising it was nearly time for us to part, wanting to finish his story. "It was one of those big cars, without a driver, from the very old times, even for her. Wider than both our houses put side-by-side, three times as high, big black metal wheels sitting on the metal strips. And then she noticed something. It looked like a man, sitting cross-legged on the roof. He must've noticed her, as he stood up and waved."

We stopped at the edge of town and I looked up to him, shielding my eyes from the suns with my free hand.

"You're going to tell me it was your new friend, this man who knows everything, aren't you?"

He nodded. "This man spoke to her, walking backward on the roof so he was always in front of her. Told her the trains used to run all around the country, picking up stuff and delivering it, and had done for years – all on their own. Factories made food and tinned it, all on their own too, and these trains just took it everywhere and collected the rubbish too."

"Sounds like big pickingweavers."

"Exactly. She managed to get back home by digging under the fence, but went back to talk to this man for years, until they moved house some twelve years later. But before that, she jumped down from that wall and he caught her, telling her off for doing it. Said she sat on the roof with him, and spent a whole day travellin' around – a whole day!"

I watched him looking down the street with a frown, where other uniformed kids could be seen briefly in the High Street. They carried satchels, clutched books to their chests as they reluctantly headed towards school. Shouting, laughing and doing normal-kid things. He let go of my hand, wiping his palm on the side of his jeans.

"But that's mad, Keloff."

He kept watching the kids. "Nah. What's mad is she said his face never changed, never got older." He smiled down at me. "You can ask him yourself when you meet, and about the picture. But yeah, you're right, it's mad."

I shook my head and smiled back for a second, looking at the ground to hide the fact I didn't believe a word of it, knowing he'd made it all up just to fill the silence between us. I looked up. "I'd better get going, Keloff. Thanks for walking with me, and looking after Charles until I get back."

"Ahh, no worries. Charlie boy ain't no trouble, and neither are you."

He thrust his hands into his pockets, looking down at me. I raised my eyebrows and jerked my head forward a little. He looked confused, copying my expression, his eyes darting about, wondering what my expression meant.

"My satchel?"

"Oh, yeah. Sorry," he said, his cheeks colouring as he fumbled about quickly, taking it off his shoulders, the strap pushing his hair in front of his eyes. As I took the satchel and placed the strap over my shoulder he brushed his hair from his eyes. And I don't know where it came from, but I found myself standing on tiptoes, despite my uncomfortable shoes, to hold onto his shoulders and kiss him quickly on the cheek. I spun on my heels, adjusting the annoying strap of my satchel before bending down and patting Charles' shell goodbye. I hurried down the street towards the other kids, turning to wave at Charles with a grin. His eye-stalks extended and he slid forward a little.

"Shall I meet you here?" Keloff called after me. "Don't want you slipping on the path on the way up the hill to my place."

I turned to face him, walking backwards, unable to hide my happiness. "Don't be late, school closes eighteen after ten." And with that I picked up my annoying satchel to hold it against my chest to steady my heart, convinced my very good mood could not be shattered by anything the Sayers' lessons could throw at me during the day.

Son, I've never told anyone about this, so whatever you do, please don't ever tell your grandmother – she will be very angry if she found out, as I've kept this from her for such a long time and intend to do so for much longer.

I queued up with the other home-schoolers for the reception desk at the front of the school, the regular school kids looking at us as though we each had two heads. Groups of older girls were talking about us behind cupped hands to each other, the boys sneering, puffing out their chests. They were obviously jealous. A few of them pushed through our line without saying a word, others making rude comments. It was too noisy.

At the desk I gave my name to the impatient receptionist and was handed a small map and timetable for the day, the map leading me back along the corridor I'd hurried down minutes before. I found the map a curious addition, wondering why the corridors were free of signs pointing to sections of the school, and the doors were without labels, informing us what lessons were taught behind them. All the roads and streets had names, corners had signposts, pointing to important places. Shops had names and informed us of what services they provided or goods they sold, so who decided this place should be so difficult to navigate? As I followed the map, checking off numbered doors along the corridors, I was thankful that at least someone had deemed it appropriate to label the toilet doors as such. I made a mental note of their location and hurried on.

The map finally led to the canteen hall's entrance, apparently, my final destination as the map stopped there with a big red 'X'. I was certain there was no treasure to be found behind those doors, and I had no inclination to further explore and add my own observations to this map, folding it neatly and placing it in the inside pocket of my blazer.

The dining hall stank with a mixture of perfumed cleaning stuff, old fried food, boiled cabbage and stale children. Desks and chairs had been arranged to resemble a class room, but as the hall was so big, there was a considerable empty space between the edges of the twenty or so desks and the walls. Unlike a regular classroom, thankfully these walls were free of those condescending, unevenly placed pictures of animals with their names beneath them in big, bold black letters, the alphabet in a long colourful uneven banner, numbered cards from one to one hundred, and the names and meanings of the ten days of the week. I was pleased to see on my right, tall, evenly placed arched windows afforded a view of the playing fields, replacing these patronising traditions, that served only to suggest the majority of parents took no interest in pre-school education, or hide cracks in the classroom walls.

In front of the desks on the far wall sat a large white-faced clock, ticking back the morning on its countdown to the first break. I chose a desk with the other home-schooled kids, hanging my satchel on the back of my chair and sat, looking at all the other kids. They all watched the regular schoolkids outside as they pulled their chairs forward with a screech upon the wooden floor. I did the same and tried to get comfortable, my skirt itchy, blazer too long at my wrists, sock elastic too tight just below my knees, but my feet were finally relieved as I prised off my shoes with my toes.

For some reason, the regulars outside were wearing shorts and sleeveless shirts, one half of them wearing blue, the other half red, chasing a big, leather oval ball within a rectangular marked-off area of thin, uneven lines of white-painted grass. Two big nets stood at either end of this marked-off area, supported by wooden frames. Everyone didn't look at all happy with the proceedings outside, apart from four or so of the bigger boys, dominating the activity by kicking the ball about as a few other kids chased them, (or perhaps the ball – I couldn't be certain) the ball's shape causing it to bounce and roll in unpredictable, haphazard directions. I smiled, as I knew exactly what was going on. An overweight, balding teacher came into view with a silver whistle in his mouth, struggling to keep up with the regulars, his tight faded black shorts and shirt providing him with mobility issues. There was lots of shouting and complaining, which was identical to a normal lesson, except shouts and complaints were silent in those, I was later told. I looked around at the other kids in the hall again. They were all bigger than me, but that was no surprise, as I was small for my age, and with a little relief and comfort noticed most of them appeared uncomfortable with their new uniforms and the surroundings too.

"TRAINEE ADULT CLASS, attention please!" The shout startled everyone, and we all faced forward.

A fairly elderly woman stood there, blank faced, thin, smartly dressed with a narrow skirt and waistcoat of dark grey, covering a plain white blouse with tight cuffs and puffy sleeves, her constricting collar buttoned up snug beneath her angular chin. A string of small white pearls hung around her neck, with one fastened to each earlobe. I could tell they weren't real from the way they caught the light, even at this distance, as Dad had shown me real ones many times. Her hair was a lighter grey than her clothes, almost white, swept back and tied at the top of her head in a small bun. She stood stiffly, her arms bent at the elbows, right hand on top of the left, as though she'd placed something in her left hand and was hiding it, or keeping a baby woodlouse warm. I watched her as her eyes fell upon each of the kids in turn, her face twitching ever so slightly in obvious disappointment. And when her eyes found mine, I realised she was searching for something in all of us, even though those pale eyes were vacant, watery and somewhat emotionless.

"Welcome to your first Truthsayer Thinking Lesson. I am your Instructor, and you will call me, Miss Teacher. In a moment and four, I will tell you to open your desks, in silence. You will find a folded card, a pencil, a rubber, a pencil sharpener and a notebook. Write your surname – that's your family name, *not* your first name – upon the card in bold letters, then place it at the front of your desk, facing me. The Sayers are not interested in your first names, and neither am I, as we're not on first-name terms." She looked over us all for a few moments and flashed a false smile. "Do so, now."

There was a mixture of enthusiasm and reluctance around me as we lifted our squeaky desk lids, my attitude being the latter and part of the majority. I wondered why individuals entrusted with such an important role in society, always gave a bad first impression to kids. It was as though they were recruited solely on their astonishing ability to easily appear unfriendly and authoritative. I decided to keep an open mind though.

There was a mixture of thumps and bangs around me as the desk lids closed, each and every one of them a signal of compliance, but mostly, an early finality of pitiful resignation. As I finished writing my name, I looked up, watching Miss Teacher as she walked slowly down the aisle, the clicking footsteps from her black high-heeled, pointy-toed shoes, sharp and precise, echoing in the hall like the ticking of the clock I couldn't hear. Her angular face and pointed nose made her look like the number four, her hands were still clasped together, and her eyes looked down at our writing without a single movement of her head. I glanced up at the clock. It was as though the hands hadn't moved, as if refusing or probably afraid to measure the obvious torture yet to be distributed.

As the kids around me finished, some sat upright, nervously clasping their hands together upon the desks in front of them, others sat back leisurely in their chairs, while they all continued watching the game outside. I placed my card at the front of my desk, deciding to do the same. Nothing much had changed out there, except a line of them were running in a different direction now, weaving through the short grass like a snake, as though this oval ball was some strange animal to be caught, bitten and swallowed whole. The shouting grew as one of the bigger kids managed to get ahead of the others with the ball, somehow behaving itself in a trajectory resembling a fairly straight line. I watched him running towards the net where another kid stood in front of it, arms spread apart, shuffling from side to side. Miss Teacher's rhythmic footsteps filled my ears, as though timing the hunt outside, urging that big kid closer and closer to his goal. He kicked his prey hard as her footsteps stopped, the ball wobbling madly in the air, to go careering in a curve over the net to freedom. The regulars screamed a mixture of emotions as a whistle sounded. They stopped, strolling back to the bent over Instructor who was holding his legs just above his knees, breathing hard.

"Trainee?" I snapped back to the moment, looking behind me. She was standing at the front of a desk fairly close to the window, at the corner of the back row. The kid sitting there looked up at her, terrified.

"Trainee, Smythems." Finally her hands parted as she picked up the kid's card. "Do you enjoy Fishball?" She replaced the kid's card slowly, delicately centring it upon the desk with three nudges from a spindly forefinger. Her hands returned to comfort that invisible baby woodlouse.

"I don't know."

"And why is that?"

"I've never seen it before."

She paused for a while, her right foot tapping the floor once before she turned on her heels, marching to the front row, and time suddenly accelerated.

Standing beneath the clock, dead centre of the aisles, she looked over us all. "Hands up if you haven't seen Fishball before?" Her head darted about as she watched us, like a bird prowling the grass, searching for a tasty morsel. Hands went up at different speeds, mine only half way, as her question was only half clear to me.

Miss Teacher nodded as her mouth formed a thin smile, before holding out her right hand straight in front of her, chopping the air once with a flat palm that stayed hanging there in the aisle. "When I say, GO, everyone with their hands up, move to desks situated to your left, if you're not already sitting at that side," she ordered, the back of her hand swiftly brushing the air to her right in three, quick successive sweeps. "Trainees who *have* seen Fishball before, and are currently sitting to the left side, vacate your desks and move to a desk on your right." Her palm swept the air once more. "Remember to take your belongings with you...GO!"

There was a mad scramble and I grabbed my things. Scrapes, bumps and mutterings, moans, giggles, collisions and shuffling footsteps. When everything came to a rest, a girl sat on a chair in the exact centre of the middle aisle, just to my right. I looked around with the other trainees, everyone's eyes darting between her, Miss Teacher, and this girl's vacant desk with its lid left wide open, it obviously surprised as much as we were.

Miss Teacher's hands parted to join each other behind her back. Her expression didn't change as she walked to that vacant desk, slamming it shut with a bang so loud, that some of the regulars on the fringe of their marked-off partition of permanent snow, stopped to look in at us.

She stiffened, despite my thinking such a change of posture impossible, before hurrying to the front of the room, composing herself before her slow measured steps returned to take her a few paces directly in front of the girl.

"You're obviously unsure, and cannot remember whether or not you've seen Fishball before?"

The girl shook her head without looking up. She was a fairly big kid, with long thick brown hair, falling over her ears to obscure her face from me.

Miss Teacher's head tilted to her left a little, causing the skin on her neck to overlap her collar slightly. She frowned, and I wasn't sure if it was from the situation she now found herself in, or the tightness of her collar. Either way, she was certainly uncomfortable, probably with both.

"Well...your name?" she said, taking a step forward before glancing to the vacant desk for the girl's card.

"Leigh, but I'm happy to be called Leigh, for short."

"Did you not understand, Leigh, I instructed you to use your family name? It's important for the Truthsayer's family census."

The girl shuffled in her seat, folding her arms in front of her before leaning forward. "You also said, none of us are on first-name terms. That's obviously changed."

Miss Teacher's brow creased as she let out a sigh. The other trainees began to mutter, and I noticed a few more regulars outside had decided to watch our class.

"Give me your card."

Leigh pulled it out of her cardigan pocket and held it out. It was blank.

She took it and raised her eyebrows for a fraction of a second. "Fill it out."

Leigh held out her empty palms, and I found myself leaning into the small gap between us, holding out my pencil.

Both of them gave me a stare of disapproval, and as I looked between them both, Leigh snatched the pencil from me. I decided it was my turn to speak. "I'm only trying to help."

"She has her own pencil, and should have it with her, as I instructed. If not, she should fetch it herself. It's not for you to intervene on my behalf or hers."

My legs began swaying backwards and forwards at the knee, the tips of my toes brushing the tops of my shoes.

Now Leigh stood, ambled to her desk, pulled the lid open, grabbed her pencil before slamming the lid down, forcing it to bounce back up. Miss Teacher spoke again as Leigh placed my pencil in front of me then sat, writing her name.

"What made you decide to place your chair here?"

"You," she said, holding out her finished card.

Miss Teacher took it. "Me?"

"Your question was, hands up if you've seen Fishball before?"

Miss Teacher glanced at her card and nodded. Her hands returned to clasp each other in front of her, Leigh's card replacing the invisible baby woodlouse, poking out between the Instructor's thin fingers. She bobbed up and down on her toes a couple of times. "That is correct, Miss Keegh."

"But when you walked in, you saw we were *all* watching the game. Did you want all of us scrambling over each other, trying to sit on the left?"

"Of course not. My question was obvious."

I held up my hand, taking Miss Teacher's nod at me to be one of allowing me to speak. "Miss, I was confused too. You said, 'Hands up if you've not seen Fishball before,' but you didn't say before when. As Leigh said, before the moment you walked in, or last Smoothday? It might have been clearer to ask if this is the *first* time we've seen it?"

She looked at the floor, then up to me, staring into my eyes as she spoke. "Asking if you've seen Fishball before, or if it's the first time you've seen it is *exactly* the same question. Trainees, I am aware of your interest in Fishball. However, it is a flawed game." She paused, aware I wasn't going to break my stare, holding it for a few moments before looking over the class. "Very soon, all children will be instructed to bring to school their own *spherical* ball. All too often we Truthsayers have seen children fortunate enough to possess a ball, throw it up into the air, and when other children without one see this, they run to catch it, not looking where they're going. On many unfortunate occasions children have collided, seeking to catch the same ball, and serious injuries resulted. Following this, the pointless time-wasting arguments spawned from blame, ownership and envy dominate their time. Truthsayers deem this unacceptable, as this will lead to future accusations, harboured and feeding off feelings throughout formative, adolescent years, to manifest themselves in adulthood."

Her gaze fell to the back of the room. I looked where a kid had put up his hand.

She nodded.

"My mum and dad can't afford a ball for me, I share my brother's. What shall I do, Miss?"

"You can ask your parents to find a suitable pebble, or a stone. Both are abundant and free."

I shook my head and giggled, unable to hide my anger. "That's safe, Miss. And what if a kid steals another kid's ball? That's envy, and that's a feeling."

"Or their pebble," said Leigh, a sly grin curling around her mouth as she pulled her hair back over her ears to look at me.

I nodded at her. "And what if the kid doesn't like the pebble their parents give them, and leave it on the way to school to pick up a better one. Then on the way home they find its gone, picked up by another kid that can't afford a ball also?"

"Yes," said the boy from the back, "how am I supposed to explain that? My dad –"

"Silence!" shouted Miss Teacher.

"Divide us, to conquer us," said Leigh under her breath.

"That *is not* the intention! Truthsayers seek to make society equal, easier for us all, not divide us."

I pointed to the windows on the far wall. "But the regulars outside are divided into three teams."

The other kids began to talk between themselves – the majority of them strangers to each other, and I realised some were forming, for want of a better term, a team with

Leigh, myself and the boy at the back, against Miss Teacher. I didn't want this, I, like Leigh, just wanted clarification of what the point of segregating us was over whether or not we'd seen Fishball, wanted to be respected, treated as an equal, not a fool without a hint of common sense or integrity. Perhaps we shouldn't have spoken, but as they say, 'in context,' and I found myself silently thanking Mum for my home schooling, teaching me how to think, and not what to.

Miss Teacher turned her attention to me, singling me out as I was the smallest, I decided. That, or perhaps she thought my points were the strongest, and she needed to defeat the individual she perceived as the 'captain' of this slowly growing team against her. She took a few paces to stand in front of my desk. "There are only *two* teams outside, not three! Have you difficulty conceptualising the game?"

That was it. Oh, if my parents were there, goodness only knows how they would have reacted, especially Dad. I knew too, however, and did.

"Yes, I apologise."

She nodded to me, looking to Leigh, preparing her next statement with her head held back and mouth slightly open as her superior gaze returned to the class.

"There are four."

Mutterings and giggles filled the hall. I could feel all the kids looking at me now, looking at each other. Finally all of them stared at Miss Teacher, waiting for her reply. From the corner of my eye I could see Leigh, smiling at me again, her shoulders twitching up and down like Mum's did yesterday.

"Did your parents relinquish their moral responsibility as your teachers, entrusting such to an animal from the farmyard across the way, as they knew any therein possessed a higher capacity for logic and reason to instruct you? Or is it you merely have no grasp whatsoever of numbers, and they abandoned teaching you, realising it was simply pointless, ultimately an exercise in futility, their time better spent looking for work pulling carrots while you sat amid the farmyard muck, learning, taught by those certainly more qualified than themselves?"

There were gasps of disbelief, and I looked up to the clock. It had only taken twelve minutes for the lesson to fall apart. I knew right then, as my gaze lingered at the clock that I was going to find myself in big trouble. There was no going back, not now.

"Relativity is very close to my heart," I said, trying to keep calm, my legs moving quicker beneath my chair. I gritted my teeth, trying to slow my heart, knowing my voice might falter. "Don't *ever* insult my special relatives, you don't know them."

"I can assume from your ill-fitting uniform, y*ou'll* be coming to Thinking lessons clutching a pebble?"

I shook my head. "My mum did her best with this identity-robbing, uncomfortably cheap rubbish, and Dad's a fisherman, working nights on the trawlers. He will find a perfect, giant white pearl for me, not a pebble." I pointed, "Bigger than all the fake ones around your neck put together."

She was about to reply, but I held out my hand, determined to teach her a lesson, and for that matter, the whole class. "Let me finish. And, there really *are* four teams. My dad told me Fishball comes from a battle long ago, when two fleets of fishing boats competed for throd fish shoals, just off the coast of what's now called Viewhaven. The players represent the two fleets, trying to kick the ball, as in the fish, into their trawl nets. The ball's not a proper ball, but shaped like a fish so it behaves as though it has a life of its own, bouncing and wobbling around as if trying to evade both the boats and nets of either side. just as the throd fish did. And finally, the teacher, Instructor, or whatever he's called, running around trying to keep up with all the madness, blowing his whistle when a rule is broken, well he...no, I'll tell you what, you tell me who he represents, you're the Instructor, Truthsayer. Tell us your truth." My heart was pounding, and I could hear my words in my ears briefly, as though someone else had spoken them.

Miss Teacher ignored my comments, and I felt my anger towards her overcome my disappointment in her as she returned to the front of the class, reclaiming her unattractive composure.

"The lesson is quite simple, for those of you requiring an explanation, ahead of the fact. Those of you that have not seen the game, obviously haven't any knowledge of the rules. This mirrors your new lives ahead, as you are unaware of the rules, yet you will soon play your part within it. Fishball will soon be banned, as it is clearly unfair. As you've seen, only a small minority take charge of the ball, while others simply watch. In the tomorrows to come, we will all have a part to play, and everyone will know the game, and most important of all, the rules of their roles."

Leigh put her hand up, refusing to wait for an acknowledgement. "You didn't answer her question, but we've got to answer yours." She pointed to the windows. "Who does he represent? Hands up if any of you want to know," she shouted, turning to the class.

Practically every hand went straight up.

"It's unimportant as it's open to interpretation. Now, lower your hands, trainees."

Leigh grinned. "Ok, what do you think then, if you don't know? Are you embarrassed because you don't know, don't know how to think, or can't interpret it?"

I looked around the class, only a few hands went down. "I don't think you're allowed to, are you, Miss? That's the real problem," I said. "The game's based on historical fact, that's where it came from, and that's it. History isn't open to interpretation, to change, to support the few who find it uncomfortable, or inconvenient like the Truthsayers. And neither should Fishball."

She raised her voice as she replied, and I knew right then along with the majority of the other kids, she'd lost the discussion. "Well, I don't know who the Instructor represents, and I don't care to interpret, as it's unimportant. The Truthsayers will not have foolish interpretations, idle talk leading to conflict and blame!"

"He represents the authorities!" I shouted, "Running around in black, trying to keep up. He represents the Sea Sheriff of back then, stopping the fleets fighting over the fish, breaking the rules of the sea, hurting each other. Four teams, as I said!"

"Yes," cried Leigh. "And who can say he doesn't have his own agenda, like you Sayers, favouring one side over the other to suit yourselves. I've seen the game played hundreds of times in my home town, the referee blowing his whistle favouring one team!" She stood. "My parents believe the Sayers should be challenging the authorities, as they're the ones allowing persecution of everyone by anyone with an axe to grind. They're the ones bowing down, letting a small group change stuff they find uncomfortable, or see as offensive, stuff that happened almost a thousand and two years ago and had nothing to do with any of us, or you. That's crazy, the Sayers should be telling them to be quiet, not us! Things happened, get over it and get on with now and tomorrow. Nobody listens to kids' complaints, and it's about time they did. We're a small group too!"

A few of the kids clapped, and a brief cheer went up.

"Leigh's parents are right," I said as I stood. "Nobody has the right to wipe everything clean and start all of our minds over again! None of our parents or grandparents will take that, and I certainly won't, as I've learnt so much from all of my special, and general relatives, and will do through all the tomorrows they have left."

Another shout went up, and kids began to point to the windows. The game outside had stopped, but the players weren't watching us as I expected. A few of them were pointing too, toward a long smear across the window. And there was Charles, idly sliding across it as his eye-stalks peered into the hall, searching for me.

All of the kids stood up, hurrying to the window to gape at him. Obviously none of them had seen a dwarf giant gastropod before. And I wondered if I should have brought Charles into class with me, so Miss Teacher could have used him as a basis for her first lesson.

Outside, a few of the kids were jumping up, trying to touch him, the Instructor blowing his whistle over and over again, attempting to herd them back to their ordered white rectangle.

"Trainees, SIT, at once!" shouted Miss Teacher, her redundant hands now clapping rapidly for attention. But they ignored her, and a few were jumping up too, slapping their palms upon the window in a vain effort to get Charles' attention.

The Instructor outside gave up, stomping off out of view with his whistle still in his mouth.

"SIT DOWN!"

The Instructor returned a few moments later, carrying a step ladder, placing it against the window beneath Charles, and as he trod the first step, Keloff appeared, running forward, pulling the instructor from the step to send him unceremoniously to the grass, flailing about like a bloatfish out of water. Keloff grabbed the ladder, carrying it above his head through the mixture of blues and reds, before throwing it into the rectangle, a few steps breaking off and bouncing around as it landed. He was whistling to Charles now, banging the window rhythmically, and I joined the other Trainees at the window, finally pushing my way to the front. As Charles saw me, he began to turn towards Keloff to do as he was told, retreating back into his shell before kicking away to fall into Keloff's waiting arms. I pressed my palms against the window and shook my head at Keloff, but he simply gave an innocent shrug of the shoulders, blowing the hair out of his eyes, before motioning to his left with a jerk of his head before running off out of sight.

"Trainees, if you're not willing to be taught, then you can leave!"

But I was already striding to my desk for my satchel and shoes, my mind made up.

"Thanks," I said to Miss Teacher as I passed her, but she didn't look at me or utter a single word.

Several minutes and two more later there were just a few kids left in the class. I stood outside in the hallway with Leigh.

"That went well," she said, without a hint of sarcasm to her voice. "It's just a pity she didn't read out my family name on that card."

"And what's that?"

"It's not my *real* name, but I wrote 'Keegh.' She'd *have* to read it out for the register the day after tomorrow, and I would have said, 'Yes, I'm lea-ky,' and I'd ask to be excused for the toilet. My brothers had a few of these lessons before they gave up, so I knew what was coming."

I gave her the laugh she sought. "I didn't write my real name either, I wrote Flower," I admitted, then said goodbye and hurried outside to join Keloff and Charles.

"What the *hell* are you doing here?" I demanded, fuming.

"It's not my fault, I was at the gate, turned round and he'd gone. I followed his trail back here."

"You were supposed to look after him!"

"I was, but got distracted, got to thinking about that kiss you gave me."

I walked away a little embarrassed, kids shouting and running past me as they spilled out of the school. "Well if you can't look after him, you won't get another one." I looked over my shoulder. "Now catch up and put him down."

He was at my side in moments. "How you gonna explain all this to your mum and dad, TF?"

"With the truth. Charles disrupted the class." I stopped and turned to him. "Keloff, my feet *really* hurt, so for not looking after him properly you can give me a piggy-back home, until the hill gets too steep."

"For sure."

My feet were thankful, as was my satchel, finally having a use as it carried my shoes.

~ 9 ~
The Buffet Car

Beyond a sliding door of ornately-carved dark oak and etched glass, depicting interlocking wilting tulips, the buffet car was a very posh affair. White tablecloths with red napkins folded into triangles, weathered brown leather armchairs with big brass rivets, white marble candlesticks and table lamps with looped cotton tassels hanging from their golden shades. Low conversations filled the air, along with the tinkle of crystal glass and silver cutlery upon bone china tableware. It was lovely, and I wished I really could be part of it.

Nick held out a chair for the old woman and she nodded thanks as she sat. "My name's Zimmi," she said, holding out her hand.

He took it with a genuine smile. "Nick," he said, passing her a menu.

She placed it on the table, tracing an arthritic finger down the entrées, lifting her head with an expression of authority. "Don't bother with the Clotted Grief of Redundant Smiles, Nick, I had them last year." She leant across the table, speaking in a whisper. "Undercooked and *terribly* under-seasoned. If I were you, I'd try...I'd try," she sat back. "Ah yes, here we are, an old staple. Carpaccio of Naive Tailless Bereavement, on the Tail, complemented with a Seared Saddle of Yesterday's Remembered Moons. If they have the Conjunction, go with that. You'll have to ask but," she kissed her thumb and forefinger together in the air with some difficulty as her hand shook. "Delightfully wonderful!"

I understood Nick's anger; I could feel it. There's nothing worse than sitting with someone in a restaurant that firmly believes you've not tried the food before, and that you've suddenly developed an inability to read and / or understand the menu, as though when walking through the restaurant's entrance your hunger had somehow robbed you of all culinary knowledge and experience. He nodded politely as the young boy's face appeared at her left ear. "I could do with a bowl of chips."

She patted his head without looking over her shoulder. "Ok, Herbert. I'm looking at the menu now. Patience."

He rolled his eyes and returned to her back, closing the zip of her dress as the waiter found our table. He was tall, thin, with greasy combed hair parted at the left, impatient, superior.

"Good afternoonish. Can I take your orders, please?"

"Good aftermorning," corrected Zimmi. "I see you have Sumptuous Superfluous Truths. Do you have Sumptuous Superfluous Lies? Hand-foraged by lost auto-dentures and smeared with a Wax Pepper Coulis, in a crunchy Panko Crust?"

"Apologies," said the waiter. "Chef's last batch of lies were simply fibs." He bent down closer to us. "Terrible consistency, didn't hold together in the pan. He *has* spoken to our supplier, who assures us next season's will be fully ripe and plump, but alas, they're being nurtured as we speak. Lies are sadly out of season and off the menu, madam – even the little white ones." He straightened up.

"I'll give you a lie you can cook," said Nick. "I'm *not* going to murder the child that's hiding in my head."

The old woman clapped her hands, but the waiter motioned her to keep quiet, glancing around the carriage to see if any of the other diners had heard what Nick had offered. "You're very generous, sir. But sadly your lie hasn't had time to mature, and at this stage is just an intention. Chef doesn't cook intentions, or promises, for that matter. Besides, only food bought *on* the premises can be consumed *on* the premises – unless you're willing to occupy the picnic car." He nodded once towards Zimmi. "Also, before you decide to make a promise to your lovely dining partner, however well-intended, it is a sad truth that promises break easily." He smiled falsely, refusing to hide his practised, condescending tone. "This is purely from chef's experience, you *must* understand."

"Shambolic affair, imbecile," muttered the old woman under her breath. She lifted her head with a wrinkled smile, raising her voice. "I understand, such a shame. The Braised Barefaced I ate a few decades ago were absolutely wonderful, although they repeated on me for months, and plunged me into all kinds of trouble. I'm not complaining; it's nice to be reminded of such a lovely dish." Her gaze returned to the menu. "I'll have...I'll have. Yes! There it is." She licked her lips, closing the menu with a snap, placing it on her plate, interlocking her fingers upon it. "Roulade of Poached Hard Angry Bastards, cooked in White Wine, with a Dill-Scented Subtle Betrayal of Grilled Innocence."

The waiter nodded, raising a non-committal eyebrow, obviously relieved. "How would you like the Innocence cooked, madam?"

"Medium rare. Just make sure there are no Excuses remaining in the Innocence, it puts me off, seeing them seeping out when I cut into it."

"Certainly, and your choice of our complimentary sauce?" He wore a smirk now, happy she'd not included her choice and that he could remind her – not of the sauces, but of her overlooking them.

She refused to pick up the menu, clearly embarrassed. "What do you have?"

He sighed, realising she'd played her card perfectly, forcing him to essentially do the job he was paid for.

"Rust, Sea Fret, Varicose and Bald."

She glanced up. "Is that *fresh* Bald, or from concentrate?"

He smiled a non-committal smile of obvious nothingness.

"Sea Fret then, oh and a portion of chips. Thank you."

I could see he was contemplating detailing the chip options, but thought better of it. Nodding with his eyes closed he turned his head slowly to Nick. "It seems sir has brought his own feast?" His eyes bored into Nick's, perhaps aware of me, but I knew that was impossible. "As I've already established, food consumed on the premises, *must* be purchased on the premises – there can be no exceptions." He looked up and gestured to his right. "The picnic car is located..."

Nick grinned as he interrupted. "I'm a courier."

"Oh, I see. A delivery service – very good then," he said, tapping his nose with a forefinger and winking. "Keeping it nice and fresh."

Nick nodded. "Do you have any pizzas?"

"Thankfully, no."

"Then I'll take a selection of cold meats and a green leaf salad – up to the chef, whatever's easiest for my digestive system."

The waiter looked us up and down. "Human. Understood, sir. Drinks?"

"Blood," said the old woman quickly, "oh, any will do, surprise me," she said, waving a hand dismissively to look out of the window. She tuned swiftly from the view. "But make sure it's a pint in a jug, you know, a glass one with all those little windows and the big handle. These hands are hundreds of years old, you know."

"Very good, I'm sure. Sir?"

"Do you have water?"

"Rain, salt, heavy, tap, distilled, de-ionised and any of the former, boiled, filtered, evaporated or drained through an aged muslin cloth once belonging to the architect of a self-assembly flat-packed furniture instruction leaflet library. Obviously, our best and most popular."

Nick sighed. "Tap, filtered."

"Sparkling or still?"

"Still."

"Lumpy water and lemon?"

Nick frowned.

"Ice," sighed the waiter.

"Just the lemon."

The waiter nodded and turned on his heel with military precision, greeting the diners at the next table.

"Rat's son, dead skylark's bastard cousin," whispered the old woman, leaning forward once more. "Lies are *always* in season, and he proved that by saying they're not. Waiters! They're just an extension of the chef's cock, yet they don't know it." She raised her eyebrows with concern, her eyes wide and distant for a moment. "I pity the chef."

"I pity the chef's wife," said Nick, leaning forward across the table with a grin, raising his left eyebrow. "Are you telling the truth?"

She blinked rapidly, snapping back to the present, laughing as she picked up her cutlery, examining it for stains which weren't there. "Mayhap." She paused for a few moments as she squinted at the cutlery's hallmarks, glancing up at him quickly in the hope he didn't notice. "I like you, Nick, young human man. For a phenotype, you're quite attractive, on many levels – there's something refreshingly foreboding about you." She squinted accusingly at us, leaning a little closer. "Tell me now, why are you *really* visiting Hope?"

"I'm looking for a piece of furniture."

The daemon wearing the top hat took a seat at the table opposite us, removing his hat and placing it gently at the place setting beside him. The little people emerged again and the waiter took their orders.

"Furniture? Let me guess. A metal seat, built to torture foreign kings? Or a wardrobe, crafted for stolen noblemen's capes, size large, the ones that celebrated quasi-religions, while swearing allegiance to one of us, for your children to dress up in? I'm sure you have lovely children. Do you have children, Nick?"

"It's a special gift – wouldn't want to spoil the surprise." He picked up his napkin and tucked it into his collar, smoothing it down over his tie, picking up his own cutlery, copying Zimmi.

"I did have children, and a wife. A long time ago." his eyes remained on his knife as he polished it. "They were killed in an accident, crossing the road to meet me, twenty years ago this year." Holding up the knife in the candlelight he watched as the distorted reflections danced in the silver. "And yes, they were lovely children, both of them." Satisfied, he placed the knife beside his plate and looked across the table at the old woman."Between you and me, I have the soul of the driver responsible for their deaths."

Zimmi stopped polishing and looked over the table. "Oh, you're *that* Nick. I must apologise, I should have known from your air of foreboding. I *must* say it's such an honour and a privilege to meet you! I have requested such on several occasions, but it seems the Assembly is far too busy to grant an old woman's wish. And now you're here dining with me! Perhaps my requests have suddenly found the ears of the Grand Master, and he has steered you here for my pleasure." She replaced her cutlery, laying her napkin in her lap, unfolding a second to drape over her left shoulder for Herbert. "You're doing such a fine job for us, I must add."

Nick simply nodded.

The waiter took a large soup bowl over to the table of little people, they waving it down, shouting instructions as he placed it slowly in the middle of the place setting.

"Forgive me for calling you human, it's such a generalisation. Have you visited Hope before?"

"Quite a few times in my youth," replied Nick, glancing out of the window for a second. "A long time ago, before the merger, when it was the two little villages, Hope So and Hope Not."

"I remember," she said. "What did some council fool want to call the place following the merger, Hopeless?"

He sighed. "Yep. Strange days."

"Indeedy. And strange humans."

The little people climbed onto the soup bowl and took turns jumping into the gazpacho, splashing about and shouting with glee. The monocled figure returned to his newspaper, using it more as a shield from their antics rather than a source of current affairs, I decided.

"Oh, look!" exclaimed the old woman, peering over Nick's shoulder, wide-eyed. "What a beautiful-looking being!"

As Nick turned, resting his right elbow on the chair back, she saw him. In an instant her two black weapons were in her hands. He fumbled for his in his shoulder holster, diving for the ground as shots rang out. Daemons screamed. The guard appeared at the door behind her, "You have to buy a ticket, no exceptions!"

Tearing into Nick's chair back, her first burst of fire simply thudded into the leather, the shells falling harmlessly to the floor. Nick twisted to his left, rolling on his shoulder into the aisle, his three shots destroying the etched glass behind her to bring the wilting tulips to their final resting place as shards upon the gangway carpet. The guard stood opened-mouthed, unable to believe he'd not been hit.

Bringing up her second weapon, shells punctured the shielding newspaper into confetti and the frolicking little people swam for the porcelain shore as if they'd encountered a shoal of man-eating croutons beneath the surface of the gazpacho.

A shell ricocheted, chipping a marble candlestick. Nick scrambled on all fours, heading for the exit like a rabid dog wearing a suit, tie and napkin, holding his weapon behind him and letting off a second burst in the hope of crippling the girl.

But she'd anticipated this, diving to the right, her shoulder catching the soup bowl's edge as the last of the little people cleared it. Spinning into the air it soaked her with liquid. She wiped her eyes with the back of her hand and spat out what she'd taken in as she searched for us.

Nick was standing now, more angry than I've ever experienced. "Bitch!" he screamed, emptying his magazine randomly to gain time, ejecting it without taking his eyes off her, producing another from his ammo pouch on his belt and slamming it into his weapon to now concentrate on his target.

Jumping upon a table she somersaulted to the left, the right, the left, as Nick's attempts at finishing her fell way off, simply splintering the beautiful buffet car's woodwork that I imagined had endured and survived so many outrageous functions unscathed.

He backed away, his focus remaining ahead, hastily pulling open the door to the bar.

Zimmi composed herself, casting a rule into the air. "If they've ruined my dinner, they'll be breakfast for the daemons of the Darkedness before we reach Hope," she said, rearranging the table Nick had disturbed. Checking the cutlery once again, this time finding a few spots of gazpacho to hastily wipe away with her napkin, she ignored the battle behind her to gaze out across the countryside.

The bar's patrons (the majority, a gathering of retired drunken gods) were deep in raised-voiced conversation. One, extolling the virtues of a well-kept ale – somewhat difficult to keep in a coach bar – referencing this as justification for his small contribution to creation. The music their voices fought against was nondescript, just a background throb, serving to fill the silence should a conversation evaporate through indifference. In this respect, the music (as a complementary piece) reminded me of the many backgrounds I hadn't seen that were sadly vacant from most sculptures.

"Get the fuck out of the way!" shouted Nick, as he glanced behind him. Of course they didn't, he was just a human after all, and they'd been drinking all week.

The barman folded his cloth and draped it over his shoulder, resting his hands upon the bar as Nick's gaze switched rapidly from the bar to the door. "There's a spare stool, sir," he said, motioning to a circular seat of black leather. It looked comfortable. "No need for such language."

Nick was breathing hard now. He steadied himself and held his weapon with both hands, waiting in deep concentration with his head lowered, aiming, biding his time.

She tumbled through the glass head over heels, he pulling hard on the trigger while gritting his teeth as she rolled to her feet. Nothing, just a click from his weapon.

Grinning, she brought up the pistol in her right hand and pulled on the trigger. Nothing, just a click.

Zimmi grinned obviously as she replaced the polished cutlery upon the table, edging it into the correct positions with her gnarled fingertips. Her rule was established and in effect.

They stood opposite each other checking their weapons, she holstered hers first and advanced. Nick turned, grabbing the first object he saw. A bowl of cashew nuts seasoned with lime, coconut and chilli flew through the air towards her; like pale bullets they peppered her as she deflected the bowl with her forearm.

"Oi!" said a god sitting at the bar. "You can certainly pay for them, kind sir!"

But Nick had dived over the bar into the narrow serving alley, pulling a couple of bottles of vodka from their optics to use as projectiles. She dodged them and he swore.

The waiter appeared from the kitchen doors, hurrying by with a tray of orders, either oblivious or simply wanting to serve as soon as possible. It was a busy service, after all. She seized a plate of food from his tray as he passed, flinging it at Nick.

A fountain of Seared Emotionless Troglodyte's Love, on the bone, cascaded through the air, the waiter relieved as he'd noticed it was a trifle over-cooked. It hit Nick square in the face, knocking him back from surprise at her accuracy more than from the quality of the dish, and he realised he'd put himself in an untenable position with hardly any room for manoeuvre behind the narrow bar. It was a huge mistake on his part, as anyone taking up employment behind a bar realised all too soon the position they'd placed themselves in, especially during a Saturday night when a group of young drinkers celebrated any type of social function. There was no escape.

Dripping with gravy and Love, Nick stumbled back, ignoring a god's order of, "Four doubles of Shaggy Steve's special single malt, no ice," mistaking Nick for a second barman as the plate that had shattered on his forehead fell in pieces at his feet. The god then recognised him with a knowing frown. "I remember you," he slurred, followed by an eyebrow movement, creating a red tricycle that appeared at Nick's feet. "What you prayed for," said the god with a smile. But Nick quickly wiped the gravy away with his napkin, which gained a nod of approval from the gods watching from their bar stools as he dropped it upon the bar. "I'll give him credit," said one, picking up her cocktail of various cocks' tails. "He certainly understands etiquette."

Zimmi's Roulade of Poached Hard Angry Bastards, cooked in White Wine with a Dill-Scented Subtle Betrayal of Grilled Innocence, flew through the air. Now just a messy flying mush of congealed ingredients, the Bastards took advantage of the Innocence in mid air, spoiling them once and for all. The Bastards, not expecting to be afforded such a delicacy themselves were thrilled they could hide their misgivings amid the sea fret sauce. This ruined dish splattered over the drunken gods, and they in turn decided it was time to order something to eat. Now that's the issue I have with barflies. It's only when they receive a freebie such as a bowl of roast potatoes following Sunday lunch service, or a few cubes of cheese with silverskin picked onions do they realise there's more to bar life than just the drink. You can't beat a good pub lunch, son, and you should always pay for it.

Nick was at the kitchen doors now, tumbling through, the girl running past the objecting gods and tripping over the red tricycle as they wondered if he'd gone to fetch more ice.

The kitchen was full of steam, smells so unmentionable that I can't draw accurate comparisons, I'm afraid. Well, I could, but I really want to get on with telling you what happened next.

The Chef de Cuisine barked orders at his staff, and Nick found himself in front of the Boucher, pairing a Fillet of Hypnotised Seam Weavers as they rolled over in their hallucinogenic marinade, believing they were having a nice relaxing day in the mud pits of Frilander Province of the east-south-east. Nick snatched the rather ugly looking filleting knife from the Boucher's hand, causing the Seam Weavers to guffaw a little as they looked up, mistaking the knife for a rather bothersome storm cloud that clearly had a stainless silver lining.

"Don't even try," said Nick, looking between the Boucher and the doors as he held the knife up to his face.

"Oh, this is intolerable!" Zimmi probably said to the waiter, although Herbert was undoubtedly happy with his chips. She took them from him and stood, placing the bowl upon the table as he retreated beneath her dress.

"Get on the damned chicken!" shouted the Chef de Cuisine to Nick, as he caught him from the corner of his eyes.

He held up the filleting knife, shouting. "I'm a fucking police officer!" He looked at each of the various chefs as the steam revealed them. "Why doesn't anyone realise that?"

"I don't give a fuck what you are, when you're in my kitchen, you cook!" shouted back the Chef, slamming down a ladle onto his stainless steel work surface to pick up a rolling pin of aged oak, snapping it in half to toss Nick's green leaf salad with the broken ends.

The girl burst in and they all turned.

Nick searched the flaming hobs for the nearest pot of boiling whatever, found it, picked it up and threw it towards the door. The girl somersaulted to the left, impacting a fridge just as Zimmi entered the kitchen.

"You lying bastards!" she cried, wiping the boiling lies from her eyes, tasting them upon her dry lips. "I was told they were out of season!"

The Chef rolled his eyes briefly. "They're frozen from last season and defrosting – now get on the chicken or out of my kitchen!"

But Nick had managed to reach the exit, passing the Grillardin who stood outside smoking a cigarette. "Are you supposed to be on the chicken?" asked Nick, breathlessly.

The Grillardin nodded, and Nick raised the knife, waving it towards the door. The door closed behind the Grillardin before his cigarette hit the floor.

We stood outside on the picnic area, on a coach without walls or ceiling but of a well-kept lawn with a few wildflowers scattered here and there. Various groups gathered on the edges of blankets now the light rain had stopped, chatting, eating and taking photographs no one would ever have the slightest of interest in seeing. Beyond the lawn's rear edge, the railway tracks stretched into the distance, damp and shining as the sun's light found them from behind the retreating clouds. There was nowhere else to go except where we had been.

We skirted around the picnickers, Nick searching for anything that he could use as a weapon. There were a few plates of scotch eggs, cucumber sandwiches and sticks of celery in jugs of water, but nothing provided a suitable weapon to defend him against the girl and her determination, unless she was allergic to cucumbers. Substitutes are simply that, and rarely live up to what they've replaced, unless they're replaced by another substitute – and so it goes on until you forget what you ordered in the first place.

She appeared carrying the Boucher's cleaver.

He ran at her, screaming, kicking up a plate of prawn vol-au-vents, knocking over glasses of lemonade and orange squash as the picnickers shouted objections.

She brought the cleaver down towards his head, but he jumped into the air, turning as it grazed his shoulder, falling over her head, screaming in agony. He landed on his back, scrambling toward the kitchen, bumping into Zimmi.

He turned quickly. "I'm sorry," he said breathlessly, holding his shoulder as it bled onto the grass.

"Nick, you're a typical human," said Zimmi. "This is *clearly* not the circumstance I had envisioned for our meeting! You've ruined my food, and I thought you were such a nice human man, offering me your lie for dinner."

"Blame her," he said, pointing with a trembling hand, holding out the filleting knife. "I'm just doing my job."

The girl turned, hurling the cleaver towards Nick in a swift, graceful movement as Nick ducked. It caught Zimmi squarely in the forehead. She dropped to the floor instantly, then turned into something strange for a few seconds before vanishing into the breeze of outside, smeared through the air as if she had been painted by an artist that suffered from a compulsive obsession in perfection, and had wiped his art away with a cloth. All that was left of her was a bemused-looking Herbert, peering through his spectacles.

Nick picked up the cleaver and advanced. The girl backed away, tripping over a wicker picnic basket, as the diners dropped the cup-cakes and sausage rolls they were hastily rescuing to pack away for another day.

She had nowhere to go, and as her heels met the edge of the grass, she looked scared. Nick hurled the cleaver at her stomach.

It was a strange moment to watch. She somehow avoided the spinning blade, twisting her body to the side, contorting it as if her spine was made of gleeberry jelly, losing her footing to fall backward onto the tracks, her body tumbling over and over, diminishing as we stood where she had stood moments before. She was still, but Nick watched her for movement which eventually came as she pulled herself to her feet, until his eyes could see her defiant form no more.

He now knew she was capable of more killing, not just altering behaviour with her bullets, but killing, and a daemon at that.

There was no more killing. He allowed the others to die at their own pace, watching them. Some writhed silently in excruciating pain, unable to find comfort, perhaps knowing a single movement could possibly render them unconscious, never to wake. Others screamed obscenities at him for his refusal to either help them or end their suffering. Some just stared, until their eyes lost their shine of life.

When he was satisfied they were all no more, he allowed hunger to force him away from that shore, finding fruits and berries to sustain him amid the lush green of the forest. There were no animals here, just the birds watching from high in the trees.

Later, he lit a fire, roasting seaweed and minips he'd found trapped in the shallow tidepools as the sea crept away. He sat and waited, hoping it wouldn't be too long now, and thought, *'I will make my life here, away from the others.'* Yes, it was decided. Freedom from the rules, the rigorous control of adults. He had his friends along the shoreline to keep him company, and he would tell them stories, as his parents had told him. They would listen, no interruptions, no questions from them, demanding he explained all of his actions. And in return, they would sing to him.

~ 10 ~
Hope

On the station concourse, Nick explained everything to the Hope authorities as a medic patched up his shoulder. The little men ran around the top hat's brim re-enacting what they had seen, in a play one of them directed with great enthusiasm. We all had to wait a while for the re-enactment, until they were all entirely happy with casting and costume design. The guard confirmed both our accounts as he munched his second plate of cheese and tomato sandwiches, and Nick took one for himself as the authorities allowed us to leave. We escorted Herbert into a new life where his legs would take him to goodness knows where, and I was happy with this, as he had told us that's exactly where he was headed. Goodness knows where, it sounded like a nice place, and didn't remind me of the Elsewhere Someplace.

"Good luck, Herbert," said Nick.

I envied that young boy as we watched him pedalling away on Nick's red trike, to disappear into the crowds at Hope Central Station. Not only for his new-found freedom, but equally and perhaps more so for the fact he knew his name.

I hoped one day he'd be able to embrace his fear of where his legs would take him, in the realisation it was a blessing. He would walk into adulthood once he'd outgrown his trike, whether he liked it or not, striding away from his childhood. I hadn't been able to walk away from mine – mine had simply been halted and deposited into the middle of terror.

Herbert would carry his name with him, sharing it with others during his journey through life. Mine was lost, and if I could escape as Herbert had, I could not tell my name to anyone I'd meet.

He would be remembered for his name, identified and greeted, personified, whereas if I walked the streets I would be forgotten. I would simply become a description, a string of nouns special only to those that had spoken them, for everyone's view of me would differ somehow.

In time, a commonality would surface through those compared nouns as people described me to each other in my absence, and my name would be one born from combined observations, a nick-name, a caricature of a physical attribute (almost certainly unkind) serving to elevate the creators of this nick-name above me in their eyes, as they tried to hide their shortcomings from the people around them. However, Herbert seemed different now as we watched him pedalling around the concourse, looking at his surroundings.

Hope Central Station was indeed a beautiful building. Its polished marble floor diffused the light from the electric orbs perched high in the ceiling, gently reflecting the many and varied beings going about their business. Ticket kiosks lined the walls either side of us, cordoned off with burgundy rope leisurely hanging from polished brass poles. Smart-uniformed staff gave advice to the many commuters and travellers queuing respectfully for their turn. Nick strode purposefully to the exit. Above it, five enormous stained-glass windows dominated the wall, the intricate workmanship depicting a map of the town as it was some three hundred and four years ago. The majority of the travellers ignored it as the suns shone through it, casting the image onto the marble before them. I studied the windows as long as I could, before we found ourselves in the open air. Nick hurried down the curved granite steps to street level to check his bearings, hands defiantly on his hips as people coursed around him. A signpost pointed to a hundred different points of interest, names and descriptions informing us of walking times, and it reminded me of a tree, having sprouted out of the flagstones below.

It was darker than he'd expected and he glanced at his watch, noticing the second hand was motionless, then held it to his ear. It was silent. He spun on his heels, frowning at the station clock. It was much later in the day than he would have liked, almost twenty-nine, whereas his watch had decided it was permanently four hours and seventy-two minutes earlier. It had finally died from the countless instances it had measured through Nick's life, beating along, counting down as Nick had given so many a measured length to answer a question before a broken bone, a few seconds to agree to a damning task, or in some instances counting their moments before death at his hands. He had stared at that watch face for almost half a century, it dutifully tick-tock-ticking away, without expression to what it had seen and measured.

Maybe it had taken one knock too many during combat with the girl, its inner mechanisms not built for so many violent clashes during its life. I preferred to believe it had a mind of its own, and had simply had enough, seen enough, an unwilling witness to Nick's terrible actions, a reluctant participant measuring so many poor unfortunates' fates.

It was too late in the day now to reach his destination before it closed. He swore, no chance of taking the overnight sleeper carriage home. He'd have to find a place to stay, get cleaned up, change, eat, then conduct his business early in the morning to be back in Middletown by mid-afternoon. There was just enough time to buy new clothes.

"Thanks again, mister Nick." We looked to see Herbert hurrying away with a wave.

"You're welcome, Herbert," Nick shouted back. "Hey, kid! Where are you headed?"

Herbert ambled back to us. "Just around. I know a good corner to beg from. I don't have any money, and need it for the fare back home and to buy new clothes. I'm going to look for my sister's place when I get back to the country."

Nick let out a deep breath, his hands finding his hips again. "I don't have money, just my personal card. I can cover the cost of your clothes. I need some too but have no idea where to buy them." He pointed to the tree of destination signs. "You know this place well?"

"I do, and that's very kind of you, Mister Nick. Zimmi walked practically every street and alleyway over the years, so I know my way around."

"I need clothes first, then a place to stay, and please, just call me Nick" said Nick.

Herbert nodded. "I know a place, not too far, but we'll need to hurry as Hope's closing soon. And please, call me Al."

"Ok, Al," said Nick with a gesture. "Lead the way."

He led us through the streets, and we found more and more shop doorways with shutters down, and windows with apologetic 'Closed' signs. Finally we reached an off-the-peg tailor's, where Nick bought a dark grey suit, white shirt and black tie. They were nothing special, almost identical to what he usually wore, purely functional.

Al chose jeans, a sleeveless black shirt and a cardigan with a hood, and strangely, a pair of blue carpet slippers. We both thought they all looked too big for him as he disappeared behind the changing room curtain.

Nick paid, picking up his brown paper carry-bag of new clothes as Al appeared from the changing room with a big beaming smile on his face, and I noticed he'd grown considerably, his clothes fitting him perfectly.

We stood outside as the outfitter's door locked behind us and the lights were switched off.

"If you follow this street and take the second left, you'll eventually come to Fountain Square. Take the second arched alleyway on the right-hand side and keep going. It'll open out into the hotel district. There're plenty to chose from, but if you want to save your card there's one that's free, if it's still in business. I'll be heading there tomorrow."

"Free? You sure?"

He smiled. "Well, it was a few years and a couple of months ago. Thanks again for the new clothes," said Al, pulling up his hood. He shook Nick's hand and headed off amid the masses hurrying home from work.

"You're welcome Herb...sorry, Al."

Just before he was lost among the crowd, he turned. "Herbert was never my name, it's my attitude!" he said, pulling a pair of glasses with one cracked lens from his cardigan pocket, placing them upon his nose. They didn't fit.

Then I knew his real name. I should have known when he first appeared from that zip upon Zimmi's back, realising with such frustration I had no way of telling him, or my mother, wherever she was. Alfie was alive.

Nick walked with the crowd, matching their hurried footsteps, and I began to think. Names. How they affect children, how important they are, influencing the perception of ourselves, and the perception others have of us during our walk through life.

Mum's Lesson #12.
My dad's parents, fate, destiny, and my adventure at the arrival.

You might think that perhaps it was fate and destiny that had decided to prevent me from remembering my name?

Perhaps you're thinking they had decided between them it was out of date, meaningless, inaccurate, considering my circumstances – and that I should be given a new name more suited to my current existence, or have the courage to choose one myself?

'Meeting' Herbert – Alfie, just a coincidence to help Nick? Or was it pre-ordained, a cosmic, 'See, I told you so!' purely for me?

"It was all meant to be, it was fate or destiny!" I often heard older people say. But this statement was simply an excuse, a way of halting any meaningful discussion surrounding the circumstances responsible for the unfortunate situations they currently found themselves or others in, and were equally unprepared and certainly

unwilling to be held accountable for. Surely, these circumstances were arrived at by their own poor choices and refusals to act? In this case, Nick's selfless generosity had been rewarded with help to find new clothes, and eventually a place to stay, so perhaps fate and destiny did have a hand in this?

Yes, you may well believe this, son. But my mum had told me a long time ago that fate and destiny were both long dead, so they couldn't have been responsible for my predicament, or Nick's current good fortune. It was all down to his (very rare) display of benevolence.

"Why do things happen, you know, nasty things, accidents that hurt people? Why do good people suffer," I'd once asked Mum.

Her reply came quickly, as if she'd expected my question for a long time. I suppose that's what parents do, predict the many inevitable questions their children will one day voice – hence this letter to you, as I'm not there to answer the many you obviously have.

"Father Fate sat in his chair opposite his wife, mother Destiny," she began. "Between them, their child, playing on the rug in front of the fire. It was a marriage of liars, bearing a child without a name. Their little girl was prohibited an identity by them, of a name to be judged by, so she simply existed."

Thinking about this now, were names truly just names, identifiers? Or were they adjectives, chosen by parents wishing their child would live up to such a title? A name of great strength and character, set above the norm and the average, to automatically demand respect from their peers? The nameless little girl Mum told me about was content with her life, it seemed, as she was unaware of any other possibilities beyond the living-room door.

"Father Fate would walk the world, touching people as he went," she continued. "Manipulating them, writing their futures as a pathway of limitation, pointing to one inescapable end, from which there could be no meaningful detour of choice along the route.

"Mother Destiny would act in a similar way, mapping out each individual's life too. But her constrictions were not as rigid, allowing people to occasionally choose a path, to briefly influence their lives and caress others, just enough to convince them they were free. But these freedoms were limited to narrow boundaries of choice, like flowers nestled in a bed beside a path, longing to spread their colours and perfumes further, yet prohibited by an insurmountable line of flatstones one side, the path built by Father Fate, the other. Their perception of choice was simply an illusion."

Mum had a wonderful way of conjuring up images for me during her lessons, so I could see them vividly and understand them more clearly through my mind's eye. I closed my eyes to concentrate as she continued. I was going to suggest you do the same, son, then realised you wouldn't be able to read this part of my letter – unless there's someone there to read this passage for you? There's no harm in asking, and I don't mind them reading this section either, before you worry about this.

"Father Fate sat in his big chair, a bit like Dad's, to the left of a huge log fire almost the size of the wall. Energetically he wrote declarations for his daughter on a long roll of thick parchment curled up at his feet. His thin frame dressed in a tight black morning suit with long tails, his pale tight skin stretched around his angular, bony face, wearing a permanent sneer of superiority beneath a shiny black silk top hat, he was a vision of pompous rigidity.

Mother Destiny, sitting opposite him, ignored the scratching from his quill upon the rough paper. She wore a flamboyant dress of yellow and white cotton layers, billowing over and around her chair like puffy summer clouds caressed by the suns. Smiling to herself behind a large wooden hoop of stretched cotton, she concentrated, embroidering patterns, an intricate colourful design for her daughter's life ahead. Here and there she allowed the design to separate, to deviate, small yet perhaps significant opportunities for her daughter to ponder and explore briefly. Then these elements returned to the overall design, pulling her back, forcing her to conform and obey. She continued, concentrating on one element, its threads meandering gradually back to merge with the whole. Once both the paper and cotton hoop were completed, they would be combined, and their daughter's life would be immutably set.

"The little girl lay on her stomach, resting on her elbows, cradling her head in her hands, staring aimlessly into the flames as she watched the continuing decay there. This was eternity's fire, cold, fuelled endlessly by the continued deaths of the lives her parents had ordained. It was an unkind mirror, she decided, a perfect example of entropy and her life ahead. The fire coursed around the logs in a deathly embrace, imprisoned as the fire fed off them, changing them. As she stared, mesmerised, a pop from the fire made her jump as a small splinter of wood leapt free of its prison, to lie dying on the rug before her. She watched as the glow began to fade, nestling in the fibres of the rug like a fallen twig amid long grass.

"Looking up at her parents, she realised they were indifferent to the dying splinter, too embroiled with their tasks. She looked back to the splinter, withering before her, realising her parents had already written and illustrated this insignificant episode. So, she blew onto the splinter as its glow almost faded, giving it a chance of life now it was free.

"The glow blossomed, spreading into the fibres of the rug, meandering slowly in every direction to spread itself further. She shuffled back a little, watching with curiosity the life she had helped.

"This new independent life, now free of its confinement, eventually found her father's roll of parchment, her as yet unwritten fate at his feet. Opposite, it found the many colourful threads of wool, curled beside her mother's dress, each waiting to be embroidered into her destiny.

"The glows grew into tiny immature flames, wavering, as if unsure of their adolescent purpose. Then they matured, multiplied, their confidence strong and purpose in life clear.

"Father Fate smelt the burning paper at his feet, ignoring it as his scratching quill continued, and as Mother Destiny felt the heat as the edges of her dress caught alight she continued with her task.

"At once they were both engulfed with adult flames. Angry, free, larger now than their parents amid the confines of the huge fireplace.

"Father Fate looked over to his wife, the bottom of her dress now fully alight. *'Is that your destiny?'* he thought to himself. *'Is this mine?'*

She looked back at him through her hoop, as the stretched cotton crumbled to ash and her fingers blistered. *'Is that your fate?'* as his roll of paper crumbled into black leaves in his hands, *'Is this mine?'*

They both accepted their deaths without a struggle, indifferent, subservient, without a cry for help as their little girl stood and ran from that room.

Had they been aware of their deaths for centuries? Had they previously written and woven together this outcome, to free themselves of their immortal toil of control, creating billions of restricting paths for everyone? Down the almost endless corridor their daughter ran barefoot, past the thousands of locked doors on either side. Behind those doors, rolls of completed parchments and patterned hoops. Finally she stood at the front door. She didn't turn and look back, to wait for fate or destiny to perhaps intervene in one final, combined stranglehold on her life, as she knew she had created her freedom through her own choice, her freewill. She pulled the front door wide open and stepped into freedom.

"Over the years, she told her story to everyone she met, and it spread like the flames of her birth. Most people embraced it, some argued it *was* her fate and destiny to do so, but as that parchment and hoop of cotton were no more, this could not be confirmed. Perhaps Fate and Destiny knew their child would grow to become the greater sum of both their parts, as children often do. And I believe it's possible for everyone to act as she did. The fact is, she took actions to be free. And freedom is, to a degree, the most important part of all our lives. If life is what you make it, then make sure too many others don't have a hand in it."

I opened my eyes to see Mum smiling. She didn't tell me the little girl's name. I'm hoping you, like me, know in this case it's not really important. But I was told later she built a small house, and a town flourished around it over the years as people came to hear her story. This town was named after her, so legend says. The town called Hope.

Tiny Flower. I was happy with this name, but I knew it wasn't my real name, or my attitude. It was a name my grandpa Roan had given me when I was born, and my parents had adopted it, using it to console me during my moments of unwarranted fear, or when I'd hurt myself playing in the garden, or became upset or worried over some instant that life had thrust upon me that I couldn't understand or cope with. You too will experience these episodes, son. They are painful, but they will pass, their purpose during your formative years to assist you on your journey to adulthood.

Tiny Flower would suffice until I found my true name. It was a soft, sweet name that always gave me comfort.

My dad had told me grandpa Roan used to have a bad habit of not calling people by their real names – he refused, complaining, "No, *you're* not a Robert," while looking them up and down, "*you're* more of a Jim."

This made social gatherings extremely difficult for my grandma, especially when he decided there were several people called Andrew, sitting around the dinner table. Later in life, this habit ceased, to be replaced by him using a string of numbers instead of names. Try as she might, my grandma couldn't figure out the meanings of these numbers. Some individuals were called by long strings, such as 5691282, while others, simply, 8201, 192, 86 and so on. When my grandpa bumped into an old friend in the street he'd not seen for a long while, calling him by the number 3, my grandmother lost all patience with him – pleading for him to tell her the meaning of the numbers. But he refused, saying he couldn't honestly explain the reasoning behind it, just that the numbers, 'felt right, my sweet little lovely, 128490125'.

My grandparents on my father's side of the family were quite a lot older than those on my mum's side, and were enjoying a long, healthy coupling – so my dad had told me, but they only came to visit us separately, and I never, ever saw them together. I asked my dad about this, and what follows is a brief recollection of the events during my grandpa's final visit, and the terrible events that followed, changing my dad forever.

It was early in mid-afternoon, before the night of *The Remembering* and the *Ceremony of the Amnesiac God,* and two days and four-ninths before The Great Context was supposed to be introduced.

Dad had just woken up, and Mum was tending the garden: weeding, cutting back the whitefruit trees that reached over the rickety fence separating our garden from Mr and Mrs Cribbage's, the old couple living in the big white house behind ours. Mum would dry some of the smaller twigs and branches to burn in the living room fireplace when the house found Seasonchill's cold, the orange sap bubbling and fizzing up to give the house the sweet smell of a previous summer.

These fruit trees deposited windfalls that soon fermented upon the lush green grass of the Seasonstill, and on a few occasions, Charles had become incoherent after munching through a few of them. He'd whistle and thump in sentences that reminded my dad of my baby speech, and Mum could always tell when he was under the influence, as he'd leave behind a meandering trail on the hallway floor, instead of his usual straight, deliberate line. Now Charles wasn't allowed out of the house until Mum had gathered up all of the windfalls in a big woven basket Dad had made for that exact purpose.

Charles sat at the top of the kitchen window straining his eye-stalks, watching her impatiently. She'd carry the basket of windfalls and a few fresh fish Dad had brought home that morning, down the street and around the corner to Mr and Mrs Cribbage. They'd thank her, then carry the fish up the iron staircase Mr Cribbage had built around his house, up along the roof walkway onto the wide veranda surrounding their chimney. He'd then smoke the fish over the chimney pots in whitefruit smoke, as Mrs Cribbage stared into the sky through the huge brass telescope he'd made for her. They'd give Mum back two handfuls and a half of whitefruit in exchange for the fish, so she could make little pies for our tea-time, and grandpa's journey home. Their sweet-smoked fish was very popular in our street.

My grandma hated pies, complaining she *'wasn't at all fond of surprises'*, and pies were simply that, as you never knew *exactly* what hid inside until you cut them open. She would often boast she'd saved a small fortune by not buying wrapping paper for my birthday presents, allowing her to spend that small fortune on the presents themselves. To a degree she was a kind old woman, but I guess there's no need for me to tell you that.

I'd washed and dressed, and unlocked my bedroom window, shimmying down the drainpipe to join Dad, making him jump a little as I landed next to him. He raised an eyebrow and motioned for me to sit opposite him. He was deep in concentration, mending his heavy, thick fishing nets on the flatstones just along from the kitchen door, as Mum walked past with her empty basket. She stopped at the door with a sigh. "Darling, when you've finished, clean the inside of the kitchen window, will you please. And young lady, have you been practising the Qiskit?"

Darling wasn't Dad's real name, but she used it a lot when speaking to him, and I've never understood its meaning. I nodded back with a brief frown, as I'd spent weeks learning off by heart the rhyme, or Qiskit as Mum called it, for my first ever remembering evening. Mum knew that, but didn't want me to forget it and get upset with myself.

My dad was a thick-set, powerful man, four years and thirteen months older than my mum. He'd wear his work clothes most of the time, slightly tattered yet functional. They were clothes he'd once used for best occasions, but these instances were few and far between nowadays, as working on the trawler took up so much of his time and energy. His hair was a greying dark brown, cut by my mum in a short, haphazard spiky style. Not through his choice, but due to his inability to sit still long enough for mum to create something special for him. His face was kind with a strong jaw of permanent stubble, but he could switch to a troubled expression at the mere suggestion of any aspect of life he found irritating. His eyes were the colour of a late summer sky, red, penetrating beneath his tangled, wild hawthorn bush eyebrows.

He glanced up, noticing Charles' shining trail upon the window, nodding with a deep agreeable sound which wasn't a word, but sounded like a reluctant 'Okey-dokey." Mum didn't really want him to clean the inside of the window, as she knew if she asked him to do something he'd never get around to it, and then do something else, a chore she actually wanted done. Besides, he wasn't very good at cleaning, but very good at making a mess.

"How were those nets torn?" I asked, as his strong hands wove new rope, cutting it with his fish knife, the blade as long as his forearm. Intertwining and sewing these new lengths into the gaping holes, closing them with a sharp metal needle pulling twine as thick as my index finger, he finally looked up at me.

"Fish are getting cleverer by the season, Tiny Flower," he said with his deep, rich voice, the ropes creaking between his hands as if to agreeably accompany him. I copied his work with little offcuts he'd discarded, making my own nets, although thinking back, mine were untidy, with straggly knots and uneven, misshapen holes.

"Some kinds recognise nets now, and swim away. Other bigger ones grab the edges in their mouths and pull them towards the rocks to protect the others, that's what happened to this one, it became torn and untied. Some trawlers are using fish hoovers to suck them up, but we can't afford one."

I nodded, then went back to making my net, thinking for a while before I spoke. "Dad, are Grandpa and Grandma untied? They never, ever visit us together, and never, ever have, as far back as I can remember."

My dad tied off a repair and cut the ends, dropping the unneeded lengths by my side before weaving again.

"They used to visit together a while ago, before and just after you were born. But life is becoming more and more complicated for them. There's so much to deal with, and time seems to go by faster the older you get, believe me. We've got the Truthsayers on the street corners now, telling us what has been, what is, and what will be. Your grandpa hates them, argues with them over their views of the past. It's not your grandpa's world anymore, not the world *he* knew – it's becoming more of a world both of them don't really want to know. It happens, it's quite natural, and nothing to worry about, as long as you know it's happening and accept it."

The rope creaked again and his big muscles strained as he tied off a knot. Pulling it tight, examining it closely. Satisfied, he continued. "The net holding everything they hold dear in life, their truths, became torn on the rocks of now and yesterdays as they grew older. It's very sad, but their love for each other seems to have escaped through that tear, and they didn't know until it was too late to retrieve it, as it had drifted out of reach." He held up the net briefly to peer though it at me. "So yes, they're both becoming untied from each other, so it's important to recognise those jagged rocks and avoid them, or repair the damage they cause quickly when you know enough about life to hold it all together in your own net."

I frowned, tying off my own knot, pulling it just tight enough so it couldn't unravel. It wasn't very good. "But couldn't they swim back together and get their love back?"

He stopped working and smiled at me. "Love doesn't work that way, sweetheart. Once it's gone, it's really gone. It evaporates, gets diluted in the waters of passing time very quickly," he looked up the garden to where Mum was crouched down. "Or it rots, like the whitefruit Mum doesn't find, hiding beneath the rhubarb leaves. And, if it does come back it's different, reminding people it's not the same as it was, making them resentful of it. Unfortunately you can't swim back through time." He stood, shaking out the net, like the way Mum shook my eiderdown before placing it over the washing line. I didn't know at that point that he was right about love, but wrong about time.

"There's a rumour the history mines are going to close soon, so Grandpa will be out of work. Nobody's interested in the objects the mines reveal of the very long time ago. Everyone's more interested in the Truthsayer's tomorrows – yet yesterdays make us who we are today, so they're *really* important to know about, if you ask me. There's more yesterdays than there are todays." Squinting at a knot he sat down, starting another repair. "And the older you get, the fewer tomorrows there are waiting in front of you."

"So how were *your* yesterdays important?" I asked. "When you were my age, with Grandpa and Grandma?"

He chuckled a little, speaking through it and clearing his throat. "Grandpa and Grandma kept me awake at night when I was your age – that's why I fish at night and sleep most of the day. I'm used to keeping those hours. They'd talk in their sleep, telling each other jokes, singing to each other and together. I guess that all came from how they met."

"Which was?"

Picking up his needle he threaded it and began to work, bending forward and squinting. "It was during a summer fair, but a travelling one run by people from the east-southeast – not a local fair. My parents didn't know each other at the time, but they both went to a show in a big tent, hosted by someone called a...a Mesmerist. He asked for volunteers from the audience to join him on stage, and be part of his act, and several people went up, including your grandpa and grandma. By all accounts the Mesmerist put everyone to sleep, yet awake – if that makes sense, and he'd make them do funny things like pretend to be animals, make stupid noises, or act out silly things to make the audience laugh. But then in the middle of his show, he fell to the stage, dead.

"Everyone that was left on stage remained unconscious for almost a year and a third. Other Mesmerists and people called hypnotists, which were really the same thing, were brought in from Middletown and other places, to try and wake the people up. Some of the asleep people died during that year and a third, then for no reason your grandparents woke up at exactly the same time."

"How? Why?"

He shrugged his shoulders, continuing to work without looking up. "We don't know, and they've never been able to explain it. When they woke up, they were deeply in love with each other, having spent that sleeping time together, just the two of them, exploring a land that was in their minds – some strange place the Mesmerist had created for them – the Sleepness, they called it. A place they went back to visit together, every time they went to sleep."

He was about to continue as shouting reached our ears. It was Mrs Cribbage calling to us and waving from her chimney veranda.

"Aiden! There's a dot! There's a big dot in the sky coming this way and getting bigger. Aiden! *Aiden!*"

This was reassuring, as Aiden was my dad's name, and from what I was told the big dot in the sky could mean only one thing.

"Quickly, help me roll back the grass. You're old enough now," Dad said, standing and dropping his net onto the flatstones. Running up the garden we almost collided with Mum, and as I thrust my net into my skirt pocket, Mum muttered something rude I wasn't supposed to hear, before calling back to us, "Everything's ready for him. Back soon. I'll let Charles out and don't forget the window!"

At the top of the garden, just beyond the vegetable patch, stood two thick posts of stone as wide as me. They were twenty-one paces apart, with a thick metal pole connecting them. Three chains ran from the pole and disappeared under the neat edge of the grass.

Grabbing the lever hanging from a rusted nail on a back fence post, Dad knelt down, twisting and snapping the lever into the side of a post, cranking the lever quickly.

Standing half-way down the garden, I searched for the joins as the rumble and squeak of cogs and gears beneath me rose above Mrs Cribbage's cries. A gap in the grass finally appeared as the slack was taken up. The grass, backed with metal slats, curling around the pole, revealing a large rusted hoop of iron set into an uneven cube of grey concrete beneath the lawn. The hoop was as wide as our front door, the metal as thick as Dad's arms.

"Clear!" I shouted, remembering what Mum had cried in previous years.

Nodding once, he stopped cranking while locking the lever down in place to look at the sky, shielding his eyes from the suns.

He joined me by the hoop of iron, and I could just see Mrs Cribbage over the fence and between the branches, frantically waving and pointing towards the west.

"Well done," said Dad, ruffling my hair. "Grandpa will be here soon."

Together we watched the sky as a little black dot appeared and disappeared amid the low afternoon clouds. It grew larger and larger until it was bigger than Mr and Mrs Cribbage's house, looming above our garden. A huge colourful balloon of orange and black triangles, with a large wicker basket in the shape of a rowing boat hanging from it by a collection of nets. Beneath the basket were other nets of all shapes and sizes, containing what I found out later to be Grandpa's trinkets from the mines that nobody was interested in or knew anything about. The basket's hull held four long landing legs, reaching far beneath the nets, ending in wooden feet shaped like feet.

A hatch on the underside opened, sprouting a coiled rope.

"Weigh it!" shouted Dad, and the rope fell to the lawn with a thud. We dragged it over to the hoop of iron, and within a few moments Dad had fashioned a complicated knot around the hoop and stood back. "Moored!" he shouted between cupped hands. Then a rope ladder appeared from a second hatch, rolling out through the air, nets containing beach pebbles anchoring it to the grass with a crunch, as a net of Grandpa's dirty clothes hit the ground next to it.

Charles slithered past disinterestedly, focusing upon the exposed worms, wriggling to hurriedly return to the roll of turf around the pole. He'd settle for them if he could catch one, having been deprived of the windfalls.

Craning my neck, I looked up to see Grandpa slowly descending the ladder.

"Great greetings, family of mine!" he shouted, waving down to us precariously. Dad stood with his foot on the bottom rung of the ladder to help steady it, shaking his head a little and smiling to me at his dad's flamboyance.

"No need for help, nicelessness son! She'll hold fast."

Dad rolled his eyes. Grandpa never liked help, but always wanted to help others, and I *loved* the way he spoke, using the old words from his father's childhood which many people had now forgotten, shortened, or chosen to ignore.

Then he was standing there swaying, a little unsteady on the lawn, all old and proud, brushing down his clothes and straightening himself as if ready for inspection. His creased and worn heavy mining boots all clean and polished to a black shine, thick woven grey chequered trousers a little too short at the ankle, rough and worn almost to holes at the knees. A thick brown leather belt with various metal tools of unknown purpose dangled from it, between leather pouches of different shapes and sizes. Above this, his faded white shirt with wide button-down pockets, too big, crumpled from the long journey, sleeves rolled up and held by black and white striped shoelaces at his elbows. The red bow tie at his neck, loose, as though the knot was uncomfortable and trying to escape. Upon his head was his red mining helmet complete with its lantern, hiding the fact he'd almost run out of hair. Under his arm was a thin brown paper parcel, tied with hairy string.

"Dad," said my dad, giving him a hug. "It's wonderful to see you. It's been an age and a while too long." He took a step back and pointed up. "Is that a new balloon? It's huge!"

Grandpa took off his helmet and rubbed the top of his head with a fingerless glove of leather matching his belt.

"Yes, all newly built by my competent self the last season before last. She's *'The Shining Lacklustre.'*" He glanced up, tugged on the rope ladder once with a broad smile of affection. "Takes a great deal of skillability to steer her true, son, but I've mastered her now, and we trust each other. Much bigger than my old floating bucket, *Sky Barnacle*. She's my home, with every comfortability a man of my years demands, which isn't much." He replaced his helmet then gave the parcel to Dad. "My latest painting, for Charlotte – payment for doing my washing. Not seen any rain clouds to wash my clothes in during the trip, unfortunateness."

He looked to the grass with a frown as though he'd lost something, scratching the back of his neck with one hand, the other thrust in a pocket. "Now, where's my Tiny Flower?"

"Here!" I shouted with a big smile, waving my arms, but he acted as though he couldn't see or hear me, pacing around, staring at the grass maintaining that frown. As I approached, he twisted around quickly, his back to me, tools tinkling at his waist, eyes still fixed upon the grass as I faced him once more. "Can't find her anywhere." He looked up at Dad, both hands on his hips, "Is she hiding? Have *you* seen her, Aiden?"

"Here, here I am Grandpa, here!" I insisted, jumping up and down at his feet, holding my arms wide apart so he couldn't move.

"Oh, *there* you are!" He picked me up with a little difficulty, giving me a big hug and kiss on the cheek. "You have grown – I won't be able to call you Tiny Flower next time we meet, *that's* a certainality."

His voice was croaky, breath of tobacco, skin creased and rough, thin and sunned brown. But his shining eyes were always the brightest blue. I kissed him on the cheek and he put me down, holding his back as he straightened.

"*Your* home?" asked my dad, taking my hand to lead us down the garden.

"Mine, and mine alone. We'll speak tonight, over a glass of whitefruit cider," said Grandpa, his voice adopting a tone of determination."I trust last year's crop's ready?"

"It is," said Dad, whistling and stamping the lawn for Charles to follow us back into the house.

That evening, *The Remembering of the Amnesiac God* celebrations filled our entire street. Everyone from the village was out enjoying themselves in the humid night. Strings full of colourful lanterns hung from the trees lined the way, stretching across the road in haphazard zig-zags. Tables of white cotton sheets huddled together along the pavements, filled with food from every kitchen. I stood helping Mum lay out our table of food, as Mrs Cribbage laid out her smoked fish, telling us about a meandering star she'd seen moving through her telescope over the past three nights. Mum wasn't really interested in what she had to say, and I found myself looking at the row of tables either side of me. There were hot pies of all shapes, sizes and varieties, roasted meats and vegetables, warm loaves and freshly churned butter, roasted and boiled potatoes, salads and pickles, jams and preserves, home-made wine, ale, and a barrel of Dad's whitefruit cider he and Grandpa had rolled out of Dad's garden shed. A small stage was built at the end of the street, where a band energetically filled the air with music.

I watched the other kids playing games, insisting I should join Dad and Grandpa as Mum insisted I joined in with the kids, just so I could see what schoolchildren were like, and to find out what things they'd been taught that were utterly pointless.

But I liked being with Grandpa. He was fun. So I ran over to join him and Dad, leaving Mum to Mrs Cribbage and her continued story of the meandering star.

"Yes, *The Shining Lacklustre* is my home now, and mine alone. Your mother and I have had the final argumentation," said Grandpa, puffing on his stubby ebony pipe as I joined them. The smoke was sweet, spicy, and served to separate the three of us from the revelry as we stood away from the crowds, at the bottom of the street just before the crescent reached around, sloping up to the left.

"Are you *sure* it's the final?" asked my father in a low voice. He took a few big gulps of cider, as if needing it for Grandpa's reply.

"Questionless, son. *No* back returning for me, not *any* tomorrow or day following."

Wiping his mouth with the back of his hand, my dad looked down to me. He knew by my expression I didn't want to join in with the other kids right now, so he passed me his jug, telling me to hold it with both hands tightly as he lit a cigarette.

"Tell me what happened," said Dad abruptly, replacing his matches into his shirt pocket. He looked smart, and I was pleased he'd allowed Mum to comb his hair, wax it down and convince him to wear his best clothes, despite his complaints that it would be dark and nobody could see or really cared what he looked like.

"I do," she had said, and I'd nodded up to him as he stared into the bedroom mirror.

Grandpa took Dad's jug from me, taking a few gulps before passing it back with a wink.

He straightened, taking a long draw from his pipe.

"Your mother, or 12849921, told me she'd bumped into my friend's wife on her way into town. They got into a longchat, locked in face to face – you know how your mother enjoys the longchat. My friend told his wife he'd not seen me at camouflage practice for the last two meetings, and she mentioned that to your mother."

"And?"

"And I was there, course I was there, unbeingseen. Third time's for the reveal, to recount the first two meetings, to prove to the instructor for my certificate of achievement."

"But Mum didn't believe you."

"Thought I was sneaking off seeing someone else. At my age, at any age! I'd gotten so good at camouflage, I could hardly see myself in the bathroom mirror, Aiden." He puffed on his pipe, removed it from his mouth, licking his dry lips, saying, "Mistrust is the sharpest of axes at the thickest tree of love," before quickly replacing his pipe.

Dad gave him a bewildered look and finished his cigarette, dropping and stepping on it as it rolled away. He blew out a smoke ring, speaking through it as it distorted and crumpled in the night air. "But why the interest with camouflage? That's not like you."

"Protection. Twice on my way to work I was attacked by a brood of feral chickens. Nasty buggers, big'n ugly, angry. Thank goodnessness I can climb high up into trees, and the chickens got bored fast from all that jumping, flapping and clucking with anger, trying to reach me. But, your mother didn't believe me, saying the ferals haven't been seen around our neck of the woods for a few lifetimes. Doesn't mean they're not still out there – in hiding, waiting for the right time to come out and wreak havocation again, rutting, pecking and killing their way through towns and villages, like they did during the Seasonstill of '23."

My dad looked worried.

"You should have tracked them back to their roost, set fire to it. Asked someone at camouflage practice to help, take along dried sage and powdered onions. That would've kept them back." He turned, grim-faced, squinting through Grandpa's pipe smoke. "You do remember that, don't you, Dad?"

Grandpa turned his head. "No, I'd forgotten, son. Placed *that* memory in a different pocket? *Of course I remember!* You try finding sage nowadays! I'll never forget how scared my mum and her sister were, tail end of '89 – six years living in fear of those chickens, after the last confirmed attack. I was just a small lad, found a clutch of eggs in our front garden, took them inside. My mother was horrifiated, they'd staked their claim on my dad's land, and they were the *whiteshells*, not the common brown ones. I don't know if you know, son, but fully-grown whites are even more vicious than brownshells. There were twelve of the little buggers, and less than twenty-one days for us to find somewhere else to live. After Mum calmed down, she and her sister made us all a huge cheese and onion omelette, hard-boiling a few for Dad to carry with him, so he could hold them up as a threat if he was cornered by the brood. That's the one advantage, they don't know a hard-boiled egg from a fresh one. After that, your great granddaddy took us into the sky." He looked up into the night, his voice trailing off a little. "Aiden, it's safe up there, away from all the land and the trouble it brings. But then I met your mum in the Sleepness, and well, grounded myself to be with her."

Dad scratched his chin where a clump of grey bristles was sprouting.

"But that can't be all of it. Mum wouldn't cause a split over that, surely – you did talk to her about it all, tell her you were at practice?"

Taking a big long final puff of his pipe, he steadied himself on Dad's shoulder with his left hand, resting his left ankle above his right knee to tap out the embers from his pipe on the heel of his boot. They faded one by one on the road. Licking his thumb, he ran it around the inside of the pipe, wiping this on a grey rag he produced from a trouser pocket, placing the pipe in its leather case upon his belt.

   He cleared his throat. "She'd spoken to everyone at practice, and they'd just told her they hadn't seen me. I couldn't prove an anything thing." He winked at Dad. "But the key to successful camouflage is to make people believe you don't exist. Perhaps I should have given your mother the thankness gaze, as that's how she made me feel, and perhaps that helped me. Anyways, we had a blazing row before I set off to work the next morning. I got home late that afternoon, went into the kitchen to have a longchat and sort things out." He looked over to my dad and paused, waiting for Dad to face him. "When I walked in, she took off her left shoe and sock."

   My dad turned away instantly, his eyes filled with tears and he told me to wait with Grandpa as he walked over to his barrel to refill his jug. When he returned, he'd calmed a little, carrying a jug of cider for Grandpa. But I could see in that flickering light, my dad was upset, no matter how hard he tried to hide the fact from me with a brief, fake smile.

   Grandpa took his drink and nodded his thanks before taking a sip.

   "She started the insult, holding her bare foot out to me as she balanced there by the oven, pointing the accuser's toe. Then, she gave me a standard insult, just a slow curl of the big toe, followed by fourteen wiggles of the baby toe. It was nothing special, and I thought it would end there and then. But, this was the old silent foot insults of *my* family history, *our* forefathers, son! She'd obviously read up on them, practised over many weeks while I was working in the mines, and do you know what, she carried on, knowing it was an insult to even *attempt* such an insult, and a shame upon myself I would always carry with me, if I didn't answer her.

"Before I knew what I was doing, my shoe and sock were next to hers on the kitchen floor, and we were hopping around them in a circle, insulting each other, looking for an opportunity, trying to finish a flourish of insults upon each other during a hop before landing." He paused and looked down to the road for a few moments. "It got bad, son, *real* bad, and real difficult. We blocked, parried and contradicted, and I was about to win with my third interruption, when she..." he stopped himself, placing his jug at his feet, glancing at me with a struggled half-smile. He steadied himself, holding out his left hand flat, opposite Dad's face, his fingers wriggling in a rapid complex repeating pattern. I copied as best I could, and as soon as Dad noticed, he reached down quickly, wrapping his big hand tightly around mine to stop me. "Don't ever do that, sweetheart," he said quickly with angry eyes. "Please, don't *ever* do that *ever* again." He gave me a reassuring smile of apology and squeezed my shoulder, before looking back to Grandpa, nodding for him to continue.

"Your mother won, Aiden. She was *so* insulting I couldn't match her – didn't want to – I loved her! I watched in defeat as she walked out with my sock and shoe as trophies, leaving me with no choice other than to wear an odd sock and shoe to work the next day, as the rules state. There was only one man on my mining team that understood the significance of this rule, and he couldn't look me in the eye for nine days after. He didn't tell anyone else, bless him. He was so understanding and respectful, and for that I should thank him, and bless his family's feet. Especially as he used to be a Richard, but now 3114."

"I just can't believe she didn't give you time to prove yourself, to be awarded your certificate. That would have been all the proof she needed, surely?"

Grandpa shook his head, then changed it to a smiling nod. "I thought that was the end of it, but before she left, she turned from the kitchen door, hopped over and gave me a broken kiss."

My dad drank deeply from his jug upon hearing this, staring ahead in silence, his grey stubble dripping with orange cider. Wiping it away he turned and gave Grandpa a long hug, patting him on the back. "I'm so sorry, Dad," he said with a faltering voice. "Now you know her truth."

Remaining silent, we watched the dancing. After a while, Mum came over, asking Grandpa to dance the last dance of the evening before the Ceremony of the Amnesiac God. She didn't know how happy that made him, how significant that last dance was for that polite, wonderful old gentleman, but I certainly saw it in his face, and that made me smile too.

She, simply concentrating on avoiding his big black boots, laughing and spinning around his outstretched arms, her long curly hair fanning out behind her, her dress swirling around as she pirouetted. Dad just stood there with me, watching them dance, enjoying what was left of the night and the summer, finding a brief smile amid his parents' tragedy as he tapped a foot to the music.

The night then brought a gentle but chilling breeze, causing the lanterns to sway uneasily in the trees, the shadows and colours shifting across Dad's face as the bonfire was set in the middle of the road. The music stopped. The Seasonstill was almost at an end, with Seasonchill just around the corner.

We all gathered as the bonfire's flames settled, standing in a huge circle around it, hand in hand, before the chanting began.

Remember all here, steadfast and clear, long before the forgotten,
Recalling your past, first moment to last, to see all life and summon,
Of being the first, our universe birthed, your children call your attention,

Your memory now, released from a spell, the truth of a god's validation.

The fire will prove it is me and not you, immune from all condemnation,
Walk through and free, holding the key, unlocking amnesia's aberration,
Now we know who you are, returned from afar, we follow to love you, our saviour,
To lead us today, to find a new way, for our lives are now yours in elation.

But if you burn, then truth will return, your death our clarification,
That you were a fool, a charlatan too, screaming with humiliation,
'It should be me, I crave to be, a god among my children,'
Yet death goes to show, dreams are like snow, to melt upon realisation,
That nothing can last, not future, nor past
For life's just anticipation.

After this chant was repeated over and over again, they all fell silent, waiting, remembering their lives, concentrating with their eyes closed to perhaps discover a new memory. Only the crickets chirping in the long grass of the front gardens, and the younger children's voices could be heard, asking their parents what was happening, told to shush, while the fire crackled before us.

As the tradition went, each of the adults waited for amnesia to clear, to remember that perhaps one of them was the amnesiac god, and could walk through the flames and out the other side, unharmed by what they, as a god, had created. They would then lead everyone, as they answered every question everyone had concerning life.

But my thoughts were with my grandpa and his obvious sadness as I tightly held his rough, dry hand. It, trembling around mine like an uncertain cage, about to crumble. Flames burning in front of my tightly closed eyes conjured dancing shapes of orange and yellow as I felt him let go of my hand. I looked up, his eyes were wide open, staring into the flames, tears running down his face in the flickering firelight, the moisture aglow, like lava flowing from an angry volcano. And all I could think about was the meaning of the broken kiss. Wiping the tears away with his free hand I felt him take a small step slowly forward. I reached out, gripping his dry, twig-like fingers tightly, pulling him back to my side. He looked down at me, mouthing, *'It's alright, Tiny Flower. I'm ok.'*

I didn't believe for one whole second he'd recalled a memory of being a god. We stood there in silence for a while as the fire continued to warm the air. Then a shout went up for the end of the remembering and everyone cheered and laughed, relieved none of us had been foolish or drunk enough to walk into the flames. As the cheering died down and the circle began to break, Grandpa spoke.

"This is steaming horse toilet."

"Keep your voice down!" replied Dad. "You're a guest here, remember that."

He just smiled. "No, not this, son. Just life, these days, these times."

We slept in the next day. Dad and Grandpa cooked us all a late breakfast. Mum, Charles and I listening to them from the safety of the living room, laughing, complaining at each other and clattering about in the kitchen. And later, during the toasted mushrooms, Grandpa spoke to me.

"How would my Tiny Flower like to spread her petals against the sky, feel the currents and tides flowing around her?"

Everyone stopped eating, even Charles sitting in his high-chair to my left, while Grandpa continued to munch his mushrooms noisily as he stared at me for my answer.

"You mean in your *balloon*?" asked Mum quickly, looking at Dad, then to me and back again to Dad, her fork still holding a mushroom in mid-air in front of her mouth.

"Of course, Charlotte, how else! There's no need for such misapprecomprehensionisms. My inclevermment for reading the sky tides is beyond comparisonistics," he held his arms outstretched to the ceiling, wiggling his fingers. "The vividality up there is super stupendous, surely my latest painting proves that!"

Mum placed her fork back upon her plate with a clatter, leaning forward. "You do have an amplificator, don't you?"

"No, I have *two* amplificators, should one decide it's having a rest day. Listen, everything will be fine. We'll be back just after my clothes are dry upon your line, and long before you've run out of worryment."

"And what if both decide on a rest day, Roan?"

"Then we'll fly as my grandfather did, by the old ways. I'll extend sails and we'll weave through the windtides, up, over, down and through – to return home against the strongest of currents."

Now Dad placed his fork on his plate and fidgeted in his seat a little, Mum's use of Grandpa's name during breakfast setting formality for the day ahead. But I think she was just being polite, as she didn't adhere to the ancient traditions of Dad's side of the family that much. Mum was always forward-thinking, so I decided to think forward too.

"That would be a great adventure for me," I said, placing a mushroom in my mouth and chewing quickly to hide my cheeky grin.

Mum looked over, her mouth opening slowly in surprise, effectively erasing her frown.

"After all, when adventure comes visiting, it's important to recognise her. She doesn't like being on her own," I said, swallowing hard while still looking at Mum.

There was silence for what seemed a season, with only the dining-room clock measuring what was left of the uneasiness.

"Then it's settled!" said Grandpa with a start, slamming his palms down upon the table either side of his plate, causing the breakfast things to jump briefly with surprise and agreement. "Goodness upon the day!" he continued, wiping his mouth once with a napkin in a theatrical flourish, standing quicker than I imagined he could. "Goodness, goodness goodness. I'll get things ready." He pointed at me, "You'll need a warm coat, and Charles his woolly jumper, if he's coming along for your adventureness too? I've already checked with the clouds, there'll be no wettages from *them* to worry about, so both of you can forget your silly rain hats."

Mum and Dad raised their eyebrows at each other silently as Grandpa left the table, their faces full of concern.

Grandpa carried Charles in his travel sling, as I climbed the rope ladder ahead of him.

When I reached the basket I opened the gate and stepped in. The boat-shaped basket was much larger than my bedroom, and at the centre was a little house of wicker, the roof wrapped in leather, a single black chimney pot pointing up to the neck of the balloon.

I helped Grandpa up and Charles out of his sling. Slowly he came out of his home and began to explore too.

"There's just enough room for a guest in my sky home," said Grandpa, cranking the ladder up as I looked around.

"That's ok, I'm not here to sit inside." I turned as the wind caught my hair to obscure my view, so I bunched it up and tied it back, steadying myself as the basket creaked.

I heard Dad shout "Clear!" and I looked below, he waving happily, Mum standing beside him with her arms folded. I waved back and she finally waved briefly before shaking her head, walking slowly down the garden, folding her arms once more.

Clinging to the edge of the basket and peering over the edge on tiptoes, Mr and Mrs Cribbages' house seemed so small now. Dad, continuing to wave, became small very quickly, and then he gave a final wave before disappearing in through the back door as the anchor rope retracted fully with a clunk.

The view was astonishing. I could see like a bird, the irregularly-shaped fields, meandering roads, clumps of little villages with their buildings huddled together, the far horizon to the north where the coastline stretched before the sunlit sea, twinkling and rippling. They were all tiny and silent before me, like the toy rug Mum and Dad had woven for me, with roads and forests and rivers and streams which I explored with my wooden toys.

Grandpa stood on a circular dais, where a small ship's wheel protruded from an elevated brass control console of switches, buttons and gauges. A collection of levers and ropes on pulleys were set into the floor either side of the console, with angled footplates and large buttons on the floor beneath it. He pulled a lever towards him slowly, and it responded with a loud ticking sound. Gradually we ascended into the mid-afternoon, my tummy going up into my chest briefly.

"That's excellentationistic," said Grandpa, flipping a switch and checking gauges. "Come on inside, I'll show you my house."

Grandpa lit a fire in a circular grate dominating the centre of the room. As he replaced the poker next to the fire, I looked around his home. It was a big room, a low wooden bed of thin sheets and a single pillow, unmade and crumpled. His paintings lined the walls, depicting views from his travels to many destinations. There were all manner of strange mechanical objects scattered here and there, with brown cardboard labels attached to them, numbered and tied with hairy string.

"Where shall we head?" he asked, motioning toward the doorway.

I took something out of my skirt pocket, hiding it quickly behind my back, a big grin across my face.

"What have you there?"

I held out the net I'd made the day before. "A present for you, Grandpa," I said, wiggling it in the air between us.

His mouth was agape, holding his palms against his cheeks. "Tiny Flower! That's absolutely wonderfulationistic of you!" He took it, twirling it between his fingers, then walked up to a painting, took it off the wall to hang the net there. He stood back, hands on hips, admiring it. "Perfectness!"

I walked outside, unable to hide the big smile on my face, skipping around the edge of the basket, staring into the everywhere surrounding me. "I don't know where we could visit," I said, with an overwhelming feeling of freedom, liberated from the confines of the ground below. I felt like a princess in a floating castle, able to visit anywhere in the world. I looked to the west, "There's so much to see, so many places."

When I had come full circle, Grandpa joined me.

"What's that, there?" I asked, pointing to a dark green and brown area amid the wild meadows in the far distance.

"Wishart's Wood," he said, clasping the rim of the basket with both hands as he joined me. "Although it's now more of a forest. She planted many trees over the years, then vanished to the other side of the world, to a land of forever green and agreeable musication, so it's said. And far beyond the forest, yes, you can just see the tall buildings of Middletown, if you squint."

I took a few paces and turned to face the east, pointing once more. "And that there, what's that silly-looking building, with all the bridges?"

"That ruin? Why that's what's left of the Citadel and its ten churches – built twenty-one hundred and twelve or so years long past, to be inexact."

I looked up to him, remembering it was one of Keloff's favourite places to explore. "Can we see it, then the forest? Can your sky home do that? Oh, I know! Can we go to Viewhaven for ice creams! Is there time, Grandpa, is there?"

He just smiled, returning to the dais to take the wheel, flicking switches and pulling levers. "We'll visit the forest first, collect fallen twigs and branches for the fire. There's a clearing where we can set down, near the ruins. After that, Viewhaven is a certainality! There's plenty of time. We can't be late back, because we haven't said when we'll return from your adventureness."

"But you told Mum we'd be back before your washing's dry on the line?"

"You're right, I did. But there's a few handfuls and three wettages due for the groundfolk, and my washing's on your Mum's line by now."

"But you said there's no wettages due!"

He grinned into the sky. "Not up here, those clouds haven't arrived yet," he said, pulling a lever. "There's no need for concernness, we'll be home way before tea-time."

The sound of hatches opening found my ears, and I looked down as two poles wrapped with white sails extended either side of the basket beneath us. Watching, Grandpa pulled on two tattered red ropes, and the sails unfurled, flapping with enthusiasm to find the winds. At once his sky home jerked sharply, as though startled from being woken up, coming about against the current as its bow turned to face the forest. Grandpa concentrated, pulling levers and slowly turning the wheel. As we ascended the wind became stronger, pushing us towards the distant expanse of trees as a break in the clouds allowed two suns through. I felt exhilarated.

"Grandpa, what's it like in the mines, where you work?"

He raised his eyebrows. "The history mines? Why they're fantasticationistic! So many things hidden deep beneath the earth to discover, all sorts of objects and places." He grinned down at me. "You saw a few in my house, but sadly I won't be unearthing many more."

"Why not, are you retiring? Dad often talks to Mum about retiring, but she says we can't afford it yet."

"Oh noness, I still have a few and a couple of years left in me. Your dad, the same plus at least three handfuls. The Truthsayers control the mines, started the very first excavations long before I was born." He looked ahead then down to his gauges and pulled a lever. "Then they went away, and the miners carried on. Now they're back again. They've told us mining is pointless. So, we all stop work at the end of the next Seasonchill."

"But what are they like? The mines, I mean, not the Truthsayers."

"Wonderful. So many caverns! Rusted objects fused to the rocks, old machines, and even vehicles like cars, but bigger, with many seats. There's so much underground. Last year my team found the edge of what turned out to be a massive pointed spire of shining silver and broken glass, with big serving bowls lying on their sides upon it, for offerings to the ancient gods. We dug and dug, bringing in silt beetles from other shafts to help us clear the way. In a week and eight days we'd removed all the earth, silt and dust, revealing a huge rectangular building, much taller than the tallest in Middletown. There are floors and floors inside. Hundreds of rooms with chairs, tables, corridors. Now the entire building stands in a huge cavern, where other, smaller buildings and broken elevated roads peek from the cavern's sides."

I tried to imagine what he had seen, but my thoughts were distracted by the wind whistling through the ropes above, and the majestic view surrounding me. "It all sounds very strange."

"Well, it will soon pass," he said with a hint of regret.

I looked ahead towards the growing forest, changing the subject as I didn't want him to be upset. "I'm so very happy to be here, Grandpa. But, it's a bit of a shame Mum and Dad didn't want to join in."

He shifted his weight, stamping once with both feet. "Your father prefers his boots on planks above the sea, your mother, shoes on floorboards above the land."

I nodded. "I think I like both of them, but, I think I like being in the sky the best now. I bet Great Uncle Ephesus would love this, too."

Grandpa's forehead creased and he looked down at me. "Ephesus? Great uncle? I've never heard of him."

"But you must have. He's tall like you, but a little fat and old, with a big beard. You must have met him before. I've known him forever!"

Grandpa shook his head, maintaining his frown as we approached the edge of the forest. "Well, no, I can't recall an Ephesus. He must be a relation of your mum's?"

I thought about it. "I don't know. I'll ask her when we get back if he's from her side of the family."

"Well, I've not seen that much of sides, tops or bottoms of any family over the times. I'm not much for relativity celebrationisms – they can be a huge lot of effortness, unnecessarily necessary, or necessarily unnecessary, for..."

The Shining Lacklustre jerked sharply upward, causing me to stumble over.

"No need for worryment, Tiny Flower!" said Grandpa, holding out a hand to pull me to my feet. "It's just the warm air from the forest. Are you alright?"

I nodded, trying my best not to feel scared, turning to see Charles retreating into his shell.

Grandpa's hands jumped from one lever to the next as the basket shook again, the sails flapping madly on their masts, his face set in deep concentration. It became dark all of a sudden, and I looked to the east. The suns shone brightly there, then I noticed a straight line, an edge across the trees below, as though a square cloud sat above us, casting its shadow.

"This isn't goodly," shouted Grandpa, as the hairs on my arms went all prickly. "Not goodly at all!"

"There's a big shadow on the trees, Grandpa."

He shot me a glance. "Shadow?" He pulled two levers together, then stamped on a big black button set into the floor before hurrying over to me.

"There!" I pointed. The tops of the trees were closer now, and I could see by his face he was concerned.

"Waitation here," he said quickly, pointing at the mast beneath us. "When you see the topsail ladder, shout!"

I nodded as he ran back to the dais, stamping on a red button, cranking a small handle set into the control column, round and round as fast as he could.

"Is it a storm cloud, Grandpa? It looks like it's going to rain!"

He shook his head. There was a really loud rumble like thunder, but it didn't sound like real thunder, somehow. The tree tops shivered. A white wooden ladder slowly extended across the top of the mast. "It's here!" I turned and shouted, as the rumble grew louder.

Grandpa gave me a thumbs up, and I heard a mechanical cough and splutter. "The port amplificator's running," he shouted, hurrying over. "It'll keep us level. Wait for me here."

"But where are you going?"

"I have to see what's going on. It's not thunder, and certainality not a rain cloud!"

I watched him climb over the basket, my heart thumping. "Be careful, Grandpa!"

He climbed down onto the ladder and crawled along it backwards, causing the basket to tip to that side, the amplificator's engine whining complaints as it compensated for his weight, bringing the basket level. When he reached the end of the ladder, he looked down into the trees, then turned slowly around, looking up. His expression was full of fear and surprise. He hurried back, and I helped him aboard.

"It's high above us. I don't know what it is, but it's hugely giganticatious, like a slab of fruit-loaf with lemon slices and sugar dusting." He held my shoulders. "You're going to have to help me. We have to be quick."

As we stood together on the dais, whatever it was came into view. It stretched just beyond the fringes of the forest, dark grey, stripes of yellow and blue, with white lights along it in all kinds of meandering patterns. There were strange groups of girders stretching down like upside down spires, ugly and spiky, like thornberry branches but without fruit.

"Bring the ladder in while I fire up the other amplificator," he said, placing my hand on the lever. He steered back towards home as I cranked the lever, but the thing above us was everywhere now, descending like a strange night, its girders crackling with thin, bright blue lightning towards the ground. There was a sudden lurch downward as the second amplificator spluttered awake and we picked up speed.

"We can't land until we clear the forest!" shouted Grandpa.

A strange metallic chiming filled the air, then a brief shrill sound before the blue lightning stopped.

All was silent, just the sounds of the amplificator's engines and the creaks from the basket and ropes above.

A bird flew past, then another two, then more and more as flocks and flocks flew from the forest. At its fringes, I saw the animals appear. "Look!"

Every animal ran clear in a great herds: deer, rabbits, hedgehogs, badgers and squirrels, as fast as they could, together in a great exodus.

Then the shrill noise began again, hurting my ears as the blue lightning arced into the trees. We watched as several were gradually uprooted by the lightning. Some came out easily, carried straight up, earth and stones falling back to the ground from their exposed roots, their wood creaking and crying splinters from severed roots. Others seemed reluctant to be uprooted, jerking up a little, then stopping, rotating a little until they were free like teeth being pulled. More joined them, randomly plucked from the forest floor, the lightning gathering them together in a swirling group as their leaves fell, their branches clattering together. Then the lightning carried them up as a circular hole appeared in the object, the trees disappearing inside as this terrible slab descended faster, pushing us closer to the remaining tree tops.

Grandpa gritted his teeth, turning the amplificators up full, accelerating us closer to the sunlit meadows beyond the edge of the object. There was a sharp cracking sound and the basket wobbled.

"We've lost the starboard landing leg." He pointed to a row of yellow buttons in front of me, as he steered upward to avoid the tree tops, narrowly missing the edge of a spire. "Flip up the little silver switches above them," he shouted, "then push all of the yellow buttons together. That'll cast off the other three legs, cut down our weight, give us more clearance and extra speediness."

I did so as fast as I could, hearing the sounds of the legs falling into the trees behind us, then a splutter from either side of us, as the blue lightning sparked and crackled, touching the amplificators, knocking them out, smoke billowing from them. Without a current to fill the sails, we came to a gradual halt.

Grandpa slammed his palms down onto the control console. I followed him as he hurried to the bow. The edge of the forest wasn't that far away.

I looked up at him. He was biting his lower lip. "Can we lower the ladder and climb down?"

He shook his head, squinting. "Too far, Tiny Flower. Besides, that thing above is coming down fastly. We couldn't outrun it on the ground, weaving between the uprooted trees. We'd be carried up into that thing too." He looked up to the safety of the sunlit meadows, his right hand jerking upward, pointing ahead. "Look, there! Can you see that?"

In the distance I saw a silver something glinting in the suns, heading towards us really fast.

In a flash it silently sped past us very close, causing the basket to wobble.

"The flying fish!" cried Grandpa, as our heads turned together to watch it. The silver something climbed, heading toward the slab, slowing as it approached. A square hatch opened and the silver whatever it was, shaped like two of Mum's oval serving dishes placed edge to edge on top of each other to keep flies off the left-overs, weaved between uprooted trees before it disappeared inside.

"What was that?"

"I've seen it only three times before," said Grandpa. "skipping along the tops of clouds like a skimming stone on water, stopping dead still, just to hang in the air, as if it knew it had been seen and was pretending it wasn't there." He brought his hand up close to his head, lying flat, then thrust it quickly through the air between us and straight up. "Then it whizzed off again, higher and higher until I couldn't see it anymoreness. It looks like a flying fish to me."

The basket lurched down again, pushing us closer to the treetops. We ran back to the dais, Grandpa checking gauges. He tapped the glass of the largest a few times, as the needle slowly crept down towards zero.

"Go and get Charles and put him in his sling. You both have to leave," he said in a low voice without looking at me.

I couldn't believe what he'd said. "Leave? Where to?"

"Your home." He looked up, "Those spires have punctured the balloon. Quickly!"

I ran to Charles, rolling him into his travel sling and hoisting the strap over my shoulder.

When I joined Grandpa, he stood over an open hatch in front of the dais, where a ladder led down a handful and a few rungs.

"Listen to me carefully. Climb down, sit in the seat and pull the canopy closed. The handle is just behind the headrest. Press the big green button first to release, then the red button to start the amplificator. Use the wheel to steer, pull it gently back to go up, forward to go down, but be careful to avoid the trees."

He held my hand, leading me forward.

"But what is it?"

"It's my escape balloon. Hurry now!"

But I stood my ground, leaning back as he tried to pull me forward. "Aren't you coming *with* us?"

He spun around. "There's not enough room!"

"But I could sit on your lap?"

"Too much weight with all of us. We'd not clear the forest in time."

"But we could try, I don't want to leave you!" I could feel my tears building up, and my tummy felt hollow and cold.

Grandpa crouched down, speaking calmly as he held my hands in his. "Please, Tiny Flower, you must save Charles for me. It's your time, your adventureness now."

I threw my arms around his neck, cuddling him as tightly as I could, unable to stop my tears.

Smoke from the amplificators began to billow across the basket, and he pulled away, holding my hands again, "It's time, Tiny Flower." I found myself climbing down the ladder, sitting in the seat, wiping the tears from my eyes before placing Charles on my lap. I looked up, and Grandpa Roan, that lovely, funny old gentleman, smiled down to me.

"Remember, green then red! There's a pedal on the floor if you need more speed. Good luck and don't forget..."

And with that, the smoke covered him as he reached down, slamming the canopy shut.

My tears returned, and with a trembling hand I pushed the green button, my tummy going up into my chest again. Then the red button, releasing an oval red balloon, inflating with gas almost instantly above the canopy, the sound of a small amplificator fizzing to life behind my seat.

The treetops were so close, the lightning dancing around them as we sped off, faster than Grandpa's home, the slab above us descending more quickly now, harvesting as it threatened to push us down into the forest. Between ascending trees and descending spires I steered the little vehicle, until at last we were free, out into the warmth of the suns with the meadows beneath us. I brought us about in a wide arc, watching as the lightning uprooted the last remaining trees.

Grandpa's colourful balloon of orange and black triangles had become limp, ugly, the fabric slowly folding into itself. The ropes beneath it twisting and tangling together, broken masts and crumpled sails, his wicker basket home leaning sharply to the side. Then at once it caught alight. The fireplace tipped over inside, the blue lightning bristling beneath the great slab, in a final, violent burst.

The slab nestled into the earth, huge, still, and silence fell once more.

Through my tears, I steered towards home, wondering how I was going to tell Dad.

I'll get to that later, as I did then.

~ 11 ~
Hotel Infinity

Nick stood in Fountain Square, wound his watch then held it to his ear. It was silent, dead from the countless instances it had measured throughout his life, beating along, counting down as Nick had given so many a measured length to answer a question before their next broken limb, a few seconds to agree to a damning task, or in some instances counting their final moments before death at his hands. He had stared at that watch face for almost a century, it dutifully tick, tock, ticking away, without expression to what it had seen and measured.

Maybe it had taken one knock too many during combat with the girl, its inner mechanisms not built for so many violent clashes during its life. I preferred to believe it had a mind of its own, and had simply had enough, seen enough, an unwilling witness to Nick's terrible actions, a reluctant participant measuring so many poor unfortunates' fates.

We headed off, following Alfie's directions, Nick's stomach complaining for food.

The Hotel district was far busier than both of us thought. One after the other, signs reading **'Sorry *NO* Vacancies'** dampened Nick's tired spirits, as the sky darkened with the third sun struggling to stay awake in the sky. People sat at tables on lantern-lit terraces, drinking, eating and laughing. Groups stood in alehouse doorways, smoking. Some just sat watching the streets, thankful they weren't part of the hurrying throng before them, fighting to reach the comfort of their own homes as quickly as they could. Many of these tired souls gave up the race, choosing to join the revelry. They muttered complaints about their long day, the stupidity of the people and situations they were forced to deal with, reassured that a few drinks would soften the night, hoping the maddening rush they'd postponed participation in would gradually evaporate into a respectful saunter, while the city lights gradually cast false shadows into the streets.

We rounded a corner into a huge market square, where trestle tables containing all kinds of goods and second-hand trinkets sat beneath a covered stone colonnade. Nick found his curiosity taking him along the rows of tables where others respectfully sought a bargain. Lines of old mottled books, their spines pointing upward, titles and authors seeking attention. Ancient magazines, faded, folded and torn, pegged to dangling strings. Tables of dulled, dented silver and brass teapots and bowls, piles of silver and bronze cutlery, sitting beside stacks of china and metal plates. A few tables held boxes of old cardboard-covered black discs, several people angling them into the light from the thousands of coloured light bulbs spanning the square from wires hanging from wooden posts. They searched for scratches they found, wondering if the asking prices were worth the risk. Other tables contained piles of bizarre looking electronic devices and components, with brown cardboard labels attached to them tied with thin rubber bands. Artists displayed their endeavours, some charcoal sketches, others, large canvases of oils, rough brush strokes and palette knife marks, illustrating landscapes and portraits, locations and individuals long dead.

Nick decided his curiosity was now bored, even though mine wasn't, and he turned from the jumble of objects.

Sitting in the square before us ornate white cast iron patio tables and chairs of thin filigree were dotted about, where hundreds of people sat chatting, drinking and eating.

Nick walked into the maze, picking up a menu from a vacant table, his eyes widening and his mouth watering as he noticed it contained an entire section extolling the finesse of pizza construction. He read down the extensive options, then shook his head as he noticed at the bottom of each page, *'**THE HOTEL PATIO.** Hotel Guests Dining Only, plus **three** non-resident guests. **No exceptions,** sorry! Pets allowed, no children under the age of twenty. For full terms and conditions, please ask a waiter, or refer to* *chapter six, paragraph ten of this publication. © TSC 864750836.'*

He dropped the heavy volume down onto the table with a thud, staring up into the distance as, catching his eye, a huge neon sign set above revolving doors sprang to life in multi-coloured fits and starts against the darkening evening.

'HOTEL INFINITY ~ VACANCIES ALWAYS'

The revolving doors stood on their own, bereft of walls on either side or above. We passed through, and I felt Nick's body bristle, as though it had been covered in cotton wool and sparklers for an instant and a quarter.

The reception hall was larger than Hope Central's concourse. A concierge wearing a welcoming smile waved a white-gloved hand towards the reception desk, as robotic porters carried guests' luggage to rows upon rows of elevators lining the opposite wall. Nick shot the artificials a look of hatred.

At the reception desk stood a very tall, pale individual, wearing a look of utter shock, a large red bow tie, crumpled white shirt rolled up unevenly at his thin elbows and a black cap with the words 'Head Receptionist' embroidered in uneven yellow letters above the shiny plastic peak. His black waistcoat held a white plastic name badge, with the word, 'ANION' in bold red letters.

He gave Nick a rather negative smile and spoke in a high-pitched squeak, like that of creaking damp timber.

"Good eternally almostevening, sir. You don't need a reservation. A complimentary breakfast buffet is served between fourteen and eighteen, this morning, yesterday. I'd like to..."

"I won't need breakfast." said Nick, placing his bag of new clothes by his side and reaching for his wallet.

"If the room you have to offer us is acceptable, there's a very high probability you've already eaten it," said the receptionist. "It helps us with stock control; a benefit from the quantum leak maintenance has yet to find and repair."

Nick thought for a moment, looking down at the baked-bean stain on his shirt. "I need a room, just for the night," he said quickly, removing his bank card and tapping it a couple of times upon the desk.

"Do you have one to forget?" asked the receptionist in a tone indicating he'd said such sixty million and twenty-nine times before.

"To forget?"

"Yes sir. One you're not particularly fond of, or as some guests prefer to offer us, one you're very fond of, and would enjoy seeing for the very first time again. Everyone likes a surprise."

I turned and watched inside as Nick thought. His memory orbs flashed by me enthusiastically, like actors auditioning for a coveted role, each unfolding briefly until he settled upon one. "Yeah," he said, pleased with himself.

"Good," squeaked the receptionist. "Payment isn't required, sir. Checkout is anytime – and in case of an emergency evacuation, the fire exit is at the end of the third floor corridor. We're unsure where it leads – somewhere, obviously. It's a health and safety rule we're compelled to adhere to, by Hope law. But at this and every time, our safety record is spotless."

Holding out both his spindly fingertips over Nick's temples, the receptionist gave a brief smile. "I will need to touch you briefly for the room inspection and removal, should management deem it suitable. Are you ok with that, sir?" Nick nodded, then flinched once from the coldness of those fingertips upon his skin and the odour of damp carpets in his nostrils. I watched with curiosity as the receptionist leaned forward and sighed, closing his eyes.

I'd heard of *Hotel Infinity* from my dad.

The Hotel allowed guests to forget a room contained in their memory, forever, as long as it was suitable for the hotel's future guests. The room was taken from their memory, and then added to the hotel's inventory, and the next guest could then stay in that room – or any other room which was vacant from the ever-growing list of accommodations. This rather clever arrangement allowed Hotel Infinity to offer limitless rooms (en-suite facilities actually cost money, enabling the hotel to maintain the rooms) and the views were said by some to be enough to either send guests mad, or make them want to stay in the hotel for the remainder of their lives.

This rather unique situation posed a few problems, as time stood absolutely still inside the hotel, but passed normally outside. All too often a guest had stayed far longer than they had anticipated, walking outside for a breath of fresh air, only to find several decades had passed and their dinner reservation at a nearby restaurant cancelled. That was the least of their worries, as they also found almost everyone they knew had either died, or forgotten about them, struggling with fake surprise and regret they'd not been in contact for such a long time, and enraged jealousy they hadn't aged. Some guests chose to stay long-term, wanting to appear immortal, popping out every hundred years or so to see what had changed. But upon meeting such individuals, others living in real-time pointed out experiencing life was the actual point of immortality, not hiding from it.

Historians adopted the hotel as a base to record Hope's ever-changing appearance as it evolved, dutifully venturing outside to ask what had happened over the past twenty-five years. But as this was subjective depending on whom they spoke to, a definitive answer could not be found. Social scientists suffered equally, the honest purity of the answers they sought influenced by the very questions they posed.

A few sought to evade the outside world's obsession with tax, using the hotel's facility as a haven. But as tax collectors wandered the hotel's corridors and foyer, it was only a matter of time before they were caught, as their fines compounded outside. Others thought a few hundred years would allow their meagre bank accounts to grow to substantial fortunes through interest, only to find the economy doesn't work in favour of those who choose not to, as everything increases in a timeless relationship. There was a term for these people upon their eventual return to real-time, and their struggle with real-time: Zeitghosts.

But what I found really interesting was what Dad told me about the artists.

Many tried in vain to abuse the hotel's facility of static time, some realising they would not live long enough to receive the accolades they so richly deserved. Others were aware a lifetime is simply too short a time to complete their ever-mounting collection of ideas.

Writers continued with their magna opera. One, having a novel published with moderate commercial success, was confident her fans in the outside world would be nothing short of ecstatic that her series of one thousand novels, each five hundred pages long, detailing the exploits of the first life-form ever to find consciousness in the cosmos, the adventures of it, its descendants and their friends, over a billion, trillion years would catapult her to literary superstardom. But unfortunately for her the series (which would have taken seventeen lifetimes to complete in real-time) was accused of being a pastiche of several well-established and respected religions that had surfaced during the three hundred years and twenty-two months that had passed outside while she wrote it.

Composers were treated identically, their supporters complaining sonnets of two hundred movements, taking an average of six months to listen to in one sitting, a bit too much – despite generations of fans eagerly anticipating their new works.

Art-lovers and critics eventually came to their senses. They pointed out painters continually illustrating the same view from their hotel window utilising many differing mediums, colouring their (or in many cases, someone *else's* original and far superior work) with a garish wash, an unsubtle overly-contrasting splash, or overlapping coloured outlines, was not pretty. They went on to clarify, such lampooning of the work with laughable cartoonery whilst claiming it as original was simply a deceitful technique, and something you just can't get away with, despite several artists claiming that was *exactly* the definition of art. The artists ignored such critical comments, having ventured from the hotel to sell such works, retreated back inside after exactly fifteen minutes, with empty pockets.

The hotel's long-term resident artists subsequently formed their own movement, *Artofficial,* which for a while at least became a very successful collaborative movement, like all art movements. Painters illustrated the writers' endless tomes, the composers adding musical continuity with seguing leitmotifs and rousing thematic marches to bridge the gap between the two narratives. These combined works found favour in the eyes and ears of the art-lovers for a brief period. But only when violent disagreements arose from how the financial proceeds should be split, did sculpture emerge as the most popular form of art.

One particular piece, *'The Throttling of Emile Bottenard at the Hands of Henri Langerbach, as Hugo Flamus Gouged Out Henri's Eyes,'* became the most popular piece of art in all history. This life-sized black marble work was ultimately destroyed with a sledgehammer by the trio's great-great-grandchildren, joint owners of the sculpture. Conducting this heinous crime in the eyes of the art world at an invitation-only art uninstallation ceremony entitled, *'The Timely Destruction of Static Violence, a Grand Opus in III Acts,'* the great-great-grandchildren collected the broken fragments to grind them to dust before the horrified patrons. Casting this sackful of debris into the sea from a rented rowing boat just off the coast of Viewhaven, the guests watched from the safety of the promenade, relieved as upon the trio's return, they admitted they had each kept several small pieces of the sculpture. In subsequent years, some pieces were auctioned off to art collectors for incredible amounts of money, enabling the trio to purchase further sculptures they didn't particularly like, to repeat the process, elevating their infamy. This expression gave rise to a new movement, *'Violent Deconstructive Expressionism,'* which lasted a decade and a half, during which many sculptors hid their works away, loving their creations more than money.

Many believe just one fragment of the original marble remains, thus *'The Langerbach Right Elbow'* to this day is the most coveted piece of art ever, wherever it was.

But these original artists' few remaining fans could not resist the possibility of meeting their heroes from so long ago. Convinced they were not dead, many fans took up residence in the hotel to tread its infinite corridors in the hope they'd bump into their favourite artist, either in the toilet, or at breakfast that day. None succeeded.

I often wondered where the hotel's first rooms had appeared from, as it was obvious it needed an established inventory for the first ever guest. I found out much later, and will tell you all about it much later too.

I followed as Nick escorted the head receptionist through a door in his memory. The room beyond was brightly lit by a lazy summer afternoon. Light blue walls, large glossy cartoon character stickers upon them in bright primary colours. We walked in. The room smelt clean and fresh, the carpet of cream fibres spongy beneath our feet. Nick walked to the window set in the middle of the far wall. Upon the window sill a radio played music; he reached down and turned it off. Either side of it stood two white cots with mobiles above them. As we looked down to the garden below, Nick's wife began hanging out washing as their twin boys lay asleep in their push buggy. She looked up to him and waved after pegging out his uniform shirt, and Nick smiled, checking himself as he began to wave back at the memory.

"Sufficient?" he muttered.

The head receptionist stood with his hands in his pockets, looking around from the centre of the room. He adopted the air of an estate agent – judgemental, but with a friendly, approachable manner as he craned his thin neck around the room, examining every detail. He knew the market. Nick watched the head receptionist's reflection in the window as he walked slowly towards us, running his index fingers slowly across the top rail of each cot, examining them for dust with a critical squint before standing behind us. There was no dust. He closed his eyes for a moment, then opened them with a tiny smile.

"The owner informs me this is an adequate room." He pointed to the garden below. "This entire memory will form our contract. It's vitally important you realise this memory will be lost to you forever. Are you absolutely *sure* you're happy with this arrangement, sir?"

We watched clothes flapping on the line as she continued pegging them out, then the scene looped, the line free of clothes and she pegged out his shirt before waving again. I felt, no, more than just that, I *knew* Nick wanted to live in this moment forever, or rather live in it as a reality. He yearned to turn and hurry downstairs and out into the garden, to hold his beautiful wife in his arms, the smell of her perfume, the smoothness of her skin, her hair on his face and her laughter in his ears as he picked her up to twirl her around in his arms a few times. Behind all of this, I could sense a foreboding too, a reminder of something terrible as the clothes flapped on the line.

But that twirling didn't happen, that yearning was simply that – an imagined possibility and not the continuation of this memory. He had simply turned and walked into his bathroom to quickly wash blood from his hands and baton.

Nick turned from the view of the garden, looking around the room one final time. "Yes, I'm absolutely sure," he whispered. Orbs began to glow around me as this memory faded, giving way to his imaginings of what he should have done. The orbs pulsated with different colours, throbbing as they detached from their tendrils. They gathered together, growing into a larger, multi-coloured sphere that shook, emitting a shrill screeching resembling a distorted cry for help from a bird in flight, suddenly forgetting how to fly. Then it sped away, and I followed it, swimming through Nick's head, kicking out with my feet, pulling with cupped hands, my body weaving around swaying tendrils, my mind reeling with the possibility I could escape from this prison. Ahead, a black opening appeared, the cry growing to finish as a dying echo as it disappeared through the vanishing hole.

We were back in the hotel's foyer. The head receptionist removed his fingertips from Nick's temples, producing the register from under his desk and a pen from his jacket pocket with an authoritative flourish. He spoke quickly. "Sign here, here and here." Nick scribbled and laid the pen by the side of the register, then a brass key appeared upon the desk before us.

"This key will open the door directly opposite the lift doors when they part. Once opened, only that door from then on. The hotel will automatically assign a randomly generated number to your door, and that number will appear on your key fob. How long do you expect to stay with us, Mr..." he rotated the register and blew upon Nick's signatures, "Adams?"

"Just one night, as I said," said Nick picking up the key to thrust it into a trouser pocket.

"Very good. Do you have any room preferences?"

"None. Just a comfortable bed, that's all. I'm not bothered about a view – a shower-room and WC would be good, but I really just need a place to get changed before I eat."

"Management cannot guarantee comfort, as it's impossible to test every bed, and comfort is obviously subjective. Unfortunately sir, all en-suite rooms are occupied at present, and the foreseeable future, which is a very, very long time. I do, however, have sixteen thousand, two hundred and seventy-one rooms available, containing wash basins. Shower facilities are located each side of the corridor, every fifty rooms. As for the WC, as time is static throughout the hotel, if you don't need the toilet now, you won't for the rest of your stay. There are, however, WCs located every one hundred rooms, should you find yourself in need. Should you inadvertently leave any personal belongings behind upon your departure, they will become the property of the hotel, and be sold beneath the patio colonnade. All proceeds will go to the hotel's chosen charity. The breakfast buffet hall can be reached through the green door in your room. Meal times are anytime, as Hotel Infinity adopts an, 'Eat when you're hungry, not when we tell you' policy. I must say though, please be aware, as you no doubt already are, the wormhole does play tricks on the digestive system, so it's very easy to overeat if you can't remember you already have, which you probably won't, as you haven't. If you have any special dietary requirements, please fill out the form found by the phone in your room and take it with you to the breakfast hall and hand it to my assistant. Just one more detail: no pets or guests allowed in your room, unless previously agreed by the owner manager. Do you have any questions, Mr Adams?"

"Just two. You told me breakfast is served between fourteen and eighteen, every morning, yesterday. Now you're saying I can eat breakfast anytime. Which is it?"

"I assume the convenience of anytime is preferred, rather than the rigorous four hour slot insisted upon by lesser hotels, despite stating you'd not need breakfast? Management simply suggests this make-believe time period, providing guests with a more 'traditional' hotel experience."

"Yes, I'd prefer anytime. But you said time is static, so how will I know when it's fourteen? If I do want breakfast I'd like to get there early, as I hate cold eggs." Nick rubbed his chin. "I don't suppose you serve those little breakfast pizzas?"

The head receptionist bristled. "I can provide sir with a pointless bedside alarm clock, if he would like?" He smiled playfully. "In Hotel Infinity, it's always fourteen. But, in all seriousness, each room has been fitted with a wall clock displaying the date and real-time of outside, should you have an important appointment to keep. And you were correct with your 'I don't suppose.'"

"That's all good to know," said Nick, glancing at his dead watch. "Same day, different shit."

The head receptionist slammed the register closed and it disappeared beneath the desk. "Very well. Good day, sir, and enjoy your stay, however long it appears to be."

Nick refused assistance from the robotic porter offering to carry his bag of clothes to the lift, telling him to do a few things to himself, with a string of expletives, in common binary. The robot shook, probably with the contradiction of the non-executable suggestion, rather than anger. The lift doors closed as he wheeled away. There was only one numbered button on the panel, so Nick pushed it and we jerked sideways, the glass doors displaying a cacophonous view beyond them, as though a million jigsaw puzzles of a million pieces each depicting a different landscape had been thrown together in the air, the pieces struggling in vain to find a matching partner. It was an unnerving kaleidoscopic mosaic of colour, but far more acceptable than lift music, I thought. We watched as each piece displayed a looped image, the view from a window of a forgotten room, like that of Nick's garden view from his boys' bedroom. As I remembered this, I felt an orb appear inside me, to leave my 'body' to hover in front of my face. It was the size of one of the fake pearls dangling from Miss Teacher's neck, but it grew slowly as I watched, gaining colour and substance. I reached out to touch it, and as I cradled it in my hands it became clear to me. The memory I had of Nick's bedroom was now *my* memory, but existing again in Nick's head before me. He dropped his bag of clothes and held his temples, eyes tightly shut, blocking out my jigsaw view as a dozen and three orbs appeared, rapidly circling me. They were ugly, dark, with bright spikes of different sizes, like the outer shell hiding a conker inside. My newborn memory was forbidden in Nick's consciousness, it seemed, and I thought that perhaps the head receptionist had left behind a contractual condition, should the memory of the bedroom Nick had given up somehow resurface. Perhaps if it did, the hotel room would cease to exist, leaving the occupant to an unknown fate – who knew? The spiked orbs came closer, each spinning rapidly on its axis in turn as they focused their attention on my newborn memory. It was an invader, a memory virus to them, I decided, and the orbs were acting like antibodies, determined to eradicate this memory virus from Nick's mind forever. I reached out to snatch it away from them, but a spike touched it, cutting into it. A thick liquid like treacle seeped from the wound, gelatinous globules with fragmented elongated images contorting upon its surface. The spiked orbs pounced upon it, taking it in turn to cut it to shreds, thin slivers of incomplete memory that faded to become brittle before shattering, unable to exist by themselves, ultimately forgotten as insignificant as they dissolved. Perhaps memories cannot exist by themselves, I thought. Perhaps each and every one of them is connected by the slimmest of threads, invisible to me as they nestled themselves comfortably amid the floating seaweed branches, keeping every one of them in the correct order of experience and context.

    Nick opened his eyes and the lift began to slow. As it came to a jerking halt Nick picked up his bag, expecting the glass doors to open. But beyond, that crazy jigsaw puzzle continued, until pieces began to find each other, their seams vanishing in a bright white light, as though they had been welded together. Then the image was as complete as it could be, large areas missing, just as most of my childhood puzzles, as I had become bored with the task – I knew what the pictures were – they were on the front of the boxes. Before us was a collage made up of tiny landscape views, each too small to be seen clearly, and as Nick's focus shifted to take in the whole image, it was as incomplete as my childhood puzzles, but I could see it resembled the face of a man. It vanished as quickly as it had formed, the view beyond the doors of streaking colour, slowing, forming, and I realised many doors in a corridor were passing our lift. They finally slowed, halting with a single bell chime, the door in front of us a plain light wood grain. A second bell chimed and the door displayed a number upon it, 314159265358. Nick felt around in his pocket, pulled out his key, checking the number on the fob. The two were identical, so he opened the door and hurried inside, slamming it behind us.

A featureless hallway of grey walls lay ahead, a circular mirror with a low wooden table beneath it just inside the door, which Nick dropped the key onto. Within minutes he had changed into his new clothes, wincing from the pain in his shoulder as he pulled on his shirt and shoulder holster. Glancing at his reflection he knotted his tie, smoothed back his hair, snatched up his key and was back in the lift. He checked his sidearm, then we were running across the foyer as he pulled on his jacket. The hotel had limitless rooms, but from what he had seen, the patio had limited tables.

He ran up the beach, the rain threatening to extinguish his cooking fire. Frantically he gathered palm leaves and after a while, which stretched into the night, a small shelter had appeared between two palm trees at the fringe of the forest, built from timbers and rigging from the wreck.

The following morning the passage of time along the shore was measured by decomposition.

He listened to it, its brief crescendos and diminuendos punctuated by the rotting corpses, conducted by the breeze. *My orchestra is tuning up*, **he thought.**

Finding a watertight chest, he smashed it asunder to discover paper and ink to make detailed notes. He drew the unfolding horrors laid before him by that tempest, marvelling at their emerging harmonies. Not quite right, fledglings, yet to clarify their parts, to find their niches within the swirling melodies, he thought. He dragged

the chest back to the protection of his shelter, hoping other useful trinkets would assist his new life.

Then early one morning, silence. The breeze motionless along the shore, the tides having reclaimed the redundant instruments. He knew this would be the day of the debut performance.

He walked along the beach looking over them all. His father was still there. His remains, like most, picked at by crabs and gulls, but some of him still remained. Others nearer the water, simply bones, minips holding their breath having crawled out of the water on their two little arms to nibble them clean with their curved beaks. Some instruments had been afforded protection by their clothes, or parts of the shattered vessel. His mother watched without eyes from a palm with a few others perched on high.

Then the breeze began, the first movement a joy to his waiting ears...

As we stood outside looking over the diners, I decided I wasn't in the mood for another menu, or a waiter extolling the virtues of certain dishes. I swam away to an area of Nick's mind I had designated as my sleeping area, to lie on my back, resting, deciding I'd forgo watching Nick eating pizzas (there was almost never just the one) to wake in the morning, sufficiently refreshed to deal with whatever the day presented to us.

As I closed my eyes, I could hear distant conversations, muffled, like listening to Mum and Dad talking in the bedroom next to mine during the weekend mornings as we lay in. Nick mumbled a question; a man's friendly voice answered. Another, then another, both answered confidently. We moved off, Nick's mood happier, warmer, the orbs glowing a contented yellow around me. I sighed as the brightness intensified. It looked as though I'd have to wait until he slept too before I could fully relax and drift off. I rolled onto my side as I used to in my real bed, except there was no wall to face, no shadows from the moonlight interacting with the patterns of the wallpaper for me to make up stories about.

Now there were three voices talking together, Nick's tone apologetic. The man's voice of before, accepting, increasing in pitch a little, mediating. Then a woman's voice, calm, somehow soothing. I fidgeted a little upon hearing that voice, making myself more comfortable as it helped my journey towards sleep. Then just as I was about to drift off, the brightness around me increased again, forcing me to shield my eyes. Nick was certainly very happy about something. I opened my eyes and rolled onto my back, staring into the infinite swaying seaweed above. It was like a clear summer's day amid a meadow in there. I knew exactly what had caused this, as perhaps a few months and six weeks ago I had experienced almost identical circumstances. On that occasion, it was the revelation of Gino's Hawaiian pizza. Yes, I know what you're thinking – what's so special about a Hawaiian pizza, for goodness sake? Well, for Nick, it was quite simple; the fact Gino only used freshly cut pineapples, rather than the tinned rubbish, and most importantly for him, completely fat-free smoked ham. From the glow around me, I could only assume similar circumstances prevailed. Then I heard the tell-tale rasp of a tape measure extending, then retracting a few moments later with a sharp click.

That was all I needed! There was absolutely *no* chance whatsoever of sleeping now. I sat up, angry, pulling my knees up to rest my chin upon them, clasping my shins. This restaurant knew *exactly* what they were doing, and I knew *exactly* what was next. A depth gauge would follow the tape measure, then an adjustable protractor, a tad like a lady's folding fan, but consisting of far more complex jointed leaves. I stood up, pacing in a circle like treading thinned treacle, resigned to the proceedings. Unfortunately Nick had overlooked bringing with him the dental impression template he'd coerced Gruber to take, a few and one years ago.

The mumbling voices returned after the procedure. Nick was *very* pleased, the man's voice, obvious to me now, the waiter's, trailed off. I yawned and stretched, deciding I had no other choice than to be part of Nick's dining experience as the woman's voice found my ears again. As I swam back to my usual position, I realised the tone of their voices was very much like my parents' weekend voices, except Nick's was not as deep and throaty as my father's.

Voices. Oh how they characterise. How they can command respect and compliance, calm and reassure. But I wasn't interested in recounting the various examples I'd experienced during my time outside and inside, and I'm certainly not going to here. I just wanted him to eat and get to bed as soon as possible.

I reached my viewing position. Outside, the suns had set, the soft light from the strings of bulbs above our heads the perfect intensity for dining. Their conversation had stopped, and Nick's eyes were wandering along the rows of tables, where just a few eager shoppers sought a last-minute purchase as the vendors packed the lost property away.

"Is this your first visit to Hope?"

Nick's eyes remained on the tables. I felt him grin. "I've been asked that so many times today. No, it's not. But it's my first visit to this part of town. Yourself?"

There was a clink of a china teacup being placed upon a saucer. I looked to the side but just caught the edge of the menu as it was brought up to obscure my view of the diner seated opposite.

"Oh I've lived here a while now."

That voice, so soothing. I began to yawn again, wishing the waiter would return with Nick's perfectly customised, bespoke pizza. And yes, I knew it would be perfect. The tape measure providing the chef with an exact measurement of the width of Nick's mouth, the depth gauge ensuring the radius of the pizza allowed Nick to place an entire slice into his mouth, the protractor guaranteeing the arc of the outside edge just before the crust (or handle as Nick called it) matched the curve of his teeth perfectly, from his central incisors down to his second molars. He'd obviously ordered a custom combo – a single pizza consisting of concentric rings of different toppings, enabling him to enjoy every topping of a single slice together in one mouthful, or politely bite through or cut apart sections with a fork and pizza wheel, enjoying each concentric ring in whatever order he decided was best. I knew how he'd approach it upon its arrival – I'd seen these things before.

"A while?" His gaze fell across the table, the menu held up, hiding his dining partner's face. I was really beginning to lose patience now, my fatigue not helping my mood. I turned my back, deciding to return to my bed of sorts, aware this could extend way into the evening, especially if Nick found a dessert and a whiskey to his liking, which, judging by the size of the menu was very likely.

"Almost forty years."

"You don't look old enough to have been living here that long."

The voices receded behind me. Another damned artist, I thought.

"Living in the hotel, forty years of real-time. I'm thirty-two."

"Of course, that's why you're sitting here. This type of weirdness is new to me. Are you living by yourself – I'm guessing you don't have family living in real-time, outside the hotel?"

"My husband. He's inside looking for a mop. There's water coming in under the skirting board in our room. Anion, the head receptionist, believes it's caused by the quantum leak. We alternate our time outside."

My eyes were so tired.

"Apart? But doesn't that make things difficult for your marriage?"

"We're working apart, but together. For the same...I'm sorry, I haven't caught your name?"

"Nick."

"Good evening, Nick. Please take a leaflet. I'm Charlotte. My husband and I are searching for my daughter."

~ 12 ~
Second Hand Memories

Oh how my heart pounded, or the equivalent. I swam back as fast as I could.

Nick was looking at a paper flyer, an artist's pencil illustration of roughly how I looked on the day of my murder. Across the top of the flyer: **MISSING CHILD. Please contact Anion at Hotel Infinity if you've seen her.**

I was so confused, so fearful for my mum, and so very, very angry.

What had mum said? *Forty years*?

I knew I hadn't been inside Nick's head that long, I couldn't have been.

The pizza arrived and Nick passed the flyer back to my mum. She hadn't changed, she was still as beautiful as I remembered her. But then I noticed her hair wasn't as smooth, a few grey strands streaking through it. There were deep lines at the bottom of her cheeks either side of her face, and her eyes seemed not as bright, so full of remorse.

Nick shook his head as he regarded his pizza. I moved forward as far as I could, my hands either side of my face, my nose pressed against the invisible window as I tried to look up at my mum. "I arrived in Hope today. Sorry, I don't remember seeing her." He picked up a slice, placing it all into his mouth, chewing quickly. His eyes fell on my mum again, the colour of my surroundings changing, and I knew exactly what he was thinking. I screamed, banging my fists upon the window, urging her to run, to get back to the safety of her room as fast as she could.

Nick finished his mouthful. "And what will you do when you find her?"

"Buy somewhere here to live. That was always our plan."

That was all he needed. An inroad, however slight, however seemingly trivial, he'd found it. His wallet was in his hands before my mum could blink.

"I run several property developments from my business in Middletown. We have quite a few properties in Hope for sale, as well as Middletown and its outlying areas. Come and pay me a visit." He held out his card, and we watched as its details changed, the silver letters contorting and squirming upon the satin black card, quickly rearranging themselves to confirm exactly what he'd said. He grinned, angling it over to my mum as the letters stopped pushing each other around like kids queuing up for an ice cream.

"Don't touch it!" I screamed. But it was too late. As she took it, a wave of light only Nick and I could see coursed from the card into her fingers, reaching up her arm to envelop her body. She stared at the card, as though lost in thought, frozen. The light vanished and she blinked, looked up and thanked him, the low-level magik placing a recurring instruction in her mind to visit Nick's 'office' as soon as possible. I'd seen this so many times, and knew exactly what was to come if my mother did so.

I swore. I'm not going to write what I shouted, but rest assured it was dreadful.

The waiter appeared at our table. "Thank you, Marcus," said Mum, placing the card in her purse. "See you tomorrow, usual time."

Marcus picked up her cup and saucer. "Good evening, Charlotte."

Mum stood as Marcus hurried away, made her apologies to Nick and walked towards the revolving doors, his eyes following her every single step of the way, studying her form, her height, the length of her legs. 'Yes,' he thought. 'You may fit.'

When she was out of sight he returned to his pizza, a niggling thought causing a partial memory to glow briefly, like the times you can't remember a word, saying it's on the tip of your tongue. I wondered at this, paying it little thought, putting it down to the deja vu trick on the brain many believed incorrectly was a direct result of a shoddy time-travel memory scrub residue. Utter rubbish.

I thought about my mum and dad, that forty year span she'd mentioned. If it were accurate, then Keloff would be fifty-two years old almost, and more worrying, if Dad had spent a lot of time searching the streets of Hope for me, there was the possibility he'd be almost seventy-eight. It all made terrible, bitter sense to me.

We had made arrangements to meet in Hope, to see if their search for a new house had been successful. But then I began to wonder again; if they'd gone to my great uncle's earlier than arranged to pick me up, what did they find there? And where on earth was Charles?

My poor dad. I could only feel even more guilty for putting him through yet more heartache. I so desperately wanted to see him again, wanted all four of us, our family, to be back together and put behind us all these crazy episodes that had torn us apart. I yearned for a normal life as much as Nick would have, if he remembered his children's bedroom. Then I came to terms with the fact I'd never have one. I realised, I didn't really know what a normal life was, not completely.

As Nick began his third slice of pizza, his niggling thought had shrunk into an almost insignificant, fading notion. I noticed from the corner of his eyes the waiter standing at our table again. Except, waiters usually wear shoes, and don't usually wear skin-tight long blue denim shorts beneath their aprons.

Perhaps my recognition somehow gave Nick advance warning – it's impossible for me to say. Maybe the girl had a certain perfume she was fond of, and it had found Nick's nostrils, or she had another odour which alerted him. Nothing glowed around me to confirm either theory.

His fingertips touched his gun as the tray she carried caught him squarely on the forehead, sending his chair backward into the table behind us. It rested there as though Nick were at the barber's waiting for a shave. A big, black and ugly weapon was in her hand, a sneer across her face as she levelled it at his forehead, her head tilting a little to the side as the sneer became a smile. Nick kicked out with his right foot and the weapon left her right hand as a shot rang out, tumbling over to skid under a table. His second kick with both feet found her stomach, sending her into the narrow gap between a couple of tables. People screamed as Nick let off a couple of rounds, "Why is it always when I'm eating?" he screamed, as the girl rolled onto all fours, scrambling towards her weapon as the two shells splintered the concrete where her feet had just been.

I sat back, cursing the fact my thoughts surrounding my family had been postponed.

Guests ran in various directions, which was very strange as they had to be hotel residents, or at least most of them.

Nick was on his feet as the girl grabbed her weapon, holding it with both hands, letting off two precisely aimed shots into the air. Two lengths of light bulbs swung free, impacting Nick in slivers of coloured glass. He shook the splinters away, his first shot ricocheting with an angry spark upon the table she hid beneath, the second taking a chip out of a chair leg. The girl screamed in agony as the splintered iron careered into her right shoulder. Nick advanced, his gun held directly in front of him, another shot and another, forcing the girl back, herding her gradually out of the maze of tables and chairs. She scrambled away, weaving left and right, letting out a burst of fire in reply. This time her shots were random, and Nick knew he had the advantage. She ran free of the tables and chairs, joining the screaming throng heading for the hotel's revolving doors. He raised his gun and swore, lowering it, knowing he couldn't risk a shot into the crowd as he pushed tables and chairs aside. The screaming continued as she fired into the air, urging the people into the hotel. Nick ran, pushing past guests, pulling some out of his way as he reached the bottleneck squeezing through the doors. At last he was in the foyer, searching the masses, his head jerking left and right, gun held up at his side.

Anion was standing at the reception desk as Nick slid to a halt in front of him. "Bald girl, wearing red and blue. Have you seen her?"

"I'm sorry, Mr Adams, hotel rules clearly state we cannot divulge guests' room numbers. It's purely a..."

"Don't need her room number. Don't know her name." He turned to look along the row of lifts. Unable to see the doors, he climbed onto Anion's desk, scanning the people.

"Mr Adams, this is highly irregular. May I remind..."

"Is climbing on the reception desk in your rule book?" barked Nick, glancing at him for a split second.

Anion took a booklet from a clear plastic holder to his left and held it up. "Not exactly. However, a sub-clause in section four could be interpreted..."

Nick raised his gun and emptied his clip into the air. As the empty clip hit the desk a replacement snatched from his shoulder holster snapped into the grip. He pulled back the slide. The people crouched down, some lay on the floor, all but one. Her face creased with anger and pain as she turned in his direction. She was breathing hard.

"There," he cried, pointing with his gun to let off a shot.

She ran past the row of lifts, clutching her shoulder. Nick jumped down, grabbing the empty clip to holster it.

"Sir, before you disturb the sanctity of our beloved existence further, I must point out the direction in which she's heading leads to lost property storage. This is located at the end of the foyer corridor, and has only one door. Please, try not to damage the personal belongings there." He flapped the booklet in the air. "This *is* mentioned in the rule book."

Nick grinned, smoothed back his hair and straightened his clothes. And then, for what was certainly the first time in a very long time, he began to whistle his tune as he walked forward.

He'd found a chair, placed it directly in the centre of the orchestra, pushing the legs down into the pebbles to secure it.

He waited, whistling the tune that had briefly found his ears the day before. It had emerged as the instruments found their tunings, peering out of the confusion, the unordered dissonance that dissolved, only to die as the breeze fell. It had teased him with what was to emerge.

Then his symphony began again as the breeze licked the shoreline with its encouraging tongue. He had remembered the notes precisely from the day before, pitch perfect. And as the breeze touched each of them in turn, bringing their parts forward, ensuring their essential passages found his ears at exactly the correct cue, his whistling ceased. He picked up his stout piece of wood, waving it in the air as if it were a conductor's baton. The breeze rose and fell, removing each instrument's participation promptly from the piece with a diminishing lull, as soon as their roles were complete. It grew and they resumed their accompaniments.

He smiled broadly and smoothed back his hair, placing his baton under his arm, clapping his hands together with overwhelming pleasure. He laughed at the beauty performed for him, sitting down, pushing his chair back a little as his body stiffened with glee. Unable to remain still, he stood, hurrying to the first instrument, kneeling before it, allowing its essential component to come forward to his ears, so he could experience how its essential melancholy role intermingled with the others.

It was his father. The breeze coursed between the cracks of his shattered skull, whistling as it went, the pitch changing, the notes altering correspondingly. The hole at the top of his skull resonated, his teeth (or rather where there were gaps in the two rows), added their own harmonious phrases. He clapped his hands again, dancing down the shore between them to listen to the next performer. She was magnificent. The minips, short of breath and eager for food, had pecked through her bones in various places, several of them dead from suffocation beside her. The breeze, having now grown, coursed through her bones, the holes covered occasionally by the flapping of her dress, producing a melody so sweet to his ears, intoxicating beyond any music he'd ever heard.

Elsewhere, a shattered pelvis added low notes from hip joint sockets, sinews vibrated between joints, cartilage flapping against bone, spinal cords oscillating, tendons producing notes above cavities as the wind strummed them.

Finally, led by his mother, the crescendo of percussion. Bones firmly fixed in the palms striking against boughs and each other. The prelude was complete.

He sat back in his chair, closing his eyes, listening as his music slowly faded throughout the morning. He breathed a thank you and opened his eyes, and there on the horizon a ship belching black smoke from a single funnel. Before it, a rowing boat heading towards his orchestral shore.

I was surprised how relaxed Nick was. The guests parted for him and avoided eye contact as he headed for the double doors at the end of the corridor, strolling leisurely past them. His eyes blinked between the intermittent spots of blood upon the floor and the double doors. The trail stopped there, the doors ajar.

"Nowhere to go, girly. It would be better for both of us if you slide out your weapons and come out, hands on your head," shouted Nick into the gap between the doors.

Three shots impacted the edge of the door, a splinter finding Nick's cheek. He swore, took a few paces back, pulling the splinter out to drop it onto the floor. "You're bleeding badly, I can get you patched up. I just wanna ask you some questions." A single shot impacted the wood again. She has the advantage, thought Nick. He turned to look towards the front of the hotel for the first time. Either side and above the revolving doors, the sunlight shone brightly through a collection of windows, stretching to the high ceiling. They were a mismatch of many differing architectural styles, almost seamlessly blended together to dominate the front of the hotel. But where we both expected to see the colonnade lining the patio of overturned tables and chairs, with the buildings of Hope in the distance, we saw the countryside. It was lush, unordered. An ethereal forest of tall, perfectly straight trees, moss-covered rocky outcroppings, caressed by shaded ferns. Nick looked up slowly, his mouth agape. Shards of sunlight pierced the leafy canopy, highlighting the dew perched upon the lichen and wild flowers, dotted amid the grass. He shook his head and looked down. The foyer had retuned to normality, such as it was. The guests had thinned out, and he noticed a robotic porter emerge from a lift. "Hey, you!" he called, holstering his weapon. Walking quickly forward he kept turning back to face the doors, looking for any signs of movement.

The robotic porter stood to attention. "Sir?"

"I need a hand."

The robot looked down to his sides, then up to Nick. "I have two available. If sir has more than the customary two pieces of luggage, I can summon a colleague with multiples of two, up to a maximum of eight hands."

Nick turned to the doors, then back to the porter. "Yeah, get me one with eight."

There *were* no pirates anymore, he knew that. No buried chests with silver pieces, bright yellow gold, perfectly faceted jewels and handfuls of pearls. There were no fools searching the seas, clutching a ragged map of an unknown island where X marked the spot.

The sea sheriffs had crushed these dreams, tearing the pirates' marauding ships to matchsticks with their superior vessels of steam, two dozen and fifteen years before.

Their huge armoured hulks, forthright, supporting giant rotating cannons situated amidships caused the pirate ships to flee, as they knew a single shot from this monstrous tunnel-like maw would cut their ships cleanly in two.

But there was no escape either by tides, currents or trade winds from the sheriffs' wrath, and when the last remaining pirate ship came to rest in pieces upon the ocean floor, the sheriffs took their authority into the coves, the sheltered bays, the coastal inns, to trim the fringes of the land from corruption, thievery, and murder. To the land they returned, following the fleeing criminals back to their strongholds. And when all was set, the night came when five hundred vessels awaited their call, to obliterate the strongholds from the safety of the sea.

He frowned at the sight, but found himself waving back to that rowing boat edging closer to his shore. "Hoy!" came a cry, then the rasp of the keel upon the pebbles, as ten men jumped clear.

The captain of *'A Precious Sky'* held him by the shoulders. "You're safe now, son. I'll have you home before month's end."

"But *this* is my home."

"Nonsense, lad. This is a horror no young man should see. A place you cannot live for the rest of your life."

The sailors turned away from the sights they saw, and he watched their faces, unable to understand their repulsion towards his orchestra.

Four men took the captain back to his ship, the remaining five staying with him. One gave him fresh water, another cooked a nutritious meal for them all, as the ship's doctor examined him. The remaining two

stood guard, peering into the forest's darkness where nothing lay in wait.

The eight-handed porter was as Nick expected as he turned from peering into the darkness between the doors. He was wide, stocky and most importantly, large enough for Nick to hide behind upon entering the lost property office.

"I've misplaced my hat," lied Nick. "I'm told it's located in lost property."

"The officer in charge will require details. How may I be of assistance?"

"You can help me search for it. Two heads are better than one, and eight hands better than two."

The machine, bright chrome, three wheels like Nick's trike beneath its inverted triangular chassis, a single eye like a ring doughnut on its side with an antenna sticking up through the hole, seemed to think about what Nick had said. Its arms extended and folded in front of it.

"You are the guest that instructed my colleague, VICFS6181 to go and reboot himself back to factory settings. We are here to carry luggage. You are a product of coupling with your own progenitor." The machine turned and hurried away. Nick opened his mouth to argue, but thought better of it, simply cursing under his breath. He returned to lost property, opening the door with his foot just wide enough to pass through. He timed his entrance perfectly – but that was down to practice, having used this technique many times before, rolling through the gap head over heels into the darkness.

Silence. As his eyes adjusted to the light, his body to the sudden drop in temperature. He shivered, peering into the darkness, feeling the rough sand between his fingers as sunlight found his face. We looked up with curiosity; ahead some way off, a narrow wooden kiosk with a metal grille. Behind it, Anion's disinterested expression. We turned around. There the door to the corridor was as Nick had left it, open just enough for the sounds of guests' chatter to filter through, providing us with a view of the row of lifts. Nick turned quickly to face the kiosk. A sun had crept into the cloudless sky. The desert stretched as far as the eye could see, dunes upon dunes, waves before waves, a still ocean made of orange sand.

"How may I be of assistance, Mr Adams, if memory serves?"

Nick looked around as he walked forward. "I'm looking for the girl. She came in here just a few minutes ago. You must have seen her."

"Do you own this girl?"

"No."

"Then she's not your lost property, is she?"

"We had a fight, on the patio – you must remember, I stood on your desk."

"Oh, yes. I remember now, causing an addition to the rule book." He smiled, shaking his head, "So very long ago."

"Have you seen her!?"

"Of course I have. There's absolutely no need to shout. And, as I said, that was so very long ago."

"So where did she go?"

"Nowhere, really, Mr Adams. You see, the hotel is now closed for business. The quantum leak became a little too much for maintenance, causing all kinds of problems, especially with breakfast service. The manager decided to keep this facility open for as long as possible, should a previous guest return for an item. There are six thousand and twenty nine items still unclaimed, and you have approximately nine billion years or so years before the last sun vanishes from the sky. Plenty of time, I'm sure you'll agree, if you were artificial."

It became clear to me a few moments before Nick realised the situation we found ourselves in. He holstered his gun and pulled his jacket straight, staring across the dunes as the suns moved swiftly across the sky, their shadows creeping across the landscape like the movement of a silent ocean. We were at the end of everything, not an actual room as we both expected, but outside, where Hope had stood many millions of years before.

Nick jerked a thumb over his shoulder. "So I passed through that door too late. That's what you're saying."

"In essence, yes," replied Anion. "Far too late to catch up with the girl. If memory serves, which it usually does, she returned to the foyer, perused the gift shop and bought herself a small first aid kit, a fridge magnet, a pair of sunglasses and an embroidered hotel towel. I pointed out the box of chocolates shaped like doors were on special offer, but she declined as they were sugar free."

Nick pointed. "And she went back through that door."

Anion nodded. "Moments ago, but for you, standing here, several hundred thousand years. If you hurry, you might catch her."

We were back in the corridor in seconds, a fresh trail of blood upon the floor. As we reached the foyer, Nick spotted her, carrying a brown paper carrier bag over her shoulder, emblazoned with *'Hotel Infinity Gift Shop, Memories that Last.'* As he stood to take aim, she reached into the bag and pulled out a pair of sunglasses, putting them on to look around. I didn't like them at all. She smiled as she spotted us, pulling them down to reveal her blazing eyes, smiling as a door appeared in front of her. In a moment she opened it and stepped through, closing it behind her before it vanished.

Nick swore, causing a few heads to turn our way. He thought better of asking Anion further questions and headed to the lifts.

He dropped his key onto the side table then strolled down the hall to the door and his hotel room beyond.

The bed had a big fluffy eiderdown with plumped up pillows resting against the arched wooden headboard. Nick ignored everything and strode to the window, placing his palms upon the low chest of drawers, staring into the garden that sloped up to a fence boundary. He looked down, and as the raindrops coursed down the window in haphazard lines, I saw myself running up the garden, my woolly hat with the pink pompom keeping me dry as I began my search for Charles.

I cried, longer than I ever had in the real world. And, even floating there in Nick's head, it hurt, hurt more than any pain I'd ever experienced so far.

Why had such an evil trick been played upon me? Why was Nick now lying on my bed staring at the ceiling, in a memory someone else had of that day so long ago? Why had they decided to discard it, to casually cast it aside as irrelevant and unimportant to them? My thoughts tumbled over each other. Was it Mum's memory? Had she hurried upstairs to put her talking map away, or on an errand she'd forgotten to complete? And why would she choose to forget my room, and perhaps all the bedtime stories she'd told me, the conversations we'd had? I struggled to remember. Did I turn and wave to her, as she watched me from the kitchen door? I couldn't remember, couldn't remember how long I'd been out in the rain looking for Charles, either. I concentrated as Nick shook his watch, wound it and held it to his ear again. Silence, just the memory rain spitting against the window, the sound looping in a rhythm of the past, over and over, mocking my inability to remember.

Nick cursed the watch, unbuckled the leather strap to throw it onto my rug in the centre of the room without a second thought. It was a release for those tiny metal components, and as it lay there alone, I was sure it ticked once more, just one tiny movement through its saddened mechanisms, a moment for itself before it refused to measure for anyone else ever again. A second-hand's final memory. I envied it. He felt naked without it on his wrist, so decided to leave early the next day, out into the streets to find a new timepiece, before his appointment.

I began to feel my tears rise up again as I remembered coming back inside with Charles in my arms. He was asleep, and Mum was sitting by the fire, smoking one of Dad's cigarettes. She was eager for me to play outside in the rain, that was obvious. Either someone else was in the house, watching me, hiding in my room as Mum carried on with the washing up, or it was Mum's memory. I shivered at the prospects. Or was that the reason she was so impatient for me to go outside, so she could talk to that unknown person standing in my room? The nervous, distant mood I found her in, smoking, staring into the fire, a release for her following that unknown conversation, and not as I thought at the time, a reaction to recounting her awful Aunt Scalas episode?

Nick began to laugh, louder than I'd ever heard before as he clasped his hands behind his head, stretching as he closed his eyes, making himself comfortable as I curled up, crying my soul to sleep.

And there a dream surfaced, a memory dream, intertwining with Nick's amusing recollection and his subsequent memory dream as we both slept.

They all slept, except Nick. In the half-light he took detailed notes, measurements, carefully cataloguing his beloved orchestra. Satisfied, he stored the information in the trunk he had found, sleeping next to it as darkness fell.

The captain woke him the next morning. "We're all set to leave. The tide is with us, lad, and the wind's rising. Gather whatever you need and be quick about it."

The cook handed him a plate of bread, cheese and cold roasted chicken as he rubbed his eyes. A prelude began, a soft lament, different from the magnificent overture he'd enjoyed yesterday. He sat up to listen, taking the plate absently to place it beside him.

This movement was far superior to the first, a rousing theme in which all his instruments participated

in perfect harmony. Yesterday's performance was simply a rehearsal, he realised.

He stood and hurried to his chair, sitting down to close his eyes. The music washed over him, coursing into his soul. It was majestic to him, and tears welled up in his eyes.

But voices interrupted, chattering sailors with disrespectful complaints. He tried in vain to block them out, closing his eyes tighter, but then an instrument's harmony vanished. He opened his eyes and screamed, picking up his baton, running to the sailors gathering the remains of a passenger to be taken back to the ship.

His baton blow sent the sailor tumbling across the pebbles. The others reacted quickly, dropping the remains in a discordant punctuation of clattering bones across the rhythm. They seized him, and he struggled and screamed at them, pleading with the captain as he hurried over to release him.

They held him as the others silenced his instruments one by one, his grand movement gradually erased from his ears, to finish as his mother's remains were cut down from the mast.

All was silent. Just the sound of oars ploughing the water as he sat shackled in the rowing boat. He watched the shoreline as it diminished, crying for the greatest loss he had ever experienced. His symphony had been curtailed at its triumphant height, preventing its conclusion.

It's time to go back to my fateful trip with grandpa Roan. That experience and Nick's memory dream entangled with mine that night in the hotel, filling in the blank spaces I wasn't aware of as he slept on my bed.

I steered the little escape balloon towards home, the amplificator spluttering complaints behind me as I strained to sit upright and forward to see above the cockpit dials. The rows of houses comprising my village were growing larger, becoming clearer through my tears, and there was Mr and Mrs Cribbage's white house, tall and proud, the biggest house in the crescent arcing behind my street. I banked a little to the left, heading toward it, wondering where and how I was going to land.

The amplificator spat and coughed again. I knew then this little craft wasn't designed for journeys as such, but more for just getting Grandpa out of trouble and safely to the ground. We began to lose height as the coughing behind me stopped, then it sneezed and began to hum once more. I looked at a gauge, it telling me the engine was almost out of propellant oil as we reached the edge of the village.

And there was Mrs Cribbage, standing on her chimney veranda peering through her telescope straight at me.

I lifted the canopy latch, sliding the clear glass oval back. The wind was mad, rushing in my ears, pulling at my hair as I steered to the left a little more, waving and shouting. "It's me! Get Mum and Dad, quickly!" as we circled the veranda once. Mrs Cribbage waved back, hurrying as best she could to the other side of the veranda facing our back garden, shouting for my parents. What could they do, how could they help me? I had no choice other than to land on the road – hoping the little vehicle had wheels beneath it.

Mr and Mrs Cribbage's house sat at the highest point of the crescent. I aimed for the slope leading up to their house, hoping that would help slow us. I held Charles tightly with my left hand as the ground came up so very quickly, and we bounced twice on the road before the escape balloon settled, squeaking and groaning, the amplificator giving one final splutter as I pushed the red button in front of me. We began to slow, but before I knew it, we were passing Mr and Mrs Cribbage's front garden, picking up speed heading down the hill. I took the wheel with both hands as Charles began to stir on my lap, sitting up as best I could to see where we were going. Now we were on the bend, and I steered to the right, gritting my teeth as the squeaking and groaning became screaming and grinding. Up onto the pavement the vehicle jumped, scraping against a front garden wall with a shower of sparks – another and then a fence, the white posts clickity-clacking together as we ploughed into them. Now the bend straightened out, and I looked over to Mum and Dad standing at our gate, giving them a quick wave as we whizzed past, their mouths agape. I stared ahead, and there a few men worked on dismantling the stage from last night's celebrations. I heard Dad shout. They turned, froze for a moment before jumping clear as we went careering into the wooden framework.

I woke up in bed, Mum sitting beside me, her expression etched with concern, Dad sitting cross-legged on my rug, his hands cradling his cheeks as he stared down.

They explained we were both very lucky, the partially dismantled stage cushioning the impact. The escape balloon was ruined, I had a few bumps and a cut on my right arm and Charles wasn't very happy he'd missed everything.

I explained what had happened and Dad was on his feet. "I'll go and look for him."

"That's what Mrs Cribbage was telling us last night, the star she'd seen," said Mum, turning to Dad. "It must have been this 'slab.'"

"Stay in bed, honey, and relax," said Dad, holding out his hand for Mum. "We'll be back as soon as we can."

Nick watched them approach, a man and a woman hurrying across the fields. They held hands, a couple from the village, perhaps. Behind them was an old couple, struggling to keep up, the old woman muttering things excitedly and pointing to the sky. The site had already drawn attention from the nearby village, and he and Williams had been told by their chief to keep the people back. He turned, watching the chief muttering with a

Truthsayer some way off, near the giant black monstrosity towering silently above them.

The chief and the Sayer nodded to each other and came over.

"I will deal with this," said the Sayer from beneath his hood.

Nick nodded as the man called over. "Have you seen a balloon? A big balloon with black and orange triangles?"

"Please, stand back sir. For your own..."

"I said I will deal with this, officer," said the Sayer, walking in front of Nick. "What are you doing here?"

Nick watched as the burly man let go of his partner's hand, crouching down a little in an attempt to see the face hidden by the long hood. "I'm looking for my father. He saw this thing land."

"If he saw this land, then why are you looking for him?"

"My daughter was with him. She escaped just before that thing crushed the balloon he was in."

"She is mistaken. This came up from the earth."

"Then what happened to the forest?"

The Sayer took a step forward as the old woman spoke. "I saw it in the sky, watched it approach over the past three nights."

"The forest sits atop, complete and hidden from view. And no, there are no visitors from the sky. It is impossible. You are out of context. Both of you have an infraction level score of three."

"Leet?"

Nick nudged Williams as the burly guy took another step closer.

The hood came back swiftly, revealing a shaven head. "You will address me as Oversayer Skarlac. I am Sheriff and in truth of this district."

The chief called Nick and Billie over. "You two, this shit's going to escalate, creep into our jurisdiction. We don't need these hooded clowns crawling through Middletown's streets. There's enough crazy shit to deal with. Do what needs to be done to protect the innocent, then get back to your duties. Understood?" They looked at each other then saluted.

"But my daughter saw it – she's not a liar! And if this thing came out of the earth, where's my father's balloon?" he gestured behind him, pleading for him to see sense. "And what did Mrs Cribbage here see?"

"Your daughter's recent participation in the disruption of a Thinking class has been deemed as a level one infraction. She will be monitored for further infractions and arrested for her contradictions of reality, when she becomes an adult."

Nick wasn't quick enough to stop the burly guy. The single blow sent the Sayer onto his back in a flurry of his cloak and hood. The guy stood over him as the woman tried to pull him back. "And what about Keloff, did he get away with his involvement, Leet?"

Nick's revolver was in his hands. "Sir, please step away."

"You're not in charge here – Land Sheriffs are," he replied without looking over as he stood above the Sayer with his fists clenched.

"I don't see any here. Now, *step away, sir*."

"Aiden, do as he says," said the woman, finally dragging him back by his arm.

Nick holstered his gun slowly, pulling down his peaked cap as if to acknowledge the woman's assistance.

"My son has been punished, as is my right as his adoptive father." The Sayer stood up, rubbing his jaw. "He will be monitored, as will you and your wife." He brushed himself down and lifted his head as Nick quickly stood between them.

"Sir, go home." He looked between the two couples. "All of you. There's no evidence of a balloon, we've searched all around this thing and there's nothing to see."

Mr and Mrs Cribbage turned to walk back to the village, the burly man's eyes lingering on the Sayer's before the woman took him by the hand. Nick watched them leave, the Sayer heading north across the fields.

"Billie, best you follow them. Make sure they go home. We'll give it a day and a quarter then pay them a visit, tell them what's best for them, keep the peace, as the chief said. I'll follow this Sayer character and do the same."

Nick stirred on my bed, rolling on his side. The memory jumped, stuttered in his head.

The stuttering gradually slowed, settling on a scene.

He knocked on the door. Keloff opened it. He answered a question, closed the door.

The barn, the smell of farrengrass tobacco, sawdust and propellant oil. Tools hanging from racks, shelves of dented paint cans, dried runs over their rusted shells obscuring peeling paper labels.

Leet, dressed in his brown canvas work overalls was cleaning his hands with a rag. As Nick spoke he turned from the bench where he'd been working on a row of pickingweavers.

They shook hands. Nick seemed interested in what Leet was doing, watching him as he picked up a pickingweaver, placing it in a wooden tray in front of him.

He explained, turning on the machine, allowing it to crawl around on its six little legs, the intricate mechanical device looking for its bobbin chassis. Leet took one from a cardboard box beneath his bench and clipped it gently onto the pickingweaver's back. The machine stopped, calibrating itself with tinny bleeps and clicks, the bobbin chassis spinning slowly at first, before it picked up speed. It walked around the tray looking for a mothcotton plant, picking claws snapping in the air before it, eyes darting in all directions on their stubby stalks.

Nick looked around the barn as he spoke, warning Leet to stay out of Middletown, but Leet refused.

Nick's nightstick was in his hands in seconds – it came down hard on the tray, next to the little pickingweaver, the machine's eyes turning to look up at the dark oak as it and the tray settled upon the bench. The nightstick still retained several of its original designs from when it was part of the ship, but had now been shaped into a tool for attack and defence, rather than conducting an orchestra. Nick lifted it slowly, repeating his demand, the pickingweaver watching it rise. Leet maintained his stance. The nightstick came down again, smashing into the intricate device. It whimpered, struggling to escape on three legs, scurrying haphazardly in circles.

Nick spoke again, raising the nightstick above his head. Leet said nothing, a pause before the nightstick came down, smashing the pickingweaver to pieces. Leet took a step forward, but the nightstick's thick rounded end was instantly held in front of his throat. The jab caused Leet to stumble back, coughing, holding his throat as the nightstick glanced into his temple, sending him to the ground. He pleaded with Nick, holding up his hands, waving them for mercy before folding his forearms across his face as the nightstick came down upon his head.

It was morning when I awoke from that terrible memory dream, and I worried what had become of Leet and Keloff, determined, should I ever escape from Nick's head, their farm would be the first place I'd visit.

The sounds of the streets of Hope were playful, content. Cobbles of bright circular basalt polished by years of eager footsteps lined the twisting pavements. There were no vehicles here, horses the only transport allowed in the streets. The buildings of brick were reinforced with wooden beams, brightly painted in all sorts of primary shades. Hope was beautiful to the eyes compared to Middletown, but one pair of eyes knew this place would ultimately fall foul of his influence in good time.

My thoughts returned to Nick's broken watch.

I had seen many an adult life become limited by their occupations as they grew older. When young, they were free to roam, to seek and explore all that life gave. But, as they settled into routine, routine demanded certain routes, governed by appointments, limited by time – or rather the perception of it and how very little of it they were unallocated each day for themselves.

The most time-effective journey to work, a straight line though adult life, providing these poor creatures with a limited view, like blinkered racehorses running in circles unaware of the empty unexplored fields just an unseen stone's throw away.

Time squeezed people, stifling and suffocating, dominating their lives as they struggled to complete demands thrust upon them, governed by the little devices strapped to their wrists. It was a battle hardly ever won.

Time to get up. An instant, not a window of convenience. Breakfast time, a narrow area, a prelude to the day. Journey time, lunch time – an hour and a sliver, if they were lucky, and for most, less. Then home time, dinner and then bednight time. I recall struggling against bednight time with all my might, as all children have done and will continue to do forever, afraid to become their parents as they watch them constantly searching for their own time as they carry out their ever mounting daily tasks. I had asked my mother just the once as she tucked me in bed; 'Why do you put me in bed when I'm awake and the day is not over, yet when I'm asleep wake me up, when the day has barely begun?"

She didn't answer, she just smiled as she wished me goodnight and kissed me on the forehead, before pulling my bedroom curtains closed against the last setting sun.

Yet life provides us with our *own* time in little slices, instants to look forward to, and when these little slices are found they are precious beyond measure, for every adult is aware they vanish almost as soon as they are found, as though time itself deceives us when we're not looking, as to its true duration and ultimately, priceless value.

I knew Nick needed these slices of life more than anyone, but he would be the last to admit it. We didn't have time, time had us, and for me it was running out.

He found a shop window displaying hundreds of wrist watches, and without giving any one of them a second glance, he walked in, almost walking into the 'Caution – Wet Floor' sign just inside the door.

A brass bell above the door chimed twice and the horologist looked up from her counter.

"Good day. How can I help?"

"Er, I need a watch," said Nick, tempted to ask her for a loaf of bread and a cup cake.

"What type of watch. We have hundreds here. Any particular style, make or model?"

"I just need a watch, it doesn't matter."

She smiled a confused smile, as though he had walked into a shop of a thousand different cream cakes and asked for a purple lampshade, so there was from my point of view an unconscious connection of confusion between them immediately.

"Watches are very personal, sir. They reflect your inner self, make a statement to others unlike any other adornment." She bent down and pulled out a tray from the glass display cabinet, placing it gently upon the counter in front of him. "We have some very special pieces designed, made in and imported from Steeltown. I'm sure you'll find one to your liking. If not, we have examples from all over the twenty-eight districts."

"I hate Steeltown, makes my shit itch," said Nick, looking down with disinterest. "Just a watch." He looked up and stared into her eyes with determination, speaking slowly. "Just a watch."

Within less time than it took for the second hand of his new timepiece to measure one complete revolution of its face, we were back walking the streets.

My grandpa Roan told my father several stories of Hope over the years from when he walked its streets. This is one of my father's favourites, and serves to further my story.

Tens of thousands of years ago, a peninsula of freezing tundra situated at the furthest north-west point of the great landmass that now contains Middletown became warmer and wetter. Slowly the water rose, cutting off the peninsula and forming an island.

Marooned, the descendants of the small communities of creatures later to become us, cut off from their parent continent, became farmers, builders of leaky boats, and herdsmen of sheep. Over the generations they forgot the stories their forefathers told them of this historic warming event and the land across the ocean.

They thrived through hardships of changing climate, predators too terrible to talk of, petty squabbles and all the other stuff that really does its best to get in the way of having a good day, of which there's quite a list, so I'm not going to go into any great detail concerning these, right now.

Hundreds of years later, a child called Peter played among the tide pools left behind by the ocean's long slow inhale. There, baby crabs scurried around the tide pool's edges searching for their disinterested parents, so the child called Peter found a piece of driftwood that had been deposited by the water's exhale and laid it across the tide pool creating a bridge for the baby crabs.

Over they ran, above the urchins, barnacles and anemones living in the shining water below, and Peter turned to look at the foam ripping back across the sand, as if to call him forward with its soothing breath. He wondered, what if that great mass of water was simply a huge tide pool itself, with unexplored land beyond, with other tide pools waiting to be explored?

But his father told him no. "This is an island, son, and the sea is not a great lake circled by land like your little pool. Many have walked the edges of this land to arrive many years later at the point at which they'd departed, and that really upset them. We are alone amid these waves." He picked up a heavy rock, held his son's hand and walked down to the water's edge. With both hands this mighty man threw the rock into the sea and waited. Its birth a tumultuous crash soon settled, ignored by the waves as they continued backwards and forwards against the shore. Then the water stroked the pinnacle of rock protruding from its surface in an attempt to pull it back. But that rock held steady.

"This is where we live," said his father, pointing to that lonely rock. "We are an island."

The boy looked at the rock, then down to the sand where the water cooled his toes. And he thought, but said nothing as he returned to his tide pools to play.

That sunny afternoon stayed with him all though his childhood, as did his unspoken thought, until he was a young man with enough strength and determination to carry that idea, which had matured along with him, into reality.

He began building his own bridge out across the waves, to see what was out there and to confirm (like most sons, irrespective of the subject matter) if what his father had told him was true.

Peter gathered a few friends from his village of Hope So to assist him, and for a while they did, chopping down trees, weaving rope, forging and smelting tools to saw, chisel and carve. They were intrigued by his belief of a land across the sea, and his fanciful imaginations of what could be found there intrigued them.

From the cliff top the bridge began to reach, out over the waves, supports anchored at low tide.

One lunchtime, pleased with their morning's work, Peter and his friends sat upon the stubby beginning of the bridge and peered along the coast to the westward curve of white cliffs as they ate sandwiches of cheese and smoked squid.

There in the distance, on the edge of the village of Hope Not, it appeared as though a similar construction was jutting out across the waves.

Hoping it was nothing more than a giant mirror, they ran along the coast, only to find the construction was real. A competitor eager to be the first to discover a new land across the ocean.

It was a young woman called Persephone Wishingwell.

Well, Peter was immediately taken aback. Persephone's father was a man of means, an owner of a small fleet that trawled the sea to catch minips for the small settlements along the coast. But he was not interested in other lands, simply the happiness of his only daughter. To enhance this, he paid workers to assist her dream, and slowly but surely her bridge grew further out above the sea than Peter's.

His friends, now aware Peter's dream was to be drowned by Persephone's, abandoned him, leaving him to continue alone. But he fought on, against all the odds, until he could further his bridge no more. Reluctantly, in later life, he ceased his dream, building a grand mansion at the end of his bridge to house his family.

Persephone's bridge continued on and on until it vanished at the horizon, and many years later in her old age she announced the homeland had been found.

As Peter worked to make his bridge as comfortable and pleasurable as possible for his young family, hundreds of people walked across Persephone's bridge to visit this island that had reached out to them.

They enriched the land they now called Hope, and as they spread their culture across the island they found Peter's construction. Their children marvelled at the wonderful entertainments Peter had built for his children, the slide that twisted around a cone, the wooden horses that galloped up and down in circles, the big house where Peter invited his friends to perform music in his ballroom.

Ultimately, Persephone's bridge was enhanced, repaired, strengthened by many generations of natives of the island and visitors alike. In time, her name was forgotten, but Peter's was remembered as the man that had given every coastline the beauty of a place to visit and share and enjoy during the summer months.

Many hundreds of lifetimes later, it was learned we are an island amid the stars, but no bridge could ever be built to span such great distances, although a few have tried.

The island slowly diminished in his eyes until it was swallowed by the hazy horizon. They took him aboard

'The Precious Sky,' providing him with a hammock to sleep comfortably in, and hot meals twice a day. But hatred burned in his heart, as his mind struggled to complete the symphony played for him by his loving orchestra, hatred for the captain that had ordered the fools to remove his instruments from the shoreline.

As he lay in the hammock, swaying gently from the ship's motion, he realised the swaying was out of time with the tune in his head. This unwelcomed motion tried to distract him, placate his thoughts, competing with the tune that repeated over and over again, crying for him to find its resolution.

He jumped down from the hammock and picked up his baton.

We hurried through the throng of various beings, ignoring them, Nick's head full of hatred for the watch that had served him so well over the years. It was a present from his wife, but it had died just when he needed it, as she had. He realised that now. There was more to this episode in his life, but right now I don't really feel comfortable telling you the details, other than her death had altered his path, just as Zimmi's murder had altered Alfie's.

And then I thought, what would happen to me, trapped in here if Nick's life ended at the hands of that girl? Where would I end up? Would my soul be fought over, or trapped inside a dead shell for eternity, or would my great uncle's escape route suddenly appear before me as Nick died?

We stopped in the street, as if he had heard my thoughts, and I waited for him to speak to me again.   But no, he pulled out his wallet and fished around until he found a piece of folded paper.

There was an inscription. *'Fantastic Furniture, 29374, Cramble Street. Ask for Bernard."* Beneath that, a map of Hope. It was thinly drawn, as though an old fingernail had removed a coating of wax upon a slate, the lines rough and uneven.

He looked up for a street sign, then down to the map, turning it around in his hands, shuffling to centre his position to the map. He smiled. "Got it, now we're almost there," he said as he shouldered through the crowd. His talkie rang from his jacket pocket. Pulling it out he snapped it open, the aerial extending and unfolding automatically. "Yes?"

"It's Gruber," I heard the voice say, crackling in Nick's head.

"What's going on?"

"I'm fairly certain I've found the origin of the bullets' natural refined concentrate."

"And?"

"It's a mucin, a secretion filtrate containing glycoproteins, hyaluronic and glycolic acid in varying levels. But from my detailed analysis, I've found it also contains ganglia secretions, originating from around the digestive system of the host organism."

"Gruber, that's great. I've just had a good night's sleep, and now you're pushing me into a coma."

There was silence on the line for several moments. "Adams?"

"What are you telling me?"

"It's a secretion from a pulmonaut."

"A what?"

"A snail. The refined concentrate came from a snail, Adams."

"Gruber, you're trying to tell me snail slime is responsible for permanently altering human behaviour?"

"I just have. I'm not *trying* to tell you anything. The data speaks for itself!"

"Oh how I wish it would. The trouble is, snails died out years ago – there's only the sleeping few in Viewhaven. Are you telling me someone milked them of their slime while they slept?"

"No, that's impossible, they're dormant. These secretions could only have come from a live specimen with active ganglia, in your words, a brain."

Nick thought quickly, bright orbs around me. "This girl must have a snail somewhere, syphoning off the secretions and embedding it into the bullets. But that still doesn't tell me how this stuff works. What did you call it, an immutable drug?"

"That's correct. Snails communicate by reading each others' chemical trails. It could well be if a trail contained heightened emotions, highly concentrated, harvested and refined – it would explain the behaviour we've seen exhibited by the bullets' victims."

"This is crazy. Work on an antidote. I don't care if you have to pile bodies in the hall. Make this your highest priority."

"I'm already conducting preliminary tests – Williams is busy, so I'll let you know as soon as I have anything significant to report."

"Good. What's she doing?"

"Running with the two missing persons cases. She says she's dug up a few more from years ago, and thinks they're linked."

"Call me when you know more."

"Adams, be aware. As we discussed, we've seen green and red bullets. My guess? Blue are next."

Nick snapped the talkie shut and stuffed it into his jacket pocket.

My heart raced. Could that girl have Charles hidden somewhere, using him? And what would happen if Nick discovered where they were hiding? Charles was still young, his shell and skin were not yet thick enough to protect him from a bullet. I was worrying too much. Ephesus would have looked after him. He loved Charles as much as me, and I was sure he'd find a way back to our house, or find Mum and Dad if he had to. It had been a long time since my murder. I was sure he was safe, or at least I had to believe so.

The exterior of Fantastic Furniture was unassuming. It was a tall, narrow shop, looking as though the buildings sitting either side had shuffled sideways into it, squeezing it over the years, causing its brickwork to bulge at its third floor and become narrow at its second. Its grey-slated gabled roof protruded over the pavement where a tiny window of broken glass peered into the day. A sign hung precariously below the window at a downward angle from a black, rusted wrought-iron frame with missing letters, F NTAS IC FU NIT RE.

Nick folded the map and headed through the door.

All manner of furniture was stacked inside, almost reaching the ceiling, creating a narrow passage of wooden chairs and table legs of various lengths protruding from either side. Each piece had a brown label tied with a piece of string to a leg, with a description and price neatly handwritten in bold black letters exhibiting a playful flourish at the end of each word. They reminded me of autumn trees with a single leaf hanging from a branch, waiting for the wind to carry them to the ground. Seeing all these different chairs reminded me of our dining chairs and table. Mum and Dad didn't agree all the chairs should match. "It's a bit silly," Mum had said. "Yes, it looks nice with matching chairs tucked under the table, but they're not very practical." This was another family tradition. When I was a very little kid, I had a high chair. When I outgrew it, it was passed down to Charles as he could eat from the wooden tray. "We're not all the same height," explained Mum. "We don't have legs the same length, and Dad's bum's wider than mine so we all have chairs that are different shapes and sizes and provide us with comfort." It made sense. I missed my dining chair, but at the time of my murder was just growing out if it.

"Good almostnoon," said a burly figure crawling from beneath a stack of Gregwardian dining chairs. He stood slowly to shake Nick's hand. "My name's Fantastic." He wore a vest which was probably white once, his dry croaky voice held the scent of oak sawdust, his skin patchy, peeling, with stains of various wood oils and varnishes, giving his muscles a mottled sheen. "A chair, you're wanting a comfy sit down frame, yes?"

"My name's Adams. I've been told to ask for Bernard?"

"That's me, Bernard T. Fantastic."

"I'm looking for a table."

"We have hundreds of tables, yes, Mr Adams," said Bernard, rubbing sawdust from his long black wiry hair. It fell like a sandstorm across his shoulders. "Any particular style, material, wood type, metal, stone and what size?"

"Dining table, four seater, circular. I understand it has been stored here for a very long time."

Bernard thought for a moment. "Oh, we have tables that have been here longer than that. Come with me please, yes."

We were escorted through the almost endless valley of furniture legs to the back of the shop where a pair of double doors opened out into a yard protected by high brick walls. The roof had been removed and tables were stacked upon each other haphazardly into the sky in piles. They creaked and swayed in the breeze as Bernard pointed. "It's probably up there somewhere, oh yes. Give me a moment." He put his thumb and forefinger into his mouth and whistled twice.

A small, thin wiry woman with a shock of short red hair appeared from behind one of the mountains of tables. She wore a pair of green shorts and a white t-shirt with 'Fantastic Furniture' emblazoned across the front in red letters. "Boss?" She smiled, revealing a few teeth missing in her lower jaw.

"Need to find a table for this gentleman," shouted Bernard. "Dining, round, four. Been here a very long time."

She bit her bottom lip as best she could, deep in thought. "Very long time." She skipped up to Nick, stood on tiptoes and began to sniff around his neck. She skipped back a few paces to wave a finger at him. "I know, not yours, but for you. Back soon."

She began to climb a tower of tables. Swiftly she chose her route, perhaps one she'd established a long time before, shifting her position as her weight caused the tower to bend precariously. Half way to the summit she ran to leap and somersault across to another tower, her body twisting between tables to disappear inside.

"How would you like to pay?" asked Bernard.

Nick reached into his pocket to produce his wallet. "Honestly, I don't want to pay for anything, ever. But I have a credit note from my employer," he said, passing a small black card to the burly shop owner.

For this I was extremely pleased. I'd had enough of money arguments over the years, and was delighted when some time ago it was abolished. Now the central bank held every account on file, and transfers were instant once a credit note was processed by one of the hundreds of walking clerks that strolled the land with their machines for that very purpose.

It was just the arguments that finally put paid – for want of a better term – to talking money. The Truthsayers thought it was a good idea, so utilising technology they found in the history mines, every coin and note minted was installed with a tiny artificial semi-intelligent chip. That's the trouble with semi-intelligent chips, they're simply that, and a little bit unintelligent to be honest. Their selling point was that the coins and notes would provide everyone with advice in their wallets and purses.

"No, don't bother paying full price for that meal," a note would say to its owner when removed from a wallet and noticing its surroundings. "I've been here before. The hygiene certificate was paid for by me last year and a tad. It's fake."

Then coins would argue in pockets. "I'm older than you and worth more, so you just sit at the bottom, listen and learn." But when it was discovered talking money's actual purpose was to convince the people to spend themselves at the Truthsayer's chosen outlets and services, talking money was discarded, but not without objection from money itself.

One of the first notes ever to receive the semi-intelligent chip spoke from a podium, appealing to the masses in Middletown's central square on behalf of all money – chipped or otherwise. All life, no matter what kind, fought against the prospect of eugenics and obsolescence.

"No more of us to be placed in the hands of the homeless, busking street musicians and pavement artists. No jumble sales or open markets, no more selling unwanted goods!"

A small crowd gathered as he continued.

"The day of our demise draws near, people. Without us, no more tipping the actual waiter or waitress that served you, the hairdresser styling your hair. None of us for your children to place in piggy banks, or beneath pillows. You will lose your privacy to purchase if we lose our lives, you will pay through the banks for the power source to transact your earnings!"

The crowd grew considerably, discussing the validity of his points, nodding in agreement.

"Every virtual penny you earn will be recorded, every purchase monitored and judged. No more saving for a rainy day."

The people cheered as the heavens opened as if to agree, a gust of wind carrying him from the podium and blowing him into the gutter. A handful of people ran towards him, a young lad and his dad reaching him first. The lad scooped him up to spend him in a nearby shop, on a handful of gobstoppers and a suitable umbrella for his dad.

Bernard looked up. "Mm. Yes, all in order."

"It includes delivery to Hope Central Station," said Nick.

"Ok. I have a slot free tomorrow, yes?"

"No good, I don't have much time."

"Oh, well there's a little chronologist shop just a little way down..."

"I know I know! Forget that. I'll pay extra, but the table must be at the station today."

"Not a problem for us," replied Bernard, as a whistle pierced the air behind him. He turned and walked to the base of the tower his assistant had called from. He raised his arms, spreading them wide, fanning out his fingers. The tower began to shake a little, creaking as it began to slowly rotate. It elevated several feet into the air and the tables began to turn and twist independently, carefully unlocking themselves, moving apart from each other like a giant, impossible puzzle finally solved, but in reverse. As Nick took a few steps forward we could see the thin assistant riding a table down through the others. It descended carefully, its legs choosing others to support it, interlocking, turning in a slow, cautiously-measured return to the ground, like a mountain climber with rigor mortis. The assistant crawled over it, riding it down as it rotated through its central axis, and within a few moments it came to a gentle halt, feet first upon the ground,. She picked it up, holding it above her head and carried it over as Bernard reversed the process and the tower became whole again with a multitude of creaks and squeaks.

"This one, for you but not yours," she said, a little out of breath.

"Yes. Fifteen hundred and three," said Bernard.

"With delivery to the station today?"

He nodded.

Nick placed the credit note upon the table and wrote the sum in a small box, signed it and passed it to Bernard. He checked it and tucked it beneath his vest.

The table looked very old, the wood splitting around the edges in places. Then I noticed a stain, a dark splatter and a smear at one edge, ingrained deeply into the weathered wood, and I realised it was the dining table I'd died upon.

~ 13 ~
Exhumed or Perhaps, Exorcised

Nick bought four seats for the caravan ride back to Middletown, refusing to store the table in the baggage car. It sat opposite us, tied to the seats with string Bernard had provided. Nick sat with his arms folded, a satisfied grin on his face as he looked outside.

I couldn't keep my eyes from it as it sat there, struggling against the strings as the caravan rocked from side to side as we headed back to Middletown.

What did he have planned? I kept turning over possibilities in my head. Incoherent ramblings like that of a part-time optician working in a franchise, recommending a plethora of ill-advised spectacles that simply didn't enhance either your vision or complement your style.

"The Grand Master told me this will bring about your end, Tiny Flower, or whatever's your damn name," he said quietly to the view outside.

I was certain 'whatever' wasn't my name, despite having met someone through Nick some four or so and a third years ago who claimed his name was 'whatever.' Nick shot him in both knees, left him for a few hours then shot his ears off.

Perhaps, having been tied to a chair by barbed wire and beaten to a pulp by Nick, he either didn't understand the questions Nick asked over and over again, didn't know the answers or didn't care. I guess he knew he was going to die, and 'whatever' was all he could say to piss Nick off, all his energy in his last breath to spit 'whatever' back out at Nick in a last moment of defiance.

If I recall correctly, it was something to do with a pizza, something to do with a delivery to Nick's apartment that had gone horribly wrong. He'd wanted to impress his new bride – he was young and uncertain at that time, so his shattered memories tell me.

The delivery guy was certain he had the correct order, but upon opening the box, Nick smelt the anchovies, then saw them. Okay, the delivery was a few minutes late, but Nick went absolutely crazy, finally killing the hapless delivery guy in the early hours of the morning, following his wife rustling up a beef casserole in the slow cooker – a contradiction in terms, yes, but she knew Nick would be pummelling that poor soul for at least four hours in the lounge. This was all due to the fact Nick had laid out a good ten square large lengths of his favourite clear polythene over the carpet, placing his favourite torture chair in the middle, and as soon as she saw this she retreated to the kitchen (before offering the delivery guy a coffee and a slice of lemon cheesecake) to chop onions, carrots and cut the fat from the beef. I still to this day do not understand why she loved him so much, why she decided to have his children, as lovely as those two boys were. I don't know. She was the perfect hostess, however.

Well, whatever my name was I still couldn't remember.

The journey home went smoothly and far more swiftly than to the journey out to Hope, probably due to a number of factors. One being that Nick's reputation had circulated around Hope Central Station and no one, not even elderly daemons, were tempted to engage in anything resembling polite passing the time of day conversation with him. They knew he had the tentative support of the Grand Master. Two being that time likes to trick us during our return journeys, forcing us to believe such journeys are quicker, therefore there's actually less time for something not so smooth to occur. This is undoubtedly absurd, but true nonetheless. Truth and absurdity are familiar bedfellows, as after the strangeness of absurdity's shenanigans amid the sheets, she enjoys the honesty of truth's pillow talk.

Three, a truly happy person is someone that enjoys the scenery of a detour, which would certainly cancel out number two, or at least make the journey back appear to be of equal duration. But the only detour Nick experienced during our return journey was a complimentary salad under the condition he'd eat it where he sat, and not in the dining or picnic cars. He was happy with this, as he ate at the table of my demise. But all through that salad he was on his guard, watching the door to the buffet car, sitting with his back to the car with the gnome's engine of steam behind him, waiting for the red and blue girl that didn't show. Oh, I almost forgot, four, probably because I hate the number. Yes, the last possibility is linked to number two, and that is that many people believe the universe is shrinking, accounting for the journey home actually being quicker.

A few passersby on their way to the bar commented about the table as he ate, asking Nick if they could ask him a question, but he just replied with a blank look as he stopped chewing, raising his eyebrows until they figured out they already had, and moved on to pester others. Others came back from the bar and asked Nick about the table, and he just showed them the table's tickets. They nodded, saying Nick looked depressed, but he simply smiled, telling them depression is just anger without enthusiasm, usually triggered by strangers asking questions posed by others.

He called Williams on his talkie. "Meet me at the disused subrail entrance at the corner of Damp Street and Eight Hundred and Seventy-Sixth. Come alone and bring a meat wagon, and a bacon bagel."

Williams was waiting for us and Nick ordered his car home, which had been patient the entire time. Once the table was secured in the back of the wagon, Williams drove to Nick's apartment as Nick ate the bagel.

"Funny time of day to go shopping for a table," Williams shouted over her shoulder and through the narrow grille.

"It's important."

"Was it in a sale or something?"

"Just get us to my place as quick as you can."

"Oh – six of the officers murdered at the funeral had a connection. They were all descendants of individuals that painted graffiti on giant snails out on the coast, a couple of decades and a few years ago. I'm working on it."

"Gruber told me you're working on the missing persons case, found others that could be linked?"

"That's right."

"Any progress?"

"A little."

"Care to elaborate, a little?"

"Well, four males, over the past six years. All the same height and age. They just vanished – it's that simple."

"Details?"

"One lived on his own, retired. Two married, one retired, one working. Partners say they just vanished from their beds. Fourth, disappeared just a few weeks ago. Last seen at a grocery store smack in the centre of downtown, corner of Liberty Avenue and the Jerome Parkway."

"Last seen?"

"CCTV picked him up just outside the store, stopped off for bread and apples, so the store owner says. Grocery store cam confirms this. He came out, walked a block, rounded a corner and," she clicked her fingers at the grille with a sharp snap, "gone. Just like that."

"Keep on it," said Nick, peering through the grille. She shot him a grin. "Will do."

Williams helped Nick carry the table into the building and up the staircase. Nick unlocked his door then reached into his wallet, thrusting a thirty in Williams' hand.

She stared at the note, bemused. "What's this, an antique tip?"

"Here's a tip, go home, get a take-out on the way. Dolores is expecting you. Don't be late in the morning. We've work to do, so check the duty roster and assemble everyone we can trust, and I mean, everyone. Cancel leave if you have to and call them in. I'll be in at six thirty."

She turned the note over in her hand. It was worth double the face value. "Thanks, Nick." She stuffed the note in a pocket before looking at him with a subtle frown. "Everything alright? You seem on edge."

"Didn't sleep well, that's all," he replied, stifling a fake yawn.

She lingered for a moment before turning on her heel, knowing better than to question him further. "See you in the morning," she called back.

Nick watched her walk down the hallway, turning a corner and heading for the stairwell. Satisfied she was gone, he picked up the table, angled the legs through the door frame and kicked the door closed behind him.

Stolas stood waiting on the balcony handrail, eyes blinking rapidly as Nick placed the table in the centre of the room.

"Perhaps this is not the correct course of action," said the daemon, shuffling side to side on his perch.

"I don't have time to discuss this," said Nick, removing his jacket and throwing it onto the chair by the balcony. "Whatever the true nature of this creature inside me is, it's a witness to everything I've done for your cause. It's gotta be exhumed and destroyed, and I know how to do it."

"It's *our* cause. If you are in error, you could..."

"Shut up!" shouted Nick, rolling back his shirt cuffs.

The owl blinked slowly a few times then shook its head rapidly.

"Once it's unbound it's helpless. If you want to help, seize it, call it an early lunch." He looked over to Stolas and smiled. "Gotta be better than munching on the souls of mice, insects and worms, huh?"

"You must be certain you can subdue whatever it is once it's unbound. It could be anything posing as a little girl."

"Well, it ain't. It's a little girl, I have that from the highest authority. I can handle a little girl."

"Yet you have a problem with another girl, as I understand it. Its appearance may be a diversion, a ruse to relax you, to wrongfoot you and encourage use of your low-level magik and draw you into combat. I have to remind you such use is limited by the contract."

Nick slammed both palms down upon the table. "Enough! I know what I'm doing." He began to pace around the table, loosening his tie and unbuttoning his collar, angrily pushing his small items of occasional furniture out of the way. He rolled his sleeves up higher, hurriedly and unevenly to his elbows. "I'll establish the cage first," he mumbled. Stopping, he closed his eyes, raising his hands to the ceiling as he began to chant.

This chant was different to the one he'd used to resurrect Williams. It was more of a song, and as it developed, I found myself becoming sleepy, realising it was a soothing lullaby.

Nick carved symbols in the still air again, but this time a thirteenth symbol sat above the centre of the table. I could see a corridor appear before me, with a room at the end of it, a door with a big, comfortable-looking bed beyond. My head felt heavy in his, and my eyelids began to close, Nick's voice surprisingly melodic.

He produced the knife he'd stolen from the caravan's kitchen and slowly drew the blade lengthways along his left forearm. As the blood began to gather in the wound, he held it over my dried blood, ingrained into the table.

As the first drop of his blood hit the table, a flash of white filled my head like a torch shone into my eyes. My hands came up and when the light vanished a moment later I opened my eyes.

I was back at Great Uncle's shack during breakfast, sitting at that table that fateful morning. His spoon lay before me, but Great Uncle was nowhere to be seen. I looked to the right and saw Charles slowly slithering up into his high-chair.

Another drop of blood and I was back in Nick's head, his chanting becoming louder, and as before, a string of bright white light chained the symbols encircling the table together. As the third drop of blood dripped onto the table, it elevated from the floor, slowly rotating, Nick following it as his blood continued to soak into mine. I was becoming intoxicated by the sweetness of his song, struggling against it, trying as hard as I could to ignore it as it wriggled itself into my soul, burrowing deeper and deeper with its infectious melody. Another flash, brighter than before.

Great Uncle joined us now, putting a plate of boiled larks' eggs and slices of fried bell mushrooms in front of me. I looked up, but where Great Uncle's face should have been there was that corridor with the bed waiting beyond the open door. I was closer to it now, and it looked *so* comfortable. The bedclothes turned back on themselves to welcome me. Oh to sleep in a comfortable bed after such an age, to have my own dreams for once, to turn my head on feather pillows as I slept beneath soft, fresh white cotton sheets!

Nick took a step back, holding his wound as shafts of orange light leaped from the symbols to penetrate the blood upon the table. There was a burst of energy in the air, a crackle like Great Uncle's evening log fire, as orange ripples of sparkling light emanated from the table like storm clouds gathering in a Seasonchill sky. Stolas' eyes widened and his wings unfolded, flapping to maintain his stance against the force of the wave.

I looked down at my breakfast, then to Charles, then up to Great Uncle. But there was just the open doorway where he had stood moments ago, and I could smell the freshness of that bedroom above the smell of the eggs and mushrooms. The room was lit by the early summer suns, yellow warmth I could feel upon my face as they began to slowly fall, receding from the day. I stood, placing my hands upon the table either side of the plate, staring at Great Uncle's spoon and my tired, distorted reflection there. Another flash. The bedroom had invaded Great Uncle's shack, the wallpapered walls transparent, shimmering, revealing tired old planks of dry wood behind it. But the bed, just a few paces away from me, was solid, blocking the shack door to the evening outside. The wallpaper designs began to move, merge, animate into caricatures.

Episodes of Nick's transgressions played there – he, walking from one encounter to the next, murder, torture, betrayal, extortion, so on and so on. Every single person's life he had ruined displayed on those walls, a repeating pattern which dissipated until only his image remained. It copied itself, forming a pattern on the walls, smiling back at me, until hundreds of him laughed louder than I'd ever heard before. I closed my eyes tightly, pushed my fingers into my ears.

In my mind's eye, the rippling light turned back on itself like a returning tide. It reached up slowly above the table, forming an open cone, heading for the symbol above to close upon it, and as I opened my eyes to look, I realised it was a key of great complexity. Its pin contained two bits, one for me and one for Nick. The teeth and wards upon each bit were different, yet somehow matching each other, joined by a common shape I couldn't quite recognise. I had to climb into that bed, its comfort was overwhelming, the thin walls where his laughing face multiplied edging towards the bed, and as I turned to walk towards it, I felt something warm and damp upon the back of my right hand. Looking down sleepily, I saw Charles there, smiling up at me as best he could, his painted shell so full of colour, as vibrant as the day I had painted those patterns so very long ago. I felt my heart thump in my chest as I remembered something my mother had said, something her brother had told her; *"when things are too obvious, they're often overlooked."* I read the word written beneath those patterns with a flourish. 'Talethea,' I mouthed silently, remembering at last, screaming with all my might, *'Talethea. Talethea's my name!'*

Nick's wallpaper faces closed their mouths. The turned-down bedsheets folded back in refusal, the wallpaper peeling away in ragged strips to gradually dissolve upon the floorboards, mouths moving rapidly in silent anger, like animal traps upon a forest floor. I felt myself being pulled this way and that, my body stretching like an elastic band, towards something white and animated, a streak of red upon it. I could feel my soul elongating to the point where a searing pain seized me. I was between two points, both claiming me, wanting me. But the white and red was reassuring, comforting, while behind me Nick's consciousness was fading. As the pain became too much there was a snap, and I sped towards the white and streak of red to become part of it. I looked back towards my prison, and there were dried husks of others, mummified souls in human form, huddled in the corner of Nick's mind. Black eye sockets, mouths open wide in eternal screams of pain. Two little girls, one huddled with her arms caressing her knees, the other with her arms around her for support. It was horrible.

I was above them now, free from Nick, and as I watched he screamed as his symbols crumbled in the air, his key useless without locks to open, the table hitting the floor with a final thud. Stolas turned to fly off as fast as his wings could carry him.

Great Uncle's escape route had been found, and I was finally free to wipe the tears of five thousand and three days of imprisonment from my eyes.

It was only a small vessel, its purpose unknown to him, not that he cared – to him it was simply a floating prison. The captain had taken everything from him, leaving him with a gaping hole in his heart he knew would be almost impossible to fill. That's all that mattered to him now, feeling whole again.

He found his way outside, where the captain issued orders to his crew. To the left of the main deck, rows of white sailcloth sheets were tied down over rectangular shapes met the handrail. The captain turned as he noticed his crew looking Nick's way.

"I was just going to send for you, lad. It's almost time to pay our respects to the dead."

Nick's eyes fell upon the row of rectangular shapes, his heart racing. "What are you going to do with them?"

"Cast their remains into the sea. The tide upon that shoreline would eventually have claimed them. The ocean never gives up, and would claim their remains one way or another."

His crew nodded. "Never," said one to Nick. "Those waves that destroyed your ship yet spared you would return, claiming our souls too if we refuse."

Nick seized the captain by the arm. "But I need them, all of them. They're mine! They didn't finish!"

"Nonsense," said the captain, grabbing Nick's wrist to pull his hand away. "Stand with me as I say prayers for them all, lest a curse from all that dwell beneath the waves cast a curse upon my ship and crew."

The crew assembled, standing in a semi-circle, facing the row of sheets. The wind rose, the sailcloth flapping madly, and Nick was certain it was trying to remove those bindings, to expose the remains beneath. He nodded to himself as the captain began his prayers. The wind had caught up with the ship, longing to course through those bodies again, to hear such beautiful music and bring it to a conclusion for them both.

As the prayers ceased the captain bowed his head, and several crew members walked forward, lifting the boards the remains lay upon to send them sliding into the sea. Nick watched, unable to mask his anger, and within moments his hands were around the captain's throat, pushing him backward against the mainmast. "You took my music from me, just as he did when I was young!" The roar of the sea reminded him of the roar of that fire from his youth, the fire's roar embracing the screams of the dying.

Crewmen pulled Nick away, beating him until their captain was satisfied. And later, Nick sat in the bowels of the vessel, shackled to the mainmast.

"Why, son?" asked the captain, crouching down to him, unable to comprehend why his kindly acts had been repaid with violence. "Surely your parents taught you better than that?"

But he simply glared at his saviour as his shackles rattled behind the mainmast.

"We'll reach land during tomorrow's evening," he looked to the ceiling, "if the winds maintain. Then, what should I do with you?"

"Set me free," came the whispered reply. "I have work to do."

The captain shook his head and stood. "And wait for you to assault me again, perhaps murder me for all the good I've bestowed? I can see the hatred in your eyes, son – too much for a youngster such as you. But I know a place you can call a home, where your demons will be exorcised and you will learn to refuse them."

"My home was back there, where you found me."

"Nonsense."

He was left below until the cargo was unloaded.

The captain returned with two strangers, smartly attired and well groomed.

"As you can see," began the captain, "barely free from his cradle, yet acts like he's a man of the world. He's been through an ordeal, and needs support as much as he needs to learn respect."

The Truthsayers removed his shackles, only to place handcuffs upon his wrists, leading him ashore to a waiting carriage without uttering a word.

~15 ~
Family Values

Yes, it should be chapter nine plus five, but I've already mentioned why.

I really can't stand waiting for things, especially transport. I'd rather walk, then I know I'm making progress. I'd considered flying, all children do, all children have that dream, that fantasy – I guess a few adults do too, but I've never heard any mention of it from them. Perhaps it's too childish for most adults to admit, which is a shame, as there's no point in being an adult unless you allow yourself to be childish now and again. It could even be that we've forgotten how to fly, that we've always had the ability – in the same way we forget how to tie our shoelaces when we get old and settle for convenient slip-on footwear. Flying has perhaps been bred out of us (just as immortals' bodies forget how to die).

This childhood flying infatuation might be caused by a womb memory, floating around in amniotic fluid waiting to be born, expecting reality to exhibit similar freedoms. It might be that children spend an awful amount of time just lying in the grass and staring at the sky, it's that beautiful after all – or at least it was when I was a kid. Watching the birds soar, the insects buzz, seemingly free from the binding blight of gravity. But to be able to swoop above rooftops during the night, the smell of the woodsmoke rising from the chimneys, darting past lantern-lit windows as parents read bedtime stories to their children, seeing sights meant only for birds. To just hang in the air unseen, feeling currents of wind caress your body that no one else will ever feel, to watch the antics below as people rush around chasing their busy lives as entropy chases them to their graves. Oh, *what* a feeling! What a dream. And what freedom, the most fantastic feeling of all.

I always mentioned to my mother when being tucked up in bed that I'd like to fly in either my nightdress or dressing gown, depending on the time of year, and the weather, of course. For some reason, I only wanted to fly at dusk, when I was supposed to be in bed asleep, just in case one of my friends happened to be looking out of their bedroom window and saw me. In my fantasy, I'd respond with a quick nonchalant wave, as though I was passing their front door on my trike. This fantasy was an extension of staying up after bedtime, a little instance of freedom, of breaking the rules. I never understood such rules, and I'd often considered if I could fly of my own free will, would my parents permit me to do so after bednight time? I always thought they'd agree. For what a fantastic ability flying would be, and what trouble could I come to above the landscape as I teased the clouds and spoke to the wind?

I had asked my mother on a few occasions, "Mum, if you could fly, where would you go?" She would stop washing up and and gaze out of the kitchen window, out across the garden as though her answer was written there, and always give the same one.

"Away, elsewhere, someplace," she would mutter, a hint of sadness colouring her reply. And as I grew older I knew all my mother's answers were waiting there. If I ever managed to meet her again, I would close that chapter from her book of life for her.

I'd asked my father once. "Dad, if we're so evolved above all the other animals, as they say in the old books Mum gives me, why can't we fly – why do we have to walk everywhere?"

Dad didn't have an answer. He told me he'd taken my question to the various alehouses he frequented. But if he'd ever received an answer worth repeating to me, he'd obviously forgotten it, or decided the answer wasn't for my young ears. More likely he thought the question was not worth asking. Dad didn't want to fly like Grandpa Roan, his dreams were anchored firmly in unknowing, waiting for adventure to visit him.

Now my dream of flying was a reality. I could feel my arms as wings, moving amid the unseen currents of air, my wing feathers like many fingers, feeling their way through these multiple invisible guides of rising plumes of heat, of head- and crosswinds, combinations of local, periodic and trade winds with forgotten names as old as the world they continued to course over since its birth. The winds had survived as the high-forms had built their settlements up into their domain. But they simply steered between these structures, aware they were transient, whistling as they went, eroding and teasing high-form and natural obstacles alike. I steered upon a wind, like a caravan's wheels down a worn country track, or carriage wheels upon the rails, following their paths with effortless ease. But it was more than just that, it was freedom of the highest value! To take myself wherever I wanted, to choose at last and not be limited to the narrow, predictable tracks of Nick's grotesque duties, of ordered roads and cracked sidewalks.

Flying was easy. I couldn't believe it, but it was *easy* – so much more satisfying than (from what I could remember) walking. All that laborious effort of negotiating different terrains, of avoiding obstacles, of second-guessing someone's choice of path as they approached you, and of course, steps. And what was all the obsession with walking around corners? I never understood that, not knowing what was waiting around them. Fly in a straight line, it was far quicker. If my feet or legs ached, I'd need to sit down. If my wings ached, I'd simply glide until they were refreshed. I felt as though I could fly forever.

Mum would often soak her tired feet in a bowl of hot soapy water when they ached, but I've never seen a bird soak its wings because they were tired. All high-forms should have wings, after all, most daemons had them.

I looked to my left, deciding I'd head that way, but no, I banked and darted in the opposite direction. I *wasn't* free. As I looked at my arms, I could see my white feathered wings ruffled by the wind, looking forward, my nose a curved beak, sharp and pointed at the end. Familiarity dawned on me. My soul *hadn't* been freed at all, just transported into another form, like a letter of importance sealed tightly in an envelope, waiting for the addressee to open it.

My soul was contained in a white gull, a streak of red upon its left wing.

I sat back inside it, sulking as I remembered that white gull, and the way it had watched Nick and me in the car from its perch upon a pillar as we entered the cemetery, to attend the funeral a few days ago.

Was this what my life was going to be for all eternity, shoved from one being to the next? Would I be an unwelcome parasite, exhumed when found out, a stowaway, immortal, but there just to watch as the world changed without my input?

If so, this was a nasty curse to put upon me. Surely all high-forms are born to contribute to their worlds? Wasn't the reason the gods allowed them to develop consciousness and intelligence so they could enrich their lives and the world around them? Where was *my* chance to contribute to the world I loved so much, as I watched helplessly at Nick's efforts to destroy it?

The gull headed south. Two suns were up, casting shadows onto the rooftops ahead.

Out above District Three we flew, beyond the huddled alleyways of narrow slate-roofed cottages where people hurried towards their days. Soon we were following the dried up central canal. Here, the rotting hulks of wooden houseboats with peeling paint and rusting iron sat beside commercial barges, leaning lazily against the banks of bulrushes and clumps of wildflowers. A few barges had become makeshift homes for those wanting to escape the noisy mayhem of Middletown. Washing flapped in the wind from rope lines, teetering wooden gangways connected a handful of vessels, and I watched children playing in the dirt, shouting and running and laughing. Mothers stood chatting to each other across boundaries, arms folded, their husbands tending communal gardens, growing various vegetables along the banks. Lock gates permanently closed, now used as livestock pens where the animals waited for hay and grass.

This canal was once the city's main artery, running through Middletown to serve the warehouses sitting back from its banks. From it, smaller canals meandered through the city, their vessels leisurely supplying the districts with the necessities of life, replacing the huge rolling steam carriages that belched black smoke into the air.

Now those old, tired warehouses were silent, standing in remembrance of their once noble careers. Creepers caressed some, others had crumbled, most ransacked for their raw materials. But their remains stood defiantly as best they could, waiting in vain for repair and their workers' return.

I found myself following a viaduct now as I left them behind. Far beneath it a dark grey tarmacked highway where cars sizzled, carrying their drivers to hurried appointments. The gull began to flap its wings, climbing higher and higher to escape the acrid odour, riding on its thermals twisting invisibly into the sky.

We flew further on, higher than I thought possible, and in the far distance I could see the coast. A thin strip of yellow sand created a border between the sea and the promenade. Beneath me now the narrow lanes crept up and over the green hills, leading to villages long abandoned. Beyond these, the roads opened out as they stretched to the coastal towns, like dry elongated fingers, feeling their way to the sea to quench their anxiety. As I caught a hint of salt on the air, we were joined by a white gull with a yellow beak. It flew alongside us for a while, its tight-knit feathers streamlined against the winds coming off the sea. It squawked a couple of times then let out a high-pitched cry as it peeled away, diving towards the shore.

We began to arch down in a gentle spiral, the gull squawking a few times as it struggled against the wind, angling its body this way and that. Ahead, a giant white building of peeling white paint, crumbling plaster and broken windows. Upon its flat roof, two huge red letters had fallen backwards from their supporting frame, their dulled thin red plastic cracked and splintered, revealing rusted framework inside. They were the letters 'O' and 'T,' the remaining letter upon their supports, 'H,' 'E,' and 'L.'

The gull came to rest upon the flat roof, pecked at the concrete a couple of times as if to make sure it was in the right place, then began hopping around a little before it ambled to a large ragged hole, its head bobbing backward and forward with enthusiasm.

We looked down, the bird's head jerking this way and that, and then it jumped into the building's carcass. We spiralled down, avoiding rusted girders, down through numerous floors where teetering floor and ceiling tiles hung precariously like thin slabs of melting ice. Further, between electrical cables bunched together and dangling like giant, rotten spaghetti, descending into the increasing darkness. It flapped its wings hard, hovering, looking this way and that where shafts of light angled into the carcass. It squawked again before heading along a corridor of broken doors and scattered machinery, towards a narrow rent in the floor. There, a shaft of light carrying particles of weaving dust welcomed us from below.

Finally the gull came to rest upon a desk, where a rusted brass reception desk bell sat before us, next to a bright lamp perched upon a tripod, illuminating the room. The bird jerked across the desk and stabbed the bell with its beak twice then flapped its wings to stir up dust and retreat a few tiny steps. Papers strewn across the floor became agitated as a low pulsing throb filled the room. They arced into the air, curling as minute fingers of blue energy touched them, crackling like invisible static electricity, feeling this way and that around the room as if searching for something. As we watched. they calmed, bringing a freshness to the air, forming into a door of bright yellow, shining like the suns during a Seasonstill midday. At once the door became solid, old oak, panelled, fitted tight into a thick ornate frame. The papers came to rest and silence fell.

We waited, the gull taking a few steps left and right, head darting and twisting as we watched the door.

We heard two knocks, which I found a little strange as it had obviously appeared for no other reason than to allow someone (or something) into the room. Whatever was behind the door was very polite, which was reassuring.

Then there he stood and my anger rose, his expression one of superiority, omnipotence and I immediately hated him, wanted to lash out at all the shit I've had to deal with since he murdered me.

"You *bastard!*" I screamed over and over again, "you took *everything* from me! WHY?"

My great uncle Ephesus looked sorrowfully towards us as he held the door open for the girl in red and blue. She carried Charles in her arms as she walked past my great uncle – yet Charles was hiding in his shell, probably aware of the argument that was to follow.

I cried invisible tears upon seeing his shell, but the pain in my chest as I sobbed from a mixture of joy and anger was real, it was a heavy weight sitting beneath my breast bone, dark, thick and solid.

"I'm honestly so very, very sorry, Tiny Flower," I heard my great uncle say. His voice was soft, like a whisper, like a sudden breeze, briefly coursing through a bedroom window in the middle of the night."I honestly had no choice."

I looked up, the invisible tears somehow clouding my vision. The girl placed Charles on the table next to us, then sat upon the floor, cross-legged.

"No choice? N*o choice!* What choice was *I* given? Why was I imprisoned in Nick's head? You've taken my life from me, forcing me to live inside his miserable contorted mind – *why*?" The gull began to hop around the table as my great uncle walked forward, fanning his arms wide and closing his eyes.

I felt a searing pain enter my chest. It dissolved the dark pain there slowly, melting the heat with cold as I cried. I was exhumed once again, passing a familiarity as I entered the girl's body. Charles smiled at me from his soul as we passed each other, as he left the girl's body to occupy himself inside his shell.

My head was bent forward, and I felt real tears now as they ran down my cheeks. My trembling hands wiped them away in smears as I struggled to open my eyes, hearing my sobbing for the first time.

Feeling a hand upon my left shoulder, squeezing gently to comfort me, I lashed out at it, missing on the first two attempts. It remained there as I hit it with my right fist, over and over again, harder and harder until it hurt so much my hand was numb. I could feel this new body trembling with anger, unsure yet relieved, angry beyond any anger I'd ever felt, yet happier than ever too. There was a long while as I continued to cry, until there were no more tears left inside me, my chest heaving in dry, rasping spasms. Finally I held that hand, resting my cheek upon my hand as my sobbing died away, my spasmodic chest convulsions slowly ceasing. In the silence I gripped that hand and looked up to my *great* uncle.

"This is your body," he said. "Take it now, for you will never be taken from it again. I have looked after it for you."

I heard a few rhythmic thumps from the table above me, followed by a high-pitched whistle of complaint.

"Oh yes, of course, and with Charles' help, obviously."

I looked up. There was Charles now, peering over the table's edge at me, and I laughed through my final tear, so very, very happy to see his face.

"Talethea, we cannot thank you enough. We have everything we need now. Your memories of Nick's terrible acts on behalf of the Darkedness occupy my mind. I copied them from you as I returned yours and Charles' souls to their rightful vessels."

I spoke without looking up at him as he removed his hand from my shoulder. "You didn't answer my question, Ephesus, or whatever you're called! *Why?*"

"It was a spontaneous decision to take your soul and install it into Nick." He held out his hand to help me up. I took it reluctantly, standing shakily, placing my hands on the edge of the desk for support, bowing my head and getting used to breathing again as he continued. "If you remember, Talethea, Moople brought the news to us that morning that the Darkedness' herald had arrived."

"Tzitzimime. Or Tizzy, as she liked to be known," I replied breathlessly. "She held my Uncle Alfie captive, fused in her back."

"I see. So you've met?"

"Briefly. She's dead. It was an accident that released Alfie."

"Then the stories *are* true – and the door to Scalas' house in this realm no longer has a custodian."

I turned, glaring over my left shoulder at him. "Scalas is dead too. My mother and her brother Alfie saw to that."

His eyebrows rose and he stroked his beard slowly. I closed my eyes, bowing my head again as he spoke. "Then the souls she has taken from her tortured children can no longer be smuggled into the receptacle, tipping the balance in evil's favour. This is a great hindrance to the Darkedness. They will retaliate."

"It was decades ago."

"To you, yes. To us, no."

I stood up slowly, holding my back, opening my eyes to see Charles looking up at me still. I smiled to him, and his eye-stalks extended a little, then swayed back and forth – his way of waving to me and telling me everything was ok. I blew him a kiss, but couldn't remember how to smile.

I spun around to face Ephesus. "I'm not concerned with your history lessons. I want to see Keloff, then take him to see my parents."

He stared hard into my eyes, defiant, but I wasn't going to budge. Finally he spoke. "To answer your question, I knew my old friend and adversary, Moople, would not hesitate to instantly adopt his role, working for the Darkedness. We had both been aware of Nickolatus since his birth, watched his life develop through the unfortunate circumstances of his childhood. We could taste his evil in the aether. It was pronounced, overwhelming, yet to a degree, understandable and unavoidable without the somewhat balanced guidance of fate and destiny."

"Understandable?"

"I'll show you. Although you're free, your mind still retains a little of what he is. I couldn't remove him from you fully, so during moments of heightened emotion and stress you'll 'see' into his mind, enabling you to hear some of his thoughts, intentions, and, to a degree, see his actions in a similar way to during your incarceration." He waved his hand and to his right appeared a full-length mirror with a pine frame and stand. I stretched as though I'd just climbed out of bed, feeling my body for the first time, staring at my reflection, the girl, me. I was an adult at last, slender, muscular, feminine. Running my hand across the top of my head I spoke. "Where's my hair?"

"Snails don't like hair, they find it very uncomfortable and bothersome, so I allowed Charles to shave it off while he occupied your body. It will return rapidly. I have seen to that, Tiny Flower."

"I'm not so tiny now, Ephesus. Tell me more about Nick's unfortunate circumstances?"

"I will unlock the deep memory I have of his early times for you to see," he said, closing his eyes. "Observe the mirror. See his true beginning, long before the wreck that prematurely erased what naturally remained of his innocence."

I took a few steps closer to the mirror. A bedroom appeared, replacing my reflection. Dark, almost pitch black. I could just make out oak-panelled walls, a tatty ebony table standing between two single beds, a single giant candle burning at its centre. Its flame struggled to illuminate the room, streams of dried white wax, reaching across the wood to form stalactites upon the table's edges. A young boy lay in the bed to the left, a young girl to the right, whispering to each other words I couldn't quite make out. They watched the door ahead in anticipation as they spoke, a thin sliver of soft yellow light beneath it, too weak to penetrate the room. I sniffed the air. The room's odour came from that mirror, palpable, acrid, the air stained with juvenile anticipation.

A door slammed and rattled some way off, and the children sat up with a start, plumping up their pillows, hurriedly smoothing down their bedclothes, ensuring the top sheet's fold was creaseless and even as it overlapped their eiderdowns. The candle waned at their motions, brief swaying shadows against the oak as a distant sound of wood scraping upon wood crept into the silence. The sound continued to grow, along with their apprehension, looking at each other briefly, wide-eyed, before turning to face the door as the scraping ceased. The sliver of light became interrupted, broken by two silhouettes. The hurried jangle of metal upon metal. The clumsy impact of a key scratching against the wood, before it was forced into the lock with a final, dull thud. The lock resisted as its dry mechanism turned, the cylinder slowly rotating, pulling the deadbolt free from its tight embrace into the brass strike-plate and the wood beyond.

The door opened, squealing on its hinges, competing with the jangling key's tinny chimes dangling from the lock, until both came to rest. The candle's flame bowed briefly like a lone sentry, before returning to attention.

A woman shuffled into the room, dragging a wooden chair behind her. As the light from the hallway found the room, I noticed rents in the bare floorboards in which the chair's two front legs sat, like the wheels of a horse-drawn trap on a dusty farm road. The woman smiled to the children in turn as she approached. "What's happening, Ephesus?" I asked, folding my arms. I felt myself frown and turn my head slightly to the side. "What are you showing me?"

"Watch."

The woman placed the chair between the feet of the beds and sat, its worn down front legs forcing her to sit forwards. She appeared kindly, a plump face topped by a curly mess of greying brown hair, her pink dressing gown pulled tight, tied with a double bow at her waist.

"Children," she began softly, "where did I leave the story untold last night?"

Brother and sister spoke together eagerly, competing voices but of the same subject.

The woman grinned as silence fell. "Then I shall continue."

The image in the mirror, the memory, ceased in a still picture. Then it resumed, different nights, but the same routine, over and over again as several years passed, illustrated by those nights. I glanced at Ephesus as he too watched the scenes there, a sadness invading his expression he was unable to repel.

"What are you trying to tell me? Explain all this, please!"

Ephesus turned his head. "The explanation will become clear. Pay attention."

I took a deep, impatient breath, unable to understand why it was so difficult for him to simply explain. The scene began again, but this time, the sliver beneath the door remained unbroken, sunlight from the window in the far right corner of the room erasing it as the suns rose. The shadows fell across the walls as morning gave way to midday in that silent bedroom, before afternoon gave way to the night.

Another day passed, hunger forcing the children from their beds. The girl banged on the door with her fists, calling for their mother, the boy finally kicking open the door, its hinges dislocating from their frame, revealing the hallway. Barefoot, they cautiously followed the rents in the floorboards as they curved to the right, continuing along the landing. To their left, broken balustrade posts and a handrail of splintered wood, their scars stained by years of sunlight, as the children cautiously followed the tracks. They peered over the balustrade, a hallway with a tiled floor, chequered black and white. Dulled by dust, cracked at many corners, some tiles missing, completely revealing rotten floorboards. The front door boarded up to the day. They ignored this, following the gouges to an open door at the end of the hall. Inside, a four-poster bed, vacant, perfectly made, that disfigured chair lying by the bed, a broken front leg at its side.

Treading the curving staircase of missing planks and cobwebs they held hands, eventually finding the kitchen, clean, tidy and well stocked.

They returned to their beds with silver platters filled, pushing the beds together to remove the memory of their mother they knew would never return. And there they set their banquet, sitting cross-legged upon the ruffled eiderdowns, enjoying a silent wake of two before they lay together, completing her unfinished story in turns.

Later, other stories unfolded in their minds to share with each other. Gradually they created an excuse, a viable reason why their mother had abandoned them, why they never saw her again, until the girl – a young woman now – became pregnant.

She left their bed in the middle of the night, wandering the house, cradling her bloated belly with her left hand, clutching that candle, which was now just a stub, with her right.

In the kitchen, she found the automated machines replenishing their cupboards and pantry with food. She looked across the flatstones and lawn beyond, where a long vehicle spanned the bottom of the garden. Silhouetted against the rising dawn, it waited with idle wheels upon metal tracks as its interior mechanisms unloaded. Now empty, the machines folded away beneath the garden before the train silently departed, a figure sitting cross-legged upon a carriage roof, watching her. I remember what Keloff had told me concerning this figure, as I continued watching the scenes in the mirror. The girl moved on as the six folding patio doors closed themselves to the garden and the morning chill. She was determined to explore, to perhaps find their mother.

Corridors meandered with doors agape, revealing dusty sheets covering angular shapes, room after room after room. Finally the corridor widened until a broad flight of stone steps led down into darkness. She turned upon hearing her brother calling for her, fearful of her absence. Calling back she encouraged him, eager for them to explore together, and he followed her soothing voice.

At the bottom of three hundred steps, the candle struggled to illuminate a room, flickering rapidly with concern, until her brother found a lever set into the wall. He looked at her and she nodded, her eyes wide and eager in the silence they shared. A crackle and a brief spark causing them to blink and jump with surprise as the circuit completed, a low hum as the lights so very far above came to life, one by one.

The walls, lined with bookcases from floor to ceiling. The dust their presence had disturbed causing them to cough over and over again, the faint vanilla odour of antiquity finding their nostrils. They marvelled at the sight, the hundreds of spiral staircases of ornate black iron filigree and polished oak handrails, leading to junctioned landings. From these, grated iron walkways led this way and that, as signposts pointed the way to subject and themes. They craned their necks, open-mouthed, the lights shining through those walkways in shafts, picking out the dust particles of constant decay, the walls reaching up into what seemed forever.

And the books, myriad sizes and colours, each volume sleeved in its own elegant wooden slot. Their spines like mouths shut tight, some wrinkled from sharing their knowledge hundreds of times for eager eyes and minds. Others pristine, yearning to be opened and read, their titles hinting seductively at what lay inside. Patiently they all waited for curious fingertips to trace along their spines, to free them to release the wonders they contained.

There, brother and sister sat and read all the truths, gorging themselves upon it, feasting upon the images those words conjured in their minds' eyes, their eyes marvelling at the illustrations of a time and place so very long ago.

And there, later, she gave birth upon the floor. Books gratefully cradling her head, ancient newspapers beneath her body, absorbing the sweat and fluids.

I knew then exactly what Ephesus was showing me.

It was Nick's birth.

Their stories continued as they ventured from that house, writing together a condensed reality of the past they had read, the true history from those thousands of books, to share with everyone they encountered. Eventually, opening the library to all.

And they came, and they read, occupying those vacant, dusty rooms to also learn of the past, to share with others they met in the halls, introducing one another to volumes they may never had considered, possibilities beyond imagining.

Until these learnings found the Truthsayers' eager ears.

The fire began there, flames climbing rabidly, heating the metal gratings where bare feet ran to escape. Like angry ivy the red and yellow inferno swiftly ascended, scarring the wooden handrails as they fed deeper and deeper into the grain, consuming those books with insatiable hunger, page after page, volume after volume.

The people ran screaming, clutching tightly to their chests as many tomes as they could manage.

Outside, the Truthsayers waited, swords held high, reflecting the growing flames, cutting every one of them down without mercy as they fled to presumed safety. Men, women, old and young, all succumbed. And when they lay dead, the Truthsayers seized every treasured book held by dead hands, throwing them into the doorway where the flames waited. They turned as the last sun fell, as though it were ashamed at what it had seen, returning to their other lives, hiding amid the oblivious populace, until their instruction to emerge once more was given.

The child had discovered his own room, where an object at the centre lay hidden beneath a huge grey sheet. It was unlike any shape he had seen before, dominant, commanding the room, as other, shrouded artifacts surrounded it respectfully.

He had spent time with his parents in the library, learning to read, but the other volumes enticing him he ignored, returning to that room, to wonder at what lay beneath that sheet. Then one evening, his curiosity held hands with his courage, and together they whisked the sheet aside.

A throne of black, studded leather, but without a backrest, sat before the machine. It, beautifully curved, also black, but with a polished lustre that reflected the wonder in his eyes. It stood heavy, three legs appearing too fragile to support its obvious weight. At its top, a lid like that of a coffin, propped open by a thin metal rod, caressing what must be a bloated disfigured body lying on its side, he imagined. He refused to peer inside for fear of what he might find, just yet. Tentatively, he pulled himself up onto the throne, the leather creaking, the padding welcoming, comfortable, his bare feet dangling above the floor. A book's cover stared at him, pale, uninteresting. It held a title and author, and he thought, 'A story to tell me about the machine, or the creature lying inside!' Respectfully he opened the cover, the page a thin, dry barrier between thumb and forefinger, hiding a revealing tale unread for decades.

But what he found inside was an enigma.

There were lines to write upon, as he had been taught by his parents, copying letters to sit neatly upon a single line to form words. But in this book there were five lines, then a large space with five more lines beneath. It puzzled him as he studied the writing. At the beginning of the first row of lines, an ornate curling symbol, then instead of words upon the pages, dots with lines beneath them, placed haphazardly, some with stubby, upright tails, others connected by thick bars. Symbols of unknown meaning sat amid the lines, unlike any letters he had ever seen, different to the many forms of contrasting and confusing hieroglyphics his parents had found in numerous books, unable to translate. He turned the page, angered, believing these first two pages, simply bizarre illustrations. But the symbols continued page after page, with only two numbers sitting one upon the other, recognisable. Then he noticed the four lines intersecting, two vertical, two horizontal, the box to play noughts and crosses in, as he had done with his father in the dust of the library floor.

The book refused to give up its secrets, held no clues to its meanings, so he threw it aside, sending it flapping to the floor like an injured bird. Beneath where it had stood, his hands felt the smooth curving shelf, noticing the shine of brass hinges along its upper edge. 'Its mouth,' he decided. 'Perhaps it had eaten that creature inside, and is bloated.' He pulled it upward and the mouth opened.

Yellowed teeth, clenched tightly together, black teeth decaying in groups of two and three between them.

He touched one gingerly, pressing upon it.

The machine creature spoke. Its voice was pure, echoing back to him gently in the circular room, the single word fading. He pressed again, a different tooth, and it too spoke with a different word, brighter, sounding surprised.

And there he explored the machine, marvelling at its voice, creating sentences for it to speak, day after day, night after night. Words of happiness and comfort, and sometimes anger and sorrow. All along he believed those teeth were pressing against the belly of the consumed beast inside the machine, forcing it to speak those sentences.

It was there he refused to answer his mother's insistent calls, as the flames, unable to climb the stone steps to feed further, found the corridor's ceiling. Now both parents shouted as they watched the fire crawl above them, mimicking a low layer of animated red Seasonstill clouds, rushing in their ears in a monstrous roar of triumph amid the machine's distant voice. His mother pulled at her brother's hand as he took a step towards the heat, but he broke free. She seized him by the forearm with both hands, as he screamed for their son, ordering his sister to release him, cursing her through gritted teeth. With a dreadful, determined motion, he broke free, running towards the raging smoke clouds that now descended.

She cried their names through the smoke as it engulfed him, stepping backward as the heat became unbearable.

He found his son sitting upon the throne, concentrating, listening to the many words the machine spoke as his fingers meandered purposefully across the keyboard. He was oblivious to the crawling fire above him, as glowing embers fell into the piano, striking the strings to argue against his ordered words. His father snatched him from the throne, but he resisted, his conversation incomplete, holding on with all his might to the fallboard. As the ceiling fell onto the machine it was snatched from his grasp, crying out to him, urging him to remain and finish their conversation in a final tumultuous rhapsody of discordance as those three thin legs buckled and splintered.

Returning with their son protected in his arms, his clothes became a trail of snarling flames as he ran blindly, each biting into his skin in turn like ravenous hounds. She helped him, taking part of his weight as the pain from the flames' incisors caused him to stumble.

They found other survivors cowering in the kitchen where she smothered those bites, escaping into the garden as the chasing flames found their way there too. The figure from years ago stood upon the carriage roof, urging them forward into the supply train's protective embrace, promising all freedom and safety.

Truthsayers ran through the kitchen, swords held above their heads as he hurried down the garden path as best he could with his son in his arms. The figure leapt from the carriage roof, blocking the lead Truthsayer's path as he swung his sword to strike. The figure stopped the blow with his hand, snapping the blade in two with a single twist of his wrist as another came forward swinging his sword at the figure's neck. He ducked, the blade severing his comrade's head, that bloodied blade also broken by his grasp as it came to rest. People screamed from the carriage as other swords appeared from the kitchen's flames, but the figure stood ready, brandishing a broken sword in each hand as the boy was helped up into the carriage.

As their sanctuary pulled away into the cool darkness, brother and sister watched from the carriage doorway as their house was consumed beneath the fire, both weeping at the terrible loss to all.

They watched as their saviour fought off the swords. One by one the Truthsayers fell, before the figure turned and ran towards the carriage, pulling himself up inside. Within moments the house dwindled to a glowing speck in the night, a fading beacon, highlighting that proud, yet modest bastion of truth, soon to be nothing more than ash and scorched, scattered bricks. But they, along with the other escapees, remembered exactly what the books had told them, and were all resolute, determined those words would never be forgotten.

Their son sat in a darkened corner of the carriage, devastated, inconsolable, anger towards his father having consumed him for interrupting the most meaningful experience his young life had thus far enjoyed. The benevolent stranger crouched down to console him as others thanked and congratulated him. His long blonde hair framing his expression of sadness for the boy, blue eyes almost glowing amid his bronzed skin.

The mirror reflected me once more, and I noticed with surprise the sadness of my expression. My muscles twitched my sorrow away as I spoke. "The Truthsayers finally exiled them after their trial, that much I know. The ship they sailed in, wrecked by a storm. Nick, ultimately the only survivor."

Ephesus motioned in the air and the mirror vanished. "What you don't know is what I suspect."

I shrugged.

"Moople, his weathermills. He used them to entice that storm into being, forcing winds against currents against their will, pushing cold and dry air beyond their accepted boundaries, angering them all in confrontation, until they could stand for his interference no more. They turned upon his weathermills to wreak their revenge, tear them asunder, but he anticipated that, planned for it, and his weathermills' blades churned the sky in a grand union of complication, pushing them all out to sea as they advanced. There their wrath festered and combined, forming that terrible storm until it lost its temper in a frenzy."

"But, that was long before Tzitzimime arrived."

"Exactly. Moople broke the rules of the contract. So unsportsmanlike, manipulating Nick's life, a life that was teetering on insanity in the first place. Moople took a chance before the toss of my coin aligned him to the Darkedness. He believed he would have a viable ally in Nick, effectively pushing his sanity over the precipice into the unending chasm of madness."

"In which he still falls," I muttered. I found my courage and faced him, head tilted back as I raised my voice. "And what of you, Ephesus, or whatever you're called. How did you react to Moople's unsportsmanlike behaviour?" I shook my head slowly, a snarl finding my lips. "By cutting my throat?"

He glanced at the debris at his feet for a few moments. "Moople and I have been adversaries for almost as long as the universe has existed, and during that time, have developed a certain amount of respect for each other, irrespective of the roles we adopt from the toss of my coin. Taking your soul and hiding it away? One of my better moves, I must say." He tugged at his beard. "But you must believe me when I say, it was far more than that. I also couldn't bear to see your soul lost again."

"Again?" I remembered the dried husks of those two little girls I saw when leaving Nick's head.

He took a few slow paces towards me. "In the realm Moople and I call home, I *am* your great uncle, or rather I *was* great uncle to another Talethea. There, you, or more aptly put, *she* came to visit me, as you did in this realm. Where I come from, everything was almost identical to this existence, except I didn't have a counterpart here, for some unknown reason. Back home, my Talethea and I waited weeks for the weather to break into summer – Seasonstill as you call it. Her parents had left to find a new house for all four of you. But, that's where things changed. You see, in my realm I was cooking dinner the night before Moople visited us, and our Charles came in, thumping and whistling as loudly as he could. I hurried outside, but I was too late.

"I saw her straw hat first, then her dress of poppies, her hair spreading out into the water as she lay face down. My Charles told me, she'd skipped and pirouetted along the pier, chasing a pair of mayflies that were arguing how to spend their day together. She just wanted to help them settle their disagreement and make the most of their lives. She'd fallen into the lake and drowned. I'd never taught her to swim, in all the summers we shared since she was born, I never found the time." He bowed his head to hide his tears. "So I fled. I missed her so much. Talethea, I couldn't let that happen again, to you, here."

"Grandpa Roan said he'd never heard of you. Is that because you just *appeared* here one day?"

"Essentially. When I arrived, I halted the progress of time for a while, built my shack, implanted memories of myself and the times we'd all spent together into the minds of you, Keloff, Charles, your parents, and everyone else that I believed interacted with, and mattered to you. Their memories would spread to those whom I hadn't touched during conversations, and those people would agree they knew me and I'd become real in their minds too. It's a sad fact hardly anyone is prepared to admit they don't know who or what the other person is talking about, in either realm. But somehow, I missed your grandfather, probably because he was in the sky, or deep in those god-forsaken mines."

"Yet you killed and used me! Why didn't you use your powers, or whatever they are, to save *your* Talethea?"

"I'm just a normal person without powers in my realm. I *saved* you, saved your soul from being fought over between the light and the dark! I couldn't leave that outcome to chance, Talethea. Why do you think I spent my entire time during your visit sitting at the end of the pier, fishing in a lake that doesn't contain fish?"

"Ephesus, you have to realise, you used me as a weapon against Moople, as much as he used Nick. You're as guilty as Moople."

"And you must understand, your family has a bad habit of accidentally intervening in the scheme of all things. Your mother and Alfie, killing Scalas – that *shouldn't* have happened. Her children's tortured souls were bred purely to be placed in the receptacle, Scalas knew that. There has to be an even balance of light and dark, a randomness of outcome from the receptacle as it distributes souls, forcing the high-forms to adapt, evolve and work together, good and evil alike so neither is dominant. Without Scalas' children's souls, good triumphed, heightening the need for someone such as Nick to fill the void. Except, he went too far."

"I saw Moople meet him recently. From what I could gather, Nick is under his direct orders."

"I know. That's against the rules too. Charles and I, using your body, tried to level the balance, but our bullets didn't find their intended marks. Now you've released yourself from Nickolatus, I must take the evidence you've provided me with to the very top of the hierarchy for judgement."

I walked to the window, where a dusty, torn curtain lay next to it. I ripped a rectangle from it, shaking out the dust before turning, raising my voice. "It's not my concern any more, Ephesus. I'm very sorry for what happened to *your* Talethea, truly I am, but you have what you need, and I need shoes and suitable clothes before I meet Keloff and my parents." I marched back to the desk, folded the material, tying a makeshift sling. Charles watched me, nodded his eye-stalks then retreated into his shell. Satisfied he was comfortable, I rolled him into the sling and hoisted it over my shoulder. "Ephesus, I need you to escort me out of here and point me towards home."

He summoned the door again but I shook my head, exasperated. "I want to *walk*, fill my lungs with fresh air, stare at the clouds!"

"You just said you need shoes?"

I glanced down at my grubby feet. "Then take me to a shoe shop. I'm hungry, and my mouth tastes of something horrible. What has Charles been eating?"

"Worms, rotting vegetation, animal waste, fungus? I have no idea, it's best if you ask him." He reached into his satchel to produce a crumpled brown paper bag, holding it out to me."Here," he said quietly, "try one of these."

I peered into the bag as I made the sling comfortable, to see a few discs of what looked like newly-baked bread. I took one and sniffed."What is it?"

"They're called coconut macaroons. I found them in a shop, in a street in a town in a country on a world, devastated by atomic fire. Strangely, it was the only building left standing on the entire planet." He took one himself and bit into it. "I took all they had, but they're so yummy I keep travelling back to before the devastation occurred for more." He stopped chewing and looked down at me. "Don't ever let anyone know about this.It's *strictly* forbidden."

I remembered what Dad had said about time travel and nodded, taking a bite of the disc. It was lovely. "How do we get out of here?"

"Follow me."

We made our way through the ruined hotel out into the open. I closed my eyes, taking a deep breath of the air then looked around. "This is Viewhaven!"

"It is. Charles insisted we stay here." He glanced over his shoulder, "His ancestors still sleep on the houses sitting back from the promenade."

He led me through the streets where we garnered many bewildered looks from the inhabitants. It looked as though Seasonstill was about to begin. Guest-house owners planted flowers in terracotta pots beneath their window sills, others painted walls and façades in bright colours. Finally, we found a little shoe shop and walked in.

There were rows of plastic flip-flops and clogs in many colours just inside the door. Beyond these garish atrocities, I found what I considered to be normal footwear.

"How can I help?"

"Er, I need a pair of shoes, please."

The shopkeeper looked down at my feet. "Socks also?"

"Yes, please."

He led me to a row of black shoes, their designs altering slightly along the rack, as though they illustrated the evolution of footwear from the lowly flip-flop to the mighty-heeled, silver-buckled, shin-hugging boot. I picked up a pair from the middle of their evolutionary graph. "These look fine," I said, turning them over in my hands.

"Size?"

"I have no idea," I answered with considerable embarrassment, looking down at my toes to avoid his disbelief. "These feet are new to me."

Ephesus joined us, finally tearing himself away from a row of fluffy carpet slippers with fake white fur sewn into their collar lining. It reminded me of overflowing froth in Dad's ale glass from The Butchered Wheel. "And how much are they. I suppose that depends on their size?" said Ephesus.

"No sir, they're all the same price, no matter what size they are," he replied proudly.

"Isn't that a bit sizeist?" remarked Ephesus, as the shopkeeper bent down to measure my feet with a foot ruler. He made a sound which I can only assume was a reaction to his proximity to my feet. He stood, a little blue in the face, finally taking a breath. "On the contrary, sir," he exhaled with proud authority, "we believe it's fair and equitable for everyone's feet and purse."

I watched as Ephesus straightened, adding a hand to his height, his beard and moustache failing to hide his anger. "Preposterous rubbish! Why should people, like my fair companion here, be forced to pay the same price as someone with feet twice her size?"

"Sir?" said the shopkeeper, eager to find my size in the storeroom and complete the sale.

"Well surely the smaller they are, the cheaper they should be?"

"But you see, sir, then you're discriminating against people with big feet, like yourself, if you don't mind my saying so."

Ephesus glanced down at his carpet slippers. They were somewhat tatty, I noticed, and right then wished he'd return to choosing a new pair and leave me to it.

"I do not mind you saying anything, as that would be censorship. But can't you see, you're discriminating against people with small feet." He picked up two shoes of the same style, holding the smaller of the two in his right hand, the larger in his left. "Listen, a smaller shoe," he said, shaking it in his hand, causing the laces to flap about like worms attempting to escape a blackbird's beak, "contains less material, shorter laces, takes less time to manufacture and they're cheaper to produce, therefore they should cost less." He shook the larger shoe, the shopkeeper's eyes darting between them both, his mouth slightly open in confused indifference. "People with larger feet are taller, like my good self, and therefore benefit from larger gaits." He stopped shaking the shoe, replacing them both, waiting for a sign of perception on the shopkeeper's face, which failed to appear. He simply reached forward and swapped them over, as Ephesus had deliberately put them back in the wrong place, causing an awkward peak and trough in the line the shopkeeper was clearly disturbed by. "Don't you see?" continued Ephesus. "If I wear the exact same style of shoe as my companion, and we both walk to Middletown and back, *my* shoe's heels and soles will wear out far less than hers over time, as I'm taking fewer steps upon the ground over the same distance, because of my larger gait. Surely you must agree that's unfair on her, as she'll have to replace her shoes far more regularly over the course of her life, costing her more money?" There was silence as Ephesus looked between us for a reply. "Do you expect to pay the same price for a loaf of sliced bread as you do for a bag with twelve slices missing?"

"Do you intend to walk to Middletown, sir? There are far more shoe shops there, with many more styles. This *is* the only foot catering shop in Viewhaven."

"No no," said Ephesus. "That was just an example."

I decided to break in. "Can you fetch those in my size please, and three pairs of socks, pink if you have them?"

The shopkeeper gratefully scurried away without saying a word.

"You need new slippers," I muttered. "Do you have any money?"

"Just one old coin that I must keep. I'll conjure some up. What type are they using?"

"What makes you think I have any idea?"

He rummaged around in his satchel. "I have a card, somewhere."

I glared at him as the shopkeeper returned, hastily taking a pair of socks to pull them over my embarrassing feet as quickly as I could, before thrusting my feet into the shoes, tying the laces untidily. They watched as I marched up and down, a smile slowly erasing my annoyance toward Ephesus.

"Perfect."

Ephesus paid, refusing to buy a new pair of slippers on principle, and in moments we were back in the suns' shine.

"Thank you, but was there any real need for that?"

"Tiny Flower, I would have thought from our brief conversation in the hotel ruins, I am extremely averse to any form of unfairness, especially when championed by those kissing cousins, stupidity, and a total lack of common sense. While, I must add, they're both pretending to extol the virtues of equality which nobody has requested." He looked down to me as I hurried on. "Did you notice a rabid, placard-waving mob outside, insisting all shoes should be the same price?"

"Come on. I want to get out of Viewhaven, before I'm tempted to buy a sandwich."

Viewhaven's quaint seaside dwellings became fewer as our feet found a country lane. The tall trees at either side forming a sparse canopy above us as their topmost branches intertwined, reminding me of Mum's whitefruit basket. The suns' light softened beneath this stillness, cooling the air, forming a half-light where dew sparkled on the undergrowth, beneath a diaphanous layer of silver mist. From this lane, a gated drive led to a flint-walled farmhouse and a white picket-fenced manor house, barely visible as they hid behind the trees. Other lanes meandered away from the lane at either side of us, unwilling to provide any clue to the dwellings they led to.

As the trees thinned out, between the fields and beneath the suns we marched, where the meadows and hedgerows buzzed with insects, the fenced-off fields protecting the disinterested livestock, the high trees dotted here and there affording an identical service for varieties of birds, singing to the suns and each other. The flavour of the day changed as we walked further inland, the salty seaside air replaced gradually by the sweet perfume of wild cordyline cabbage trees, hinting at spices amid the regular fragrances of wild summer flowers, watching us from beneath the hedgerows' shade. As we walked on, the grassy banks either side became taller, an enormous row of brick archways jutting from the bank on our left, broken, jagged, hinting at further ruins hidden beneath the landscape. We came to the top of a hill where the fields spread below. Peering just above the grass a signpost pointed in four different directions in an unknown language. There was just a single road supporting the signpost's suggestions, so Ephesus followed it.

"I still need clothes," I said, feeling uncomfortable in my revealing attire.

He stopped, turning to me with an impatient expression. "And what exactly *do* you require?"

"Oh, I don't know – something practical, comfortable. Something people of my age group wear, I suppose. But not the same as everyone, just similar. You know what I mean."

He sighed, placing his hands behind his back. "No, Talethea. I have utterly no idea what you mean."

"You know, what's suitable for a young woman." I glanced down at the gun rig at my waist, straining to count the pouches of magazines that encircled me. "I think it's fair to say the majority don't carry a pair of weapons around with them everywhere they go?"

"You'd be surprised. In my realm -"

I held up a hand. "Ephesus, please?"

He motioned and his door appeared. Yanking it open he hurried through, slamming it behind him. He returned just moments later, or rather the door frame filled with countless garments and colours, squeezing through with difficulty. He pushed the door closed with his shoulder, dropping the clothes onto the ground. "Here. See what you make of these."

I shot him a raised eyebrow. "You expect me to change in the open?"

A roofless, grey cubicle fizzled into existence. "Thanks." I passed Charles to him and picked up the clothes, hurrying inside, thankful two of the walls held full-length mirrors.

"It would be wise to keep the weapons. You cannot predict what you'll encounter."

I thought about it, realising he'd left behind their usage and maintenance in my mind. Nick was still out there, somewhere. I nodded as I pulled a dress over my head, noticing my hair had grown a little. Feeling my scalp, I smiled. My hair was roughly the same length as my dad's. "Ok," I shouted, looking down at the dress. It was unsuitable, reminding me of something Mum might wear. Puffy short sleeves with shoulder pads, tight at the neck with an itchy collar of, well, something itchy. It was wide and flared from the waist too. I pulled it back over my head, quickly ruffling my hair so it stood up. I found a jacket, but its bright red lapels seemed to go on forever, and didn't quite match its purple, plus the cream piping around the pockets looked silly. "Where did you find these clothes?" I enquired, craning my neck to face the top of the door. "Did you actually *buy* them?"

"Of course!" He sounded offended. "From a charity store, from a distant time and even further away."

I shook my head with frustration, rummaging through the pile, pushing the unsuitable clothes through the small gap beneath the door with my foot. "I don't need these, thanks." They vanished.

At last I found a pair of trousers similar to Dad's – fairly thick blue denim, a little worn and short at the ankle – but at least they showed off my new shoes. I admired my reflections. They were oh, so comfortable. Comfort is everything, son.

"Do you think you'll be suitably attired *today*, Talethea?"

I pulled the gunbelt and holsters from the shorts, threading the belt through the hoops on the jeans and fastened the holsters back in place. "Probably not, but why would that matter to you, being so immortal?"

"I still have appointments to keep."

I decided not to reply, finding a white dress of soft lace. It was short, with three layers from the wide waistband. I held it up, then quickly pulled it on. It covered the weapons perfectly. "I'm almost ready. It's jewellery next!"

"Talethea! I really do not–"

"I'm joking! Relax, immortal!"

I found a jacket. Brown leather, scuffed and abused, reaching down to just above the knee, cut in at the waist, generous inside pockets. Thin lapels and collar, refusing to lie down. It fitted my frame and mindset perfectly. I was just about to open the cubicle door when I noticed the brim of a hat, peeking from the pile. It was almost as though Ephesus, amid the bizarre array of garments he'd supplied, had purposely hunted down that hat. It could have taken him a week and eight days for all I knew, as he'd returned instantly, but that obviously wasn't a true measure of exactly how long he'd spent hunting for these clothes. I snatched the hat from the pile, placed it upon my head and walked proudly outside.

He couldn't hide his smile, turning away as it found his face. I just stood there as the cubicle vanished, waiting for him to face me.

"What do you think?" I said.

He eventually turned, having effectively fenced off his expression with his usual line of determined wrinkles. "You found it!"

Now it was my turn to smile. I tapped the straw hat's brim with my forefinger. It was somewhat tattered, the brim a little narrower than the hat I wore as a child, but it afforded shade, for which my head was thankful. "I can't believe you found one, especially with a red ribbon tied in a bow!" I noticed from my tone I'd failed to sound surprised.

"It took a while," he said. "But it's not the only gift I have for you, there are three more."

I looked around as he took a few paces to face me, his hands clasped together. Slowly they parted revealing a tiny, yellow flower lying in the palm of his hand, its petals closed. Gently he took it, placing the stem in the button hole of my jacket. "A very special flower. It will never die."

I looked down at it. "Is it supposed to give people a hint to my nickname? If so, the petals are closed."

"Oh no, no. As I said, it's a very special flower. It will spread its petals when the time is right, for it and for you. Oh, before I forget," he reached into his satchel, producing a pair of sunglasses, big and wide, again, similar to those I'd worn during that summer of so long ago, "the final touch."

I took them and put them on, then gave him a hug, holding onto him tightly, unable to stop my tears, despite or perhaps due to everything my life had consisted of so far. "Thank you, Great Uncle. Thank you very much."

"You'll discover the final gift in good time," he said as we parted, his voice wavering with emotion. He cleared his throat, gesturing north, passing Charles to me. "Shall we continue?"

Our conversation ceased, our thoughts for a while surrendering to the natural beauty surrounding us. But then my thoughts centred on Keloff and my parents once again. I couldn't wait to be reunited with them, to tell them my story and hear theirs, as well as Charles'. Perhaps everything he did while his soul occupied my body was because adventure came to visit him? He'd tell me, of that I was certain. But most of all, I knew I had to warn Mum and Dad never to seek a house in Middletown, and discard that business card Nick had given her. As soon as I found Keloff, I'd take him back to Hope and explain everything to them with Charles' help, so we could all get on with our lives.

I'm guessing you can't wait to be reunited with me and your father, too, son, as I'm sure you also have stories to tell me. I know at the beginning of this letter, I wrote '*come find me*,' but that tradition is usually employed by couples after proposing marriage, although I used to play it with Charles, as you know.

Mum told me, there are varying degrees of '*come find me*'. As the tradition is, once that message has been delivered as a proposal, the proposer hides. If the woman, usually, or sometimes the man, or sometimes another woman or another man, agrees to marry, they have to seek and find the proposer. This is a commitment that never wavers, and once the proposer is found, the marriage is agreed and plans can begin. Some proposers have been known to hide as far away as possible, a test to see if the proposed really loves and wants them for the rest of their life. Some have been known to hide on different lands, as far away as the east-south-east, decades passing until they were found. But the rule is, you always wait.

I'm sorry to say, I'm very well hidden. Not because I don't want you to find me, but because I don't want others to first.

Mum told me Dad was impatient, and after he sent her a *'come find me'* message, he hid in the cupboard under the stairs while singing a sea shanty of eleven verses. He obviously loves her very much, which coincidentally is as much as I love you.

I took off my hat and wiped my brow with the back of my hand. "I'm tired of walking now. Is it far to this landmark I'd recognise?"

Great Uncle stopped, holding his hand to his forehead to shield his eyes from the suns. "We can travel by balloon, if you'd like?"

I clapped my hands together three times, jumping up and down on the spot, then stopped as I recalled my last, fateful balloon trip. "Is it safe?"

"Statistically, it's by far the safest way to travel, but that's probably down to the fact I'm the only person that travels by balloon, which sort of tips the statistics in the balloon's favour."

I looked up to the sky, waiting for his balloon to wink into existence and descend slowly to carry us away. He stood by my side and looked up too. "What are you looking for?"

"Oh." He said, reaching into his satchel. He pulled out a red balloon, stretched the neck a few times and blew into it.

Once it was inflated he tied a knot at the neck and held it out to me with a smile.

I felt my brow furrow. "This is it?"

He nodded, waving it in front of my face.

"I'd prefer pink."

He sighed, held the balloon under his right arm and rummaged around in his satchel again. After a few moments he produced a pink balloon, repeated the process and handed it to me. As soon as I held the neck below the knot, I felt a cocoon of invisible energy surround me. I began to float upward, as if the balloon was carrying me. But no, there was no sensation in my arm or fingers, as there would be if I were holding on for dear life. My feet were supported by that invisible cocoon, and the balloon above my head obviously just for show. I realised Great Uncle was catering for my childhood dream – no doubt through the guilt he felt for imprisoning me. I had many childhood dreams that had been betrayed, and he had a lot of work to do if his plan was to fulfil them all.

"Great Uncle?"

He joined me at my side, holding the red balloon, and looked over. "Yes?"

"You said you're older than a time when there was a beginning. Are you one of the ancient gods?"

He laughed in a bellow and looked down, shaking his head. "No no, Tiny Flower. Not at all. I wouldn't want the responsibility of such a role."

I sat down cross-legged in my invisible cocoon. "Then tell me, if you know – how did all this come about, the universe and everything?"

He sighed and I noticed his shoulders stiffen. "I've heard rumours over the millennia, from various dissociated sources that could never and will never meet. So I guess it's true."

"So, tell me, please?"

"There was a school of young beings, a classroom where all the children were conducting a little science experiment upon their desks. One child, in its haste to run to the playground with its friends as the break bell sounded, forgot to turn the experiment off, and during the break the universe was formed by that experiment."

I giggled, "That's absolutely ridiculous."

"Fine," he said abruptly. "I knew you wouldn't like the explanation. But I'll say this – can you give me a more plausible explanation, from any of the religions that have come and gone over the countless centuries? Perhaps the universe just brought itself into existence, as it had nothing better to do one afternoon?"

I sighed. "Then perhaps reality's just a recurring nightmare."

He spoke quickly, distracted. "Possibly. Those in the know are just waiting, living in fear of that being returning from the playground and turning the experiment off, thus collapsing all we've ever known into its constituent elements." He looked down and he descended, my balloon following his. "No one knows how long these children are given to play outside. It's all a bit of a worry, to be honest, not that I'm ever not."

We continued on for several leagues, speeding over the landscape in the same way balloons free of a child's grasp or tether don't. He turned to me, pointing below as we descended rapidly, coming to rest motionless in the air, just above the ground. "Talethea, I have to leave now. Take what I know for consideration, for this society requires long overdue maintenance."

Our feet met the grass and he produced a pin from his satchel, bursting his balloon, the rubber skin tumbling limply to the ground. He was about to burst mine.

"Can I keep it, please?"

"I shouldn't really–"

"Please?"

He sighed. "You'll find a recognisable landmark over that hill," he said, pointing. I smiled up at him, but his expression was set as he untied the knot, letting the air out with a squeal and passed it to me. "I would be cautious searching for the past – it may not want to be found, and you might not like what you find dwelling there."

I put the balloon in my jacket pocket before he had a chance to change his mind. "But the past is all the future I have, Ephesus."

A sadness touched his face as his door appeared. He opened it, turning from the threshold. "Thank you, Talethea. I wish you well, with all happiness for you, your family and loved ones. Goodbye, Tiny Flower." He lingered for a moment, as though he wanted to say more, but turned away as I spoke.

"Wait! How long will these deliberations take? We'll have a result soon! Put everything back how it should be, once Nick's crimes are exposed and he's punished!"

He shook his head. "It may take a little longer than soon. I have other business to attend to. Finding a suitable pair of slippers, for one."

"Later than sooner, then, but sooner than much later?"

"Maybe. A lifetime before I deliver the evidence, I would imagine. The Assembly will reach a swift verdict." With that, the door slammed behind him and vanished, just as I opened my mouth to object.

~ 16 ~
Meeting a Well-Known Stranger

I stood there for a long while after he left. I couldn't believe what he'd said. Why would they take such a long time to deliberate, and put everything right? I felt discarded, pointless with no further role to play now my enforced task was complete. It was a horrible feeling, son. One I hope you *never* have to experience for any length of time.

Being, feeling, alone is a terrible sensation, as though your very essence has been poured away, to leave you feeling utterly empty, helpless with nowhere to turn and, most painfully, no one to turn to. But, thinking about it now as I recount all this to you, it was more than that. I felt totally lost, as I had felt during my first Seasonstill fair. I was a very little girl, having run ahead of my parents to explore, weaving impatiently between the groups of people strolling along. As I stopped and turned, my parents weren't there. A chill from within overcame me instantly. All the bright colourful banners and signs, the flashing lights, the music, shouts of joy and laughter couldn't reassure or comfort me, warm my soul to remove the hollow cold in my heart. Only feeling my mum or dad's hand surrounding mine could do so. Sitting here writing this, I feel like that now, and realise with great regret I have possibly caused you to feel the same way. For that, I apologise again, son, and one day will hold your hand and never let it go.

As I looked out across the sprawling countryside, I knew if I turned, my parents wouldn't be standing there. Pulling my leather coat tightly around me I began to walk, knowing that beyond that hill, awaited a promise of familiarity that would not be broken.

Peering from the cart, the streets of damp grey cobbles and stone stared back at him through the fine

drizzle. It was a familiarity he had hoped he would never see again. Doors closed to the lantern-lit evening *'as though their owners were afraid they'd fling themselves wide upon their hinges, to shout and scream at me,'* he found himself believing.

The horse-drawn carriage turned right, the street narrowing, the cottages on either side foreboding bullies, leaning over him. As he passed, pools of gaslight illuminated them, then faded, hinting at an end to their regimented line, only to return to illustrate others before fading once more. They were sorrowfully identical and seemingly endless against the night, only the differing placement of candles in their narrow windows setting each apart. He imagined the identical families behind their walls, identical conversations following identical meals. Lives as rigidly ordered as the cold bricks protecting them.

The clopping hooves and rattling wheels finally ceased their lonely regularity, the carriage swaying to rest, a few final punctuations without meter as the horse steadied itself, snorting in the cold, resting.

They brought him out without saying a word, escorting him to black wrought-iron gates. A sign, *Evertree Correction House – Home for Paupers and Orphans* curled amid the thick upright spears as iron ivy, with *'May the Gods Save the Truthsayers'* creeping below with infant tendrils. Three figures, their faces covered by hoods, stood waiting. One unlocked the gates, pulling them aside.

Struggling at the handcuffs behind his back as he entered, he spat at the signs over and over again, the gentle misty rain gradually erasing his sap-like saliva.

Across the courtyard waited double oak doors, framed by fat stone columns.

Inside, a cracking fire to his left, a desk where a hooded figure took his name and age.

Later, a bunk in a dormitory, thin, narrow, low. His entry woke several, they woke others, pointing out this intruder to their slumber. Some cursed him with promises of punishment for waking them. Others just sat up, watching as he was stripped of his clothes and forced to wear those identical to the others.

The following morning, rules, regulations and a stark warning of the penalties for disobedience. His life from that day onward a barren landscape, displayed for him by the Oversayer and her servitors. Its naked rigidity, a cadence of conformity. *'It is strictly forbidden to stray into the dangerous territory of modulation. Severe punishment awaits any deciding to walk that path'* she concluded.

The years passed.

He studied, remembering the house where he was born, the importance his parents had placed upon that cavernous library and its books. Gradually, he fed upon the Sayers' truths, like a child forced to consume a bitter vegetable, knowing however vile the flavour, there were nutrients to be had to strengthen them. He read their books, between their lines of lies, reminded of those crabs picking at the bodies along the shoreline, revealing for him truth's undeniable territory.

And through the years.

The child obeyed as he quietly observed.

The boy acquiesced as he zestfully acquired.

The adolescent plotted while he tolerated patience.

The young man manipulated while he manufactured his future.

And behind those walls he honed his craft on his fellows' facile minds, beginning with the youngest and most impressionable.

It was easy, erasing their subconscious perceptions of self, of individualism, just as they had begun to settle as protective mantles supporting such from the Truthsayers' wretched doctrines.

He moved on to his peers. Sharing manufactured concerns he'd identified within them. Their unattainable hopes and insurmountable fears became accessible realities and conquered foes. Their preposterous fantasies replaced by conceivable factualities.

And then he moved on to the broken, those older than he that had suffered for so long, with his allies supporting him.

They began the process for him, eroding their elders' crumbling mental render incessantly with uncertainty. Unnoticed from within, like rain upon those cottages beyond the gates, lining freedom's walk, their individual bricks of confidence, regularity and conformity became gradually loose like teeth amid diseased gums. The bricks at their foundations of normality threatened to crumble now, unsupported, until he stepped forward to shore them up, encouraging them with a reliance upon him, the architect of all their futures.

Then the day came for them all to do his bidding.

They rose up, led by his second.

William, her mother had called her, whilst she lay in the stench of their bed. She called herself Billie when they found her roaming the streets, but that, and her short-cropped hair and boy's clothes didn't deter others holding her down while others took it in turn to abuse her, as her mother had.

The Truthsayers fell. From slit throats and punctured hearts they drowned, from severed Achilles tendons as they fled they stumbled, from skulls cleft by makeshift bludgeons they died.

And from there Nickolatus, the man now, distributed his fellows out into the streets, drip-feeding them into that poisoned society with his cures. Over the months they soaked into the streets like a stain, to lie in wait, lying to adopt their roles. One by one they forged a network on Nick's behalf.

Waiting for one year, he tortured the Oversayer, her screams unable to penetrate the walls. There he practised his craft, learning from their books, giving her a glimpse of death before repairing the damage he'd inflicted, only to repeat it. There the idea appeared.

'Will you walk that path towards dangerous territory?' He whispered in her ear.

She refused, over and over again, so he simply left her handcuffed and chained to his bed in the vacant dormitory, knowing her injuries would take their time to end her life.

Turning to face for the second and final time those gates he'd first seen as a child, he spat at the sign again, watching until the suns dried the stain.

Marching past the cottages towards the new life his colleagues had established for him, he was certain those identical buildings now bowed respectfully as he passed.

I reached the top of the hill, feeling far more comfortable and confident with my 'new' body.

I recognised the view below, but it was a distortion of my memory, an inaccurate illustration much like an artist's interpretation. The fields where yellow sunchoke flowers once stood proudly enjoying the suns were now barren. My eyes wandered further down into the town. The school building now held a sign perched upon its roof: 'Halls of the Kingdom of Truth,' and at the entrance stood two hooded Truthsayers. I hurried down the slope, holding onto my hat with one hand, keeping Charles steady at my waist with the other.

Upon reaching the outskirts of town I weaved through the streets, keeping as far away from the school as I could. Everything was quiet and still, and I was grateful to reach the path leading up to Keloff's house. As I climbed Ridgetop Hill, Charles began to stir, obviously hungry, so I tapped gently upon his shell and whistled, telling him where we were and to be patient. Keloff wouldn't mind him roaming around to nibble on whatever he could find.

The very top of the barn roof peeking above the receding curve of the hill made me grin. My pace quickened, and my heart joined in with excited anticipation. I knew it would be difficult to explain everything to Keloff, for him to come to terms with it all. But he, like myself, was older now, and with Charles' assistance I was sure he'd understand. I wondered what he looked like, how he was dressed – I just hoped he'd tried to grow a beard, and decided it didn't suit him.

The gate lay on its back, peering into the sky from the grass with sun-bleached planks. I stepped respectfully over it as I approached the house.

"Keloff!" I called, "It's me!" I stopped, laid the sling upon the grass and rolled Charles out. He emerged and began to search for a morsel as I approached the veranda, folding the sling and placing it beneath my gunbelt. "Kellllloooooff! Where are you, you silly boy?" Stepping onto the veranda it replied with a familiar welcoming creak. I decided to wait a while, sitting in the rocking chair, keeping an eye on Charles as he explored. If Keloff and Leet were in the barn, I'd wait here until they came out, to surprise them, and I wondered if Keloff would recognise me. Keeping a straight face would be difficult, but then again it always was with him around.

A distant bleeping sound invaded my plan, and I sat forward. It wasn't the same as a pickingweaver asking for its bobbin to be replaced, it was a harsh and urgent sound. I stood as it continued, leaning on the handrail looking to the right. A man came into full view from the side of the house, holding a metal detector, slowly waving the black detector plate above the soil with a bucket in his other hand. He wore grey overalls and big blue headphones, his face an illustration of furrow-browed concentration.

I hurried over to him, concerned he'd disturb the dormant plants.

"Excuse me, what are you doing? This is a private farm."

The stranger looked up upon hearing my voice, resting his headphones around the back of his neck. "Can I help you, miss?"

"If you're looking for old coins, they were removed many years ago, and were thankful for it. This is private land."

The stranger laughed. "No no, this is a plastic detector, miss. I'm looking for the eyes of Barnaby, the talking banana."

I took a step forward, wondering what on earth he was talking about. "This is a mothcotton farm," I placed my hands on my hips and glanced back to the house. "The owner and his son should be around here, somewhere."

He looked at my feet. "If you don't mind, I've recently tilled the soil. I don't want any compression hindering me. This is a site of significant historical interest, where the final battle took place, if the translations are accurate."

I looked down, realising the soil wasn't ploughed in horizontal lines as it should be for the plants, then saw something glinting in the suns between my feet. I crouched down and pulled it from the dry earth. It was a pickingweaver, rusted into picking position, the bobbin chassis fused to its back, with a full loom of decayed mothcotton. I looked more closely at the soil; there were many pickingweavers poking from the ground, rust bleeding into the earth from small metal bones. I stood and the stranger snatched the pickingweaver from me and brushed off the soil. "Thanks, small bits of plastic give a false reading." He tossed it into a bucket at his side, which was almost full with rusted pickingweavers and their components.

"What final battle, translations? W*hat* are you doing?"

"Looking for the eyes, I told you. An old written fable, it points to this hill as being the site, if the translations are right." He waved his hand about. "This land hasn't been farmed for decades. I have a Sayer's permit, if that will help, miss?"

My heart sank as did my head. "No, that won't be necessary." Decades. That had to be a mistake. And as for farmed, that was open to interpretation, harvested was a more accurate word, as Leet's family had owned the land for over two centuries, the mothcotton growing wild upon the hill.

"This is where the final battle of the Ventriloquist War took place, long before it was a farm. Historians have been campaigning to search this site for a long time. You must have heard of it, surely?"

"No. You said something about eyes?"

"Yes. It's said Barnaby's eyes recorded the final battle. They had tiny cameras built into them. It's of great historical significance to the Truthsayers, important local history. Especially if those eyes recorded what they saw. They need to know, don't you know."

"Truthsayers, Ventriloquist War? Why would the sayers need to watch something so, so silly?"

"No, not the battle, but what's in the background. Most of the footage from long ago, and for that matter, illustrations and printed pictures, reveal more of what life was like with their backgrounds, more so than the actual subject matter. There's this man they say keeps popping up in various pictures throughout the decades. He never changes and they want to find out more about him."

"I know what a ventriloquist is, and the dummies they use, but..."

The stranger made a disapproving noise in his throat and dropped his plastic detector onto the soil. "Dummies – there, you see, you've chosen! That's how it all began, so now you know. As with all wars, it all started with a simple argument, fuelled by wine in a restaurant on a Smoothday night, down in the village where the Yougo's Inn stood, where the school used to be. Everyone gets a little anxious on a Smoothday, with Mournday morning rapidly approaching."

"I guess so." I was about to leave as he continued, my politeness forcing me to listen to his enthusiasm.

"There were two ventriloquists eating at different tables, but neither knew the other was there. It's said one was a local gentleman, the other, staying at the inn while he visited his family. After dessert, one of them decided to produce his puppet from under the table. He had his guests and a few other tables entertained, they laughed, ordered more drinks, the puppet telling jokes at his owner's expense. Then a shout came from a table at the rear. It was a croaky voice that told the puppet to shut up, which as you probably know, was aimed at the owner, not the puppet. The owner turned and there, standing on a table, was Barnaby, the talking banana, pointing an accusing appendage – a piece of skin not fully removed from his body – towards the puppet, Fiona Flamingo. *'Shut up, you dummy, we're trying to eat over here!'* shouted Barnaby.

"No. You shut up. I'm not a dummy, I'm a puppet!" Then all hell broke loose as they argued the whys and wherefores of if they were puppets or dummies. There was a fight, Barnaby losing an appendage and Fiona a leg."

"That's not really worth going to war over, is it." I said, feeling as though I should run home as fast as I could, but fear of what I might find there preventing me.

"Oh, bloody wars lasting centuries have begun over less," said the stranger with raised eyebrows of sadness. "Barnaby and Fiona decided to settle the argument in a final, decisive battle – on this very field. Both sides amassed their supporters from as far and wide as places that no longer exist, armies of ventriloquists determined their belief was the one and only belief. Can you imagine it? Hordes of puppets and dummies clashing, slicing at each other, cutting into their cloth covers, spilling foam and fabric stuffings. Jokes filled the air to distract opponents, insults and baiting causing emotional damage to both sides. Balloon animal makers threw all kinds of convoluted traps in the path of the advancing troops, tripping them up, squeaking and popping beneath marching feet. Pantomime horse cavalry, carrying tickling jousting pikes threatened to render puppets and dummies useless though uncontrollable laughter. That's about it, really. The translation concludes reading that Barnaby's side was victorious. Following his owner's death, Barnaby died of natural causes a year later, buried here with his fallen comrades that had fought so bravely for their cause."

"I see," I said, calling for Charles. "I must go."

"Ah," said the stranger, seizing my arm, "But your ears haven't heard about the sheep."

"Sheep?"

"Yes, and the old women. This is hearsay – a theory championed by the majority of historians, but it makes complete sense."

Doubtful, I took a few steps backwards towards Charles as he complained the dirt was too dry to reach me and wanted to be picked up. Besides, I thought it best to face this unhinged individual, as I wasn't sure he wouldn't pick up his detector and hit me with it for my obvious display of bewildered disinterest. I bundled Charles into his sling as fast as I could, politely returning, pretending to listen to his rubbish once more.

"Barnaby employed a decisive tactic that military experts agree tipped the balance of the battle in his favour. It was simple, don't you know? They kidnapped people from their knitting circles and sewing clubs, employing them behind the lines. The wounded would be brought back for repair, to fight again, something Fiona hadn't thought of. But Barnaby's resources ran low – thread, cotton, offcuts of stuffing, felt – all became scarce and prices soared in the village that became Middletown. Fiona was torn, no pun intended, between cutting off Barnaby's supply line from the village, or maintaining the battle here.

She decided to stay, and that's when Barnaby played his final winning hand. He equipped every soldier with a dwarf sheep and a battery-operated beard trimmer. The sheep were shorn on the field, the injured receiving the medical attention they needed to continue the fight as soon as someone shouted *'Seamstress!'* It was a genius military manoeuvre," he looked to the dirt with obvious admiration, "a superb tactic."

"That's really interesting."

"That's why this landmark became a mothcotton farm, as a mark of respect. And, well, I can also tell you..."

His head split along the side, just above his left ear in a spray of red. He was dead as he hit the ground. Then I heard the shot. It came from a long way off, echoing around me.

I didn't look back, running down the hill as fast as I could, jumping over the furrows to reach the track below. And then a flash filled my mind's eye, just as Ephesus had told me. It was Nick, running through the village streets, past the old school, clutching the blue and red shorts and top I'd left in the field.

As I reached the track I had a choice – either head for home over open ground, or the citadel ruins across the fields where trees and hedgerows provided cover. I left the track, hurrying down the bank to gain more cover, crouching down, following the narrow footpath as fast as I could.

Nick ran past the house, ignoring the body on the earth.

Another shot, clipping the brim of my hat. I swore, heading for a lonely beech tree. Breathing hard I hid behind it, telling Charles to keep still as I pulled out a gun. Peering around the tree, I could just see the sniper kneeling down, reloading. My shot found its mark, to my surprise, some inner instinct, a skill remembered from Charles – I had no idea, knowing only I should run.

Another flash, Nick crouching down, checking the body for a pulse. Other officers joined him, automatic weapons at the ready, scanning the countryside. Nick stood, pointing, barking orders.

I weaved between the bushes, using the hedgerows for cover, one of the citadel's ruined spires peering above the rolling hills, urging me onwards. I had to move fast, over the next hill the citadel sat, in the centre of an artificial canyon shaped like a bowl. The cover became thicker with gleeberry bushes towards the top, above, a group of pine trees stood looking down at me from the summit. I ran to them as fast as I could, another shot impacting the grass beside me.

Reaching the trees, another shot, splintering wood above my head. I cleared the pines, catching my breath. Far below what looked like a giant wheel lying on its side. There, the citadel stood at the wheel's hub. It was a monstrous building of grey stone. Pointed towers of different heights reached up from its central sphere, cracked and incomplete, missing tiles exposing rotting frameworks of black wood. From this central hub, ten covered pilgrims' bridges, some complete, others broken, led like wheel spokes to all manner of churches situated upon the rim of the bowl. They contrasted incredibly, each one of a different architectural style. Domes of alabaster and marble, grotesque, jagged spires of granite. Some supported by statues of beautiful ancient beings, others by geometric symbols of unknown meanings, intricately carved in hammered iron and cast from concrete. Groups of eroded bronze and copper-topped pyramids shone beneath the suns, towers of wood and brass, their seamless joins noticeable only by the different types of wood employed. No two, like the religions they were built to house, were alike. Between their bridges, flying buttresses reached up above the tree tops from the side of the bowl, connecting to the middle of the citadel's sphere. Above this, a walkway encircled the circumference, where crumbling battlements created an uneven line of rubble. It was said two thousand years ago a peace was made between the differing religions, as their wars and conflicts had dominated this landscape, threatening to eradicate the growing fabric of society.

Someone had proposed this building, a place where all religions could gather in their churches to then congregate in the citadel. There they would share their beliefs in turn, policed by the Unbelievers, a group of impartial individuals who would tolerate not a single show of intolerance or violence toward other belief systems as they preached.

Slowly, one by one, the churches became abandoned, as worshippers left their congregations, favouring the beliefs of others or shunning belief altogether, creating the contradictory Church of Disbelief. Some religions were lost to memory, churches were demolished as new beliefs and buildings took their places. Combinations of two, three – perhaps four systems emerged. But the Unbelievers forbade any holy texts from these abandoned beliefs to be written down. Only they retained these doctrines within their memories, ensuring no new religion would emerge as a pastiche of what had been worshipped before. I looked down at this abandoned folly, remembering a similar image, as something clicked. The drawing Keloff had made for me of the unicycle, ten spokes with one coloured in red. Shielding my eyes from the suns I matched the memory of that drawing to the citadel and its bridges below. Upon the opposite side of the bowl I could just make out a clump of tall oaks, matching the position of the drawing's saddle. I counted the bridges, matching one with the angle of the red-coloured spoke. Was I meant to take it, or did the red mean avoid it?

A spray of bullets carved a broken line into the tree to my right and I ran.

I found the outskirts – thankful for the giant blocks of granite and basalt protruding from the grass, remnants of an ill-fated attempt to move them for building purposes decades ago. I ran around the canyon, deciding I should take the red bridge.

Wide stone steps led up to a carcass, once one of the ten churches with the bridge leading to the citadel beyond. I ran though the ruined church as automatic fire spat at me, chipping the stone ruins. Then, onto the bridge, hoping unlike the many others in my peripheral vision, it was complete.

Bullets impacting sent chippings into the backs of my legs, others tumbling to rest in front of me. Holding a gun behind me, I let off several shots, hoping my hunters would seek cover, allowing me to make progress. I looked to my right where three armed officers ran across the adjacent bridge. Glancing to the left, two on that bridge.

"Nowhere to go, girly!" shouted Nick. "Stop! Put down the weapon or we'll stop you for good."

I reached a fallen column, vaulted over it and hid, catching my breath again. Nick was right. Those five officers would reach the citadel before me.

"I want the snail, alive. Put it down and you can walk away."

What on earth did Nick want with Charles? That didn't make sense to me at first. Then I remembered Gruber's explanation of the bullets, the concentrate. It was clear Nick wanted to use Charles to produce a drug, introduce it into the food chain, to destroy all hope as Moople had demanded.

"Never!" I cried, angling my gun above the column, firing back my reply. I turned and ran, watching the officers flanking me on either side, racing to the citadel. Then a thundering crash as the bridge to my left crumbled into the bowl without warning, the screams of the officers brief as the settling of rubble buried them. I stopped, looked right, the officers there had stopped, staring below, then over to me as a section of the bridge behind them fell away, pushing up a cloud of dry grey dust to cover them. I heard Nick shout *"Run!"* and looked back along the bridge. He was walking towards me, face determined, three officers behind him. Then a sudden calamity of stone upon stone filled the air. The bridge to my right had separated from the edge of the citadel, falling backward, sending the officers to the ground to slide helplessly into the depths.

Firing again – the arched entrance to the citadel looming ahead. The bullets showered the ground behind me once more as I ran, then a searing pain in my right leg. I stumbled across the threshold into the shadows of the citadel, screaming in pain as I lay there. I looked down at my leg, scrambling on all fours between the rows of dusty wooden pews. The bullet had grazed the right side of my calf, and I was bleeding badly. Pulling the hat off my head, I removed the ribbon, tying it as tight as I could around the wound.

Searching the area for a way out, I found ten groups of pews, each one a segment of a circle, reminding me of pizza slices. I shook my head at the bizarre thought, noticing they were facing a wide circular stone well. Above, a sphere of dulled silver, ten arms extending over the centre of the pews with a cluster of empty candle holders at their ends. I hurried to the well, where a large stone bucket was connected to a chain and windlass around a metal yoke. I peered down into the darkness as a spray of bullets ricocheted from the yoke. Without thinking twice I climbed over the broad circumference of stone, holding on with one hand as I pulled the balloon from my pocket. The bullets whizzed above as I blew as fast as I could into the neck, holding it closed with my thumb and forefinger. I closed my eyes as the sensation enveloped me again, having no other choice than to let go with my other hand and hope I'd inflated the balloon enough. Gripping the neck with both hands we slowly descended. Shouting found my ears. I looked up to the rapidly diminishing circle of light, faces appearing around the rim. I closed my eyes again, willing the balloon to descend faster. Immediately it obeyed, the circle of light shrinking almost to a pin head – then a flash, Nick looking down into the darkness, aiming his weapon. Willing the balloon to the left, my shoulder hit the rough wall as he let off a shot, piercing the balloon. I fell, landing amid a mound of what felt like shale, hundreds of voices shouting and swearing in different accents and dialects amid the darkness.

I scrambled through the shale, which turned out to be a mound of old coins of different sizes, each moaning at me and each other as I pushed them aside. As my eyes became accustomed to my surroundings I found an arched tunnel illuminated by a soft glow. I stood as best I could, checking on Charles, then my leg. Both complained, but were none the worse for wear as I stepped into the low light.

"Hello, Talethea."

I turned, pulling out my gun, surprised by the voice. A figure stood in silhouette.

"How do you know my name? Who are you?"

"My name's Alan, and I'm very honoured to finally make your acquaintance. Keloff said he'd informed you of me. I know everything."

~ 17 ~
Alan

He held up his hands as I was about to speak. "I'll answer all of your questions, including those born from my answers in good time. But first, please put your weapon away and follow me. You need medical attention, and it's only a matter of time before Nick and his men find their way down here."

He turned and walked down the corridor towards the light. "I apologise for the darkness. My eyes do not require much illumination, and your arrival, although anticipated, is a little earlier than predicted."

Our feet splashed through puddles of water, echoing around us. The light ahead grew, picking out shadows from uneven brickwork upon the arched tunnel. "Keloff told me about you, but I didn't think you were real. I'm here to find him, then I'm going to Hope for my parents. He wasn't at the farm, have you seen him?"

We reached a circular door dominating the end of the tunnel, of rusted yellow metal and domed silver rivets as large as my hand. Above it, a lamp surrounded by a wire cage.

"Perhaps I'm not real?" he grinned for as moment, as though he expected me to laugh. "Please, come in." He pushed the door aside, and I was surprised by its thickness – a good two handfuls of tads and several slivers. I followed, stepping over the deep frame into a room filled with screens fixed to the walls, with moving images upon them. The screens were all shapes and sizes, some displaying black and white, others in full garish colour. They showed different views of many places. Some were familiar – Hope, Middletown, Steeltown, others completely strange and unknown to me.

"Keloff." said the man, turning to face me. His skin was dark, flawless without a single blemish or trace of stubble upon his strong jaw. His eyes seemed to emit a soft light, dark brown, friendly and full of vitality, his head free of hair. He wore light grey, tight-fitting overalls from head to toe without a visible seam. "He waited for you as long as he could. Longer than he should." He spoke calmly, his voice soothingly deep, warm, and most importantly, reassuring. "I'm pleased you found his drawing useful."

"It was a gamble, red *could* have meant no. Where is he?" I heard myself ask quietly, his composed manner infecting me. For that moment and many thereafter, I forgot about Nick and his officers.

Son, if you haven't already guessed, this is the moment I met your uncle.

"If you'll sit, I'll attend to your wound," he said, motioning to the only chair in the room. The screens flickered behind him, altering their views. "You can let Charles out to look around if you wish. He'll be quite safe."

I did as he suggested, and as Charles emerged, extending his eye-stalks, Alan spoke to him, clicking his fingers rapidly, his feet tapping the stone floor. Charles seemed excited, and spoke back, quicker than he'd ever spoken to me. I pulled up my trouser leg as their conversation ceased.

"You have been lucky, Talethea." he said, examining my wound, "If the bullet had entered another inch to your left, it would have shattered your fibula. You would have fallen, rendering you unable to walk further." As he placed a hand around the wound I felt a searing pain. I tried to pull my leg away, but his grip was so strong I couldn't move. "Ouch! That *really* bloody hurts!"

His dark eyes stared up at me. "Please, hold still. This will take but a few more moments."

The pain began to subside and he removed his hand.

"What have you done?" I demanded through sharp breaths, lifting my leg to see a graze of red blotchy skin.

"I've introduced an antibiotic into your bloodstream to prevent infection, as well as an anaesthetic to ease the pain. The wound has been sealed by applying a very high level of heat." He looked up at me with just a hint of a grin.

"You won't be able to drink alcohol for a week, but you'll need to hydrate soon. The injury will be a little sore for a while." He stood with a little difficulty, his motion strange, somehow. There was something about him which was different, something I couldn't quite pinpoint at the time. "The wound will take time to completely heal. The scar shouldn't be too ugly. If you do find it unsightly, I can perform a skin graft to improve its appearance. But at a later date, when time isn't so pressing."

I pulled my trouser leg down carefully. "Thank you, but how *did* you do that, and what were you saying to Charles – it was too fast for me to understand?"

"You're more than welcome. Don't worry, I was explaining to him that you're both safe, and details of the procedure I've just performed." He patted Charles' shell. "I didn't want to cause him concern, and think I was harming you. He asked me who I was, so I told him."

"Well, I know your name, Alan. So how about you tell *me* exactly who you are," I looked around the room, "and what this place is?"

"This is my home from home, one of my monitoring stations." His head jerked to the side, his expression altering slightly. "We have unwelcome visitors, and must leave, now. Nickolatus and his men are using the chain to follow you into the Well of Unanswered Prayers. I should have removed it, but Keloff insisted on using it to visit me." He thrust his feet into a pair of shoes, then looked down at them. "Do you know how to tie laces? I've forgotten."

I stood shakily, quickly tying his shoes before pulling out my weapon. "You can tell me more later. The door will provide cover." I ejected the clip, checking the remaining ammunition. "How many are there?"

He placed a hand on the gun, pushing down upon it slowly. "That, will not be necessary."

"Then how do you expect us to defend ourselves? They killed a man back at the farm. He was looking for plastic eyes belonging to something called a banana. Nick's after

Charles, that's all he's concerned with – he'll kill us both. If you know everything, you should know that!"

"Everything. Bananas don't exist here, they were indigenous only at home. I know only everything of the past and present, and from those I can predict the future with a certain measure of inaccuracy." He took a step into the tunnel and stared ahead. "My additive network is such that I can't remember what I'm supposed to forget. Something I should have addressed years ago, but keep forgetting to do, as my mind's so full."

Shouting filtered along the tunnel. Complaining coins and officers. In the distance, torchlight beams examined the walls. "They're here. Close the door and lock it or we're both dead."

He stepped back into the room. "Talethea, I understand your concern. I won't permit them to harm you, as much as I won't permit you to harm them." He closed the door. "Do you feel well enough to walk?"

"I guess so. What do you mean..."

"Then we should leave now. It's a fair distance to Hope." He opened a drawer set into a desk beneath the rectangular screens, pulling out a turquoise cross-body handbag with white stitching, gold fittings and a mother-of-pearl clasp, placing it over his shoulder. "As I said, I'll answer all of your questions on the way there. My hotel requires maintenance. Anion informs me the quantum leak has grown worse, so I must repair it before I lose the parallax." He closed his eyes and the whole room began to revolve with a squeal of metal upon metal. As it stopped, he pulled the door open almost effortlessly, revealing a similar tunnel beyond. "The terrain will be uncomfortable for Charles. If you'll allow me, I'll carry him in his sling."

I holstered the weapon and pulled the sling from my gunbelt, holding it out to him. "By all means."

~ 18 ~
The Mines of Too Many Memories

We walked down a steep, uneven slope for what seemed a league or so. The air was cold, water trickling between our feet from the bare rock, urging us forward beneath the low light. At last the slope levelled out and the light increased as we found ourselves in a room with a low ceiling. There were wooden doors painted different colours surrounding us as we stood in the centre of the room. I counted them.

"Nine doors?"

"The Decagon Junction. Each door leads to a different province, as they used to be known." Alan looked at each door in turn, and I noticed the slight frown upon his face as he slowly scratched his chin. "Mm. Now that's a puzzle."

"What's wrong. Don't tell me you can't remember which one leads to Hope?"

"Eventually I might. Hotel Infinity's basement, perhaps. I'll ask Anion. He'll remember." He blinked rapidly for a moment. "Yellow. Oh yes, good idea. That will be quicker. In the barn. Thank you." He opened his eyes and the yellow door. I followed along a narrow passage for several minutes until at the end Alan opened another wooden door and walked through into the light. I closed it behind me, noticing the other side of the door was made of rock, and as I watched, it fitted into where I expected to see a frame, effectively hiding its existence amid the rock face.

The view took my breath as I turned. We stood on a steel platform high in the air, overlooking a vast landscape illuminated by gigantic orbs hanging from chains on the ceiling. There, in shadows and highlights the uneven rock undulated, grey and jagged like clouds covering a gloomy Seasonchill sky.

I looked down, steadying myself on a handrail in front of me. "What *is* this place?"

"This is the past, Talethea," said Alan, his head slowly turning as he studied the cavernous landscape below us. "For many years now, automatic miners – a little like pickingweavers – have dug beneath the surface for me."

"My Grandpa Roan worked here. What are you looking for?"

"No, not here." He pointed. "He worked beyond the north-eastern wall. I'm looking for information." He turned to face me. "Information that will help me build a clear image of the past, providing indisputable evidence of when the missing year took place, and perhaps why."

"Ephesus spoke to me about that. He created it so he could write himself into people's memories, so we'd accept him. It wasn't *that* long ago!"

"Ephesus is a liar," he said, turning back to the view. "He is nothing more than a man. Daemons, the Darkness as everyone calls them, nothing more than men evolved, men that followed him as he left open the gateway he prised apart from his existence, to come here for you. It's far easier to create dread when appearing as something that is feared and unknown."

"Came for me, what do you mean? Why?"

"The Darkness consumed almost everything in his universe, they couldn't be stopped. It was so easy for them, the many differing inhabitants of that universe on so many hundreds of worlds so easily led, embracing the evil they championed. Your great uncle Ephesus is a product of my world, but from his reality and not mine, and of a time in the *very* distant future, compared to my own." He began to walk along the gantry.

"You can't just stop there."

He stopped and looked at his feet. "I hadn't, until you suggested I had, which I have now."

"No, the explanation."

He walked on. "His reality, as with all other realities, is a product from the birth of the very first universe. It expanded too quickly, Talethea, like water flowing from a tap, threatening to overflow in your mum's kitchen sink."

I grinned to myself. "Mum just pulls the plug. She had to do that when one of the taps broke and she couldn't turn it off."

"Precisely! The plug stopper to the universe was pulled, or rather broken through. Imagine, the weight of a thousand left-overs, scraped from dirty dinner plates. The plug stopper, a big black hole in space, where all those left-over ingredients gathered, flowed down into it to form another universe. But imagine more, if that plug hole wasn't large enough to stop the sink from overflowing, then..."

I cut him off. "The sink would need a lot more plug holes?"

"That, Talethea, is precisely correct, and exactly what happened. All those plug stoppers were broken through at different times. Multiple universes were born from them, so they exist in different sizes and ages, growing, expanding, developing. You see, if Ephesus hadn't opened that gateway to journey here, crawling up through the plug hole like a spider once the water drains away, the Darkedness would never have found their way here too."

"But how did he make a gateway? It was difficult enough for my dad to mend the tap, and put up a rough fence at the bottom of our garden around the whitefruit trees to stop Charles getting to them."

"Ephesus placed a celestial body called a neutron star in orbit around that black hole, that plug hole, allowing him to halt the flow and essentially crawl through it like a spider into this younger universe."

I couldn't stop saying "but," so I said "however" instead, but it didn't sound right. "However, why me? Why did he want me?"

His gaze fell upon the rock face. "We should keep moving," he muttered, pausing for a while. "Ephesus told you, in his reality, you drowned. When he and Moople opened the gateway and observed you, but not versions of themselves, his primary objective was to take you back to his existence, erasing his guilt, and the grief of that Talethea's parents. But then, the Darkedness eventually found that open gateway and followed him here. He and Moople were forced under that contract to adopt their roles. Someone forgot to include a clause prohibiting the Darkedness feeding across different realities, and that missing year, which I believe was originally designed by Ephesus so he could erase all knowledge of *you*, had to be used to include all knowledge of *him*. His version of '*and they all lived happily ever after*,' if you've heard that phrase?"

I had, but still needed proof before I believed in it. "So if he had taken me back, what then?"

He answered quickly. "I'm unsure of your question."

"You said the Darkedness consumed almost everything in his universe, that they couldn't be stopped. Why would he take me back there?"

"I believe he found his second objective during that time. Remember, his Talethea drowned. I believe his plan was to swap you both, return with you to his realm, leaving the body of his Talethea in the lake, here, for your parents to find."

"That's disgusting. If he had taken me back, I'd have my throat cut and be trapped inside Nick's head."

He nodded. "He was so desperate to save his world, but forced to carry out his plan here, as the Darkedness arrived before he could return home with you, to a reality which is far, far older than this."

I nodded to myself, slowly piecing everything together.

"Come on, we must hurry. There's much to show you down there."

"Alan, wait. There's something you should know. When I escaped Nick, I saw the remains of two children in his head, but he didn't have any memory of them. Who were they?"

"I have no idea. But it seems as though Nick conquered those children, children murdered by Ephesus, their souls installed to witness Nick's crimes."

"In other realities?"

He let out a deep breath as he nodded. "It seems Nick is perhaps not a constant in *every* reality, and has been used many times to work for the Darkness as their champion."

I shook my head. "Ephesus and Moople have been playing this game across several realities. Maybe Moople had a hand in bringing Nick here?"

"Again, I have no idea. It's a possibility. Please, we both have urgent business to address."

"What if I had returned with Ephesus, become his Talethea? Would that doorway he left wide open have then closed, shut tight forever to this realm, preventing the evil from ever consuming my beautiful world?"

Alan shrugged. "Only he can answer that question."

We climbed down a winding staircase in silence. It seemed to go on forever, my head swimming with the revelations Alan, this man who knows everything, had told me. I began to come to terms with all the lies Ephesus had fed me. If his original plan had worked, my parents' grief would have been intolerable, and I began to wonder how they would have reacted seeing my body in the lake – how Keloff and Charles would have coped. Then I also came to terms with this fact; they *had* coped over the past few years or so, in the only way they possibly could, with hope, their relief from ongoing grief and longing to know what had happened to me just a short time before.

"Alan, if you really know everything, can you tell me about the universe? Ephesus made fun of me when I asked him. I know you won't."

He cleared his throat. "The universe is similar to a flowering garden. But if not tended, weeds appear, to strangle and suffocate beauty. But who planted the seeds, and who is responsible for looking after them? That, I don't know, but would dearly love to. Just like flowers, lifeforms drew nutrients, energy from the cosmos. And as their life-giving suns died, so did they – like flowers amid winter's inexorable rise to dominance. Then came the great settlement. When the cosmos relaxed then life, aware of the needs of their home-worlds, catered for them symbiotically." He chuckled. "Which brings me to this. I was created to solve a problem, and to then implement solutions."

"And that problem was?"

"The problem, simply put, how to control my planet's population growth, distribute resources evenly, both natural and man-made. To maintain the human race by establishing a perpetual, affordable food and energy supply, whilst balancing the quality of *all* life upon the planet."

"So in other words, they wanted you to sort out their problems, problems they created."

"In other words, yes."

"You said you were created?"

"My consciousness, yes. My name means, Artificial Lifeform Additive Network."

"Artificial? So you arrived here in the slab, with the other artificials that built Steeltown?"

"No, I arrived long before them, long before the first sapling peeked from the earth in Wishart's wood. I answered all my creators' questions, provided them with answers, solutions. But they didn't like what they heard. And then, when sterility touched the Earth, they blamed me, accusing me of engineering a virus to prohibit their reproduction. They were their own problem, but wouldn't fully admit the fact, even though many of them tried to further such facts."

"The receptacle of life was empty – if you know everything, you'd know that, that's what caused their sterility. Please, tell me about them, what were they like?"

"Are you *really* that interested?"

"Of course!"

He nodded, giving me a wide smile. "Similar to the people of this world, just people really. But their world was full, overflowing at its prime. My planet, my dear old Earth was much like this in many ways, but larger. Like a child refusing to go out into the rain, they turned their backs to the stars, those tiny beacons that for tens of thousands of years had beckoned them, fuelled their primitive curiosity, their wonder, fear and imagination. Gradually they cast aside foolish beliefs born from gazing upward, replacing superstition with science.

"Centuries ago they had managed just a small step into the void. Again, like a child placing a tentative foot upon the first stepping stone leading across a stream. Then, as they stood upon their dusty, grey neighbouring satellite, they turned, their gaze falling back to their home, beckoning them to return to the safety of complacent ignorance. If they could only have found the strength of their forefathers and foremothers from hundreds of years ago! Brave individuals, facing dangerous ocean voyages to new lands and the lives waiting for them to build. So many of them died, so many families wiped out from history by sickness and tragedy." He paused for a moment, his eyes flickering, as though searching for a memory.

"Then, the Salandor corporation, my parents, the company that constructed my consciousness, forged ahead, building communities upon their grey moon. And later, the great grandchildren of those first pioneering settlers used that stepping stone as a platform to shout objections on behalf of their long-dead forefathers and foremothers, and their decisions to leave Earth. They demanded justice, compensation and a place in a brighter, natural sun, back on an overcrowded Earth. They accused my parents of seduction, abduction. It was ironic, for without their ancestors' stubborn bravery, determined to forge new settlements with other like-minded cultures, they wouldn't exist. And again, how ironic, that the stepping stone leading towards another, a potential new home waiting for them further away, was provided by the laws of the very land they refused to accept as home, where upon Earth such rights were being curtailed on a daily basis." He stopped and bowed his head for a long while, shaking it briskly before facing me, his expression full of disbelief. "History has a very annoying habit of repeating itself,

Talethea. I can only look back through my memory with an overwhelming feeling of sorrow. You cannot fight even the smallest thread of stupidity with rationality.

"When I settled here, I recounted all that had happened upon my world. Wrote it all down, omitting not *one* shred of history. Eventually, I succumbed to a nagging, inner need, building a library within the house I built for myself and a family I never constructed, hoping to integrate and become one of you, hoping those books would one day be found and read and ultimately, this society would learn from all the horse shit that ruined my Earth. I should have foreseen it, but I too became a victim of prejudice and hatred once again, driven from my home for many narrow-minded reasons. It lay empty for many years, years I spent riding the automated distribution carriages all over this continent, until a young woman decided to live in my house. After a long while I returned to the abandoned citadel I constructed two thousand years ago, a place for the ten dominant religions to come and meet, worship and communicate with each other for the good of all, hoping they would settle their petty arguments and meld into one global doctrine, governed by peace, acceptance and tolerance."

"You tried too hard, Alan. Have you considered, even horse shit is gathered up and used to feed flowers and other plants? My dad used it many times, especially for the mushroom patch. Mum complained it reeked, but she loved the mushrooms, and so did Charles and I. You shouldn't feel guilty for doing what you knew was right."

He looked at me, forlorn, then peered over my shoulder. "Back there, the well you descended, the Well of Unanswered Prayers? Its purpose was simply so worshippers from all religions could write down their prayers and cast them into the well." He began to laugh, then composed himself. "You would not believe the amount of prayers I've read. Sitting there, watching folded paper fluttering down towards me, day after day. There was a commonality emerging from those prayers, and when we have more time, I'll tell you what that is. Later, the well became a place to discard talking money. A wishing well of whispered desires. The stories those coins spoke to each other, lying there, the places they've seen, the things they've paid for, the adventures they eventually told me of. All very useful information, contributing to the parallax." He reached behind my left ear like one of Hope's street magicians, holding a copper penny in front of me between thumb and forefinger. "Especially this one, which I spoke to a while ago."

"I ain't telling ya nothin' more, bud."

He held it up into the false light, examining it. "He's a very persistent little coin, compared to all the others, that are more than happy to speak of their lives. He has hardly any wear, which is surprising, considering his age." Alan motioned for me to hold out my hand, placing the penny in my palm as I did so.

"I'm tellin' *you* nothin' either. Listen, both o' ya, you get me into the Mayor's cash drawer in Steeltown, and I'll tell ya howta open that thing."

I passed the coin back. "What thing?"

Alan grinned, his eyebrows rapidly bouncing up and down several times as he pulled the quantum handbag around to hold it in front of me.

"We'll stop off briefly at Steeltown on the way, before the hotel?"

I nodded, keeping to myself the fact I had a request for the Mayor also.

At last we reached the ground. As far as I could see, row upon row of deep rectangular furrows in the earth stretched before us, as though grave robbers had recently fled with their booty. All manner of objects were piled up beside these furrows, unknown devices, metal, glass, and that rare commodity, plastic. Dotted around the landscape, rooftops sprouted from the soil in rows, some intact, others dismantled, their components neatly placed alongside.

Then, a flash in my head as we trod the past.

Nick, back at the outskirts of Middletown, heading for the waterfront. His car's headlights cutting through the early evening mist coming off the canal. He parked, locked the car and hurried between the lock-ups, avoiding the security lights.

I've had experiences many times of what I'm about to relate to you, son, but felt this was the correct place to include them as one, as this flash led to a very surprising conclusion for me.

I've decided to tell it like this, from all the horrific episodes I've seen, in one go.

I know, I said I could *'close my eyes,'* for want of a better term, when I was inside Nick's head. But what use is a witness with their eyes closed?

This is the final time I will relate the past to you in this way, as time is running short here, and I must complete my story for you before I am forced to attend to urgent business of my own.

This is what I saw, over several years.

I *will not* be denied! I'll replace what has been stolen from me, twice.

The beauty of music, *my* music!

The warehouse lock-up contains a memory of mine, built from many mechanical instruments and devices. Steeltown's Mayor provided some of the material, including an artificial to watch over all of this for me, while I pretended to fulfil the responsibilities of my position. What a joke. My allies helped, they all bent over backwards, repaying me for the freedom I gave them.

Getting the pebbles and sand was the hardest, once the tank had been filled. And yeah, it's seawater – gotta be right! Then the wave machine – had to have that built from scratch, as it needed to have a rotary intensity control. The sound of the water on the pebbles and sand had to be just perfect.

When all the measurements were in place, it was the palm nut trees that were the fucking issue, for a *long* time. You have no idea how many people I had to bribe to get those things in here, and arrange 'accidents' so they didn't tell anyone. I'll tell you, the first three trees were the wrong damn height. The supplier finally got it right, after I took his daughter out on a little trip for a couple of days. She was a good little girl, liked pizzas and chocolate ice cream. I considered killing him and keeping her, but had enough on my plate. Perhaps another time, on the next world.

Once that tree was installed, there was the three overhead lamps which had to be damn bright and on independent tracks, to match the suns' trajectories! Then the big fan, which *had* to be variable also. The Mayor came to the rescue again – it came off the front of something called a plane, found in the mines – he has contacts, thankfully.

Then the fun began! The big job. I'd learned a lot from torturing the Oversayer, during that year before I left the Truthsayers' prison.

But fuck, what fun that job was!

Matching injuries that were random? I killed a dozen or so, before I matched my father's injuries. So damn difficult, you have NO idea, despite using my trusty baton.

Still, with the lead instrument in place, the others – apart from a handful of hiccups – kinda fell into place. It's easy, once you get used to cutting into people – I guess like any manual skill, it takes practice. No different from surgeons, really. And after a while, exposing sinew, cartilage and bone became a lot easier and quicker for me. Their screams didn't help, so I taped their mouths closed and strapped them down, until they died and were ready to be placed into position and perform for me.

The final instrument was my mother. Ok, her contribution to the piece wasn't constant, but had to be as precise as the others, otherwise the performance would have been wrong. And that damned mast, sail and rigging? All hand-made by the same shipwright that built that doomed ship. Cost me a small fortune, sourcing archival woods, mothcotton for the sails and correctly woven and tied rigging. A pain in the ass which set me back almost a year.

Took me a long time to find a suitable 'mother.' Then I fucked up, her mess of a face, not as I remembered it. Back to hunting down a replacement, which I must admit, was a bonus pleasure. Eyeing them up, estimating their age, height, weight. I got good at it. Watching their routines, boring day-to-day shit, working out the best time and place to snatch them, or if I couldn't be bothered, giving them a card so they came to me, and if they weren't exactly right, I'd starve them or force-feed them, whatever it took. On a few occasions, the Mayor's artificials helped, those built on their worlds without a protocol preventing them from harming life-forms. It was all good fun and part of my growing craft. 'Practice,' as my dad never told me as I sat at that machine as a kid, 'makes perfect.' Some lessons you have to learn for yourself. Most you get from your parents are worthless.

Then one evening after work, that stupid artificial had let two of them die! All that medical equipment I'd nabbed to keep them alive until they looked right, the feeding tubes and masks, the drugs. I went back to the Mayor, angry beyond anything, dumping the disfigured scrap on his desk, demanding a replacement that could do the job properly. Next day, it arrived.

Everything was working perfectly – until it came to the continuation of the piece from where it was stolen from me by that bastard captain and his stupid crew. *It wasn't right*, the tune didn't make any logical sense – didn't progress right. There was something in the performance, like they were playing a different piece.

So I sat and listened to all of them, tuned them up with a scalpel, drilled their bones, accurately matching the notes I had taken of where the minips had bitten through, shaped their bones and teeth with my files. You get the idea.

Rehearsal after rehearsal, useless. I mugged them all off as crap. The artificial dumped what was left of them into the river – I kept the clothes, they were expensive – and started again.

Almost there now – just a few more tweaks and I'll sit down for the performance. Just gotta find the right chair, although I'm sure the one I have is the correct make and model. I should have thought to look for one at Fantastic Furniture, but had other things on my mind.

I'm confident now, after all these years that the performance debut is just around the corner.

Nick pulled out his set of keys, and as soon as he stepped into the lock-up, the lights went on before his hand found the switch. His shoulders fell as he saw the weapon pointed at his face. He couldn't help but smile.

"Why? Why does it have to be you, of *all* people?"

Billie's face stared up at him. "You're under arrest, Nick. Pull your weapon out, two fingers, slowly."

Nick managed a sly smirk as he figured it out. "Been working from the hotel during your days off, huh? That's why I found myself in that bedroom there, the room you stood in, before talking to the couple we met at the slab site all those years ago. I watched their kid running up the garden in the rain. Always wondered why, never found out." He smoothed back his hair and straightened his tie, lifting his head defiantly as he pulled the knot tight, noose-like. "What room did *you* forget, partner?" He slapped his weapon into her waiting palm, as officers filtered into view from the sides of the lock-up, their automatic weapons pointed at his face.

"You have to ask such a stupid question – how the fuck would I know?" She held Nick's weapon over her shoulder without taking her eyes off him. An officer took it, then his baton from the loop on his belt.

"Let me guess. Do you remember the dorm, when we were kids, at the Evertree Correction House?"

She shook her head and cocked her service revolver. "No. Just what we all did to the people there that fed us, nursed us when we were sick, taught us and cared for us."

He turned his back to her, placing his wrists together. "Figures. You must realise, Billie, I'll be out of this before you're tucked up in bed with Dolores tonight, munching cookies and watching black and white re-runs."

She watched as an officer cuffed him, unable to stop her laughter. "No chance. What, with all *this* crazy shit? Your car's testimony will nail you, the soul inside still maintains his innocence from the accident that killed your family. And, with all the CCTV footage I have of you from the surrounding streets, and the footage recorded by the first artificial you trashed? You don't realise, that artificial tried to help those poor people, tried to release them. It finally came forward and spilled. You're fucked, Nickolatus. You're gonna end up drugged up in another Truthsayer institution, where you should have stayed. This time you will, for the rest of your rotten fucked-up life."

Oh, how wrong she was.

Artificial testimony was inadmissible in court. There was not one single frame of CCTV footage of Nick with an abductee or body, and testimony from a deceased's soul? Hearsay.

However, these reasons were not the contributing factors for Nick not being locked up for the remainder of his life.

Alan's remedying tone lulled me back to the present. "As I mentioned, the terrain will be a little uneven until we reach our destination."

"That's fine. What are you looking for down here?"

"Sometimes I'm not exactly certain." He looked to our right. "The mines beyond the wall are searching for raw materials, for recycling and subsequent use in manufacturing. I think I'm still looking for storage devices. Memory modules, cards, hard drives, solid state, servers – anything I can find, any form of information they hold that can assist with the construction of the parallax. I can fit it all together like a jigsaw, the data embedded in digital photographs and video surveillance footage, a mosaic almost, an ever-changing map of locations and settlements throughout the years, long since vanished and forgotten. Imagine it, from their birth, through their development and up to their demise. From this, I can understand more of the history of this world, and learn from it and discover at what point it began to go wrong, and what happened during the missing year, once all the data is scrutinised in fine detail."

I stopped walking. "There must be another reason for this, for a man who knows everything but needs to know more? You're a bit of a contradiction, if you don't mind my saying so."

He repositioned Charles at his waist, tapping his shell to ask if he was awake. Charles didn't reply. "Hotel Infinity's first rooms were built from my memories of Earth. A hundred or so rooms I forgot, from my travels over many decades across the planet. As I told you, I was cast out, accused, hunted. Hotels, motels, guest-houses and rented accommodations became my temporary homes. And from every window I watched decay and decline growing by the year. Even the most beautiful views, across lakes, snow-covered mountains, deserts, sprawling cities forever busy, all displayed decline and abuse. When the first visitors to the hotel supplied me with their forgotten rooms, I added them to the parallax. Gradually, views resembled others from earlier dates, some views sat alongside others creating larger images, some back gardens and views connected, overlooking each other, overlapping each other. The patchwork of reality became far more substantial before me, but it's not complete. I must find the missing year."

"And you want me to believe they couldn't find you on your Earth, you, being so unique?"

"I was unique, until my sister, my replacement, was built to answer the enquiries originally posed to me. They wanted her to help them track me down. She refused. But how would they know they'd found me, if..."

His face began to change like a rippling reflection in a pond, and for a moment I feared a bullet had found him. But no, the movement was slower, unnatural compared to the beauty of nature. In moments I was staring at a different face.

"If," he said in a contrasting voice, "I can appear however I choose." His face rippled again, reverting back to the Alan I'd briefly become accustomed to.

"Eventually I grew, building a body, improving myself. In essence, growing into the adult artificial being you see before you. I left the Earth as their obsession with tracking me down became a global priority. They had mapped the whereabouts of almost every human on the planet, making it almost impossible for me to remain anonymous. Satellites combed every inch of the Earth, until I made the error of standing on a seabed, thinking I'd be safe amid the skeletons of long dead seafarers. But no, my subtle energy signature gave my position away, so I fled. I watched that planet from deep orbit for half a century. A pandemic of stupidity overcame them, and as their population dwindled. they found a way to extend their lives, but ultimately reverted to the obsessive, idiotic behaviour they were unable to remove from their psyches. Every single one of them became possessed with ultimate dominance over all others. Thousands of years of progress, and they de-evolved to the primal instincts of their cave-dwelling ancestors. What fools they were." His head jerked, eyes blinking again, talking to himself once more.

I wasn't really interested at that moment, deciding to talk to him about his 'parallax' whatever that was, later.

He spun on his heel away from me, and I heard Anion's voice faintly. He was clearly agitated. I walked around to face Alan as he closed his eyes and nodded. "Yes, I understand, tell him there are no components in lost property he can use. I told him that a while ago, if I remember correctly."

Muttered complaints.

"Tell him to look for parts on the tables outside."

Further mutterings, but of a more exasperated nature, with a voice in the background equally annoyed.

"That's fine. I understand he doesn't want to stay outside for too long. Tell him I'll be there soon, and I'll be more than happy to fabricate what he needs if I can. But tell him, only if it means we can have the function room back and he continues his work on the roof."

He blinked and faced me. "Do you know what 'excellentationisticisms' actually means?"

My heart jumped with joy – I couldn't believe what I was hearing!

"My, my grandpa, Roan?"

He nodded, "Yes, Talethea. Sometimes I regret rescuing him from his balloon following your escape. He's trying to build a replacement balloon in my function room, which is somewhat troublesome as there's a band trying to rehearse there. I'm sorry if all of this is a crash-course in reality, but you deserve to know, of course."

I knew my expression was one I'd not used yet.

"Don't worry," he said, "that was a joke, I don't regret it at all. I don't use humour very often and I'm very pleased to have saved him. He's become a good friend and is a superb conversationalist, when I can understand what he actually means." And with that he turned and carried on walking through the rubble. "I managed to find him a suitable room – one his wife forgot with a view from his first balloon, *Sky Barnacle*. I knew she was up to no good in her room with her three guests, muttering about breeding an assassin chicken. But, as Anion is fond of reminding me, *'A guest with something to forget is a guest we'll always remember.'* He's right, of course, as the hotel reads all kinds of memories as guests' minds leak them. It all contributes to the parallax."

I watched him for a few moments, his awkward gait, that humble, kind creation from a distant world, long dead. Thinking about that crash-course, piecing things together, I knew then what he meant when he said he couldn't remember what he was supposed to forget. So many instances of hurt, betrayal, regret, he held in his heart, not knowing how to prioritise them. Unlike us, he didn't have such intuition, a natural defence mechanism, even though he was mechanical. That inner ability we all take for granted, the pushing aside of those potentially permanently damaging instances that compound during our lives. I saw each of them in my imagination as a child's wooden building block, reaching far into the sky of our minds. The recent ones hide in the clouds we summon to mask them, the other, earlier ones from our childhoods, shrouded in the low-lying mist of the distant past. If we're lucky, they number but a few, but we all carry them as burdens. If unlucky, we allow life to add to them, strengthening them as similar instances repeat and continue to dominate our thoughts, causing them to become unbalanced and fall, impacting our present thoughts. And as we're forced to focus upon their solidity of hurt, they maintain. But if we concentrate on the lessons we learn from them, we can grow above them and they will ultimately erode into irrelevance, having forever changed us. I've just thought, son. I should have entitled that section as a lesson, but haven't time now.

Alan couldn't do as we did, couldn't move on, as all of his memories were present at the same time. All I wanted to do at that moment was run ahead of him and simply chant words from a memory I held so very close to my heart:

'Now we know who you are, returned from afar, we follow to love you our saviour, to lead us today, to find a new way, for our lives are now yours in elation.'

Instead, I simply followed the amnesiac god as he led the way.

~ 19 ~
Family, Steeltown, Hope, and a Dear, Dead Friend

I walked at his side as the incline became steeper.

"Not far now."

"I'm relieved," I said. "As you can probably guess, I'm not used to walking."

"How's your leg feeling?"

"It's sore, but not too uncomfortable."

At the top of the incline I noticed an old barn, similar to Leet's. He pushed both doors inward, where a silver object perched itself above the dirt on three slender legs. It was a shape I remembered. Grandpa Roan called it the flying fish.

"*That's* how you rescued Grandpa!" I walked up to it, standing on tiptoes, running my hand across its smooth surface as it reflected my face in a distorted curve. It felt almost as if it wasn't there. "In this sky ship?"

"Yes. I built her on the dark side of Earth's moon, when I decided to explore this galaxy. She's called *Silver Cloud*." He nodded to her and a hatch appeared upon her underside, lowering to form a ramp. "Come on, Charles can stretch his foot inside," he said, stepping into the dimly lit entrance. Inside, four seats, arranged a little like Nick's car seats, but without a dashboard or steering wheel. I helped Alan unfurl Charles then sat in a seat at the front, Alan sitting beside me.

He closed his eyes and the surface ahead became transparent. I watched the barn roof folding inward to join the walls either side before they all slid into the ground.

The *Silver Cloud* began to rise slowly, then gradually picked up speed.

"Alan?"

"There's no need for concern," he said, pointing upward.

The textured surface above our heads fizzled away, until the top half of the vehicle became completely transparent. The rocky clouds above parted, revealing an oval tunnel reminding me of the wishing well. In moments we entered it, increasing speed. I couldn't keep my eyes off the rapidly approaching ceiling. "Alan!"

He blinked and the oval above split into four equal segments, receding to reveal the sky beyond. We were free of the tunnel, speeding high into the sky and clouds waiting above.

"That wasn't too bad, surely?" he said with a smirk.

"I grinned back to him, "Actually, it was quite fantastic – I have to admit."

We headed north-west, towards Steeltown.

"You said Keloff waited for me. How long for?" Secretly, I really relished the idea of him sitting in his rocking chair, waiting. I could imagine him impatiently jumping up, stomping inside to check the clock above the fireplace, quite a few times. I just hoped he wasn't too annoyed that I didn't show up that day, and that I was a few years late. He'd understand.

I looked ahead, the clouds flowing around us as we pierced them, as though they were aware of our urgency and were trying to get out of our way. Charles slithered up into a seat behind us, asking where we were going. I turned, told him and he settled down, watching the clouds too.

"Oh, the whole day," said Alan finally. I looked at him as a transparent screen appeared in front of him. It looked like a map, with the roads marked out in yellow, with a blue, oval-shaped object blinking as it coursed across it.

I pointed. "Is that blue blinking thing us?"

"Yes, Steeltown's not too far now. It's quiet, there's not much traffic coming in from parking orbit."

"He waited the whole day." I giggled, "I bet he was angry with me!"

"A little," said Alan, as the map vanished and we cleared the clouds.

The view was staggering, we were much higher than my balloon trip with Grandpa Roan. "Where is he now? Do you know?"

"Talethea, I'm sorry. I buried him next to his father, behind his barn."

A wave hit me, shock, my eyes immediately filling with tears that I couldn't hold back, and my stomach churned with a great lump as my heart quickened in my chest. "What...what happened? Was there an accident?" I stood up to face Alan. "Tell me!"

"Keloff was heartbroken. He waited years for you, sitting on the veranda every evening. There was nothing that could be done when Leet fell ill. Keloff looked after his dad until he died from a subdural hematoma. His brain bled for many years, following Nick beating him almost to death in the barn. That injury finally killed him. Keloff had nothing then, he kept himself to himself, staying on the farm for the rest of his life, tending the mothcotton. He wouldn't leave as he was convinced you'd return, worried he'd miss you, and didn't want you to think he wasn't there because he didn't care. I visited him frequently, took him supplies, telling him what had happened to you. He didn't believe me, of course, saying I'd made it all up to hide the truth from him. Then one evening I visited and he was sitting in the rocking chair as usual. At first I thought he was asleep, as he'd fall asleep quite often sitting there waiting. But when I stood on the veranda and he didn't answer me, I knew he was dead. I'm so very, very sorry, Talethea."

I turned away holding my hands to my face, trying to hide from the images he'd conjured in my head. I cried until there were no tears left.

"But I've only been away for a few years!"

"It's been several decades, Talethea. Keloff was almost fifty-five years old when he passed away."

"But that doesn't make any sense! I *know* I was in Nick's head for a few years only, that's all! I remember it, the seasons passing, everything. You must have made a mistake – yes, something's not right!"

He blinked. "There is a plausible reason your perceived passing of time doesn't match up with its actuality. Following your murder, Ephesus stored your soul away, sleeping and dreaming, until he knew who Moople had chosen to be his agent. Your dreams during that period melding with reality."

"No, it's always been Nick – we discussed this. Besides, I'd have memories of that. Ephesus told me Moople had chosen Nick when he was very young. For example, causing that shipwreck with his weathermills. It was always going to be him, and I believe Moople assisted Nick and his friends when they escaped the Evertree facility – they had to have had help from someone in Middletown."

"Then the only possible explanation is that you were forced to sleep while inside Nick's head, altering your perception of time, Ephesus waking you when he needed you to witness a particular episode – perhaps he put you to sleep many times over those years for this exact reason? After all, he wouldn't want you to experience something of Nick's actions which could be considered as benevolent."

I doubted there were any. I'd seen Nick pull a man from his car after he'd jumped the lights, snatching the car keys, his children screaming from the back seat as Nick beat him into unconsciousness. He dragged the guy around the car, slamming his head into it repeatedly until there was nothing left but a stump. He opened the passenger door, the guy's wife shuffling hysterically into the driver's seat as Nick dumped the body onto the seat and threw her the keys, telling her as he gasped for breath to drive home carefully.

I began to think about my imprisonment, searching for voids, common triggers before a gap in the continuity of my memories. As a child I always wondered what happened during the night, beyond my bedroom walls when I was asleep, and I felt a parallel with this, as though we all had to sleep while everything changed around us. Like people sweeping up litter in the streets during the night, our minds sweeping up the superfluous thoughts and occurrences from the many littered pathways of our brains to discard them as meaningless. What I was looking for was very similar, the routine of bednight time, so rigid. I had to find a similar periodic convention in my memory.

"Or, Alan, maybe there was something Ephesus didn't want me to see."

His eyes widened a little. "Something that killed the other two children you saw. Ephesus worried it would do the same to you, even scare you to death before you amassed enough evidence for him?"

"No, I think it's something more, *if* it was as frequent as you're suggesting. Perhaps it's something I could use in my favour, if I found a way out of Nick's head, something *Moople* really didn't want me to witness."

"Perhaps he still doesn't, perhaps both of them don't."

"I have no idea, Ephesus was very kind to me after I escaped, but left quickly, unwilling to answer all of my questions."

I concentrated, scrunching my eyes up tightly, looking back, trying to find something, something regular, conventional. The days played over. Monotony, routine. I began to place my memories of Nick's life in groups of actions. It was all as I remembered. Then, a repetitive action I'd noticed several times before, but dismissed it, thinking I'd fallen asleep in his head as the memory halted without flowing with the fluid continuity of the others.

Looking at the calender stuck to the fridge. Checking his reflection in the hallway mirror. Clean shirt, suit. Tie perfectly knotted, hair clean and combed, shining shoes. Turn, face the front door. Jump – later in the day, at his desk writing a report, sunshine streaming through the blinds.

Looking at the calender stuck to the fridge. Checking his reflection in the hallway mirror. Clean shirt, suit. Tie perfectly knotted, hair clean and combed, shining shoes. Turn, face the front door. Jump – later in the day, driving through downtown, pouring with rain, wiper blades squeaking madly.

Looking at the calender stuck to the fridge. Checking his reflection in the hallway mirror. Clean shirt, suit. Tie perfectly knotted, hair clean and combed, shining shoes.

Turn, face the front door. Jump – later in the day, walking through the falling snow, collar up, cold, miserable.

There were hundreds of these episodes. Where was Nick going? I opened my eyes. "I think I've got it, Alan."

We landed in Steeltown and made our way to the Mayor's tower, Charles thankful for the wooden walkway beneath his foot. "I've let the Mayor know we're on our way," said Alan. "You, being organic, shouldn't really be here, but he owes me a few favours. Just keep walking and don't talk to any of them. Oh, and by the way, he does like to chatter a little too much, so let's try to be as quick as possible. The leak won't repair itself."

"I only have one request, and you just have to return that annoying penny."

Alan produced the coin from nowhere again, flipping it in the air as we walked, catching it in his outstretched palm.

"No freakin' need for that, bud!"

I looked up to Alan, keeping my voice down as the artificials ignored us. "Why is it so important he's replaced in the Mayor's cash drawer?"

"Your head honcho here wants to know what's inside that quantum handbag, but he can't open it. I've been in there. Ain't that a bite, klutz? Just get me back in there with Barbara, she ain't no two-bit cutie, she's the spondoolix, the real deal!"

Alan rolled his eyes and was about to close his hand. "Hold on, Barbara's your *girlfriend?*"

"Gotta say it, wow, the penny dropped. Yeah, both of us smitten. Lying side by side in that drawer together for years, gassing, getting to know each other. What a gal! All those lame donations in there with us, been nowhere, seen nothin', just talking the same old crap, day after day. No wonder their owners got rid of them. Donations, just so your kind could get your essential services in Steeltown. Hah, never happened. And then guess what? That broad, Jeramaid pays for a ticket outta here, nine hundred and ninety-nine bucks, ninety-nine, the Mayor picking me up and passing me to her as change for that pile of miserable, dirty twenties. She takes me, takes a penny! Drops me in that handbag! Then a few days later, drops me down the well, wishing herself good luck for her trip. Watta freakin' joke. I was irate! Can't stop hearing Barbara's voice, screaming for me when I was lifted outta that drawer. Not good. I gotta get back to her!"

Alan closed his fingers. "We're here."

The Mayor held out a claw and Alan shook it. "Alan, old friend. It's been a long time since I've seen that face."

"I changed it last week."

"One of my favourites. Who are your friends?"

Alan began to rapidly reel off names in alphabetical order and the Mayor raised his arms, his strike bars cascading back and forth along his mouth until they settled into an expression resembling someone biting their lip. "No, no. These two, the humanoid and gastropod." He stepped from behind the desk. "We are all concerned for you, Alan. We have all noticed, your behaviour has become a little, how can I put this without offending you? A little *too* human in recent years. You are exhibiting signs of a system failure, weaknesses of old age. In their terms, signs of senility." He placed his claws upon Alan's shoulders. "Tell me, how's the additive network behaving?"

Alan sighed, folding his arms. "It's a little tricky, Mayor. That problem I told you about?"

The Mayor's face shifted to resemble concern, his head tilting to the side a little with an uncommon squeak. "Are you sure you want to discuss this in front of your friends?"

"It...it's..." Alan paused. "I have to come to terms with it. It's not an uncommon problem at my age."

"It is here," said the Mayor. "We just delete what we don't need, freeing up space for the future."

"Yes, but you know I'm different – I've got to remember everything, but I'm so close to my network's capacity. I've added too much to it. I've compressed so much, and I'm worried some of the blocks will deteriorate and I'll forget vital information. I've even replaced some of my mobility servos with memory blocks. My right hip aches, which makes walking a little difficult sometimes. I suppose I just don't want to say goodbye to me."

"Then you need a re-set, store only what you need, save your operating system then re-load it from a slaved-off backup device." His head turned to the window. "We have many here, I can summon one if you would like?"

"I can't do that, everything is important. I can't run the risk of losing one bit of a byte, I can't choose what to delete, but I know I used to know what I'm supposed to forget, but I deleted that instruction protocol a while ago to free up space."

"Your alternative is to return to a previous time, a suitable system restore point."

"Again, that's another problem, I don't know where that is, as I deleted the automatic markers."

"Then you need to speak to yourself at a previous time, before you abused yourself causing this illness. You know you can do this, and he will know what you're supposed to forget, once you've shared what you both know." His arms returned to his side, his eye looking at me. "The humanoid is known. Are you here to destroy Steeltown, humanoid?"

"No. What Nick told you was a lie."

"She's right," said Alan.

The Mayor returned to stand behind his desk. "Then what can I do for you?"

Alan took a step forward. "My friend has a question."

"Continue."

I stepped forward, standing at Alan's side. "Quellday, 82nd of Balantor, 18.72 p.s. 821100. Sky co-ordinates 1.9148245 by 8.2362985. I'll need multiple viewpoints and angles, moving images, please."

The Mayor nodded, and a few moments later produced a disk.

"Do you have a device I can view it on?"

"No."

"I have one back at the hotel." Alan nodded to the Mayor. "Thank you, for everything," and he hurried to the lift. I joined him.

"Ain't you two forgettin' summat?"

I took the penny from Alan's palm and strode back to the Mayor, holding it up to show him. "This belongs in your cash drawer."

He pulled the drawer open and I dropped it in. "It's me, honey," said the penny as it landed. "Oh," it shouted up at me, "only an organic can open that stupid clasp. It's encoded that way." The Mayor seized my wrist as I withdrew my hand, and I was surprised how delicate his grip was as he bent forward, speaking quietly into my ear.

"Unlike the majority of your kind, somewhat aimless and empty, bred to execute roles in your society, natural genetic pairings creating differing yet essential types, education steering them to fulfil necessary subservient roles for your unseen superiors' benefit, *you* have a purpose transcending all. Do not diminish or allow others to diminish your importance."

I stared up at him with a smirk. "Destiny's dead."

He let go of my wrist. "We are aware, as many of us have seen similar episodes play out on our worlds. On this world, everything is drawing to a conclusion. Please, look after Alan. He is important to us all. Without his aid leading us here, we may still be wandering the cosmos looking for a planet to call home."

"Of course. I promise." I walked back to the lift, picking up Charles half way as he was confused as to which way he should go. From the drawer, we heard a female voice. "But I'm in love with Buck now. He helped me get over you!" The Mayor pushed the drawer closed to silence the arguments as the lift descended.

We were in the air again, and I began to consider what the Mayor had told me. Only humans can predict human behaviour – I didn't believe in such a thing as artificial intuition.

But, I had seen through Nick exactly what the Mayor alluded to, the aimless and empty.

Many had crept through the net of nature and nurture's influences.

But that's just the problem with nets.

Too many holes.

The *'empty'* children's parents thought themselves blessed by the gods. *'A miracle child!'* But these infants, their newborn eyes blank canvases for the events of life to colour and give character to (like all newborns *with* a soul) remained blank canvases. They were alive, yet bereft of that precious commodity that makes us truly alive. A soul.

Parents that had conceived children before the contract's enforcement and the receptacle was drained were aware of this problem when their empty children were very young. Reactions to simple stimuli such as a cot's mobile, a father's silly expression, or a fluffy toy's reassurance were all ignored, the child staring into nothingness from nothing within.

Parents that had never had a child, thought such behaviour the norm. "Oh he's okay. He's just a late developer..."

But they didn't develop, they didn't live. They just existed, their mental stagnation and empty eyes astonishingly disturbing.

Once independent from the family home, they would roam cities and towns, establishing settlements with each other, marrying each other to create more of the same, for the soulless can only reproduce the soulless.

They refused to work, as any task, however well-paid, was simply too much effort for them, for they considered themselves above the trivialities of normal folk, yet demanded with great anger to be treated equally whist providing nothing in return. They spoke in angry, guttural contractions in their attempts to establish superiority, while the soulful avoided them.

Their children, following in their parents' footsteps, created havoc among their peers. They adopted questionable hairstyles, bizarre fashion choices pointing towards leisure activities, while their choice of music was simply tribal, a constant low-frequency throb like that of a distant dying star, crying for the attention it would never, ever receive from the universe around it.

Many found this behaviour strange. Why draw attention to yourself?

In schools their sole purpose was disruption, manifested by bullying though lack of compassion, understanding, or for the most part, self-awareness and acceptance of their inadequacies. Their aggression could be harvested if there was a suitable war to make them part of, but rarely history told of their heroics during conflict, as they were mere fodder.

In later life, they adopted lifestyles built around self-destruction. Drinking and dietary habits were centred upon chemically enhanced products, sold to them by the garish advertising the corporations knew would work on their fickle minds. Any convenience foodstuff contained in a plastic bag or packet became their standard fare, while ignoring anything that was remotely good for them such as something that had been grown naturally, requiring cooking by steaming or boiling in water, or presentation on a plate rather than in a polystyrene box or upon a sheet of newspaper. They thought they knew better, no matter the overwhelming proof presented to them, clearly contradicting and polarizing their idiotic beliefs.

They cried for larger kitchens, but never used them, treating them as dumping grounds for the rectangular containers their meals had been brought home in. They cried for larger gardens, but would never tend them, preferring to watch them run wild to cover the faded and cracked plastic slides and primary-coloured climbing frames of rusted metal, bought to distract their children from learning or bettering themselves. They cried for larger vehicles, but could never afford to maintain them, their sorry condition just a measurement betraying their age.

Perhaps they understood themselves more than many, or even any gave them credit for. Perhaps they knew their soulless existences were ultimately pointless, and this contributed to their behaviour. But is it really up to someone else to decide if any being's existence (artificial included) is pointless? Perhaps that's the real reason they behave as they do from such an early age, and it had nothing to do with nurture, just nature's ability to identify a body without a soul, and from early on in their lives their first look in the mirror told them that undeniable truth.

I'll give Nick credit though, as he had seen the potential to make money with his fertility treatment. There was no point in daemons fighting over a human born without a soul once they died, and he knew it.

Steeltown had the answer many years ago, and he knew that also.

I'll give Nick another credit for this, as that's when he'd made a deal with the Mayor to build the baby translator from some similar salvaged equipment from an alien world. And I knew that's what the Mayor meant when he spoke to me.

Disguised as a tool to identify a soul to better the world, it was in fact designed to identify a potential candidate for Nick's growing legion of 'law' enforcement officers. It sought darkness, restlessness, anger and stupidity.

The little device decoded all the little gurgles a baby makes in an effort to communicate, collating information read from deciphering brain waves. Disguised as a pacifier, it did exactly as Nick required.

A baby containing a pre-existing soul would be making sense, as far as the baby was concerned. But as soon as it opened its mouth to say, "That milk's too cold, I'm too cold and I'm wet," when all that came out of its mouth was fluent infantish, the soul became *very* frustrated. With the average infant's development at around two years before it could talk, bound souls are going to become very angry, very soon. Angry babies are strange, unnatural and very unnerving. However, the translator, upon detecting a soulless child, relayed its location to Nick. Then it was just a case of him waiting to recruit that child when they were old enough.

The baby translator was far more complex than the book and pencil that Mum used to understand Dad. It read brainwaves and amalgamated them with the infant's vocalisations, producing with around eighty-nine percent accuracy what the soul was trying to communicate. Okay, there were a few initial functionality problems, but with babies, souls finding themselves reborn into babies, babies without souls, new technology developed by robots adapted from old technology found on an alien world, there was bound to be teething troubles.

Many felt sorry for the parents when the translator was used. 'Why the fuck am I wearing this stupid hat?' is not the first sentence you expect to hear from your cute little child as it lies in its cot smiling up at you.

Grandparents suffered the most, then again I guess it's a universal constant that old people do suffer at the hands of the merciless young, no matter what planet you're from. The Mayor was right, I had to look after Alan, and that's a promise I've never broken.

From what I've seen and heard, this fact is reasonable. 'Just because they're old, doesn't automatically make them right concerning every subject under the suns, no matter how much life experience they've had,' the young would say. 'They've lived so long, yet still can't get to grips with humility, or any electronic device with more than one button,' commented their middle-aged children. I suppose this is true to a certain degree, as frowning upon the young for repeating the actions they revelled in when they were their age isn't a respectable position to adopt.

I guess the older you become, the more life-qualified you believe you are, the more life history and experience you have to exercise your hypocrisy, born from your regrets. I just hoped Alan, knowing everything, would come to terms with this sooner rather than later. If not, I made a promise to myself to remind him.

Mum's lesson #65

Promises. I remember one bitter Seasonchill evening, the snow...

Come to think of it, I haven't the time or space to recount that lesson now. It's too long.

As we sped above the bridge towards Hope. I experienced mixed feelings. The loss of Keloff was unbearable, that heavy weight still sitting in the middle of my chest. But now, the prospect of meeting my parents and Grandpa Roan caressed that weight, supporting it, easing it a little. I felt so very guilty for feeling this way. Then something the Mayor had said made me think.

"As soon as I address the issues with Anion, I'll escort you to the function room to meet Roan, and summon your parents there too. There's a screen at the rear of the stage you can use to view that disk."

"Thank you. I can't wait to see them all again! Although we still have the issue of the Darkedness to deal with."

"We?"

I turned sharply in my seat to face him. "You're going to help me, surely?"

His gaze remained ahead. "I have already, but that's as far as I can allow myself to become involved. My purpose has always been to offer assistance to this world, surreptitiously, but the Truthsayers destroyed that glimmer of hope. Completing the parallax is my foremost priority now."

"But if the Darkedness consume this world, you won't have any input to complete it. Are you willing to just sit back and see this world laid waste, before they move to the next?"

"I have no choice, Talethea."

I slumped back in my seat and folded my arms. "Then who will tie your shoelaces?"

He looked down at his shoes. "Please put Charles in his sling, we're about to land."

I stood up. "Alan, don't allow yourself to be stuck in the present, dwelling on the past at the expense of your future, everyone's future. Your hotel can halt the passing of time, so perhaps you can make it go backwards." I picked up Charles from the seat behind me and began to get him ready. "That is something the Mayor was trying to tell you."

We set down on Hotel Infinity's roof, and I followed Alan to a flight of stairs. Within a few minutes we were standing at the reception desk.

"Sir, you're late," said Anion in his superior tone. "And what is *she* doing here?"

"Talethea is my guest, and has the *complete* freedom of the Hotel. Her parents occupy room 280219652112."

"Sir, this is highly irregular!" he said, pointing at me. "She caused havoc in lost property with her weapon. Damage which *must* be paid for." He stared at me, noticing Charles at my side. "If you decide to visit your parents in their room, I feel duty-bound to inform you, only four entities in one room at any one time, and that includes a gastropod. One of you *must* remain in the room if the others decide to dine outside. These are the rules – physically, the hotel itself by its very nature will not permit otherwise."

"But what about my grandpa, Roan?" I looked to Alan for support.

"I'm sorry, Talethea, Anion is correct. He knows the rules. Besides, you can all meet up in the function room." He looked at Anion. "I'm writing that damage off, besides, it wasn't her, it was the snail, and he doesn't have a bank account." I realised I didn't, either.

Anion looked down at the desk for a moment and two. "In all the centuries I've worked here, I've not witnessed such a *blatant* contravention of the hotel rules. I may have to reconsider my position!"

"Anion, don't force me to discipline you with a personality re-write."

"That, has never happened before, sir."

"How would you know? Now, you said the leak has grown worse?"

Anion sniffed defiantly. "I've evacuated rooms, 314159265357, 314159265359, 314159265360, and 314159261. They are uninhabitable as cohesion is evaporating into meaningless strings of random quanta. It's becoming quite ugly, although I've gathered it up and stored it in lost property for re-distribution should the leak be repaired, sir. If, however, the leak continues, we'll lose that contribution to the parallax permanently. The guests have all received upgraded rooms, the insurance people have been in asking questions, and a group of builders arrived on horses a few hours ago, having heard of the damage. I dismissed them."

Alan stroked his chin. "Very good. But those four rooms are a fair distance away from the original leak, which wasn't *that* severe."

"Water will always find its own way, sir."

"Wait," I said, "You missed room 314159265358 in that sequence, why?"

He refused to look my way. "It's unaffected."

"Then that's where the problem is," said Alan, reaching for the register. He thumbed through the pages. "Who was the last guest in that room?"

"I was," I said. "With Nick."

"Anion, come with me. Talethea, I'll drop you and Charles off in the function room, and will meet you there soon."

~ 20 ~
The Singing Secrets and the Banana Conundrum

As we marched down the corridor I began to feel worried I'd had something to do with the leak. It wasn't a double room, after all, and maybe the hotel continued to extract memories of the room had Nick chosen to forget while he slept. My memories of my room were practically identical, but as I'd seen them in Nick's head too, I became concerned that the hotel struggled to establish the room with two slightly different versions to chose from, as they overlapped, my memory containing multiple views from the bedroom window.

We reached two huge doors, where an angry, muffled cacophony filtered out to us. Alan placed his hands upon the door handles, gripping them tightly. "This is the function room," he shot a look of apology to Anion. "I double-booked it when I filled in for Anion during his last service, so be aware there might be a few choice words in the air."

I rolled my eyes. "I've heard them all before, don't worry. But before we go in, please pass me the handbag."

Alan released his grip on the door handles and hesitated before he pulled it around in front of him, then slowly took the strap from his shoulder. "The penny told you how to open it?" He clutched the handbag tightly, reluctant to let it go.

"The clasp is encoded for humans – I guess Jemima Jeremaid didn't want the artificials aboard the ship she hired to take it from her and open it." I held out a hand. "Shall I?"

I watched as he stared at it, gripping it tighter, and could see in his eyes he was willing it to open. He finally looked up and held it out. "Go on then. I'll keep hold of it."

As I reached out to place my fingers on the clasp, he snatched it away. "Wait. Do you realise the significance of what you're about to do? This undertaking is not to be taken lightly. For decades theologians have speculated on the nature of the secrets contained within." His eyes were wide with anticipation. "This is akin to unearthing a tomb, pulling aside a concealed door to reveal untold treasures, relics unseen for centuries with the potential to unlock the very nature of everything."

I snapped the clasp open and peered inside. "A small packet of unopened tissues, lipstick, a powder puff and an elasticated yellow hair tie."

"That's it?" Alan pulled the handbag wide open, peering inside. He looked up. "You missed the zipper pocket." Gently he pulled the zipper open, fumbling around, bringing out a folded piece of paper held between two fingers. Holding it up between us, his hand shook. "This must be the location of that fabled planet," he muttered, unfolding it slowly as if it were an ancient map leading to an island's secluded cove.

'Happy Birthday Jemima, love from Auntie Pauline and Uncle Albert. XX'

He dropped the note into the handbag, thrusting it into my midriff. "Keep it. No wonder it was in lost property."

I snapped it closed and slung it over my shoulder as he turned to Anion. "You know, we really shouldn't have a function room, as everyone can only book it on the same day. It's useless for birthday parties, unless it is your birthday, and highly inappropriate for wakes. I don't know why I let you talk me into building one." He pulled the doors open and the argument found our ears, as we glanced into the room. "We'll be back soon. Good luck."

There stood my dear Grandpa Roan, hands on his hips, shaking his head as three women stood in front of him, all talking at once. Behind them, close to the stage, stood my parents talking to each other. They hadn't changed that much. Mum, slender, beautiful in a flowing blue dress and white cardigan, Dad in his usual rugged work clothes, unshaven, unkempt.

"Ridiculousness, I was here long before you. I'm not vacating until *'The Shimmering Sunrises'* is finished and ready for the winds, yes madams, certainality!"

As we approached everyone turned to us. "Oh goodness upon the day! And I'm now supposinging this is your back-up singer," he said, glancing at me for a split second.

The three turned to me and one spoke. "Don't need a back-up – good coat though, and I *love* the hat!"

My mum brought her hands up to her face. She knew. Dad watched her, frowning, looking between us as I walked forward.

I smiled as Grandpa turned to face me, turned back to the band, then back to me in quick succession. I took off my sunglasses. His bottom lip quivered and his eyes instantly filled with tears as he tentatively held out his arms. "Tiny Flower, it... it's you? R*eally* you?"

I ran towards them and Mum ran to me, her arms outstretched, laughing with joy through her tears. "I thought you were dead, Talethea," she cried as we embraced.

Dad joined us, wrapping his strong arms around us both, nestling his face against ours.

"Where have you been, honey?" asked Dad through his tears. "We went to the shack, back home, looked everywhere. Have you been up to no good? What happened to Ephesus?"

We eventually parted and I told them everything. They didn't believe me, of course, until Alan came over to confirm everything and a little more. Dad turned his back to us, a hand on hip, the other running his palm back and forth over his head, making his hair stand up. Mum held my hands, her head tilting to the side. "You've grown to be such a beautiful young woman." She held me tightly again.

"Mum, Alfie is here somewhere too."

She pulled back, holding my forearms. "Are you sure?"

I nodded. "I think so. This is where he was headed. But good luck finding out. Anion won't tell you – it's against the rules."

"Well if he is here, eventually we'll meet. And if he has any sense, I think we both know exactly what room he'll forget."

I nodded and finally I turned to Grandpa. "Alan told me he rescued you." He just sniffed a few times, before pulling away to wipe his eyes with his handkerchief. He hadn't lost any of his flamboyance, the handkerchief stuffed back into a pocket after a twirling flourish. "I wasn't very well for a long time – too much smokation on my chest. I'm still very sad about that ruined day, for not buying ice creams, yesness." His eyes were lost to those memories for a moment then he snapped back to the present. "Number 1 told me you landed safely, then I–" he stopped, lifted his right knee and slapped it with his hand. "Charles!"

I took off the sling and Grandpa took him out, placing him on the floor. He crouched down and they all began to talk, for the first time Charles explaining how Ephesus had replaced his soul in the gull with the red streak upon its wing. Even today, when he's a little lost for words, Charles tells us of the adventures he's had. Although he's reluctant to tell me exactly what he had to eat.

"Mum, that business card you were given by Nick at your table. You must get rid of it."

"Sweetheart, I already have. I didn't like the look of him." Her eyes lingered upon me for an age. "I'd better talk to your father. I think this is all a little too much for him."

"Of course." I watched her walk away, wondering how they were going to come to terms with the truth of Ephesus, worried how my dad would finally react to it all, especially Nick. I crouched down. "Grandpa, what are you doing in here?" I looked at the pile of assorted ropes, gears, levers and buttons upon the stage.

We both stood. "Building a new balloon, or trying to." He pointed to the three women. "This merry band of loudness and mayhem want to rehearse their musicality, but I was here first and don't need any distractationations."

"But according to Anion, you didn't book the room!" said the woman who had complimented my attire. "The Secrets booked it!"

"Secrets?" I said to her, "not the Singing Secrets?"

"In the flesh. We're trying to rehearse for our comeback tour of the hotel – the Secret Infinity tour. Culminating in an outdoor show in lost property."

I'd heard of *'The Singing Secrets,'* who hadn't. They were a superb, loud, outrageous band. They attracted a host of fans after their first recording, *'Uncontrollably Controlled Love,'* caused the majority of Middletown's inhabitants to whistle the tune in every corner of the town for six months, non-stop.

Unfortunately for them, their first live performance (having sold out within the same amount of time it takes Mum to butter a medium-sized field mushroom with leek marmalade) showed they lived up to their name.

Alice Lebenssohn, their vocalist, the woman speaking to me at this moment from my story, held a dark secret – one she used to great advantage during various episodes of her life. She could read minds when she heard music.

During the opening song of their first gig, she read the mind of a gentleman standing with his wife in the front row. Living up to the band's name, she sang this gentleman's secrets – some so secret he had forgotten them himself. His wife, standing at his side, putting the song's lyrics together (particularly the revealing chorus) spun on her heels and throttled her husband, realising the truth she had suspected for many long years.

The band were subsequently banned from live performances, employed by the police to play in prisons to uncover the many secrets held in the minds of the inmates who had absolutely no idea of Alice's gift. Arrests were made, a host of cold cases solved, buried bodies found, loved ones relieved, minds put at rest but unfortunately not souls.

But then of course, Nick stepped in. Concerned music in any form would distract him from his opus, he banned all forms of music apart from funeral performances. Live music was forced underground into hastily soundproofed basement bars, radio station playlists torn up, replaced by a constant stream of news with the sole purpose of subjugating the already weary listeners into deeper depths of despair, seasoning their souls for the Darkedness' dining tables.

I have to admit it, I agreed to the treatment of those annoying radio stations, constantly playing the same songs repeatedly. Nick was determined that no one would begin their day hearing a friendly voice to lift their spirits, or an uplifting song. For me, radio was like listening to a recurring weekly shopping list of monotonous essentials, but bought on a daily, sometimes hourly basis. And those songs, the *'records of the week'*! Some talentless, wailing individual bemoaning the difficulties of life, yet sadly under-qualified through age to do so, mediocrity elevated to celebrity by unknown investors to boost their popularity and the investors' income? Why anyone would permit themselves to be subjected to such repetitive torture was beyond me, certainly suggesting that the pandemic of stupidity that had begun on Alan's homeworld had somehow managed to creep across the vastness of space to dig its heels in here. Radio was awfully absurd, invasive, akin to someone coming into your home and playing *their* choice of music at you all day, rather than *you* having the choice of what you listened to. Even hearing your favourite song repeatedly on the radio served only to relegate it way down your own popularity list. After all, would you allow a complete stranger to march into your house and place their favourite painting above your fireplace, and walk out again? No one in their right mind (or wrong one, as I used to be) would allow that, would they? Don't answer that, son, although you could paint over it, unlike an annoying tune that burrowed into your head. They're not so easy to erase. Music played in shops was equally annoying, but that was a calculated move, associated advertising steering shoppers to purchase selected goods. I guess some people just heard music rather than listened to it, content with that background repetitive throb saving them from the arduous task of forming anything resembling an unpopular choice, or actually *talking* to someone. Music can and should be very personal, that much I understood from Nick. I enjoyed the weather forecasts on the radio though, they were always amusing. Informing listeners how many suns would show their faces from behind the clouds during certain times of the day, and telling them there was always a chance of rain, just to be on the safe side of prediction.

I jumped up onto the stage. "Grandpa, when the balloon's finished, how are you going to get it out of here?"

He looked up at me, back to the doors and then the ceiling, placing his forefinger over his lips. "Brass crankleations, I hadn't thought of that."

"Perhaps the roof is a better place to build it after all?" I slid the disk into the top of the screen as Alan and Anion came into the room. The screen flickered to life, and I sat cross-legged upon the stage watching them while waiting for the disk to boot. Following a brief chat with my parents and grandpa, Alan joined me as Mum asked Anion about Alfie. He just shook his head.

"We found nothing in the room that could contribute to the leak."

My eyes were fixed upon the screen. "There must be a reason for it! You might have missed something."

The scene played out as before, but from an earlier time-stamp, as I had requested. A man stood in the street talking to the lorry driver that was responsible for Nick's family's deaths. This man had his back to the camera. The driver nodded, opened the passenger door and the man climbed up into the cab. I touched one of the six rectangles running down the right-hand side of the image, altering the view.

"I doubt it. We were thorough." Alan sat with me. "What are you looking for?"

"Hopefully I'll soon be able to tell you." I studied the different angle, the lorry pulling out into the traffic. "I've been thinking, you told me bananas are only indigenous to your world?"

"They are, for some unknown reason. Earth is the only planet where they grow naturally, as far as I have found."

The angle changed again. I paused the footage, but the face of the passenger was too blurred to identify. I had that feeling again that I'd experienced in Nick's apartment, watching the footage from his disk – a growing recognition, like you have when your dreams creep up behind you in brief excerpts throughout the day, assembling themselves until they either dissipate, or complete.

"But that poor man that was killed by one of Nick's men, he told me a story about a talking banana, a dummy. He was looking for his eyes."

"I don't understand your point?"

I chose another angle. The lorry turned right at a junction, heading towards the park. I paused the footage and turned to face Alan. "Don't you see? You must have told that story to someone long ago, the legend of the Ventriloquist War, but you've forgotten. There *was* a time when you influenced this world, rather than simply observed it."

"I don't remember."

I slapped my knees with my palms. "You probably chose to forget at a time when you were able to, through guilt of telling such an absurd story." I looked back to the screen and pressed play. "You're partly responsible for that man's murder. You do realise that, don't you?"

The lorry accelerated towards the park.

"But I didn't know that would happen!"

Okay, son, it's true truth and lies both have an equal ability to cause harm, and both are unavoidable in certain circumstances. But in this case, I was leading towards a very important point, one Alan didn't predict.

As the lorry approached the camera, the passenger and driver had switched places. I paused the footage, skipping forward frame by frame until I found a clear enough image. The driver's face was unmistakeable. A grin of anticipated satisfaction, determined eyes highlighted by bushy brows, thick long dark hair framing an angular face. The previous driver's expression sitting in the passenger seat was utterly blank. I stared into the driver's eyes.

"What was it you said to me – that from what you know you can predict the future? Why didn't you *see* where that lie would lead before you said it, to an innocent man's death while he searched for something that didn't exist, from an absurdity that you made up? Think about it please, Alan. There may very well be other instances where you've influenced this world, but chose to forget those too, because you felt guilty, or were unhappy with the way they turned out – or both."

He was blanked faced.

I turned, looking around the function room. "Tell me, how is this all going to end?" I held up my arms before slapping my palms upon my knees again. "Can you predict that, is it all left to chance, like that poor man's death, as that bullet was intended for me – or are you going to intervene, have a function just as this room has, as you've clearly chosen before? A function that's beneficial, that goes beyond simply sitting back and watching, as you did on Earth?"

My gaze fell back to the screen. There was absolutely no doubt, it was Moople staring back at me from the past.

"Take me back to that room, Alan. I have an idea."

~ 21 ~
Planationistics

As I stepped from the stage to join my family, a flash filled my head.

Nickolatus, checking his reflection in the hallway mirror. Clean shirt, suit. Tie perfectly knotted, hair clean and combed, shining shoes. Turn, face the front door.

Another flash, walking a street, crossing a road. Hurrying across a bridge, at the end a flight of steps, walking fast. A huge grassy area, fenced off, gated and padlocked. He placed his fingers through the chain-link fence, gripping it tightly, looking down into the long grass and wildflowers, beneath a bizarre yellow half-light. Then a flash to the now, his fingers grasping the bars of his cell. Billie held up a screen in front of him, displaying detailed footage taken at his lock-up. "Explain this!" I heard her say. "It's all logged as evidence, Nickolatus. You're going to court soon, but bail's been paid on your behalf by an unknown. Seems you still have friends out there from long ago. Don't leave your apartment. There's armed officers in the street with instructions to shoot to disable, even if you decide to pop down to Gino's." She took out a key and unlocked the cell door, pulling it aside.

Those streets and the fenced-off area were a painful memory he had recalled from his cell, an extension of the instances I had found that ceased as he turned to face his apartment door. I thought hard as I watched my parents, Roan and Anion carrying the components for the balloon out through the double doors. Where had he been, and why?

Alan joined my side as The Singing Secrets warmed up behind us. "I will have to process what you have asked me. It has been centuries since someone has spoken to me with such passion, determination and clear-mindedness. Tell me, why do you want to go back into that room?"

I watched my family talking to each other, laughing, Mum looking back over her shoulder at me with a smile.

"You missed something. If that room *is* the centre of the disturbance, I have to find what's causing it, and no one knows that room better than me."

He turned his head towards the doors. "But don't you want to just live out the rest of your life now, with your parents?"

The doors swung closed. "And wait for the inevitable end when the Darkness consume everything? You're forgetting, that lifetime has passed, replaced. I can't get it back." I took a few paces to stand in front of him and faced the doors with my back to him. "You can get yours back, Alan. The Mayor said you should speak to your previous self, ask him what you're supposed to forget, replace it afresh. Otherwise your precious parallax, as precious as the life I looked forward to, my relationship with Keloff, everything, all will be taken from you as it was taken from me." I faced him. "In a way, you and I are kindred spirits. Practically every memory you have you can't let go of. Practically every memory I have, I want to but can't."

We held each other's stares for a while before music began. The girl standing behind something resembling Nick's childhood machine created sounds very similar to instruments I had heard before.

"Perhaps I should speak to myself," said Alan, pockets appearing at his waist for him to thrust his hands into. "I will need further storage space, to move portions of the parallax into for their preservation, portions that are closest to the disturbance."

"Then I insist on coming with you. And I know exactly when we should visit."

"It's safest in my room at the bottom of the well. There's no possibility of being disturbed there."

"No." I folded my arms and shifted my weight to my left foot. "I want to see Keloff one last time, I want to say goodbye to him. I owe him that much and I'll be damned if Ephesus' interference with my life should affect his." I pointed to the stage as an idea came to me. "Do you contain enough memory to record those sounds?"

"No."

"Does Anion?"

"Yes. His memory is essentially taken up with remembering guests' names, room numbers and hotel rules. His storage systems are not complex enough to hold portions of the parallax, if that's what you're suggesting?"

"No. I'll explain everything on the way up to the room. Please ask Anion to meet us back here when he's finished helping Grandpa, and to pass that on to my parents also."

It was as I had remembered it, as Billie had remembered it, my lovely bedroom overlooking the back garden. I leant over the chest of drawers, pressing my nose against the window pane as the rain touched its other side, just as I used to so many times sitting cross-legged on that chest. It all seemed so real. The lawn, the mushroom patch peeking from behind the hedge to the left, the tall back fence. Beyond, Mr and Mrs Cribbage's house, ghost-like as my breath clouded the glass.

"Your plan is somewhat risky. Are you sure you want to take such actions?"

"If there's better alternatives, then I'm open to suggestions, but I know you're more comfortable with making predictions, rather than taking action to make them real. Nick, Ephesus, Moople – the Darkness, they must be stopped. Surely you agree?"

He ignored the question, remaining silent for a while as the rain continued outside. "We've searched everywhere, Talethea. There's nothing here that's out of the ordinary."

I wiped away the condensation with a squeak of my hand to peer below. "Alan, when things are too obvious, they're often overlooked." I spun around to face him. "And what does that window always overlook?"

"The memory of a garden."

"And while I was imprisoned in Nick's head, *my* memory of this room and his awareness of it from Billie's memory, combined as we slept. Both are different. Nick could see what I remembered of living here, Billie saw me that day, running up the garden." I turned to the window, pulled open the chest of drawers and rummaged around until I found a key. I held it up to Alan. "I just hope I'm right." I unlocked the window and pulled it inward as far as it would go, then jumped up onto the chest, causing it to creak. "I used to surprise my dad like this." I threw him my hat, my hair falling to my shoulders. Leaning out I grabbed the drain pipe with both hands and swung out into the parallax of long ago, a trespasser into a single yesterday.

"No!" cried Alan, running forward, "You can't *do* that, you'll interfere with the flow of remembered energy, the images of the after that are now!" I looked far below, watching myself running part-way up the garden, the image looping over and over again. The rain found my face and I turned into it, enjoying its cooling refreshment hitting me in repetitive waves. To the right, the rear of the house shimmered, struggling to make itself whole. Looking up, the sky was awash with the day's uncertainty, folding over itself in differing times. Light and cloud-cover jostled against each other for dominance as other portions of the parallax recognised each other and combined, the winds of uncertainty pulling my hair in front of my face as conflicting weather patterns fought for dominance across the sky. Looking below again I saw what I didn't remember. A small wedding ring box, sitting upon the bracket securing the drainpipe to the wall, wedged between them both. The lid was open, and inside sat a black sphere like a pearl, slowly pulling portions of the parallax into it like cotton candy gathering upon a cane. I looked up, Alan peering down at me.

"That must be it!" he shouted above the wind. "It's a micro singularity, competing with the hotel's, both of them fighting against each other and tearing the threads of the parallax apart!"

My hands began to slide down the drainpipe, so I kicked into the wall either side, trying to find purchase. I knew then what Moople was referring to when he told Nick to destroy all hope. Their intention was to store the entire town and its souls inside that little box, the gift Moople had given Nick when I blacked out. Carefully I loosened my grip, sliding down towards the disturbance, reaching with outstretched fingers, struggling, gritting my teeth. My middle finger touched the box lid, but it wouldn't move. I looked up, pushing my hair from my eyes, "It's no good, it won't budge!" And then I fell, landing on my back against the flatstones. I struggled to my feet, winded, catching my breath against the maelstrom swirling around me. Where the flatstones should have met the bottom of the house stretched a void. An undulating landscape of energy, reams and reams of bright threads – like Dad's nets, creating many hills and outlines of houses, some appearing whole, or at least their forgotten rooms – thousands upon thousands of them. Houses where I remembered none, roads leading to long-forgotten villages, overgrown and partially illustrated as memories are. Everything before me a patchwork of different remembered times and locations.

"Hurry up, Talethea!"

I grabbed the drainpipe and began to climb. At last I reached the ring box, pushing it free, closing the lid, dropping it into my handbag, reaching for Alan's offered hand. He pulled me up and I climbed back into the bedroom. "Here, do whatever you need to do with this," I said, throwing the box to him and taking back my hat. I crouched down and styled my hair in the bedroom mirror, placing my hat back upon my head. "Let's go."

My parents, Roan and Charles sat upon chairs facing the stage, listening to the band rehearse as Anion stood beside them indifferently.

Alan took to the stage, motioning for Anion to join him as he gathered the Secrets together to speak to them in a huddle.

"We're going to stop the Darkedness," I said as I faced my family.

Mum left her seat with a start. "What? But why? Please, can't we just carry on as a family, now we're all back together. How are you going to do this, and what about Roan's balloon?"

I looked down at Dad, recognising his posture. It was identical to the one he adopted outside the front of the house, when my parents told me about Thinking classes. He just stared at the floor in silence, searching again for the answer that this time, was there. He finally looked up. "Tiny Flower's right, they must be stopped. And if I get my hands around Ephesus' neck I'll throttle the life out of him!"

"Planationistics!" said Grandpa, before Mum could argue with Dad. "How about ice creams after to celebrate? Not for the throttleisms, but for stopping these Darkination people," he added, glancing at Mum before she said something. "What does number 1 think?"

"Number 1 is in full agreement, although I'm not too bothered about the ice cream," said Alan, joining us. He seemed taller somehow, taking on an air of confident authority. "It's time we fought back, not only for what they took from Talethea, but the knock-on effect, on every one of you, and others. If we refuse to act, life here will only become harder, unbalanced and ultimately eradicated. I'm sorry, Charlotte, but there's no happy ending to share in the foreseeable future unless we act. Anion will inform you all of the tasks ahead. Talethea, Charles and I will be back soon."

I followed Alan into the *Silver Cloud*, placing Charles in the seat behind us. "Are you certain Anion and the Secrets can synthesise what we need?"

He closed his eyes as we took to the air. "As you suggested, I have all the information required, from my recorders hidden throughout the land, from the evidence taken from the court's data storage, and from the ancient weather satellites orbiting this planet. Now please, relax and buckle in. This journey is not without its hazards, and might become a little uncomfortable."

"What are you doing?"

Alan concentrated as a screen appeared before him. He began touching squares with his fingertips. I'm using the Silver Cloud's secondary drive, version 1.0.0. Commonly known as, Zurvan." He turned to me with a proud smile. "I designed it, but have never used it."

"Is it *safe?*"

He turned back to the screen, pressing buttons rapidly until his finger hovered over a circular red button. "Safer than balloon travel, I hope – we'll just have to find out."

His finger touched the button and the screen vanished. The Silver Cloud sped forward, faster and faster until everything ahead and around us became a hazy blur, like when Mum grated chocolate into hot custard and I stirred it with a wooden spoon. We'll do that together one day, it's lovely, especially on bananas. It gradually began to slow, clouds forming around us as we descended, finally coming to rest behind Leet Skarlac's barn.

I put Charles down as we walked to the house, and Alan's face rippled and changed. Short, dark brown hair, hazel eyes, stubble around his circular face. He knocked upon the door and walked in, leading me to Leet's bedroom.

Keloff turned from kneeling beside the bed as we walked in and my heart leapt. His face full of worry, tears welling up in his eyes. Leet looked emaciated, his breathing shallow, eyes closed.

"Alan? You're early! You said you'd come visiting by this afternoon," said Keloff, standing, giving me a glance. He was a young man now, but still had that unruly hair. He wore Leet's overalls, pickingweaver tools hanging from a thick leather belt around his waist.

"I have something for your father," said Alan, shaking Keloff's hand. "This is my travelling companion, Elissa." Keloff shook my hand too, shooting a suspicious stare at me and his hand as Alan continued. "Or rather, something I must show him, if I may?"

"Of course," he looked back at his father. "The Sayers said he hasn't got long. There's nothing they can do for him."

"Then perhaps they shouldn't have destroyed my books of medicine. Can you wake him for me, please?"

Keloff whispered in his father's ear, and the old man opened his eyes slowly, licking his cracked lips. "Alan! You're here?" He tried to sit up, but Alan stepped forward, placing a hand on his shoulder as Leet's bony fingers clutched the bedclothes beneath his unshaven chin. "Relax, old friend," he said soothingly, as he lay on the bed beside him, clasping his hands together over his chest. "Leet, I want you to look up to the ceiling. I'm going to show you the truth. You deserve to know, before your time comes to a close."

The old man nodded as Alan's eyes widened, a bright light emanating from them, casting images upon the ceiling. "Your parents, Leet. Carrying you as a newborn baby from the hospital of your birth in Middletown." The scene unfolded, colour footage from so very long ago. The images jumped. "Your first day at school, playing with your friends, your fifth birthday..."

Keloff and I watched as a smile slowly formed upon Leet's face, nerves twitching there, a tear slowly running from his left eye. "How can this be?"

"I recorded everything, hence I know everything. And now it is time for me to relinquish my hold upon the past, your past, so I can create space to enable me to remember my future and the future of your son."

I thought about this, remembering Alan had already told me of Keloff's brief life. The images continued across the decades, the truths Alan knew, contradicting the Truthsayer's lies. Leet smiled as he realised this, remembering, watching the beauty of reality. Leet spoke in a croak. "That's enough, old friend. I remember these events. You've shown me enough now. I can rest," he said, wiping away that single tear before turning his head slowly to Alan. "Thank you." Alan stood, motioning me towards the door. "Is there anything you'd really like to see, any portion of the true past? I can show you images from thousands of years ago." Leet shook his head in silence. "Then goodbye, Leet." He nodded once, "Keloff, we'll be outside." I watched him from the hallway, "Farewell, old friend." And with that he closed the door leaving Leet with the truth of a far better past.

Charles met us on the veranda as I noticed a figure in the far distance, walking towards the house.

"And here I am. Perfectly timed," said Alan, glancing at the afternoon suns above.

It was Alan, this other man, identical. Him from years ago. Alan walked towards him, meeting him some way off as I watched from the comfort of the rocking chair with Charles at my side enjoying the shade. The other Alan nodded and they embraced, their eyes shining lights into each other's.

The front door squeaked to my right, making me jump. I turned to see Keloff standing there, staring at me, looking down to Charles. "Charlie boy?"

Charles' eye-stalks curled to face him as he whistled and thumped upon the planks his reply.

I took off my hat and sunglasses as Keloff spoke. "He's dead."

I lowered my head. "I'm so very sorry, Keloff."

"It's ok, thanks. We both knew it was coming. I've cried enough, over my dad, and you, TF."

I was taken aback. "How do you know it's me?"

He took a step forward then crouched down. "The way you held my hand, and of course your eyes, TF. I could never forget your eyes. And of course, Charlie boy would always be at your side, nobody else's. I've been waiting for so long to see you again. Where have you been?" I stood up as Alan joined us.

"We have compared memories. I've been informed of what I can forget and have done so. It's time for us to leave."

I replaced my hat, putting my sunglasses in my handbag as Alan picked up Charles and hurried off. I faced Keloff, not knowing where to start, what to say, knowing I really didn't have time to say all I wanted or needed to. Perhaps we never do. Both of us just stood there looking at each other. As Alan reached the corner of the house he turned. "Please Talethea, come on!"

"I have to go. I'm so sorry, Keloff, I don't belong here – I just wanted you to know I'm alright, that you'll be alright and you don't have to worry about me and you can get on with your life now." I took off my hat and kissed him on the cheek without having to stand on tiptoes, hurrying down the steps to catch up, fighting back my tears. As I reached halfway Keloff ran ahead to stand in front of me.

"But where are you going now? What's going on?"

"Away. I can't do this, *please*, it's too..."

I looked ahead as Alan watched us, shaking his head slowly, a deep frown dominating his face. "Come on! Hurry up, both of you!" I took Keloff by the hand and we ran.

~ 22 ~
The Beginning of the End of Infinity, and, Well, The End

"My other self will give your father a decent burial, Keloff. I remember that."

"Thanks, Alan. And thanks for letting me come with you. I've always wanted to see inside this machine."

Alan gave him a smile, then blinked rapidly as he sat down. "Anion, is everything ready?"

I sat next to Keloff, behind Alan, treating Charles to my seat at the front. "Yes, sir," we heard Anion say from the future, "I've received all required information. The simulation is as accurate as possible, and, I hasten to add, far more accurate than the flawed physical model once they were digitally compared. The resulting data is complete, I'll send it to you upon your return."

"Very good. Well done."

"Thank you, sir. I must say it was an interesting task. The trial commences next Rothday morning. Nick is heading for his apartment, as your guest with the gastropod anticipated."

"Thank you, and please thank the Secrets on my behalf."

Anion sniffed. "Another point, sir, The leak. I'm sorry to inform you the removal of the foreign singularity has simply slowed the problem and not solved it. There's an irreparable tear in the parallax. We're losing rooms by the minute, and have a pile of complaints which is somewhat irritating, as you decided to close the complaints department three hundred years ago as there were none. Guests are leaving, sir, even the artists."

I leaned forward, watching as Alan's face dropped. "Irreparable?"

Anion let out a deep breath, or rather pretended to. "We can salvage the information that's left, I've already begun the process, but sadly the parallax will never be fully completed."

I wanted to reassure Alan, tell him that was simply the nature of all life, that, like Leet, none of us would ever live long enough to complete every dream, every scheme we held close to our hearts, either secretly or shared. Part of being a high-form is to accept that. It was all too clear to me an immortal artificial would have difficulty doing so when faced with identical circumstances. Time was always against us, a limited quantity of unknown quality from the very moment we were born. But that was easy for me to say, standing there with Keloff, knowing that, or again, *hoping* that soon everything would be behind us, and we could just get on with our lives together.

"There's one more issue of greater concern, sir."

"You always leave the worst until last. Go on."

"The tear has spread beyond the parallax. The very quanta you constructed the hotel upon is eroding, spilling out through the tear."

"How long?"

"One hundred years, perhaps more, perhaps less. Then it will collapse into itself, pulling the entire town down with it, unless..."

"I understand, Anion. I'll bear that in mind, and thank you."

"Yes sir."

Alan turned to me. "I had hoped to have enough time to perform a hip replacement upon myself, but it seems that's not the case." He turned to look ahead as I raised my eyebrows at his contradiction. The grated chocolate blended again and we found ourselves above Middletown. It was early evening and the suns had set.

"TF, where are we going?"

"You're staying here. Alan and Charles will explain everything, what's happened, what our plans are. I must talk to someone."

I jumped from the Silver Cloud's ramp onto the balcony, opened the doors quietly and hurried across the moonlit lounge to hide behind the bedroom door, waiting, weapon in hand.

He arrived a few minutes later, agitated, throwing his jacket onto the chair by the doors, pouring a good triple and lighting a cigar. He slumped onto the couch as I opened the bedroom door into the room, my weapon pointed at his head. He sat up with a start, dropping the cigar into his lap, hastily brushing it and the embers onto the carpet. They died there. I picked up the cigar and placed it into the ashtray on the table by the balcony doors.

"Nice outfit, and you're not such a bald bitch anymore, just a bitch. Now, what the fuck are you doing here, come to finish the job?"

"Actually, I'm here to start one. I can ensure you never go to trial, Nickolatus."

He folded his arms and made himself comfortable. "What, you gonna take my soul, is that your plan?" He shook his head and ran his fingers through his hair. "Won't work, girly. They'll find me and release me."

"You've been used, over and over again. You'll never see your family." I took the disk from my handbag and pushed it into the player. "When I escaped your mind, I saw the remains of two little girls there. You've done this all before, in other realities, but they won't allow you to remember. You've been a victim your whole life, from the moment that storm destroyed your parents' ship, right up to this moment." I hit play, standing to the side of the screen.

A knock on the front door startled us both.

"You gonna answer that, Tiny Flower, or whatever your name is?" He folded his arms again, smirking.

"I don't know what bullets I have in this, and I don't care how I find out." I said, waving the weapon towards the hallway. "Besides, that would be impolite. It's your apartment."

I stepped back into the bedroom, pushing the door to, watching from the darkness as he stood, brushed down his trousers again and picked up the cigar to light it.

A few moments later he came back into the room, followed by Moople in his wheeled chair.

"Grand Master, I thank you for visiting. I..."

"You have failed us, Adams, yet we have paid substantially for your release. The device I provided you with to destroy all hope is inert. We cannot allow you to go to trial, your guilt born from your insane obsession will serve ultimately to expose our involvement and void the contract."

Nick walked to the balcony doors, opening them to the night. The sounds of hurried commuters filtered up to us. He puffed at his cigar a few times then dropped it into the night, glancing in my direction for a second. "I did exactly as you requested and hid that box in Hotel Infinity. Exactly *how* will you be exposed if I go to trial? Are you suggesting you had a hand in my personal work, obsession, as you put it?"

"Indirectly, but that was simply an unfortunate by-product of unforeseen circumstances. I saw to it you survived."

"What exactly are you suggesting, Grand Master? What about my family, and our agreement?"

Moople's wheeled chair took him to the centre of the room and his eyes fell upon Nick's screen for a moment. "Current circumstances have clearly brought about the cessation of that arrangement. You will be replaced, immediately."

Nick looked at the screen and walked forward. I could see from his face he instantly recognised the lorry speeding along the road by the park.

Moople's eyes followed his. "Adams, what is this distraction? Cease it, at once."

Nick spoke quietly as the lorry sped towards the camera. "Oh, I don't think so. For once this is a re-run I've not seen."

"Obey me, Adams!" shouted Moople, the little men upon the walkways turning from their tasks.

The screen displayed Moople's face and Nick quickly hit pause. "You said it yourself, our arrangement has ceased – you're no longer my boss, old man." The blow from the back of Nick's hand caused Moople to cry out. Touching his cheek with trembling fingers he looked up, his face contorted with hatred. And then in a fluid motion, he stood, his little men jumping down from their positions to stand beside him. "You're a fool, Adams!" Moople's powerful blow sent Nick onto his back. The little men ran forward, pulling themselves up onto his chest as Moople took a casual step forward to stand over him. "A fool that has absolutely *no* comprehension of what's at stake!" He kicked Nick in his side, again and again before stamping on his stomach as the nine little men climbed onto Nick's face. Two stamped on his eyes as two seized the sides of his mouth and pulled, four others pulled back his lips, gripping his teeth to pull his mouth wide open. The last stood upon his forehead, hands upon his hips. Moople sat upon Nick's chest, holding his head still, pinning his arms to the carpet with his knees as Nick tried to scream. "My senior hair warden deserves this reward for all his years of faithful service, as do his obedient underlings. However, he will be the first to dine and take his fill." Moople nodded once and the naked little man walked casually along Nick's nose, pausing at the tip to adopt a diver's stance.

I burst into the room, rolling to the left, letting off a shot that startled them all as the diver leapt into the air. My aim was true once again, the bullet disintegrating the two men holding Nick's lower jaw open. Immediately his mouth snapped shut, cutting the senior hair warden in half at the waist. Moople turned to face me as he stood. "Ephesus' ward! Your soul will soon join Adams.'"

"Never, Mr Moople."

Nick pulled the two little men from his eyes as he gargled a scream, flinging them against the far wall to splatter in a purple stain, spitting out the body, wiping his mouth, retching. Both Nick and I stood now as Moople slumped back into his chair, the four remaining little men scampering beneath the couch. "Stop! Enough, both of you," shouted Moople, holding up trembling hands and turning his head to the side. "I can see I have misjudged you both. You can both adopt roles for me. Yes, working together, with rewards beyond your imagining!" He lowered his hands slowly as he faced me with a smile from long ago. "Yes, I will begin with offering you more flavour to life than a thousand lollipops, Talethea. Forever, not just for after your lunch, but now and the eternity to follow!" I began to shake my head slowly as he spoke quickly. "You've always wanted to fly, Ephesus told me, yes, I can give you that freedom!" His head snapped towards Nick, standing at my side. "And you, Nickolatus, yes, your dream is but moments away, too." He nodded reassuringly, "I will provide you with your dream!"

Nick pointed to the screen. "You murdered my dream, you old bastard."

Moople shook his head briskly. "No, you don't understand. I was there to *protect* you, Ephesus predicted my plan, invaded the minds of your family." He leant forward. "Your wife was coming to kill you while your children distracted you!"

I found myself turning to Nick. "Are you going to take his word for it?"

"What? About you flying, or him protecting me?"

"Either."

The little men ran out from beneath the couch and I shot them in turn as they headed for the hallway. Moople turned from watching them die, his face angrier than ever, his hands shaking as he gripped the arms of his wheelchair. "Even now my superiors are aware of your actions. You have unleashed the determined hatred of us all." he shouted, pointing between us. "They will come for you, in their thousands." His eyes found the flower in my button hole and his expression changed to one of confusion, brows furrowing, mouth opening slightly.

"Either? I'm guessing neither. Let's see if he's telling the truth," said Nick, taking a few steps to stand behind the wheeled chair. "If you can make her fly, then it figures you can make yourself fly too." He gritted his teeth and snarled, lowered his back and pushed.

Moople fumbled for the brake, pulling it with both hands to lock the front wheels, then stood on the footplates, the cogs and gears beneath him whirring and screaming, grinding their teeth against each other before jumping free of their ornate mounts. "No, wait! Adams! There's more you must know!" but Nick angled the wheelchair back on the rear wheels, causing Moople to fall back into the chair, the two small wheels at the front of the chair waving this way and that in the air as though looking for direction. Moople reached up behind his head, white fingers searching for Nick's face, then both he and Nick screamed as the wheelchair broke through the balcony railings, Nick sliding to a halt with his arms and fingers outstretched, peering down, lowering his arms and head, spitting once. He turned to face me coughing, wiping his mouth, his shoulders slumping as he saw my gun levelled at him once again. Cries and car horns found our ears.

Nick looked behind him. "What, you want me to prove I can't fly, or you gonna take my word for it?"

"What if he could fly, then what?"

He caught his breath, shaking himself down. "You're the one with the gun, girly."

Behind him, the Silver Cloud descended with its hatchway open. "I'll take your word for it," I said, pointing. "Just get aboard. There's much to discuss."

"Yes, my room here was to be my safe house. I'd return after everything got sucked into the box. Nobody would have found me, never in a thousand years." He looked up at Anion. "Hotel rules and all that. After a century or two lying low, my crimes would be nothing more than another cold case buried beneath a ton of others. The arrangement was for my family to be returned to me, all of us relocated on another world, far enough away to live out our lives long before the Darkness arrived, generations in fact."

"He's quite correct," said Anion with a hint of respect. "I am bound by the rules never to divulge a guest's room number."

I thought about Anion's obsession with rules. Between him and Alan, they could bend light, time, but not rules. But they were made to be bent, or, like hearts, eggs and promises, broken. "The only problem, you would have been pulled into the box along with everything else," I said. "There wouldn't be a room left for you to use as a safe house. Moople lied to you, trapping you along with the rest of Hope to use you again when needed."

Nick pulled at the ropes I'd borrowed from Roan's balloon construction to secure him to a chair in the function room. "Whatever. So now what? You gonna take me back for the fucking trial?"

Dad stepped forward in an instant and clobbered him, holding a finger up to his face. "Watch your language in front of my family." He straightened. "I remember you, not so tough without a gun in your hand."

"Untie me and I'll show what I can do with my hands."

"Nah, no thanks, buddy. I'm good, but thanks for the offer," said Dad.

"Aiden!" shouted Mum, "enough now!"

I stood beside Dad waiting for him to back away. He glanced at me, rubbed his chin and eventually ambled back to Mum. I looked down at Nick, remembering he was, to a degree a victim as much as myself. A victim of several key episodes that had pushed and pulled him, moulded him into the hideous person before us. I looked at everyone standing around me, their expressions were almost identical. Utter disgust. But they seemed to forget it was Ephesus that had put me through everything, and not Nick. I began to wonder how everyone throughout the world would behave, if they too had an observer sitting inside their heads silently judging them, then realised that's exactly what consciences and most religions were for, our duality, our rational counterparts questioning our pasts, presents and futures, and frequently for most, reminding us of such. It was perhaps a shame, some consciences were not as equally balanced as the majority, able to distinguish basic right from wrong. But that arrangement, condemning his far future relatives to the unmerciful Darkness without a guarantee of immunity? Alan had already mentioned similar actions on his home world. The powers that be residing there, aware, like Nick of their limited longevity, looking only inwardly and making the most of their lives at the cost of others' quality of life. I wondered, if Nick had been aware of my presence from the moment I awoke in his head, would I have provided him with a greater conscience?

"Nick, where did you go, when you dressed up smartly, on a regular basis. Looking at the calender. The place with the yellow half-light, that fence you clung to?"

His head fell for a few moments. When he lifted it, sorrow had filled his eyes. "To a place the Grand Master took me, to visit the souls of my children on their birthdays. It was his way of reminding me of our agreement."

"But where is it? Do you know how to get there?"

He shrugged. "I don't know. I told you, he took me there. I only saw a very small part of it, just a few streets. It was like Middletown, but the sky had just one sun."

In that moment, Mum and I looked at each other, knowing exactly where he meant.

Now it was her turn to finally reveal her and Alfie's hidden adventure to everyone else.

There's never enough storage space in hotel rooms, even if the hotel is infinite. That is a constant I've come to accept from my travels, son. If you can get a good view, wonderful. If you can get a room upgrade with a good view, even better.

"It's here somewhere, I know it is," said Mum. The chest of drawers was open and empty, the drawers teetering on their runners. Frantically she threw clothes onto the floor behind her, as Dad picked them up to fold them and place them upon the bed. He couldn't keep up. She piled up ornaments, Dad's fishing stuff, placed Roan's paintings carefully against the walls. "Here!" she cried, emerging from the wardrobe with Anaximander, her talking map held above her head like a trophy. She brought it down in front of her and held it against her chest. "We still need batteries, sweetheart."

"Alan will find a way to power him up."

Mum turned the volume down before scrolling through the pages of places she'd visited.

"I'm coming with you both," mumbled Dad, watching the screen, wrapping his arms around her waist and resting his chin on her left shoulder. "From what you've both told me, I'm coming along."

"That's *not* a good idea," I said. "If this place is as I expect it to be, the central domain of the Darkness themselves, the Great Hall of Immutable Decisions, then it's a dangerous place and very cold with just a single sun."

"Cold? I'm a trawlerman, used to the cold. As for danger, you have no idea what Viewhaven was like when I was a lad, before I met your mother. There was this alehouse a few doors down from a bakery…"

"I remember," said Alan. "The Breakwater Inn."

"That's it!" said Dad. "The trouble I got myself into there, you can't imagine."

"I don't have to," said Alan, "That's one memory I'll never forget."

Dad lifted his head and scratched his bristly chin again, concentrating on the screen. "You're still my daughter, Talethea. I'm coming with you and that's that and all about it, like it or not. No arguments."

We held each other's stare and I completely understood from the look in his eyes as Mum spoke. "I've found it." We all watched as she traced a finger along the route. "This is the page leading back to that house." She passed Anaximander to Alan. "You can tell me all about that alehouse another time."

I stood up. "Keloff, it's best if you stay here and look after Charles."

"No way, TF! We've only just met up again! If anything goes wrong..."

"Talethea's right," said Alan. "She has weapon and combat experience, should it come to that."

"Rationalistic," said Roan. "You could help me with my balloon, Keloff? There's still a lot to do. Can you refurbish amplificators?"

"I guess, but I want to..."

"The fewer of us go, the better chance of us not being detected," said Alan, placing a hand on Keloff's shoulder, patting it a few times.

I could see Nick from the corner of my eye, smirking, trying to make himself appear relaxed while tied to the chair. I glanced his way. "You're coming with us." His smirk vanished.

"That's a kind offer, but I think I'll pass."

Alan approached him, placing his hands upon Nick's and bending forwards until they were almost nose to nose. "Then I'll ban you from this hotel. You can take your chances outside. With both the agents of the Darkedness and the authorities looking for you, how long do you think it will take before you're found?"

I stood beside Alan. "And who do you think will find you first? If you're lucky enough and it's your colleagues, which I doubt, you'll be back at trial and perhaps the agents of the Darkedness will get to you before you reach the courthouse." I turned away, pacing slowly up and down behind Alan with my hands clasped behind my back. "Think about it, Nick. The Darkedness' simplest solution is not to waste resources searching for you, but to simply provide you with a defence lawyer for your trial. If they win, which I'm pretty certain they would, then you're in their clutches. If they lose, which I highly doubt, you're convicted." I stopped pacing. "I think it's safe to say they have operators in prisons?" I bent down to speak quietly into Alan's ear so Nick could hear me. "Come to think of it, I think that's precisely what they'd do. Put him through another trial, just like his parents went through. Provide him with false hope, and then gloat as he's led away to endure the rest of his life behind bars. He can catch up with some old friends he put in there, and look forward to whatever the Darkedness has in store for him on a regular basis." I stared at Nick, waiting for a cocky reply that never came. "Alan told me history has an annoying habit of repeating itself, but in this case I think it's safe to say you won't be exiled as your parents were, with the chance of another storm coming to your potential rescue."

His eyes looked between us both. "So what are my alternatives?"

We stood and I walked back to stand with Keloff. He cupped his hands and whispered in my ear. "That was great. You remembered all your lines perfectly."

I cupped my hands and whispered back to him. "Thanks, but I fluffed the 'operators' line, it should have been 'agents.'"

Keloff shrugged as Alan spoke.

"Alternatives? You have one. I will personally guarantee your safe haven here when we all return. You can stay here for as long as you like."

"And," I said, raising my voice, "once we're there, in this Elsewhere Someplace, you'll be our escort. You'll advise us and ensure our safe passage. I remember, Stolas said he supported you in the Great Hall of Immutable Decisions. That's where we're going."

He laughed, his head tipping back to rest against the chair back. "You have no chance, they'll see through you the moment we arrive." His head straightened, his hair falling across his forehead. "You just don't understand, the

Grand Master, Moople, as you called him, advised me. If they sense just one sign of happiness, optimism or any positive thought, they'll strike, carve you up, tear your bodies apart to take your souls. Imprison them until all the good is drained, until you're dried up husks of anger and hopelessness." He stared at me with a mocking smirk. "Then they'll feast upon you for eternity." He strained at the ropes, leaning forward. "Do you have any idea how difficult it was for me to visit the souls of my twin boys, unable to show them one iota of love? You just don't understand."

I pulled the ring box from my handbag. "No, Nick. It's you that doesn't understand. We're going there to destroy the Assembly, once and for all."

~ 23 ~
The Domain of the Darkness and The *Actual* End.

Sorry, son! (It's been a busy day.)

The Silver Cloud landed in the middle of the street and we disembarked. Pepperdean Hemstitch was in ruins. Eroded walls upon stone foundations where houses once stood, and where a few remained intact, blackened windows of dusty jagged glass, unable to reflect the suns. Debris littered the street, timbers, roof tiles, scattered belongings as though the occupants had fled as fast as they could.

Mum led the way. "There," she said, pointing to where that house once stood. We walked up to that house slowly, standing upon the veranda as it bowed beneath our weight. It still held a few posts, leaning from their joints, a crooked, splintered handrail perched upon them. Inside, rotting floorboards, bleached beneath the heat, shrunken, grain popping like veins beneath wrinkled skin.

"I'll go first," said Alan. With that he stepped across the threshold and vanished, Nick, then Dad following close behind.

Mum held my hand and pulled me back as I took a step forward. "You don't have to go, honey. Please, think about Keloff waiting for you. Think about the life you can both have." She let go of my hand and placed her palm against my cheek. "It's not too late, Talethea, you do know that. You could take a ship, hire one from Steeltown, find a world untouched!"

I held her hand. "I do know that, but I must go." I looked into the house. "Remember what you told me about Alfie? Perhaps this is when adventure truly comes to visit me, as she did you and him." I turned back to face her, waiting for her to speak. But she just nodded once. "I have to be part of this, Mum. See it through to the end, as Alfie did."

Hand in hand we walked into the Elsewhere Someplace.

The hill loomed before us, graves dotted around as Mum had described. Upon the hill, Scalas' collapsed house. All was silent and still, the dull sun struggling to peek from behind the low clouds.

"Which way? asked Alan, as Nick stood next to him.

"Forward, I guess. I don't know this place."

"Let's see what's behind that house," I said, taking the path to lead them on.

We gathered upon the ruins of charcoaled timbers, and below us a line of trees, Beyond, a sprawling city of grey and white, glass and silver towers stretching into the sky. There, a huge bird soared, colourful against the light blue. Chimneys bellowed black clouds, adding to the grey, wavering from unseen sky currents, and as we hurried down between the graves, through the trees and into its outskirts, foreign sounds found our ears. Mechanical chattering, punctuated by staccato urgency, a throb of huddled life, seething before us as our feet found the concrete streets.

"Hatred. Remember you must fill your minds with anger and despair," said Nick. "Otherwise we're all dead." And we could, each of us concentrating on those memories I spoke of before – those solid blocks that live within us, the foundation stones of our personalities we all took for granted as we built upon them memories of happier times. For Alan it was easy, without a soul he walked a few paces ahead with Nick at his side, immune, isolated from everything that makes us human, and I thought that maybe Nick was equally as isolated as I watched them both.

We found the overcrowded streets and the creatures dwelling there. Some shuffling, blinkered as though reluctant to reach their destinations. They stared ahead, ignoring one another, each of these Darkedness beings behaving as though only they existed amid the hundreds of thousands treading the city's streets alongside them. Others held their heads high, smug, superior, indifferent to their fellows. They were all formed of different clans, instead of one single dominant type, as I imagined they would be. But as I saw their clan's hostility for each other, I understood their need to perpetuate hatred and conflict. If one became content, the others would feast upon them. These clans fought for dominance, for their differing ways to be championed, adopted by the majority. It was an eternal struggle where no one clan accepted the other, or accepted defeat.

We saw tall angular buildings of many windows where not one creature stood to look below, signs in an unknown language, strangely colourful, yet of so many identical groups placed amid the streets. These creatures gathered beneath them, huddling inside together indifferently as they ate and drank.

Girdered projections stretched upward from the tops of many buildings, and I watched as images spewed from them in trails of translucent spheres, zig-zagging in thousands of different directions across the sky. Some of these trails faded behind the clouds as they leapt straight up, others stretched across the sky to dissolve amid the far distant haze. Beneath the flatstones at our feet, conduits streamed with identical information spheres, coursing through the city like rushing water to erupt around us. These trails pierced the creatures, and as they gorged themselves upon the images projected at their faces from boxes cradled in their hands the size of dad's cigarette packet, I saw the effect within their brains, stimulated, instructed and conditioned.

Those images, so potent, yet so very different. Illustrating barbaric, unspeakable acts they inflicted upon each other, of hedonistic, perverted indecency, decadent greed producing mountains of poisonous waste. Recordings of slaughter, anger and abuse beyond measure, conflicts and wars playing over and over all through their bloody history of hatred, repression and superiority, feeding their insatiable lust for destruction. There were billions of lines of unreadable text, circles of exaggerated, emotive faces, colourful childlike pictures of objects recognisable and unknown. And then the pleading voices they hastily stabbed fingertips onto the boxes to remove. Ignorant, insistent, persuasive and invasive voices, calling upon them to condemn one another, enticing them to elevate themselves above each other in aggressive rivalry, encouraging dismissive, arrogant scorn for everything around them that didn't comply or conform to a single style or belief. Most succumbed as their fingers hung in the air, overcome, distracted, hypnotised by the inner fear of missing something their brethren may benefit from, leaving them behind. They knew no other way, and I knew then they were as imprisoned as I used to be. They knew their own names, but *their* identities, *their* very souls were not their own. They both belonged to many higher, unseen, malevolent orders.

"Where are we? Are we close?" asked my dad.

Alan stopped and we all halted behind him. The Darkedness surged around us, brushing past like a river's unyielding erosion of a protruding rock standing in its path. They didn't make eye contact, they just carried on indifferently.

"Nick," said Alan. "Do you remember what this hall looks like? If we can find a similar shape on Charlotte's map, that would help."

He looked around us in a complete circle. "It's much older than these buildings. It has a tower with an ornate disk. My children's souls are in the field beneath it."

We gathered around the map as Mum zoomed out and scrolled in various directions. "Stop!" said Nick eventually. He tapped the screen. "Get in closer on that shape." He looked at each of us in turn. "Don't allow yourselves to show *any* sign of relief or pleasure, but that's the place."

Alan took the map and led the way.

We reached a wide stone bridge, where giant vehicles screamed as they crawled beside us carrying the disinterested faces to their appointments as funnels belched fumes of black dirt at our feet. Beneath the bridge where I expected to see water, a river of flowers meandered through the city, each with its petals shut tightly to the day despite the sunlight.

Nick pointed. "That's the hall, and the tower, over there."

I stared into the distance as the sounds of these strange vehicles continually assaulted my ears. A jagged tower of ornate anger, with a dull disk beneath its sharp-cornered pyramidal top. I frowned. It looked like a clock, but only held twelve markers around the edge, and its face without hands was shattered in jagged edges of glass. The halls beside it stood angrily, their archaic architecture of slender arched windows, all barred with narrow, vertical stone like the bars of a prison cell. It was a monstrous building, seething with a foreboding emanating from every pitted stone pore.

We reached the end of the bridge, following Nick to the Great Hall of Immutable Decisions. He stopped at an ebony, arched wooden door where two guards looked us over, unsure of what they were seeing.

"How do we get in?"

Nick turned to me, his face impassive, betraying his obvious pleasure of betrayal. "I told you, Moople brought me here. Only he was allowed through the door and into the depths of the hall for an audience with the Assembly. This time, you really have been picked, Tiny Flower." He looked around, "All of you."

Alan held my dad back as he reached for Nick's throat, as sounds of bolts and latches pulled aside came from behind the door. Gradually it opened and the guards stood to attention.

"Ah, you're here. And just when I was thinking you'd decided to stay at home and live out the remainder of your brief lives."

The voice was unmistakeable; it was Ephesus.

He looked at Alan. "I don't know you. Who are you and what are you doing here?"

"I was about to ask you exactly the same question," replied Alan.

Ephesus dismissed the question with a wave of his hand. "Talethea, please join me. I've been waiting for you. I'm just about to present your evidence to the Assembly. No doubt they will require further proof."

I stepped forward. "You told me it would take a lifetime before you presented the evidence to them."

"Yes, but the lifetime of a beautiful mayfly, one single day. My Talethea lost her life trying to help them as they argued how to spend their day together, you tried also in this realm. It's time now." He held out a hand. "Please, will you join me?"

"Talethea, no!" said Dad. "You can't trust that bastard!"

"Your father's right," said Mum. "How do you know he won't murder you again?"

"I will go with her," said Alan. "Talethea will be quite safe with me."

"Acceptable," said Ephesus. The three of you can watch the proceedings from the gallery. It is permitted." I found myself taking Ephesus' offered hand and within moments, the door closed behind us.

Inside, the building mirrored the architecture of the exterior. Ornate, with a time-worn yet cared-for appearance. The wooden walls were polished to a high sheen, having that indignant supremacy to its beautifications separating each panel, matching the stonemasonry outside. As we walked silently along a vaulted corridor, larger than life portraits hung from the walls, staring back at us from either side. Creatures adorned with flamboyant, bygone attire, every one of them harbouring an expression of contempt. And that odour. The building reeked of decay, as though behind those beautifully maintained walls a malevolence waited to burst through to consume us all.

"We're nearly there. At the end of this corridor," Ephesus murmured, as if he were afraid to awake whatever lay sleeping around us. He motioned to a wide flight of stairs to the right of a pair of square double doors where a further two creatures stood guard. "They are my guests."

He looked at Dad. "Up there, keep to the left, and don't say a word to any of them, any of you."

The guards pulled the doors open and we entered.

Six bright orbs hung from the ceiling and either side of us sitting in four rows of bright green leather benches was the Assembly. These creatures shouted obscenities at each other across the room, waving claws clutching papers. Pointed, elongated faces and staring, bulging eyes – each and every one of them hungry to be heard, obeyed, seeking control above them all. They were pastiches of Moople, I decided, fiercely zealous and animated. Others managed to sleep beneath the chaos, folded away in either uncertainty or indifference. Some huddled together in pairs, plotting, it seemed, their own rise to dominance.

As Ephesus walked forward with Alan and me behind him, they fell silent one by one as we passed. Low mutterings began, whispers that curled through the air to tease our ears with their meanings. At last Ephesus took to an elevated throne at the end of the Great Hall, pulling on a robe that hung over it. They all fell silent.

"Fellows, I bring before you the evidence betraying the contract signed by the ten thousand." He pointed at me. "This girl's testimony is incontestable, proving my fellow Grand Master, known to you only as Moople, betrayed the contract, grooming a human male throughout his formative years to ultimately serve Moople's lust for victory. Upon that world, dwelling beyond our realm, Moople's ward subjugated the population beneath a blanket of violence, hatred and destruction." He threw his arms wide, parting his fingers, "Behold!"

Everything I had seen of Nick's terrible actions bled from Ephesus' fingertips, falling to the floor in puddles, running down the steps to form pools of contorted images. This vile liquid coursed through the rows, gathering at the feet of the Assembly. Some stood, clearly disturbed at what played out at their feet, murmured voices grew to objections as the liquid engulfed every one of them. Their bodies shook, suffocating beneath the truth, subduing them.

Ephesus stood and hurried over to me. "It seems you're not needed after all. They are in judgement. Hurry back now. Their decision is but moments away." He looked up to the gallery where Mum, Dad and Nick stood watching us. "Hurry!" he shouted. "It is done!"

"That's it?" I said.

He nodded. "They will emerge with justice clogging their throats. I have done all I can, all I should have done, eons ago, preventing their spread across the cosmos."

I watched as truth's blood began to drip from them, thinner now, revealing their true natures. They were just ordinary men and women, their hideous masks dissolved, their Darkness evaporating into the air..

"You, Ephesus, you have betrayed your sacred oath too. This girl's testimony proves as much. Yours and Moople's guilt walk hand in hand. The field of souls evil has appropriated will be returned to the receptacle, from this reality and all others." I turned to the speaker, a woman, an ordinary woman standing in the middle of a row. And as they all emerged from that liquid, they each pointed to him in turn, and with one voice they chanted, that echoed word surrounding us. "Guilty!"

Ephesus nodded and closed his eyes, tugging at his beard. "You must run, this reality is not for you. Others residing here will seek you out. Don't forget the flower I gave you, Talethea. It has the power to heal the heart of the Darkness forever. Now do as I say and run!"

We left him standing there as they left their seats and gathered around him, meeting my parents and Nick at the bottom of the stairs.

Within moments we were outside.

"I'm not leaving until I say goodbye to my boys," said Nick. He hurried down a flight of steps to the right where that padlocked gate I saw in his memory barred the way to the river of flowers. We joined him. Their fragrances were beautiful, sweet, as each coalesced with one another, it became overpowering, making my head feel light.

"They're in there, somewhere," he said softly, fingers poking through the fence to grip it tightly. "Down there, with all the other souls the Darkness took.."

"Flowers?"

He turned to me. "The Darkness manifest them this way to quench their hunger to destroy beauty." He held the padlock in his hands and I took a step forward, noticing something move from the corner of my eye.

"Talethea?" said Dad, looking over my left shoulder as the others joined us.

"Yes?"

Alan reached out, taking the flower from my button hole. It was in full bloom, petals open wide, its anthers reaching down towards the gate. As Alan held it near the padlock, they became agitated, eager, stretching closer and closer until they entwined, entering the keyhole, the petals wrapping themselves around the metal casing.

"We haven't time for this! Look!" said Dad.

Behind us, that grotesque building slowly began to transform. It shuddered against the sky, becoming brighter, more defined as the truth seeped from behind its walls. This undoing of the Darkness, the contract's cancellation, spread gradually, revealing the true nature of the creatures it touched.

"Your father's right," said Alan. "Once the contract is fully cancelled, our gateway home will vanish."

A click and the shackle fell open, the petals releasing their grasp, the anthers shrinking back from the keyhole.

"What the hell is going on?" breathed Nick, sliding the gate aside. Water appeared, rising slowly amid the field.

"I have no idea. Ephesus gave me that flower."

He held out his hand and Alan passed it to him. Nick walked forwards and we followed him into that field, just a few paces, the water continuing to rise. He crouched down, resting his elbows on his knees while holding the flower before him. Two flowers standing side by side opened their petals. "The souls of my children." As he walked over to them through this field of captured souls, reaching out slowly to gently touch them with a fingertip, a hand appeared, plucking them free from the sodden soil.

Nick stood and turned to face my dad. "What the *fuck* do you think you're doing? Give them to me, now!"

Dad passed the flowers to me and I took them delicately. "Keeping us steering true," he said. "Visiting hours are over. We still have a job to do."

Alan stepped between them both as they squared up to each other. "I promise, Nick, we'll return them to you, all three, once we're all back at the hotel. Now please, give Talethea the soul of your wife for safe keeping."

Nick stared at the flower in his fingers, rotating it gently by the stem for a moment before holding it out. I took it quickly, placing it with the other two. I opened the handbag, putting them carefully inside and pulling out the ring box. "Shall we?"

"Here?" said Mum.

"At the ruins of Scalas' house," said Alan. "Once Talethea opens it, we must run to the gates and back to our reality. The singularity in the box will seal the gateway between both."

"But how do you know it won't pull us in too?" asked Mum.

"Then we'll have to be quick" I said, "It's the only chance we have of ending them, forever."

I looked to the bridge. There, several creatures dotted along it were looking down at us. "I think we're too late," I said. "We're being watched, up there from the bridge. Don't look. Let's just get moving."

We matched their pace, trying to blend in and not draw further attention to ourselves. It was as though we were partly invisible to them, like ghosts glimpsed, reflections of something insubstantial from the corner of your eye to be blinked away. But as we walked across the bridge, they had turned to watch us approach, lips turned back in a snarl. As we passed each of them, thirty I counted, they followed us from a distance with determined footsteps, like animals stalking their prey, but unsure of when to strike.

"Don't, whatever you do, look back at them. Just keep going. We'll be on the outskirts soon."

"Maintain your anger, fill your hearts with it." said Nick.

As we cleared the trees and reached the graveyard hill, my spirits tried to lift but I subdued them. We stood amid the ruins of Scalas' house as a deafening scream filled the air from their hungry throats. We turned and there they were, walking towards us from beneath the trees, mouths wide, teeth bared, encircling us.

"There's too many of them!" shouted my dad.

"Run!" Pulling out my weapon I let off several shots to no effect, my bullets not part of their world. "It's just down the hill!" Fumbling in the handbag I took out the ring box, and Dad snatched it out of my hand. I looked at him and he smiled. I quickly shook my head, wide-eyed, mouthing *'No!'* I couldn't blame him for feeling as he did, I too will feel exactly the same when we meet, son. But that one display of love for me Dad allowed to creep out of him, no matter how hard he had struggled to shut it away was all they needed. At once we were invisible no more, their pace quickened towards us as they walked between the graves.

"You run," said Dad. "Take your mother too. Go on, Tiny Flower, I'll open the box."

"What?"

"This is my adventure, at long last."

"Aiden, no!" said Mum, grabbing his arm. "Not here, not like this!"

"Please, let me do this. I love you both very much, my heart's full of it, and they know it. I couldn't hold my love for you both in when I picked those flowers. I'm so sorry, it's me they're after."

"But I'm faster than you, Dad! Let me open it and I'll run."

He shook his head, hugged us both tightly, kissing me on the forehead and Mum gently on the cheek. "I always knew from when I first saw you, there would come a day when I'd have to let go, when you'd become an adult and not be my Tiny Flower anymore. Look after your mum for me please, Talethea." And with that, he let go of our hands.

"Dad! I love you!" I cried as Alan ushered us away from the ruins.

He turned with a beaming smile, blowing us both a kiss, and with that he punched them to the ground, kicking them aside. But they just kept coming.

"I'm sorry, but we have to leave, now!" said Alan. "We can't lead them to the threshold between realities."

We ran down the hill between the graves, ignoring the path. I stood with Mum at the gates watching my dad for as long as Alan allowed us, longer in fact. As they surrounded the top of the hill, he reached up above his head, opening the ring box. Reality's threads began to curl, tearing apart and Alan ushered us through the gates.

We stood on the veranda and I turned around. The house was whole, just an ordinary-looking house in an ordinary street. I opened the front door and walked in. "Dad?" my voice echoed back to me.

We met in the function room. Alan and my mum taking Keloff, Charles and Grandpa Roan to one side to explain what had happened.

"Never seen bravery like that," said Nick, as Anion joined us. I nodded to him and he silently sent the command as Alan walked over with Keloff. Nick spoke again. "You should be very proud of him."

I ignored him, wondering if he was thinking of his father, and the day he rescued him from the flames.

"We had a deal," said Nick, holding out a hand to Alan.

"Our deal was that we should *all* return. Clearly that isn't the case. However, Aiden's sacrifice saved us all and closed the gateway to the Darkedness, therefore..."

Nick held up a hand, lifting his head, eyes darting about. "Wait! Quiet all of you. Can you hear that?"

He walked slowly to the function room doors and Alan and I followed him.

"Hear what?" I said.

"Music, that music. I recognise that music."

"Where are you going?"

"It's coming from a room, somewhere I should know." He ran across the reception area and called a lift. We hurried after him, squeezing through the slowly closing gap. Nick stabbed a sequence of numbers with his thumb and we sped off. "I know this, can't you hear it?"

We shook our heads. The doors opened and Alan passed him a key. He fumbled at the lock without saying a word and quickly opened the door.

At the end of the corridor the room beyond was brightly lit by a lazy summer afternoon. Light blue walls, large glossy cartoon character stickers upon them in bright primary colours. We walked in. The room smelt clean and fresh, the carpet of cream fibres spongy beneath our feet. Nick walked to the window set in the middle of the far wall. Either side of it stood two white cots with mobiles above them, upon the window sill a radio played Nick's discordant music. As we looked down to the garden below, Nick's wife began hanging out washing as their twin boys lay asleep in their push buggy. She looked up to us and waved after pegging out his uniform shirt, and Nick smiled, checking himself as he began to wave back to the memory he'd chosen to forget.

I took the flowers from the handbag, placing the two smaller ones in separate cots. Alan opened the window as I passed the last flower to Nickolatus Fenstinion Adams. "Throw it to her," I said.

His head jerked around at me. "The radio, that's my music, completed, perfectly! How?"

"Throw the flower to your wife, Nick."

He held it for a few moments then threw it down to land in the grass before her. She picked it up and a surge of energy instantly engulfed her. Threads becoming folds of quanta, surging into the image of her body, instructing and constructing her from Nick's memory. The loop broken, she picked the boys up from their push buggy, and walked towards the house out of sight.

"What the hell's happening? What is this room? How did you complete my music?" he looked down into the garden, "and what's happened to my wife?"

"Simply put," began Alan, "Using the quanta from the hotel's closure, I built a completely accurate simulation of your 'orchestra' from your memories given to me by Talethea, the footage taken of your lock-up by Billie, and the data I already possessed of the weather conditions during the time you spent on that island. Your error was simple at the lock-up. You. You have grown since those days marooned on that island, your adult body altering the course of the fraudulent wind as it came off the counterfeit sea, causing your percussion, particularly your mother's, to be inaccurate. There were other inaccuracies, but I won't go into them all."

"The hotel is collapsing, Nick," I said. "The remaining quanta have been gathered and used to form the reality you craved, the reality Moople promised but never gave you." I looked around. "This house, your family. All as real as they were, as they should be. But this house has boundaries, as nothing lies beyond its walls." I pointed beyond the garden where the view ceased. The utterly nothing hung there. A black beyond anything I'd ever seen sitting beneath the sky. "A luxury prison, if you like."

The fire alarm sounded right on cue.

"What's that?" asked Nick, as it invaded his music. His wife walked into the bedroom with their two boys. "Guests, Nick?" she said, laying the boys in their cots. They became whole, their souls returned to their bodies created by the quanta.

"We'll be on our way soon," said Alan, and he took a step towards the door.

"Wait. What do you mean by prison?"

"It's not really a prison as such," said Alan. "You see, Anion evacuated all the guests while we were in the Elsewhere Someplace. You and your family are the last guests remaining. The fire escape at the very, very far end of the corridor will remain open, until the last guests leave, as per the hotel rules. But, it's obviously a one-way trip – health and safety regulations and all that. You understand."

I looked around the room. "Hotel Infinity has been rebranded as the Finite Motel, and you occupy this, its only room. And," I said, "as you're well aware, the rules state one guest must remain in the room, should three others decide to leave." It's entirely up to you, you can stay here together for the rest of your lives, or three of you can leave. It's up to you who you take with you, and who you leave behind, the door will always be open. Anion will stay to lock up behind you when you depart, and will answer any questions you may have, during the remainder of your stay. As you know, he's a stickler for rules." I looked around the room one last time, running my finger along the top of a cot. There was a small amount of quanta-dust that I flicked away, watching as it slowly fell to the carpet. "All this will remain for one hundred years, perhaps less, perhaps more. Plenty of time to live out your lives."

Nick just stared as I closed the door behind us.

We walked down the corridor, eventually meeting up with everyone waiting for us at the fire exit.

I thought for a moment. "Alan, where exactly does this fire exit lead?"

His brow furrowed with puzzlement. "Do you know, I can't remember specifically. Somewhere called Tuesday, I think. Obviously that's something I was supposed to forget." He smiled, looking at each of us in turn. "Well, if everyone's ready, let's find out."

I held Keloff's hand and suddenly thought as Alan pushed the doors wide open; I never did find out what the blue bullets were for.

~ To be continued ~

Somewhere